# WHEN STARS COME OUT

## SCARLETT ST. CLAIR

Bloom books

# CONTENT WARNING

This book contains scenes that depict suicide.
Specifically referenced in chapters 1, 3, 4,
17, 20, 21, 22, 23, 30, 33, 37, and 42.

If you or someone you know is contemplating suicide,
please call the National Suicide Prevention Lifeline at
1-800-273-TALK (8255). Please do not struggle in silence.
People care. Your friends and family care. I care.

--------------------

Copyright © 2022 by Scarlett St. Clair
Cover and internal design © 2022 by Sourcebooks
Cover design by Regina Wamba/ReginaWamba.com
Cover images © shufilm/AdobeStock, MtysAdobeStock, jelerAdobeStock,
foldyart1980/AdobeStock, NASA/Public Domain

Sourcebooks and the colophon are registered trademarks of
Sourcebooks. Bloom Books is a trademark of Sourcebooks.

Published by Bloom Books, an imprint of Sourcebooks
P.O. Box 4410, Naperville, Illinois 60567-4410
(630) 961-3900
sourcebooks.com

Originally self-published in 2018 by Scarlett St. Clair.

Cataloging-in-Publication Data is on file with the Library of Congress.

Printed and bound in Canada.
MBP 10 9 8 7 6 5 4 3 2 1

To Mrs. Applegate,

You once said that your legacy would only last a generation, and honestly, I just can't have that happening. I need all my readers to know that without you, this book—all the books I have written—wouldn't exist.

When we were introduced, I never imagined the empowering relationship that would follow. You became a source of support, someone I knew would always believe in me. You changed my life in more ways than you know. From helping me revise my first short story that won first place in the Eastern Oklahoma Writing Contest, to writing that treasured letter of recommendation that would aid me when I applied for the Gates Millennium Scholarship, to reading all my books. Each of these things are gifts you have given me.

Teachers have such power over their students. I am so lucky to have had you: a source of motivation, a person who believes in me—sometimes more than I believed in myself—and a friend. Can you imagine the beauty that would exist in the world if every person had a teacher like you in their lives?

Your legacy lives on in your students. It lives on in these books, because you are a part of them.

Your biggest fan,
Scarlett

# CHAPTER ONE
## Anora and the Dead Girl

*I lean forward in my seat and stare at my reflection in the* car mirror, assessing my work. I took my time putting makeup on this morning, choosing a brown shadow and black liner that make my eyes look more yellow than green. My dark hair cascades over my shoulders. By the end of the day, it will be mostly straight, too heavy to sustain the curls it took an hour to fix. I practice a smile, checking to see if any lipstick transferred to my teeth but also testing to see if I can manage to make it look real. This is my chance at a new beginning, and as long as I'm careful, the past won't bleed into the future.

I glance at Mom. Even now, she keeps her gaze forward, hands tight on the steering wheel, navigating the rented Ford Focus around another bend in this hopeless road. I can't help feeling guilty. I'm the reason she has to start over too.

*You'll make so many friends*, a voice rumbles in my head. If he were still here, it's the kind of encouragement my poppa would give. I smile at the thought and straighten in my seat, clasping the round coin at my neck—my poppa's coin.

Another bend and Mom turns down a white concrete drive, flanked by a set of redbrick pillars. A black plate with gold letters identifies this as Nacoma Knight Academy—my new high school in Oklahoma. Everything about it online seemed vague. Mom said it was an "alternative" school, but I don't know what that means—is it for delinquents? Even with my background, I knew the main reason Mom chose this place was because they employ highly trained counselors, and that's what she felt I needed more than anything.

Suddenly my skin grows hot, as if the sun has moved inches from my face, and I know something's not right.

*Oh no.*

My stomach feels like it's full of wasps as I focus on the building ahead of me. Balconies outside the third and fourth floors are enclosed with black bars, making each one resemble a cage. A girl hangs by her neck at the center of the building, four stories up. I follow the rope with my eyes, finding it tied to one of several stone spindles jutting from the top of the roof.

My fingers dig into the leather seat, and there's a familiar prick in my palm as hysteria crawls up my windpipe, into the back of my throat. I swallow the scream, glancing at Mom, realizing the momentum of the car hasn't slowed.

She can't see the dead girl.

Of course she can't. My mouth tastes bitter at the thought—that's why we're in this mess. Mom can't see the dead, and from the one conversation we've had about it, she also believes anyone who claims to see the dead is a liar. Or maybe mentally ill, as if she's one to judge that.

A bead of sweat trickles down my face, tickling my neck, and I release my breath. *I can do this*, I remind myself. The dead are everywhere, and I took precautions as I was getting ready this morning. My perfume has a hint of rosemary, the evil eye dangles off a zipper on my backpack, and there's a bag of turmeric powder in my blazer pocket. Small things, but they should keep the souls at a distance. Souls, not ghosts—I don't like that word. It implies transparency. The dead I deal with look as human as the day they died: solid, fleshy, and like the nearly decapitated girl hanging by her neck over the doors, they wear their deaths.

This is just a reminder of the rules I set for myself before starting at this new school—and the reason I need them.

Rule number one: Ignore the dead.

But as we approach, I can't take my eyes off her. How hard must she have fallen? She'd been a student at Nacoma Knight Academy. Her uniform is similar to mine, except instead of a blazer, she wears a knitted sweater—longer, with two pockets on the front—and a skirt that falls midcalf. The longer skirt is a giveaway that she's been here a while. While I don't think she's one to cause me trouble, her presence is a vortex, sucking my energy. It makes me jittery, like I've had too much caffeine. This whole place feels off.

Mom brings the car to a jerky halt. I stick my hands out to stop myself from colliding with the dashboard, only to realize the bell has rung. Students dressed like me race to buildings across campus. Several move in and out of the doors beneath the dead girl's feet.

I don't move to exit the car. Once I'm outside, I'll have to worry about screwing up again. I'm the new girl, and people will want to look at me, talk to me. I'll have to make sure they're actually alive. Sure, I want friends, but I also want to become transparent, blend in so well with the crowd I'm hardly noticed. I want to be normal. If I can't manage that, I'm not sure what is next for me: Another school?

Probably not. Mom is done moving.

"Any more signs that you're seeing things," she threatened on the drive to Oklahoma, "and I'll put you in a psych hospital."

She's already been researching facilities in our new state—I found them saved as bookmarks on our computer. Unfortunately, I knew they weren't for her. Bringing up seeing the dead was the biggest mistake I'd ever made. Mom has enough to deal with just making it through her own episodes, even if she won't admit she has them.

Mom must have noticed how pale I looked after her threat, because she'd reached over, patted my leg, and said softly, "Therapy helped your poppa."

If that were true, he wouldn't be dead, I think, rubbing the face of my poppa's coin.

"Anora, stop grinding your teeth!"

I jerk, startled by Mom's sudden command. It's the first time she's met my gaze since we got in the car this morning—the first thing she said other than "put on your seat belt." I don't know if she's angry because of us having to move or if she's nervous for me. Sometimes it's hard to tell.

I let go of the coin, its heavy weight settles against my chest, and I relax my jaw, unaware I've been clenching it.

Mom sighs, which seems to soften the flicker in her eyes. She reaches to brush a few strands of hair out of my face.

"Honey, I know this all happened so fast, but this... this will be good for you...for both of us."

She smiles, so I smile back, only to make her feel better. It is damage control, something I put myself in charge of since we left.

"Would you like me to walk you to the door?"

Mom isn't smiling now, and she taps the steering wheel with her fingers. I'm probably making her late for her interview.

I lift my backpack from the floor, stifling my impulse to take another deep breath. I need to say something reassuring. Something like, *That's all right, Mom. I'll be fine. Don't worry. I love you.*

Instead, I say, "No, Mom. That's the last thing I need on my first day."

"Fine." She answers in that clipped, short-tempered tone she's been using with me for the last two months. "I'll pick you up after three."

I get out of the car, close the door, and she drives off.

Then it's just me, the school, and the dead girl.

Well, crap.

A sign to the left of the sidewalk identifies this building as Emerson Hall. I turn in a circle. Now that I'm outside the car, I feel like I've been transported to another dimension. All traces of the outside world—the street we drove up and the black fence and gate—are lost amid acres of land and trees. Even the wind is different here—quieter, like it's trapped under a glass dome, exiling street noise.

I drag my gaze back to the dead girl hanging at the center of the building like some sacrificial god. Even now, this spirit is draining my energy, making me dizzy, and the longer she hangs there, the worse it'll get. If I want to get through this day—and every one after that—I'm going to have to ignore her.

Easier said than done.

I give Poppa's coin one last squeeze, slip it under my shirt, and march into Emerson Hall, avoiding the girl swinging over my head. Right now, I have to find my new normal, and part of that is pretending I *am* normal.

Inside, several students stand in line at a counter, waiting to speak to one of three women behind a glass panel. I hang back at the entrance for a moment, surveying my surroundings, mostly waiting to see if there's an energy suck—an indication that there are dead nearby. When I'm sure everyone in the lobby is alive, I choose a line and wait. A couple of students turn to stare, but I avert my eyes, looking at anything else—the plastic plant in the corner, wooden chairs pushed against a dirty white wall, black-and-white photos of buildings and long-dead people.

A television behind the glass runs breaking news, the screen splashed with photos of a deadly plane crash, deliberately taken down by its copilot. Officials make guesses as to the motive, and the only thing I can think is that there are now one hundred and fifty more people bound here on earth, dead. My stomach clenches tight. Mom doesn't like when I watch the news. She thinks I take it all too personally.

What she really means is she thinks I become obsessed, and I guess she's kind of right. There are certain stories I invest in, and I'll follow every piece of news released on the subject.

This one is no different.

I watch the segment as images of each person who'd been on the plane cycle by. I get lost in their faces until it's past time for my first class, and no one else is left in the lobby but me. This is not a good start to being normal.

A woman with blond hair and a pink blazer smiles at me.

"Can I help you?" Her voice sounds robotic, filtered through the round metal intercom.

"I'm new. I don't have my schedule—"

"Oh! You must be Anora Silby!" She retrieves a folder from her desk and hands it to me via a small opening at the bottom of the glass barrier. Why is there a glass barrier? Does alternative school mean violent? Is she expecting someone to accost her? "Inside you'll find your schedule and your student handbook."

I open the folder and stare at the materials. My schedule sits on top. I have already zoned in on my first hour: trigonometry…a.k.a. hell.

I am terrible at math.

"Be sure you're aware of curfew."

"Oh, I won't be living on campus. We have a place in town."

"Curfew is countywide," she advises. "No one's to be outside after midnight."

"Why?"

It takes the lady a moment to realize I've asked her a question. She blinks.

"It's always been like that. Since the twenties."

"What happened in the twenties?"

"Well, you know, after the murders."

I blink. Did this woman just tell me, a student, that there had been murders in this county? What the hell kind of place is this? "No, actually…I don't know." I wave my folder around to remind her I'm the new girl.

"It's nothing to be worried about," the lady assures me, apparently realizing this isn't the sort of gossip to share with a teenager. "There haven't been any murders since then. The curfew's just in place as…a precaution. It's best if it's obeyed."

She says it like a warning, like she thinks I'm one to break the rules. I can understand curfew for campus, but if nothing has happened since the twenties, why is it countywide?

"Would you like a guide to help you find your classes?" Her voice brightens, and her smile intensifies. It looks fake, and I get the sense I'm not welcome anymore.

"Uh, sure."

It should be included in the folder, but the only things in there are my schedule and a book of rules I have no interest in reading. It's like they've never had a new student before. I'll need a map of this place in case I get lost trying to avoid the dead. The lady disappears from view, and I take a closer look at the pictures on the wall. I'm partly hopeful I'll see a picture of the girl outside in one of the photos, but I don't find her. The images are mostly of buildings on campus in their prime. Gold plates beneath the frames indicate the year they were built. My favorite is Rosewater—that sounds calming.

I run my fingers over the cold metal, tracing the name.

"You must be Anora Silby." The voice is energetic and warm, but it startles me. I tear my hand away from the plate as if I've been caught stealing and yelp, twisting to find a boy standing beside me. He has striking blue eyes, white-blond hair, and sharp features. My gaze drops to his lips, which are initially pulled into a smile until I face him, then he falters.

"Sorry. I didn't mean to startle you."

I study him for a moment—lively eyes, faint color in his cheeks, and…warmth. He's definitely alive. I guess I stare too long, because he clears his throat and says, "Can I help you find your classes?"

"Oh…um…the lady was getting me a map."

A smile stretches across his face again, brightening his expression. "I'm your map." He extends his hand to me, keeping the other in his pocket. "Shy."

I stare at his hand, confused—did he just call me shy?

"Excuse me?"

He chuckles under his breath. "It's my name—Shy Savior."

"Oh." My cheeks flame, and I want to hide. I fumble as I cradle my folder in my arm and reach for his hand. "Anora Silby…er…I guess you knew that."

"Yeah," he breathes and then quickly adds, "But that's okay. You have a nice name."

He doesn't move his gaze from mine as he shakes my hand firmly, and it is a little unnerving, especially since the pigment of his eyes is so concentrated.

"Um, are you going to let go of my hand?"

"Sorry." He drops my hand and snakes his behind his neck. "It's just…have we met?"

I laugh. "No. I think I would remember you."

Shy smiles and turns the faintest shade of pink. "You just feel so familiar."

"I hope I'm familiar in a good way."

God. I'd have to say that, wouldn't I? What am I doing? I'm breaking my second rule: Absolutely no boys.

"Yes." He narrows those gorgeous eyes, and my resolve weakens. "Yes, only in a good way."

I inhale and hug myself, feeling self-conscious. I have no idea what's going on here.

"Mr. Savior, I think it's about time Miss Silby made it to class," the lady in the pink blazer advises from the counter.

Shy turns and smiles at her. "Yes. Sorry, Mrs. Cole." He looks at me, clearing his throat. "So what's your first class?"

I'm glad the distraction gives me a reason to look away from him, because my gaping is a whole new level of awkward. I open my folder to look at my schedule. I'd seen it a few minutes ago, but now I can't remember anything.

"Um, Mr. Val, trig…in Walcourt?"

Shy laughs.

"What?" I lean away to get a good look at his face, but he just shakes his head, eyes focused on my schedule.

"Nothing. What's your locker number?"

Forty-four.

Shy directs me out of the lobby, down a hallway flanked with a large trophy case and a couple of bulletin boards covered with flyers for homecoming.

"The lockers, dorms, and cafeteria are all located here in Emerson," he explains. "It's a little inconvenient, but you just have to make sure you have everything you need for your first four classes before lunch." He pauses and nods to my locker, then the one next to it. "That one's mine."

I smile at him, and it feels like I'm falling into a trap. Fate must be messing with me. "I guess I'll see more of you, then?"

"Yeah." He grins, showing his teeth, and runs a hand through his hair. I like the way his eyes crinkle at the sides when he smiles, all things I shouldn't notice about him, considering my rules. "Yeah, you will."

The sunlight blinds me as we exit Emerson, and I blink several times to adjust my vision before turning to watch the girl overhead. She sways ever so slightly, propelled by nothing but the memory of the day of her death. Shy has stopped too, and he watches me, following my gaze to the bars.

"It was to keep people—"

"From jumping," I finish quickly. "I know."

He doesn't smile back, and he studies me. The intensity of his eyes makes me feel like he can see every layer of me.

"Why don't they take them down?" I ask.

He shrugs. "Aesthetics, history, a precaution. The windows in the dorms don't open either."

"History?"

"This place used to be an asylum before it was a school. Back in the twenties. There's a lot of history here, and most of it is kind of shady."

Oh, that isn't good.

I look back up at the bars and then around. So far so good. I haven't encountered any other dead, but that doesn't mean they aren't here.

"Do you live on campus?" I can't help but wonder why this boy would need to be in an alternative school.

He shakes his head. "No, thank God."

"That bad, huh?"

He sort of laughs, but it sounds more like a snicker. "I already spend more time here than I like. I'm local." Ah, so he probably didn't do anything to be sent here.

As we cross campus, I conduct another sweep of the grounds and notice a thin layer of decay has settled upon the landscape in the form of weathered brick, buckled sidewalks, and rusted pipe rails. These are flaws in its beauty—cracks the past has slipped through. The dead are a part of that past, and the same as always, I feel a fierce desire to fix it. The urge tugs at my heart, twines with my veins, and bursts from my palm. The sharpness is startling, and I squeeze my fingers into a fist, knowing no good can come of it, no matter my intentions.

Worse, I'll mess it up like I have before.

It's like fixing a china doll after her face has shattered— you might find a rosy cheek and an eye, but nothing prepares you for the chips in the already-broken pieces or the glue that never stops oozing from those cracks.

"Are you a senior this year?" Shy asks. His voice startles me, and though the question grounds me, I want to tell him he doesn't have to keep up conversation just to be polite. Still, I answer.

"No, a junior."

"Good. At least you don't have to start your last year of school in a new place. Where are you from?"

"Chicago."

"Why did you move here?"

The question makes my stomach churn.

"Things…got complicated." A weak response, but an answer that's true. I'm relieved when Shy nods and doesn't ask me to elaborate. "What about you?" I ask quickly. "Have you always lived here?"

"My whole life."

Surprising. Somehow, I can't see this being the only place he's ever lived. His smile seems sad too, and I wonder if he feels trapped like I feel trapped.

We approach Walcourt, which is shaped like a rectangle with large square columns running the length of a cement overhang, and ugly white rails zigzag to the doors. Inside, the place smells like must and mold. The white floor looks yellow under fluorescent lights.

We walk midway down the hall, and Shy's eyes capture mine before he nods to a door on my right.

"That's Mr. Val's class. Just to warn you…he's a bit of a prick."

So that's why he laughed earlier. Great. Shy steps back and then twists toward the door. He knocks and doesn't wait for a response. I hear a deep, stern voice.

"Mr. Savior. What can I do for you?"

"I apologize, Mr. Val. I'm showing a new student around campus."

Shy opens the door a little more, and now Mr. Val is visible. He has a thick, brown mustache and brown hair, and he wears a brown suit. He stands behind his desk, a piece of chalk in his hand, mid-lesson. I meet his gaze last and find him staring at me, eyes as black as a night without stars. I can already feel his disappointment in me, like he's set the earth on my shoulders and watched it roll off into space.

The only thing that makes me feel any better is that he looks at Shy the same way.

"This is Anora Silby."

13

"Ah." He places his chalk in the metal holder, dusts off his hands, and reaches for a clipboard on his desk. "Yes, Miss Silby. Come in."

Shy takes up half the doorway, but I brush past him. Heat rushes to my face, and I can't figure out if it is from being on display in front of twenty students or from the slightest bit of physical contact with Shy.

"You're excused, Mr. Savior. I'm sure if Miss Silby needs your services, she will find you."

The class snickers. I glance at Shy as he mouths the word "prick" before closing the door. I nod, a grin growing on my face.

"Miss Silby." My smile quickly fades, and I snap my head toward Mr. Val, who clears his throat. The students behind me laugh again, clearly amused by my awkwardness. "It's a good thing Mr. Savior isn't in this class. It already seems he is proving too much of a distraction."

Mr. Val hands me something that looks more like a work manual than a syllabus and a massive trigonometry book, then directs me to one of the only seats left in the classroom—front and center. As I take it, I notice a girl with long, dark hair staring at me. Our eyes meet, but her cool expression doesn't change. The only reason I'm okay with it is because she's actually alive.

I pull out my notebook and try to catch up on what I missed in Mr. Val's instruction and look through the syllabus. As if I need any more confirmation that my time at Nacoma Knight will be trying, I find that we have quizzes every day.

Sighing, I glance up to find the dead girl from Emerson Hall outside the window peering in. She apparently moves all around campus. I have seen the dead move before, but it still startles me. Her head dangles to the side, partially decapitated. Blood covers the collar of her sweater, drips from her nose and the corners of her eyes. My whole body suddenly feels prickly, like I've been wrapped in a blanket of spiders, their tiny legs skittering across my skin.

As if she senses my gaze, her sideways eyes snap to mine, and her colorless lips pull away from her teeth in a crooked, black-blood smile, and I know that she's come to search for me.

I look away and focus on my desk, but the dead girl's gaze heats my skin like the sun.

*Please let her lose interest in me.*

If she doesn't, I have a one-way ticket to the psych ward.

# CHAPTER TWO
# Anora and the Gold Coin

*After trig, I stop outside the classroom to look at my sched-*ule. To be truthful, I'm stalling. The dead girl moved away from the window shortly after I spotted her, but that doesn't mean she isn't waiting for me, and if I'm going to have an encounter with the dead, I don't want witnesses.

As I cradle my new book and syllabus, I bump into the edge of a locker, and my stuff tumbles to the ground. I lean over to pick everything up and turn to find three girls from Mr. Val's class observing me. The one in the middle was staring at me earlier, and while I don't read open hostility from them, I can tell they're curious about me, bordering on suspicious.

But maybe I'm wrong.

"How did you end up at Nacoma?" the middle one asks.

*Nope. Always trust your gut. They're suspicious.*

"My mom moved here for work," I mumble, gathering my stuff and clutching it tightly in my arms.

"Huh," she says, and it's clear she doesn't believe me. I wait for an accusation or a bitchy comment, but she doesn't say anything else.

She stares a moment longer before she and her two friends turn and walk away. Another girl who'd been lingering in the hallway approaches. She has eyes the color of ice, more white than blue, and her lips are a pretty, pink pout. Her creamy skin is speckled with a collection of moles that look more like thoughtfully placed beauty marks. She reminds me of a ballerina, all lithe and long-limbed, made to look even smaller by the huge cardigan draped over her shoulders, billowing around her body.

"Ignore them," she says. "Jasmine and Michelle just repeat everything Natalie says, and Natalie thinks she's queen of the castle and is always in everyone's business because her father is headmaster."

*Damn.* I'd have to draw *that* kind of attention on my first day, wouldn't I?

"Well, I guess her dad being headmaster does sort of make her queen of the castle."

"Don't let her fool you. She's not as powerful as she thinks. I'm Lennon." The girl holds out her hand for me to take.

"Anora." I shake her hand. I'm just glad she hasn't called me *the new girl* yet.

"I know. You're from Chicago. You moved into the old Foley house on Forrest." I stiffen, and Lennon must notice because she explains, "You're the only thing people were talking about on Roundtable today."

"What?"

"Roundtable. It's like an anonymous Twitter feed

17

but exclusive to Nacoma students. We don't really have much to do out here other than gossip and talk shit about one another."

"You have an anonymous app for gossip?" I ask, and holy crap, is this not something I need at the moment.

"Yeah. Normally, I wouldn't introduce a newbie to it so soon, but everyone is super curious because there was precious little they could dig up about *you*. Of course, that leaves a lot of room for speculation, you know."

"Oh, well, I don't want that. Best to get everything out in the open. I'm actually a hundred years old, and I bathe in the blood of virgins to stay youthful."

Lennon stares at me for a moment, and my face reddens. Maybe I went too far with that joke. Then a smile breaks out across her face, and she pretends to write on the books cradled in her arm.

"Virgins…got it. If I see any, I'll let you know."

We both laugh, and I'm feeling a little more relaxed. Lennon inclines her head to get a look at my schedule.

"What's your next class?"

It's biology in Kline—a building that is closer to Emerson than Walcourt, which means another trek across campus.

As it turns out, that's Lennon's next class too. We also have World History and English III together. Lennon chats beside me as we head to Kline. The path we take is free of the dead, and I can concentrate on what she's saying.

"I hear Shy Savior got to show you around this morning. You know he's a senior and the quarterback of our football team? Total cliché. He'll probably be homecoming king this year. Natalie is weirdly protective of him, so that's probably why she's cagey about you."

That turns my stomach sour, not that I should care, but I do not need to be in the middle of drama.

"I've been here for a full"—I look at my phone—"two hours. I'm not interested in Shy."

"Hmm. We'll see."

I sigh. "I hate high school." But I'd be lying if I didn't admit that I'd asked for exactly this—the normalcy of high school, even if it comes with petty drama.

Lennon sits next to me in the classes we have together and points to *the people I should know.*

"That's Maia Ledford. Her father walked out a couple months ago. She hasn't spoken since. That's Caroline Miller. She's first in the class and plans to go to Oxford when she graduates, but she's really intense. I think she had a breakdown trying to keep her grades up, which is why she came here. I'm convinced she'll kill anyone who threatens her GPA. And that…" She points to a boy sitting against the wall. His hair is dark, coming to rest on his shoulders, and his lips are curved in a classic smirk. He doesn't look interested in anything going on around him. "That's Thane Treadway. He's super rich and a troublemaker."

"He looks pissed."

She leans toward me, her chin resting on her hand. "He's just bored."

I glance at the boy again and find him looking at me. His face remains blank, like I'm the color beige or Mr. Val's math homework. As quick as he glances in my direction, he looks away, and I might have taken it for disinterest if I didn't recognize the expression. It's one I've been wearing the last four months. It's grief.

Thane has just become ten times more interesting.

19

"Speaking of homecoming, you have to go to the dance!"

I refocus my attention on Lennon, whose eyes have brightened at the topic. I shake my head. "I don't really like dancing."

She shrugs. "It's not really about the dancing—it's about the dresses."

I try imagining Lennon's lithe frame, swallowed by that huge cardigan, wearing a snug-fitting gown and can't.

"Besides, it might be a requirement for you. Rumor is the football team's considering making you their princess."

"Their what?"

"Princess...for queen's ransom," she says. "Every homecoming, they nominate one girl. It's a tradition."

I have so many questions.

"What's queen's ransom?"

"It's like...capture the flag. We play with our rival, Rayon High. Each school offers up one girl to be exchanged and hidden by the other team. Whoever finds and rescues their princess first wins the homecoming seat, and the girl becomes homecoming queen. There's a huge risk. I mean, Rayon's princess could win." She offers a small laugh. "But that hasn't happened in over twenty years."

I don't like the idea of being exchanged or hidden, and screw *waiting* to be rescued. I wanted a normal high school experience, but this is not what I meant.

"Why would they nominate me? No one knows who I am."

"Everyone knows who you are. Roundtable,

remember?" Lennon says. "Your new-girl status makes you the perfect choice for queen's ransom. They think of it as offering up the virgin for sacrifice. It's kind of a rite of passage."

Sounds more like hazing.

"Can I refuse?"

Lennon's bony shoulder pokes out of the fabric of her cardigan as she shrugs. "No one ever has, but if you're not queen, then Natalie will be."

Imagine the kind of enemy Natalie will become if I beat her out of homecoming queen. If Lennon is to be believed, Natalie seems the type to hold a grudge about that kind of stuff. If Shy is on the football team, I'll tell him to leave me out of this.

"When's the dance?" I ask.

"In three weeks," Lennon says. "Football is really big here. Homecoming is a holiday. Anyway, even if you don't get queen, you should still go to the dance. We can go together."

"What if someone asks you to the dance?"

She smiles ruefully. "No one will ask me."

"You can't know that. Haven't you been asked before?"

"No, and I won't be asked this year either," she says adamantly, as if the future is etched in stone—and maybe for her, it is. I wonder what happened to Lennon to land her at Nacoma, or if she's another one of these people who just happen to live here. I almost ask her, but prying will be opening a door for her to ask questions about me, and that's the last thing I need.

At lunch, I follow Lennon back to Emerson Hall, deposit my books into my locker, and meld with a crowd of students heading toward the cafeteria. It feels like joining a hoard of hungry zombies—they all moan about classes and can't seem to walk straight, knocking shoulders with the person beside them. I don't like physical contact, and I don't like crowds. More bodies mean it's harder to find an escape route if things go south, and I can't tell if the dead are mixed among them.

When we make it to the cafeteria, I stick close to Lennon, following her to the end of a line winding its way toward a buffet staffed with lunch ladies. I might be paranoid, but it feels like everyone's gazes are on me.

"So," I ask Lennon as casually as possible. "Are you from here?"

"No, I'm from Pennsylvania. I was shipped here freshman year, and I've been coming back ever since."

I bite back my instinct to ask why she was shipped here and instead say, "Do you like it? Living here, I mean?"

Lennon doesn't look at me as she speaks. Her eyes wander the cafeteria, like she's looking for someone. "I don't hate it."

"That is a nonanswer."

She grins. "I'm going to be here even if I hate it, so I might as well make the most of it."

"And how do you do that?"

"You watch people," she says, and even now, she studies me. "Learn their secrets, so when they come after you, you're untouchable."

Unease trickles down my spine. That doesn't feel like a normal high school teenage answer. "That all sounds a little extreme."

"You don't know Nacoma Knight."

Lennon's words must have an effect on me, because I

find myself scanning the room. I spot Shy standing at the center of a group of boys, all laughing at something one of them said. A girl breaks through the circle to hug him around his middle. His arms tighten around her, a wide smile on his face.

I look away, but Lennon elbows me in the ribs and says in a loud whisper, "Shy's on his way over!"

I will myself not to react but can feel my skin grow splotchy with heat, which makes me even more embarrassed, but I face him anyway.

"Hey," he says, coming to stand beside me.

"Hey."

"I'm guessing you found your classes all right without me?"

"Yeah, thanks to Lennon."

I look from one to the other. Shy's smile seems tight, but Lennon's cheerfulness makes me think I'm imagining the awkwardness.

"I'll be right back!" Lennon says and then bolts across the cafeteria to a group of girls. I can't imagine what she's telling them, but I wonder if any of it will end up on that app she spoke of earlier.

"I see you found another friend," Shy observes.

"Yes. She's taught me a lot."

"Oh yeah?"

"Yeah. Like about queen's ransom."

His eyes go wide. I don't know how to say this subtly, but I also want no part of being kidnapped and hidden. So I blurt, "If you're thinking of making me some sort of prize, you can forget it. I don't want that." I pause, and he looks at me as if I've grown a second head. The silence is uncomfortable, and now I wonder if Lennon was joking

23

about the whole thing and I wasn't ever going to be a princess. My neck burns in humiliation, so I quickly change the subject. "I think I met your girlfriend today."

Shy raises a brow, and a smile opens up on his face. "And who would that be?"

"Natalie?"

He throws his head back, laughing. I'm betting Natalie would be offended by his reaction. "She's not my girlfriend."

"Maybe someone should tell her that."

"She's just overprotective...and jealous."

I laugh. "Jealous? I thought you said she wasn't your girlfriend. Is she an ex?"

"No, nothing like that. We've known each other forever. Just friends."

"Well, she's nosy."

"Yeah, she is." He shrugs. "New girl at school that no one knows anything about...takes attention away from her."

"I don't want attention or people asking questions about me. And I am no one to be jealous of."

His gaze feels like an incision in my chest.

"Everyone has something someone else wants."

I blink. That's not what I expected him to say, and he's looking at me the same way he did earlier...like he has X-ray vision clear to my soul.

"You should stop doing that," I say. It feels like I'm standing next to a heater.

He looks confused. "What?"

"Staring at me like that."

He smiles a little and lowers his eyes to the floor, attempting to hide the pink coloring on those high cheekbones. I feel the loss of his gaze immediately. Where I was warm before, now I'm cold. This is not a normal reaction. There is something about this boy.

"Sorry. I…didn't mean to," he says earnestly.

I want to cram those words back into my mouth and swallow them whole, but I can't. What can I say anyway? *I take it back. Stare all you want?* This is best. Pretty boys are trouble—haven't I learned that?

Lennon rejoins us and carries on the conversation. I keep waiting for Shy to leave, but he moves through the line beside me and invites us to sit with him at an already-crowded table. My chest tightens and my stomach flutters, but not in the good way, no butterflies. This is like a spider has burrowed deep in my belly, spun a web, and captured flies. That's pretty much how I feel right now—like a fly, trapped. Especially when I notice Natalie at the table.

If I weren't trying so hard for Mom, I'd have left the congested cafeteria and found a spot outside to eat my lunch where there is no fear my true self will peek through a crack I haven't managed to seal. Then I think of that spirit who left her spot above the doors at Emerson Hall to come looking for me and decide it's best if I stay inside.

I sit wedged between Shy and another student I don't know. Lennon takes a seat diagonally across from me. Shy introduces me to some of the people at the table, describing how he knows them or who they are as if I can keep up. I keep my eyes on my plate. The lumpy thing at its center is called a soy burger. I'm wondering if it is edible when someone places the ketchup near my hand. I look beside me and meet Shy's stare.

"Just douse it in ketchup. It tastes fine."

I scrunch my nose but take his advice. It seems he's survived a few years on Nacoma Knight cafeteria food.

Soon, Shy's friends direct their attention to me. I let my hands fall in my lap, fiddling with the hem of my skirt as they begin their interrogation.

"So where are you from, Anora?" a boy with short, black hair and a great smile asks me. His name is Jacobi. From what I gather, he's on the football team and one of Shy's best friends. I notice others have started to stare, and I feel like a lion's prey. I think about Roundtable. What do these people want from me that they haven't found there?

"Chicago."

"Why'd you move to Oklahoma?"

"My mom moved here for a job." I echo the lie I told Natalie. It is the easiest thing to say—and the most normal. Lots of kids move because of their parents, right? I catch Shy's gaze as I answer. It says: *That's not so complicated.*

"Oh, that's cool," Jacobi responds.

"I heard you got kicked out of school." Natalie's declaration surrounds me like a net cast out for capture, and I go rigid, tightening my fists in my lap. She stares at me, and the voices at our table go quiet. I wonder if people believe everything that comes out of her mouth since her father is headmaster. She clearly has access to whatever file he has on me. Lennon was right: she is in everyone's business.

"Starting rumors already, Natalie?" That question comes from Shy and surprises me—why does he think she's lying?

She lifts her chin and her eyes narrow. It reminds me of the look a cat might give a mouse before it pounces. "It's not a rumor."

Everyone's watching me, but I don't owe them an explanation. Maybe I started fights, maybe I set fires, or maybe I broke down because I can see the dead. I prefer any of those over the actual truth.

At Shy's dismissal, Natalie lets the subject drop, and the table lapses into a discussion of Friday's game and next week's homecoming events. It's the third time I've heard about homecoming today, and with Shy sitting beside me, his warmth seeming to draw me closer to him, I start to entertain the idea of going...which is dangerous.

I make the mistake of looking at him and find he's watching me.

I don't tell him to stop this time.

He nods to my plate encouragingly. "The food's really not so bad."

I reach for the burger and take a big bite, ketchup oozing onto my fingers. The food is gritty, and all I can taste is tomatoes. I want to spit it out, but Shy is watching, and how attractive would that be?

*Just as attractive as throwing up*, I remind myself as I manage to swallow my mostly unchewed food, wincing as it goes down.

*That's enough of that.*

I don't touch the burger again and can't seem to gain any feeling of comfort for the rest of the lunch period, so when the bell rings, I jump out of my seat and race for the door.

Shy is quick to catch up and offers to walk me to my

27

next class. This feels way too helpful, and I wonder what exactly his motive is here.

"Oh…I wouldn't want you to go out of your way…"

"You have art in Hollingsworth, right?" And before I have time to ask how he knows, he adds, "I…uh… took note of the classes we had together when I looked at your schedule earlier."

I'm not sure why it takes me so long to form words, but Shy must assume my silence means something else, because he averts his eyes.

"That might've been a little stalker-y. I didn't mean anything by it. Sorry if I freaked you out."

"You didn't," I say. "We should get to class."

We walk quietly side by side, and I try several times to confirm that he's not going to put my name forward for queen's ransom, but I've embarrassed myself enough with that and just hope Lennon had it wrong.

Shy holds the door open for me when we reach Hollingsworth—a redbrick building with three floors, a covered porch, and double-hung windows. He walks beside me down marbled halls decorated with student paintings, sketches, and sculptures, then gestures to a room on the left where our class is located.

I start to enter ahead of him but halt when I find the dead girl from earlier blocking my path, glaring at me from that horrible broken angle. I guess the precautions I took—the rosemary, evil eye, and turmeric—are no match for the power of this soul, because she's not moving.

I wrap my fingers around the straps of my backpack, and a thin layer of sweat coats my skin, matting the hair at the base of my neck.

"You okay?" Shy asks.

*No.*

I could feign food poisoning, turn and run to the nurse's office. No one who'd seen what we had eaten at lunch would think twice about that lie...except Mom.

It's that thought that propels me forward, through the spirit. I hate this. Hate it more than my move to Oklahoma, more than my new name. Walking through the dead means for the briefest moments, I feel what they felt upon their death. A violent pain ricochets from my neck and coils in my stomach, sending a rush of fire through me, and for a moment, I think that piece of soy burger really will come back up. Then the pain is gone—as quick as a bone snapping in half—leaving an aftershock of nausea rolling through my stomach like a spiked ball.

I keep moving forward and take my seat beside Shy, fighting to swallow the acid at the back of my throat. My whole body still feels as if I've had a fever that just broke. Even my palms are sticky.

Our teacher, Mr. Seth, welcomes the class and begins to take roll. He wears a sweater vest and black-framed glasses. As he calls names, I look toward the door. The spirit's gone, but I have a feeling she isn't finished torturing me. The dead never seem to want to leave me alone, even when they don't seem particularly evil. It's like they want something from me.

"Miss Silby?" Mr. Seth's voice reaches me, and my eyes snap to his. "Miss Silby?"

"Yes?" The word comes out breathless.

"Are you all right?"

I press my clammy palm to my forehead, wiping away a thin sheen of perspiration.

"Yes."

Mr. Seth watches me as if he thinks I'll change my answer. I sink lower in my chair, and he relents, transitioning into a lecture on pointillism. I open my notebook and go to flip my hair over my shoulder when I notice blood coating the ends and dripping onto my lap. My heart feels like it's caught in a vise, squeezing until I've no ability to breathe. I reach for the matted hair glued to my neck, finding the skin is tender and coated in something sticky. I pull my hand away: more blood.

The nausea building in my stomach threatens to explode.

"Miss Silby, do you need to go to the nurse's office?"

I clamp my hand around my neck, but I can't look at Mr. Seth, because everyone in class has turned to stare at me—including Shy. Those eyes freeze me in place—hard and curious, scanning my body like a machine looking for disease. My stomach clenches. The last thing I need is to projectile vomit all over the place.

I stand, swaying on my feet, and stumble out of the classroom.

"Miss Silby!"

I race down the hallway, searching for a bathroom in this unfamiliar place. Turning the corner, I stumble through a door into a yellow-washed restroom that smells like must.

I barely make it to the toilet before releasing the contents of my stomach. I heave a few seconds longer and then get to my feet, shuddering, coated in sweat.

I move to the mirror and find a furrow around my neck in the shape of an inverted V. The marking looks like a deep, bloody moat and appears to be of the same

30

thickness as the rope the dead girl hanged from. Even as I stare at myself, the blood and markings begin to fade.

Like it was all in my imagination.

The anxiety and fear I've had since arriving at Nacoma this morning starts to bubble under my skin, transforming into anger, and I tremble with the need to unravel.

*Danger, danger, danger.*

I ignore the warning going off in my head and leave the restroom, heading outside.

The wind washes over me, cooling my heated face but stirring smells together: stale air and vomit. I round the corner of the building, finding the dead girl waiting for me, neck broken, the same ligature marks that marred my skin marking hers. I skirt around her and head for the tree line. If I'm going to confront her, I can't have anyone watching.

When I'm far enough away and hidden by trees, I stop, waiting until the dead girl appears in my peripheral. I twist toward her.

"Stay. Away. From. Me! Do you understand?" My voice sounds raw to my ears, and I curl my aching hands into fists. "If you know what's good for you, you'll listen."

I've said what I need and move to sidestep the spirit, but what she says next stops me in my tracks.

"They're coming for you." Her voice is guttural, like she's gargling blood.

"Are you *threatening* me?" I turn to face her again. There is a familiar prick in my right palm as I take a step toward her. Her eyes trail to my hand, as if she senses what's unraveling inside me.

"You'll only lead them to you faster," she says.

31

"What are you talking about? Who's after me?"

The dead girl offers a savage smile and turns to leave, but the same hysteria I felt upon seeing her rises inside me again, and the small sliver of control I have shatters as I think—what if she leads *them* to me? I reach for her, fingers spread wide, and a thread sprouts from my palm, twisting and twirling through the air like spun gold, and, like a needle attached to a long thread, spears the dead girl's head, weaving in and out of her body, perforating her as easily as paper, until she is covered from her broken head to her toes in a cocoon of gold. Beautiful and disturbing, it constricts, tightening around her form, consuming, growing smaller and smaller until she's nothing more than a coin on the ground.

I fall to my knees and reach for the coin, scanning my surroundings, ensuring no one—not even the dead—are witness to what happened. Clutching it in my hand, I peer down at it. The familiar image of a raven is raised in relief on the surface of the coin along with today's date, which keeps a timeline of the souls I have captured.

And there goes rule number three: Don't capture souls in Oklahoma.

# CHAPTER THREE
## Anora and the Confrontation

*"Anora! Anora!" It takes me a moment to realize someone's* calling my name. I close my fingers over the coin and emerge from the line of trees, finding Shy looking for me.

He stops a few feet away. "You left your things in class." He unshoulders my backpack and holds it out to me. I take it from him, hugging the bag to my chest, careful to keep the coin clasped tight in my hand as I slip it into the mesh side pocket.

"Thanks," I whisper, but I can't meet his gaze. I'm not sure I can handle those eyes, already familiar because they've studied me so much today.

"Do you have panic attacks often?"

Now I can't help looking at him. "Panic attacks?"

"Yeah. I'm assuming that's what happened in art... why you ran outside."

I bite my lip. "No, I don't have them often."

We're silent for a moment, and then I take a quick breath. "I'm guessing this will end up on Roundtable."

"So you've been introduced?" He looks down at his feet and then away across campus. "Let me guess, the ever-so-enlightening Lennon told you?"

I narrow my eyes. "What do you have against her?"

"Nothing. It's more the app I have a problem with. It's...ruined people here."

*Not what I want to hear.*

"Can't the administration or someone stop it?"

"Trust me, people have tried. It just resurfaces about a week later with a different look. It's like someone knows how to work around anything they put up to block it."

*Great.* I'll be under constant threat of having my crazy projected to the entire school.

"We should probably get to class," Shy says after a moment. "The teachers are really fond of detention."

Just as we start to walk, a loud caw makes my heart jump in my throat. I spin around to see a large black bird swoop down from the branches of a tree and fly into the bright sky—the only witness to my secret.

"Is that a crow?" I ask Shy, and when I look at him, my heart falls from my throat into my stomach. His expression holds tension and what seems like confusion.

"No." He shifts his bright-eyed gaze to me. "A raven."

I swallow hard. Thank God birds can't talk.

———

My last class of the day is physical education. Lennon and I change in the field house and walk to the football field where a black track circles the turf. Even though it's warm, Lennon wears a baggy, long-sleeved shirt. I wonder why she feels the need to hide her thin frame.

The air around me is punctuated with coaches'

34

whistles, the crack of helmets and gear, and high-pitched chants from cheerleaders practicing on the sidelines. Apparently in Oklahoma, the athletes have their last period of the day to start practice, while the rest of us have to suffer through PE. Among the cheerleaders is Natalie, who continues her routine while keeping an eye on me—a combination of skills I find equally impressive and annoying.

We merge with the crowd of PE students as Coach David instructs us.

"You know the drill. Run one lap, walk one lap—five sets," says Coach David, though he doesn't look like he's all that invested in our overall wellness. "Anyone who wants extra credit can run two laps and walk one."

*Extra credit? Who needs extra credit in PE?* Then Coach David addresses Lennon and me. "Ryder, new girl—" Students turn to stare and move a couple of steps away. Clearly, they heard about my episode in art class. Lennon's the only one who doesn't seem to know—or care. "Ten points deducted for tardiness."

*Seriously? Today is the worst.*

Coach David places the whistle in his mouth and blows. Lennon and I hang back until most of the crowd disbands.

"By the way," Lennon says, nudging me with her elbow before we hit our stride running. "He's number twenty-two."

"Who?"

"Shy." Lennon gives me a lopsided grin, and I avoid her gaze, hoping to hide my flushed face. "He's hard to forget, isn't he?"

The tone of Lennon's voice is admiring, and I

wonder if she has a crush on Shy, but what I've seen of their interactions today told me the feelings definitely aren't reciprocated. Who *has* caught Shy's attention, and how many of those girls has Natalie managed to chase away with her overprotectiveness?

We begin our lap.

"So," I say, breathing raggedly. "This curfew thing... does anyone actually obey it?"

"Yeah, it's hard not to."

"What do you mean?"

"Well, the doors lock at ten, and the only exits that work have fire alarms."

This place is more like a prison than I imagined. No wonder Shy's glad he doesn't live here.

"Apparently, there were talks about lifting it, but then about fifty years back, a girl snuck out after curfew and hung herself in front of Emerson Hall. Left a suicide note and everything."

Well, that explains a few things. Though it doesn't explain what she wanted from me.

"But why keep curfew for the whole county?"

She shrugs. "I guess they think it controls crime. Lots of people on Roundtable have speculated about it, but it's all woo-woo stuff about cults and mind control and rumors about ghosts from the old asylum cursing the whole town. None of it makes sense."

I have a feeling the curfew has to do with the dead. They have a tendency to disrupt things, especially after dark.

"You're not thinking about breaking curfew, are you?" Lennon asks.

There is only one reason I want outside after midnight,

and it has nothing to do with the dead. It has nothing to do with boys. It has everything to do with my dreams.

"No."

Lennon sounds relieved. "Good. You won't like it anyway."

"Why?"

Lennon starts to slow her pace and hesitates. "It's just...things are different after midnight. The air feels... *heavy* and all the lights flicker. Sometimes I swear the wind *moans*."

Maybe Lennon believes some of the woo-woo stuff after all. "So you've been out past curfew?"

It takes Lennon a moment to answer. "Once."

It's the only word she offers, but the way she delivers it—so light, like a feather coming to rest on a still lake—ripples through me, and I know whatever she saw after midnight is something she doesn't want to remember. Tension builds between us—the push and pull of my wish for answers and her resistance—but I don't want to press her, because I need at least one friend so I can prove to Mom I'm trying.

We slow to a walk after running two laps. I look to see if Coach David is watching—he isn't. Then I glance toward the field and find Shy looking back at me. He has his helmet cradled in his arm; his blond hair sticks to his forehead. I catch his stare before he has a chance to hide his narrow eyes and tight lips. He tries to recover, smiling brightly and waving. I wave back, but his expression makes me think what happened in art has left him both curious and suspicious of me.

"It's almost unfair," Lennon says.

"What is?"

37

"The way he's making you a target with his attention."

I'm about to say how ridiculous that is when a ball comes speeding through the air directly at my face. I snatch it quickly with one hand before it can hit me, and the momentum nearly throws me off-balance. Lennon looks at me as if I've grown two heads. I had been so caught up in the moment, I'd let instinct take over. I quickly drop the ball, but everyone's still staring, and no one moves to retrieve the ball at my feet.

"That was awesome," she says. "How did you *do* that?"

"It was nothing." I try downplaying what she saw, but Lennon isn't having it.

"I don't know many people who have reflexes like that."

I try not to move that fast usually. This is the problem with not keeping my skills in check—everyone wants to exaggerate them if they see something slightly off. Tomorrow I'll be the freak who moves at the speed of light.

"I'm pretty sure you're exaggerating. I just got lucky."

Lennon folds her arms over her chest. "You don't have to hide the fact that you're a badass. Everyone will know after today anyway, and they will be even more curious about you."

I frown. "You don't think people will get bored of speculating about the new girl?"

"You just snatched a ball out of the air like a ninja," Lennon says as a way of answering.

After PE, Lennon and I head back to Emerson Hall, and I retrieve my bag from my locker. Before Lennon heads to her dorm, she turns to face me.

"See you tomorrow?"

"If you still want to hang out with me."

She looks confused. "Why wouldn't I?"

"I'm pretty sure everything I did today will end up on Roundtable."

She laughs. "Oh, trust me—something *far* more interesting will overshadow your incident by tomorrow."

Her words raise the hair on my arms. That's a strange thing to say, but I shake the feeling off and manage a smile before Lennon heads inside, leaving me to wait for Mom.

I let my backpack slide from my shoulders, heavy, reminding me that I've broken all my rules and I haven't even been at this school for twenty-four hours. That can't be a good omen. My eyes travel upward, toward the third floor where a limp noose dangles, free of weight—free of the soul I captured. Unease crowds my mind, pricking my scalp.

I'd never worried about capturing souls until I discovered there were people who look for answers to their disappearance. People I don't want to think about.

"What are you staring at?"

I find Thane Treadway standing behind me. He is like a dark slash in the bright day.

"I was just...admiring the architecture." That is believable—most of the buildings on campus are impressive in size and composition.

When I look back at Thane, he's studying the building. I take this moment to examine him. He's tall and thin, and his hair looks messier than it did this morning, like he ran his fingers through it over and over. Maybe it's a nervous tic.

"You're Thane Treadway," I say.

39

His gaze meets mine, and I wish he wouldn't look at me. It's not the same feeling I get when Shy looks at me; this is darker, scarier. Like beetles crawling under my skin. I scrunch my nose as Thane pulls out a cigarette and lighter. I'm pretty sure he isn't allowed to smoke on campus.

"Lennon tell you about me?"

"Only what she knows." I take a step away from him. His gaze is steady as he brings the cigarette to his lips. Smoke escapes from his mouth in one heavy blast.

"That sounds a little accusatory. You think there's more than what she's told you?"

"Well, it's not like she knows everything about everyone, is it?"

Thane stares, scrutinizing me from head to toe before turning away and taking another drag from the cigarette.

"Are you sure you should be smoking?"

"Absolutely."

I frown. *Gross.*

"Unless, of course, it's bothering you."

"You don't seem like the kind of person who cares about that."

Thane glances at the cigarette, poised between his thumb and forefinger, and then puts it out against the school's white stone, leaving a smear of ash.

"I guess you don't know me very well, then." He blows the remainder of the smoke from his mouth and nostrils and nods toward the driveway. "Is that your mom?"

My heart picks up speed. Sure enough, when I look, she's there. I glance at Thane, wondering if she saw him smoking. She might assume I've fallen in with the wrong crowd, and on the first day too.

"Well, it was…*nice*…talking to you."

A smirk cracks Thane's lips. It does strange things to his eyes, and by strange, I mean they suddenly seem almost friendly.

"I look forward to getting to know you, Anora."

I hurry away from him. As I approach the car, I can't make out the expression on my mother's face, and I feel a sense of dread as I open the passenger side door and slide into the seat.

*Damage control*, I remind myself.

"Hey, Mom!" My voice sounds unnatural and high-pitched. "How was the interview?"

A tactical move—this question keeps Mom from asking about my day and about Thane and his stupid cigarettes. I bow my head, sniffing the collar of my blazer. I hope I don't smell like them.

"It went great." She smiles, and I straighten a bit. "I got the job. It's a bit of a step back since it's a different field, but I like my new boss. I start tomorrow."

"So soon?"

"I'll admit we won't be able to get the house in order until this weekend, but…we should be thankful it was this easy. It's not like I had as many options here as we did in New York."

Her voice changes—sharpens—and it feels more like an accusation than a statement. It's something Mom—whether she admits it or not—was doing even before we came here, and each comment is like a stab to my gut. During her good times, she's a good mom. But when things are bad—and they have definitely been bad since I admitted to seeing dead people—my mom doesn't really parent. It's like it's all too much for her.

41

What confidence I gained from her initial smile evaporates immediately, and I shift my gaze forward.

"Well, I'm happy for you, Mom."

She doesn't respond, but I feel her eyes on me.

"So who was the boy?"

I look at her. "The boy?"

She narrows her eyes. "The boy you were talking to just now."

"Oh." I can feel guilt like a damp cloth on the back of my neck. "No one I know, really."

The silence strains against my ears, and the air feels solid as Mom puts the car in gear and drives away. Since coming here, she's been more demanding when it comes to how I answer her questions, and I guess she has the right. I've been lying to her for a really long time.

As we leave, I look in the mirror and spot Thane staring up at the empty noose, swinging over the doors of Emerson Hall.

# CHAPTER FOUR
## Shy and the Assignment

**"You're late, Shy," Jacobi says.**

The edge of one of his long knives flies over my head. I duck, swinging my blade toward his legs. The move prompts Jacobi to jump back, giving me the space I need to straighten. We stand opposite each other in our hybrid forms, dressed in black suits as tight as our own skin. Large iridescent-black wings sprout from our backs and sweep behind us.

It feels good to be in this form, like I've dropped a heavy cloak from my shoulders, given up the disguise of being a regular teenager, and allowed the other part of me to take over. Valryns have three forms: a hybrid, raven, and human.

I actually like my human form the most, even if it is sometimes exhausting having to pretend to care about things like football and trigonometry. If my friends heard me say that, I'd never hear the end of it. I'm pretty sure there's some unspoken law that says a Valryn's favorite form cannot be their human form.

"So what kept you?" Jacobi continues.

He likes to talk when we train. I don't.

My hands tighten around the hilts of my weapons, and I glance at the black two-way mirror through which our commanders observe and score us during training. I don't really want to discuss why I wasn't on time while they're listening, but I know it hasn't gone unnoticed.

Jacobi takes advantage of my distraction by jumping to attack. What little lift he gains works against him, slowing his assault. I bring my blades up to counter his blow.

"Late and distracted," Jacobi chides. "Better for me."

On any given day, I retreat from Nacoma Knight Academy like a sting gone wrong. I hate that place. I'm forced to be there seven hours a day and assigned to patrol when darkling energy is highest, from midnight until four in the morning.

Basically, I never get to leave.

The worst part?

Nothing *ever* happens.

It's basically patrol with training wheels for knights-in-training like me, and it's not preparing us for much we haven't already dealt with. Even though the school used to be an asylum, it's also long been a stronghold of Valryn, and most of the dead tend to avoid it. The curfew is only enforced to allow us to patrol unbothered. Sure, sometimes a stray spirit or two will wander campus and scare some kids who've snuck into the woods to party, or Vera, our resident dead girl, will get a little testy and break a window (she thinks she's scarier than she really is), but that's about as intense as it gets. The

44

real action's outside the boundaries of Nacoma Knight where ranked shadow knights like my father get to patrol and fight darklings.

But today, things got interesting.

Case in point: Vera is missing.

Missing might be the wrong word. *She isn't in her usual place.*

The thing about the dead is they're as predictable as rain after a car wash. Vera is a mobile spirit and roams about campus, but she takes the same routes she did when she was alive. She'll wander into buildings, to the rooms where she had class, but at 3:05 p.m.—the exact time she hung herself about fifty years ago—she'll return to her noose over the doors at Emerson Hall. But today, she wasn't there.

I ran out of time scouting campus for her. I still need to search the woods on patrol tonight before I report her missing. Still, I know she's out there somewhere, because her noose remains. It's like a relic, tethering her soul to earth. When that disappears, it's really time to worry.

"Did the new girl keep you?" Jacobi tries again, and my blades collide with his, jarring me from my thoughts. We pause for a moment; our breathing is heavy, and the muscles in my arms start to throb. The observation is a little startling as I realize Jacobi's fighting with more force than usual. We step away from each other; our knives untangle with a crisp zing.

"No." I shift my blades in my hands to get a better grip.

I came into training thinking I could take my mind off things, which is usually the case, but today, each strike reminds me something is *wrong*.

45

Just as wrong as Anora's reaction to the dead…the second thing to challenge my complaint that nothing ever happens at Nacoma Knight Academy.

It was sort of funny, watching her interact with Vera…until it wasn't. After her first sighting, I expected her to go about her day like all the other death-speakers at our school who can see the dead—like it is normal. As sure as the sky is blue, dead people roam the earth.

But she didn't. She freaked.

I mean, I hate walking through the dead too, and Vera isn't exactly the most delightful spirit to behold. That head of hers is held on by a thread of skin, but she's nice for the most part, unless she spots a bully. We've had to shine a light through her head on more than one occasion to redirect her attention. I'm sure Anora has seen worse. I've seen worse. So if it isn't the sight of the dead that scares her, what does?

Jacobi swings his blades toward my head and feet simultaneously. I jump back, stretching my wings to keep from falling.

"I saw you talking to her." He says it like an accusation, but he's just mad because I'm not willing to have a conversation about it.

I talked to her for…*reasons*: because it's my job as a student aide, because she is clearly a death-speaker, and I need to ensure she follows the rules set forth by the Order. They're basically the Congress of the Valryn world and just as dysfunctional. Some death-speakers have a tendency to involve themselves with the dead in ways that harm the living, specifically through the occult, which makes them dangerous and puts the Order on edge.

But Anora doesn't show any signs of practicing the occult. She isn't aged beyond her years. Her hair is dark and shiny, her skin and eyes are clear—she practically glows—and she's healthy and strong. If anything, it feels like she's just a normal teenage girl. Except I'm pretty sure I've met her before.

The problem is that she doesn't *look* familiar. This is more something I *feel*. Something inside me reacts to her presence, like we're connected by an invisible thread. When she walks away, that thread unravels with her. When I don't follow, it pulls taut at my chest. Even now, I rub the spot where the feeling is tightest. Which makes Jacobi laugh.

"What the hell is wrong with you, Savior?" he says, swinging his blade toward my side. I spin away from him just in time. "You're acting weird."

He's right. And it's not just this stupid feeling in my chest.

She *did* things today that pulled at my memory just like this thread pulls at the space over my heart: laugh so that chills pricked my arms, or nervously pressed her full lips together, or tilted her head to the side as she studied me, narrowing those pretty hazel eyes in a way that made me think she finds me just as familiar. I spent all day trying to figure out where I'd met her, stared at her so much she even called me out like a stalker. I'm not meant to have a connection with a human, and I want to know why I feel this way about her.

So yeah. I'll take what I can get. The first sign she's involved in the occult, the interrogation begins. Until then, I'm going to play friend. At least being around her will dull this stupid ache in my chest. I'm going insane.

47

And, apparently, losing.

Jacobi's blade hits my shoulder. While the strike doesn't tear through my armor, it startles me. "Ah!"

Jacobi falls back, laughing again. His teeth match the soft white walls and hard floor surrounding us.

"You're so distracted, Shy. It's unlike you." Jacobi twirls his blade once and then sticks it into the floor. "Are you seriously obsessing over that pretty new human girl?"

"*No.*"

It is against the rules of the Order for a Valryn and human to have a relationship, and any offspring born of a coupling between the two races are referred to as abominations, as they're often disfigured, with bones and feathers protruding where wings and skin might have been. Something in our blood—maybe the part that gives us wings—doesn't mix well with human DNA. Not to mention a lot of my beliefs don't exactly line up with the human world. I don't believe in God or heaven or any of that. My creator is Charon, the keeper of the Adamantine Gates—the only way for spirits to enter the afterlife.

"Did you see that catch she managed when the ball was heading toward her? Pretty good reflexes," Jacobi muses.

I grunt and try to kick Jacobi's blade from where he's planted it in the floor, but he's too quick. He's right, though; Anora's reflexes matched ours, as if she's been trained by an elite from the Order herself. Another thing that doesn't sit well with me—who taught Anora to fight, and why is it necessary?

"Natalie doesn't seem to think it's a good idea for you to hang out with her," he continues.

"Natalie just doesn't want anyone to steal her spotlight."

Natalie can't stand to be outdone by anyone, much less a death-speaker.

"Ten bucks says the new girl bests Natalie."

"Don't encourage them. It's going to be hard enough for Natalie to leave Anora alone at school."

"What do you care?" I know what he's thinking—*she's just a human.*

"I don't. Anyways, we have bigger things to worry about." And if Natalie needs a reminder, all she has to do is turn on the television to see Influence's handiwork.

Influence is like a parasite. It's a chaotic energy that compels humans to commit heinous and unspeakable acts or tearing the world apart with natural disasters. The plane crash in Switzerland is the most recent antic. Last week, it was another earthquake in Haiti, and before that, a bomb on a London train. All claimed hundreds of lives, all resulting in more souls tethered to the living world and more power for Influence. The longer *it* lives, the more unstable earth becomes. Some Valryn believe Influence is the beginning of the end, Armageddon.

"Regardless," Jacobi continues. "If Vera sees Natalie picking fights, she's in for it."

Yeah, if Vera's *there* to see it.

I keep that thought to myself, instead clearing my mind of the clutter that's been distracting me and focusing on my blades. Their weight is a familiar comfort in my hands. We have been together since I started training at twelve. Unlike my suit, my blades cannot be bought. They are made from the essences of Spirit, from Charon's forges, and have protected me far better than any armor or human weapon.

The air thickens between me and Jacobi, but I'm

calm, my arms relaxed at my sides. My father's rules echo in my head. I know them as well as I know the alphabet: one, *never strike first*. Two, *never provide the enemy with a mirror*. Three, *smile*.

My lips twitch.

Jacobi is familiar enough with me that he returns the smile, but either his impatience or his nerves get to him, because he lifts his blades. That's what my father means by not providing a mirror—keeping my arms at my sides prevents my opponent from knowing when I will make my move.

My smile widens.

Jacobi strikes, jabbing with the weapon in his right hand. I deflect the blow and parry the follow-up attack from his left with my other blade. We pull away and then circle each other like prey. My wings feel like a cloak dragging the ground, and I stretch them, wishing I could take flight in this cramped room, but that's not the point of this exercise.

"I know girls melt at your feet when you flash that smile, but it's creepy as hell when you're trying to kill me."

My opponent moves swiftly, one blade swiping toward my chest and the other coming down upon my head. I jump away and cross my swords over my head to deflect the attack. Jacobi pulls his blades back and swings. I collapse to my knees as the weapons cut the air above me. The ground is not an ideal vantage point, so I use my swords as one and go for Jacobi's legs. He jumps away, avoiding the assault, but it's given me the space I need to get to my feet. We stand opposite each other again, our chests rising and falling. This time, Jacobi's smiling.

"I almost had you."

It's true that Jacobi is improving, but he has yet to catch up to me.

Motivated by his progress, Jacobi rushes to attack again, his right blade flashing under the fluorescent lights. His left remains aloft, on defense, prepared for my counter-attack. It's that blade I focus on as I charge him. Surprise flashes through his eyes, and at the last second, I slide to my knees, ducking under the blade in his left hand. As I rise to my feet, I use the hilt of my weapon to disarm him, and before he can turn to face me, both of my blades are around his neck. This is the executioner's angle.

"Down," I command.

And Jacobi kneels. I look up at two bulbs sticking out over the black glass pane. One is green, the other is red—green is pass, red is fail. In the old days, when the Order first began, the colors had different meanings, and knights could actually be put to death for disappointing commanders during training. Seconds tick by, and still the lights remain off. I hate not being able to see into the window. Are the commanders even watching? Of course they are—always assessing and recording. Every move I've ever made has been entered into the archive, and they'll use all that data when I turn eighteen to decide my place in the Order.

My gaze falls to Jacobi at my feet. His head is down, his hair spills over his face, and his heavy breathing punctuates the air. It seems like every time we enter this room, we end up in this position, and each time, it takes longer for the commanders to give us the green light. I think they hope to embarrass Jacobi into performing the way they want, but that's not how he operates. Jacobi's not interested in fighting battles. He prefers hacking databases and stealing identities. Every time Roundtable has gone down, it's been because of him.

But the Order doesn't care half as much about those skills as they do our ability to fight. Because no matter where we're placed in the hierarchy after graduation, our first duty is as soldiers.

And yet I still don't like holding blades to my best friend's neck.

Finally, the green light flickers to life overhead. I uncross my blades with a zing and step away. Jacobi exhales, and his shoulders fall. He reaches for his second blade and gets to his feet. A clear, robotic voice sounds in the training room over the intercom.

"Jacobi, report to Commander Quinn."

While those orders don't necessarily mean anything bad for Jacobi—Commander Quinn is his mother—dread swirls in my stomach. Valryn aren't really all that nurturing.

Jacobi turns to me, and though he's smiling, I still see the defeat in his lackluster eyes and drooping shoulders. Part of me wants to apologize even though I don't know what I'm apologizing for. It's just a darkness has been crowding my thoughts for some time now, a sense that every time Jacobi and I face off, it might be his last.

Which is stupid.

The only reason I've started to think this way is because I've recently learned the current head of the Order, Luminary Maximus DuPont, is dying and that his son, Roth, will ascend to his place. That means change, and change under Roth isn't something I'm looking forward to. Not to mention it's coming at a time when the world seems to be drowning under Influence, and I don't think Roth's the one who'll bring us out of it. I think he'll push us further from the surface.

"See you tomorrow," Jacobi says.

He places his fist to his shoulder and bows his head. I do the same—a sign of respect among the Valryn. I watch Jacobi leave before I move toward the door but find my exit is blocked by a tall Valryn with square shoulders and dark, buzzed hair. He's dressed like me, only far more decorated—not with medals like humans but with thread. Gold entwines his waist, crawls up his chest, and wraps around his shoulders and upper arms. They're the markings I want one day.

As he moves into the training room, he claps. The tips of his wings drag the floor.

"Elite Cain," I salute him.

Cain is the head of our branch of the Order. He oversees the commanders. Consequently, I don't see much of him as a knight-in-training, so the fact that he's crashing my training session makes me nervous.

"Bravo," he says, surveying me from head to toe. "Your father must be *very* proud."

It's hard not to roll my eyes. I look over Cain's shoulder to where my father always stands—in the shadow of his elite. He's hard to miss. I look just like him. People like to tell me that, like they think I'll forget I'm related to him. Like those eyes—the color of deep water and just as cold—would be narrowed in disappointment at anyone other than his son.

"I hoped I might have a word with you." Elite Cain pauses, watching me with unmoving eyes, and I work to hide my surprise.

"How can I be of service?"

A slow, tight smile cracks across Cain's face. "I'm sure you're aware of Commander Savior's importance to my team." Commander Bastian Savior, my father, is one of four commanders Elite Cain has at his disposal. They carry out all manner of orders—orders that take them away from their families more often than not. "Your excellence in training has been noted, and I assume you will prove an asset like Commander Savior, which is why I'm entrusting you with an assignment."

I look for a reaction from my father, but he's vacant, like a human after death.

"An assignment, Elite Cain?"

"Your first to prove if you're ready to be a knight of the Order."

I offer a nervous laugh and quickly shut my mouth. Part of training is learning to hide emotion—emotion means enemies finding weaknesses, and weaknesses mean death. "It's an honor for you to say, Elite Cain, but I haven't graduated yet. I still have nine months of training."

"Do you wish to challenge my judgment?"

"No, Elite Cain."

"You are at the head of your class, far more advanced than any knight-in-training your age. I know your father has given you no unfair advantage. This is in your *soul*."

I keep his gaze, even though his words make me feel uncomfortable. He twists on his heels, hands behind his back, and starts to make a circle around me. I flex my fingers, ignoring the instinctual pull to reach for my weapon.

"It is a simple enough task. Think of it as…a test of your loyalty."

That feeling of discomfort intensifies, raising the hair on the back of my neck.

*Loyalty.*

That word has been used a lot recently, especially with my family, and I don't like it.

"Successor Roth has requested Council and will lead in his father's stead. He's asked our best knights to attend."

My heart beats faster.

"I'm appointing you as his guard for the duration of his stay. That means seeing to his safe arrival and return to and from the airport and anywhere in between."

I deflate, punctured by the blow.

*You have to be kidding me.*

I hate Roth DuPont. And this may sound like an honor, but basically it's being his glorified gofer.

He's arrogant and self-serving, and he cheats in battle, though he claims otherwise; it's the only way he can beat me. I'm not the best choice for this job, seeing as how I'd like to shove his face into concrete. I want to say as much, but my honesty wouldn't be appreciated, especially by Elite Cain, who sees this as a lofty assignment. Who wouldn't want to protect our luminary-in-training?

Me.

Still, now that I have had time to consider, why would Roth call Council? He's not luminary yet. Did it have something to do with the plane crash? Maybe it has something to do with the shadow knight who died in New York a month ago, his soul stolen right out of his body. It is clear darklings are getting stronger and bolder. The only way to fight them is to ferry lost souls into Spirit, a gift the Valryn once possessed but lost. Now the only thing we can do is protect as many humans as possible.

It's getting harder.

Soon it will be impossible.

Those of us who still believe in Charon think he'll send our salvation—the Eurydice, the only one who is granted the power to summon the Adamantine Gates and ferry souls into Spirit to heal and reincarnate. It's also our job to support and train her.

I know I won't have answers unless I haul Roth around in my Jeep.

As bad as it'll be, I'll suffer through it to attend Council.

"When should I expect him?" I'm proud of how steady my voice is—all business—even if I want to spit blood every time I hear Roth's name.

"Friday."

"So soon?"

"I hope you don't have plans."

I know just as well as anyone that a shadow knight's first obligation is to the Order; everything else in life comes second. There is no room for negotiations. My father shows this on a daily basis, and my mother learned it the hard way. Still, the simple dismissal of my life outside the Compound makes my blood boil. I may not care that much about school, but it's still part of who I am.

"Of course not, Elite Cain. I just did not expect to serve so soon."

Cain offers the same splintered smile. I always imagine him as a doll—his features painted in lifelike color but his expression hollow. "Then this is an honor."

I place my fist to my chest and bow my head in acceptance of his task, but it feels like poison in my veins.

Elite Cain turns, and for a moment, I'm left with a clear view of my father. I haven't seen him in about three days, so it makes sense that the first thing out of his mouth would be criticism.

"Your footwork was slow," he advises.

I should hold my tongue, especially in front of Elite Cain, but I can't. "I'm not looking for your approval."

I haven't made any attempt to get along with my father recently. I'm never good enough for him, so I've stopped trying.

As Elite Cain reaches the door, he pauses and calls over his shoulder. "We expect you at precisely six o'clock, Shy." *Exactly one hour before the football game.* He turns his head to look at me. "You are lucky to be living in this time of change."

# CHAPTER FIVE
## Anora and the Coin Box

*Our new home is a two-story house with white siding and* a big front porch. Very different from the multifloor, brick apartment Mom and I moved from. I like it well enough, and there is definitely more room. Boxes are stacked all around, most of them new furniture, things to replace those we didn't get to bring with us. Photos and frames rest on the bar. I pause, taking note of the ones Mom chose: pictures of Poppy—my grandmother—with Poppa and pictures of me when I was little.

Mom tosses her keys on the counter and sifts through the mail.

"You can work on unpacking your room before dinner," she says.

"Are you sure? I can help with dinner," I offer. Mom and I enjoy cooking, especially together.

She shakes her head. "You need an organized place to study. I'll work on dinner."

I don't need to be told again. Besides, I want to be

by myself for a little while. I head upstairs to my room. It's larger than the last one. A bay window overlooks the front lawn and lets in a lot of light, and two built-in bookshelves flank either side of it. I turn up my music and start unpacking and shelving books.

After, I move to folding and hanging clothes, not that it is necessary. Coming to Nacoma Knight Academy means committing myself to a colorless life of navy skirts and white shirts—just another way to drown the old me. I use the process to mourn some of my favorite clothes—colorful dresses, comfy sweaters, geek T-shirts, and skinny jeans. The only clothing items I held on to from before are my tights.

The next box is the only one I labeled *Poppa*. It's full of his stargazing equipment: a set of astronomy binoculars, several posters of the night sky, and a cheap telescope he gave me for my tenth birthday. He had a bigger, fancier version, but Mom sold it for money for the move to Oklahoma.

My eyes burn with unshed tears as I remove everything from the box and arrange it around my room. Before we came here, I was torn between research fields: astrophysics or engineering. Did I want to discover planets and stars or orbit the earth?

But something happened the day Poppa died, and I put my dreams on hold, and ever since then, things have been falling apart.

The last item in this box doesn't belong to Poppa. It's a wood chest full of coins like the one I created today. I don't make a habit of turning every soul of the dead I meet into a piece of hard metal, just the ones who scare me. It's not something I can really control.

The first soul I captured was my poppa. It was a knee-jerk reaction. I found him just as he died, and a plume of black exploded from his body, tangled with his soul. I had never seen anything like it. The fear made the thread burst to life, and the next thing I knew, my poppa's soul was just a coin on the ground, and the black thing zipped away.

I have yet to figure out what that black thing was, but it *felt* horrible, like a burden too great to bear.

His coin is the only one that doesn't go in the box. I wear him on a chain around my neck, close to my heart.

I move to the other side of my bed and sit on the floor, slipping my hand into the mesh pocket where I placed the coin I created earlier in the day...but it's not there.

My heart beats hard against my chest as I fall to my knees and pour the contents of my bag onto the floor. Pens and notebooks scatter, but there is no gold coin.

Where did I drop it?

*The car.*

I close the chest and shove it under the bed, darting down the stairs and outside. Opening the passenger side door, I look everywhere—between the seats and under, the cupholders, the glove box. I wade through the grass outside the car and check the flower beds at the front of our house with no luck.

"Everything all right?" Mom asks from the front door. I twist to face her, heart leaping into my throat. How long has she been watching me?

"Yeah, everything's fine."

She looks between me and the car. "Lose something?"

"Just can't find a folder I thought I brought home."

Mom lifts her head, staring down her nose, and though my lie was smooth, I know she's questioning me.

"Dinner's ready."

She turns without another word and enters the house.

I make my way back up the steps, watching my feet as I go, still searching for the coin. I'll have to retrace my steps tomorrow—from the tree line where I captured the soul to the stadium. Maybe check lost and found. Hopefully some Good Samaritan turned it in, because a lost coin could mean a blown cover.

Inside, the house smells like tomato sauce, roiling my stomach.

*Oh no.*

"I made your favorite!" Mom says, smiling. The wrinkles on the sides of her eyes make her look happier than she has in a long time.

Too bad I'd basically thrown up tomatoes and fake meat today.

I swallow hard, feeling much like I did earlier— feverish and scared. Of all the days Mom might choose to let go of her anger toward me, why today?

"Thanks, Mom." I try to smile, but my mouth is coated in a thick, sour layer of saliva.

Her smile falters. "What's wrong?"

"Nothing." I take my seat at the table, trying to keep my voice light, but I've already ruined what she is trying to do here. She looks away before I finish speaking, tightening her jaw as she starts serving food.

Mom's always been challenging because of her episodes, but since I told her about the dead, she watches me more than ever and scrutinizes every word I speak. I guess it's easier for her to focus on my issues than her own.

Her movements are quick and jerky. She tosses spaghetti on a plate so hard, the whole thing crashes to the table. That fuels her anger, so she slings sauce on top, except it doesn't land on the spaghetti. It lands in a line across the table and my face.

I reach for my napkin and wipe the red pulp from my face, not looking at her. Somehow, I have gotten it into my head that if I don't meet her stare, this won't hurt as bad.

Being around Mom is confusing. It's like walking on a perfectly normal floor when it shifts beneath you, opening a chasm. The drop makes your stomach rise into your throat, but the joke's on you because you land on your feet. The aftermath remains, and you feel shaky and unsteady, completely unsure of what you did wrong. Was it a look you gave, a word you said?

Mom picks up the plate she's destroyed and disappears into the kitchen. While she's gone, I clean up the sauce. My eyes water, but nothing more.

She returns to the dining room with clean plates and serves again. This time, she's calm.

It's moments like this I wonder what it might be like to have a dad. Would he be the force field that protects me from Mom's anger? Poppa was.

Silence strains between us as Mom sits down after her second attempt serving dinner tonight. I work around my food, only eating plain pasta.

When Mom speaks again, it's like she's erased the last ten minutes from her memory. Her voice has a happy, interested edge. She even smiles. It's the turn of her lips I focus on, because I know if I meet her gaze, I won't see anything there—no warmth, no happiness, no Mom.

"I didn't get to ask you how school went today."

"It was great. There's a football game Friday. I think it might be considered sacrilege if I don't go."

"Oh. That's good. So you made friends?"

"Yeah. I met a really cool girl named Lennon and the quarterback of the football team."

"The quarterback? That wasn't the boy you were talking to when I came to pick you up, was it?"

"No." I hesitate. "He—the quarterback—was at practice."

"I was going to say...it might be hard for him to run and keep up his smoking habit."

My face drains of color. I should have known that wouldn't go unnoticed. "It's not like...we're not friends, Mom."

"Who is he?"

"His name is Thane. I think...I think he's sad." I don't *think* that—I *know* that. But at my comment, my mom looks up.

"Don't make someone your project, Anora. You can't change people."

Well, *this* is definitely awkward, and while I know the words that come out of my mouth might begin World War III, I say them anyway.

"Is that what happened with Dad?" I ask. "Did you think you could change him?"

We don't talk about Dad. What I know of him isn't much. He had a lot of problems and left Mom when I was two. She says I have his eyes. I sometimes wonder if he left because of mom's issues.

Mom halts midbite, but she doesn't look at me as she replies with a simple, "No."

63

# CHAPTER SIX
## Shy and the Hellhounds

*I stand outside on the highest tier of the Compound, a* five-story, obsidian tower and the headquarters for our branch of the Order. There are four in the United States: Oklahoma, New York, California, South Dakota, and one in every country across the world. Compound sites were chosen based on where the Adamantine Gates once stood. Our capitol is in New York. That's where Maximum DuPont is dying and where Roth will come into power.

At this height, I can see for miles—over the tops of trees to the horizon, painted blue with sky and gray by the lake. The wind is harsh, and I have to hide my wings just to stand in place. Knifelike pinnacles surround me, descending in a spiral like a dizzying set of mechanical teeth. A wall of the same glossy, black stone cuts through the woods around our fortress, covering ten acres and measuring twenty-six feet high. It's a smooth, impenetrable shield—a reminder of the Valryn's violent past.

Usually, I hang out and wait for Jacobi, but I'm still feeling the effects of my conversation with Elite Cain. Something about the appointment as Roth's guard doesn't feel right. Maybe I'm just worried about Council being called. Still, any Valryn can guess one thing they'll discuss: the growing number of lost souls on earth feeding darklings, creating new ones every day. It has been impossible to keep up. There are Valryn in the field, discovering, cataloging, and capturing them to test their skills and figure out how they die.

I spread my arms wide, step off the edge of the roof, and fall until the wind is blocked by the trees and I'm able to shift into my raven form, moving easily between the thick trees surrounding the Compound.

I fly until I find my Jeep in the clearing where I left it after school. As I land, I change into my human form. I peel off my sweat-soaked shirt, toss it into the back of my Jeep, and retrieve a fresh one from my bag. Before I'm clothed, feet thud on the ground behind me. I don't have to turn to know who's there—I sensed her following me the moment I left the Compound.

"I'm not sure why you bother driving. It's not like you need to."

Unlike me, Natalie prefers to fly everywhere she goes, and she tends to forget that she uses my Jeep as a way to explain how she gets from place to place.

I sigh. "What do you want, Natalie?"

Natalie ignores me. "Unless you think it makes you more human."

I clench my jaw. She's trying to pick a fight with me.

"Not in the mood, Nat." I meet her gaze, and we glare at each other until she relents.

65

"Jacobi's been put on probation."

"What?" Probation means Jacobi is banned from participating in patrol, raids, and stings—basically everything he needs credit for if he's going to graduate and be placed among ranks as a knight.

"Tonight was the third training he failed this month against you. You knew this was coming. Would it kill you to let him win just one?" For all that she follows the rules, she's different when it comes to Jacobi.

"Jacobi wouldn't want that," I snap. "Besides, how would that help him?"

"He wouldn't be on probation! Do you want him to rank as a knight?"

"I'm not even going to answer that." I climb into the driver's side of my Jeep. "You're not the only one who cares."

I don't look at Natalie as I speak. I start my Jeep and peel out, circling her as I leave. My tires move over the gravel road easily, but I find I can't release my breath until I hit the even surface of the pavement. Natalie's voice grates against my eardrums, and I set my teeth tighter.

No matter the situation, Natalie has to appear like she cares more than anyone else. She is pretty much viewed as a saint at school and the Compound, and she likes to maintain that reputation.

I travel about five miles down a narrow two-lane road crowded with overgrown trees before turning off toward my house. The gravel pops beneath my tires, and I come to a slow stop. I live on the outskirts of Rayon. My house is a two-story cottage with wood siding and leaded-glass windows. The roof comes to a point in two places, and my mother keeps the garden against the house manicured so not a single shrub rises above the windowsills. This house and the land belong to my father's family, and it's been passed down each generation.

It's just another thing I don't want to inherit from my father.

I head inside. Even before the door closes, my mom's voice reaches me. "Shy, is that you?"

"Hey, Mom!" I call back as I take off my shoes in the entryway. My mom's as sweet as sugar until you track dirt on her floor. She appears as I start to move into the kitchen. I look nothing like her. She's Irish through and through: red hair, green eyes, a light dusting of freckles, and an accent as thick as the woods around our house. She's also one of the best medics in our Compound, but she's been suspended from duty until further notice for basically being a good person. It's stupid, and it makes me angry just thinking about it.

I have a feeling that's another reason Dad's kept his distance…because he's embarrassed.

"Shy." She leans forward to press a kiss to my cheek while simultaneously handing me one of her homemade pizza pockets. Nothing—and I mean nothing—frozen comes into this household. "How was your day?"

"Good," I say quickly and move past her into the kitchen to grab a glass of water. "How was yours?"

She sighs. "Busy, but that will change soon. I hired a new agent today."

"Oh?" I ask, taking a seat at the table and a big bite of pizza pocket. "Who's the lucky one?"

By day, Mom's a real estate agent—the best, they say.

"Her name is Jayne Silby."

67

I was only half listening before. Now Mom has my whole attention.

She continues. "She's new to town. Just moved here with her daughter. She'll have to get her license, but I think she'll be a great addition to my team."

"Silby, huh?" Anora said her mother moved here for a job, but that doesn't seem to be the case. "I think I met her daughter today at school."

"Was she nice?"

"Very." My brows rise as I speak—nice, beautiful, odd...*familiar*. The muscles in my chest tighten as I recall her eyes—heavy-lidded and a mix of green and brown.

"I'm sure she must be pretty if she looks anything like her mother." Mom's statement is saturated with sweetness and a hint of warning. She knows just as well as any Valryn that any affection I might develop for a human is wasted...and dangerous. Then, realizing I'm rubbing the spot on my chest where the ache is greatest, I drop my hand.

"Did her mom say why they moved here?"

"Just that things were complicated back home and they were looking for a fresh start."

The answer disappoints me, but I can't really blame them for keeping their business to themselves. It just means I'm going to have to work harder to discover the information I want.

I pop the last bite of pizza pocket into my mouth and move to stand. I have patrol tonight, but I need a shower first.

"Did you see your father at the Compound?"

I pause and turn to face my mom. "How many days has it been since you've seen him?"

68

Mom doesn't respond, suddenly busy with the dishes. I know the answer; I just want to see if she will admit it.

"It's three, Mom. He hasn't been home for three days."

Dad's day job is as a petroleum engineer for Malachi Black's Oil & Gas, and once that shift is over, he goes to the Compound where he carries out a variety of orders issued by Elite Cain. There are times when he's home at four in the morning, but at least I see him at breakfast. That hasn't been the case the last few days.

"I'm sure he's busy. You know this whole thing with Luminary Maximum has him stressed."

It is stressful for all of us.

"That doesn't mean he can ignore us." Well, I'd prefer he ignore me. I might escape some of his scrutiny that way, but I know it hurts Mom, and that's something I can't stand.

"Shy—"

"I know...don't talk about your father like that." I mimic her voice poorly.

"No...just." She pauses and takes a breath. "Give him the benefit of the doubt. You don't know what he does for this family."

She's right. I don't.

But I'll do anything for Mom. I sigh. "I'll work on that," I assure her, giving her a quick kiss on the cheek before hurrying upstairs.

After my shower, it's close to midnight and time for patrol. I climb onto the roof beneath the starry sky, shifting into my hybrid form. They say the night through human eyes is beautiful, peaceful even. But I'm not human, and when stars come out, so do the dead and those who hunt them.

I'm not complaining. Truth is, I enjoy the chaos after dark. The night is my playground. I just wish I got to experience more of it beyond the borders of Nacoma Knight Academy. I glance at my watch: I have fifteen minutes before I have to be at the school, and though I'm anxious to look for Vera, I'm not in a hurry to be back on campus, which only encourages me to stop by Anora's house. Besides, the more I learn about her, the more I'll understand my connection to her.

I spread my wings and take off into the night, telling myself it's just a routine check. Often, when people move to the area, knights keep a closer watch, as darklings find newer energies more enticing and easier to prey upon.

As I near Anora's, I shift into my raven form and land in a tree outside her house. She has pushed her bike to the edge of her lawn, one leg swung over as if she's ready to take off, but she's not moving. Her fingers flex on the handlebars.

I know exactly when the clock strikes midnight because the streetlights begin to flash and the wind picks up, lifting her hair. Her scent fills me: she's sweet, like a rose. Finally, the streetlights go out completely, and I guess that's enough to convince her not to take off, because she unhooks her leg from over the bike and walks it back to the house. Then she scales the lattice and crawls into the middle window on the second floor. The light in her room remains illuminated a few moments longer before it goes out. That's when a pair of bright red eyes ignite in the darkness around her house, followed by a growl.

*What the...*

A massive doglike creature moves out of the shadow. Skin and matted fur cover parts of the dog, yet in places, bone and muscle peek through. The stench coming off the animal is horrific—decay.

It's a hellhound, a creation of Charon's once used to guard the gates into Spirit, normally not a threat, and yet this hound growls at me, bowing low as if to pounce. It can probably sense how much I hate it. I don't like dogs in any form.

I fly from the tree and away from Anora's house. The hound follows, howling and slinging slobber as it chases me down the road. Once I've left the last house behind me and am surrounded by trees, I shift into my hybrid form and land on the ground, widening my stance. The hound halts before me. His back looks bent, and his hips are narrow, as if he's been run over.

"You're an ugly bastard."

The hound howls, blowing sticky, rotting breath in my face. I choke on the stench and unsheathe the blades on my back. "That"—I jump into the air and come down on top of the hellhound—"was rude."

My blade sinks easily into the demonic dog, and the howl that escapes the creature's mouth is more like the whistle of a freight train. He starts to move and shake his head vigorously, trying to throw me off and get the blades out. I pull my knives free and jump off, landing in the middle of the road. The hound tries to run, stumbles, and falls, finally halting some distance from me, dead.

I let out a breath, relieved the creature wasn't harder to destroy, but then something inside it starts to move. A sick feeling settles in my stomach as the body of the hound explodes and several smaller but equally terrifying hounds emerge. There are five in total. They all turn and growl at me, baring razor-sharp teeth.

71

"Dammit."

I'm pretty sure that isn't supposed to happen.

The hounds attack all at once. I slash at the creature closest to me and then jump into the air, hovering over the others as they snap at me. I land behind them and strike, charging at the pack. I manage to hit the hound on my left and the one in front of me with my blades, but the third grabs my right arm, his teeth sinking deep into my skin. The pain is cruel. I drop the blade and rip my arm away, jamming my second blade through the dog's eye. It yelps but only springs back into formation with the other four, unharmed hounds.

This is not how I was taught to defeat a hellhound. In practice, we are made to fight holograms, which are programmed to act just like the real thing. Hellhounds are all but indestructible unless you skewer their brain, or so I thought.

They crouch low and bare their teeth, growling in unison and collectively smelling like a pit of dead bodies.

Sometimes my job is the worst.

I tighten my grip on my blade and pull a small scythe-like weapon from the holster on my thigh, wincing at the shot of pain that bolts up my arm. The hounds inch toward me. I mimic their stance, bending my legs, preparing to jump before they attack.

Then the hounds halt and go quiet, and their ears perk, listening to something I can't hear. After a moment, they turn their heads up to the sky and howl. The sound pierces me, like an arrow through smoke, and I pray to Charon they aren't summoning more of their kind.

Suddenly, the hounds bolt, moving together in a pack down the street, and while I'd prefer to be rid of them,

I can't let them cause havoc. Most importantly, I need to figure out where they came from, but the hounds are fast, teasing like will-o-the-wisps, disappearing into the tree line. I fly overhead and drop, wingless, below the branches in an attempt to follow, but the hounds are out of my sight. The only indication that they're still running is the sound of breaking branches.

I follow the tracks until they disappear—not into a hole or a lake or anything, just until they vanish into thin air. I halt, breathless, tangled in the tree limbs.

"Dammit!" I hit the tree with my fist. "Ah!" Pain fires up my arm, and I sink against the trunk. My heart throbs in my chest, causing the rest of my body to vibrate painfully.

I sit for a while, attempting to gain control and make sense of what happened. I don't think a Valryn has ever reported a hellhound attack. I should have been more careful, but I had no reason to suspect the hellhound would chase me—or multiply or not die. We are both Charon's creations; surely it could sense that.

I should jump at the chance to turn this information over to the Order. It's not my job to question the whys. This could aid in my placement as a commander or even an elite. And yet something about the incident and their presence at Anora's house keeps me from getting out my phone and making the call.

I swallow hard and rub the spot on my chest where my skin is pinched and uncomfortable. My arm screams in protest. If I could reach in and rip out the hold Anora has on me, I would, but I don't have anything to grasp, no thread that might lead me to the answer of who she is, and until I figure it out, until Council is over, I'm going to keep this whole ordeal to myself. I just have to treat this wound before it becomes infected. I wonder if Mom has any medical supplies lying around from before she was suspended.

Like her, I'm choosing the rules I want to obey.

# CHAPTER SEVEN
# Anora and the Boy Who Sees the Dead

*Everything about this morning is a disaster.*

I woke up to Mom yelling I'm going to make her late, five minutes before we were supposed to leave. Now I'm crossing campus in the uniform I wore yesterday: wrinkled skirt, smelly blazer, with the exception of a pair of knee-high, navy tights. Nothing else, my makeup-free face and frizzy hair, gives the impression I tried.

The only reason I overslept in the first place is because I kept myself up thinking about the coin, trying to decide if I could ride the distance to Nacoma Knight on my bike, then deciding it was too dark to find something like that in the grass. I finally convinced myself I would locate it once I retraced my steps—either between the trees, at the football field, or maybe someone turned it into lost and found. I just hope it isn't discovered by the *wrong* person, because there are people who want what I create.

There are people who want *me*.

But my plan to search campus before school is on hold as I increase my pace from a fast walk to a run in an effort to make it to class on time. The absence of the coin has burrowed into my chest, creating a perfect nest for anxiety, and whatever creature takes residence there is growing bigger and bigger as every second ticks by.

*It's okay*, I tell myself, inhaling deep in an attempt to relieve the tension. *I'll search at lunch.* It's only a few more hours.

I reach Walcourt and round the corner, slamming into a body. I put my hands up and push away from the person, stumbling back.

"I'm so—" My apology dies on my lips when I see who I've run into—Thane Treadway. He smirks at me. I hold my breath to keep from inhaling his cigarette-infused scent. We stand apart, staring at each other. I'm not sure why I can't bring myself to break away.

After a moment, he speaks. "Maybe you should reconsider this whole school thing."

"Excuse me?"

He shrugs. "Nacoma fosters obedience. You can't even make it to class on time. Trust me, they notice when you don't fit their mold."

"I'm sure you know that from personal experience." His smile remains unchanged, but his eyes glitter. Like he's proud of that fact.

What does Thane know about me? I can fit into a mold. I've done it before. Stuffed myself into sharp corners and uneven surfaces. And I fit. Until I didn't. Until an arm came free from its binding and the thread unwound and ruined everything.

That's what doesn't fit in the mold. The thread.

"Or maybe you want to be bad at this," Thane says, narrowing his eyes. "Maybe you like the attention."

I lift my chin, challenging him. "Excuse me while I go fit the mold." I try to sidestep him, but he blocks my way. "Move," I command, glaring at him.

He puts his hands up, and I brush past him, hitting his shoulder. "Oh, but I did want to ask you—what happened to Vera?"

I have to give him props. He got straight to the point, no false friendships or feigned interest, just business.

I turn to face him. "Vera?"

"Yeah." His lips lift, and his eyes gleam like obsidian. It's unsettling and makes me hyperaware of everything. "The dead girl who usually hangs outside Emerson. Where is she?"

How does he know about the dead girl? The creature that's taken up residence in my chest has claws, and they dig deep, deep, deep, just grazing my heart, beating hard in my chest.

*Fit the mold, Anora. Don't let him know about you.*

So I say, "Are you high?"

Thane's unfazed and takes a step toward me, closing the distance between us, and suddenly the air feels heavier. I imagine him as a monster with long claws surrounding me like a cage. His heat is not like Shy's, which is somehow calming. Thane feels like a burden. How can two boys create such different sensations inside me? And why?

"You aren't the only one who can see the dead, or did you not know that?"

I avert my gaze, staring at the wall—staring at

anything but his abyss-like eyes. I swear I can see flames in them, like he's the incarnation of hell.

"They will notice," he continues. "And they'll search and search and search until they find her...and when they can't find her, well, they'll come for you."

"Are they people like you?" There is bitterness in my voice.

He laughs. "No, not like me. They're not people at all."

Those words hang between us—a threat, needlelike, sharp. It draws the air from my lungs and awakens my body like a live wire. I clench my fist tight. The thread's desperate, burrowing out, grazing the surface of my palm.

"What makes you think I know what happened to Vera?"

"You're the newest thing to grace Nacoma Knight's campus in four long years," he says.

"So you have no evidence?"

He raises a brow—perfect, arched. "Is there ever evidence?"

No, there isn't.

Didn't I know that from experience? Evidence doesn't mean anything, only accusations.

My nails bite into my skin, and the pain releases me from the cage Thane seemed to put around me. I start to turn away when an icy hand grips my left wrist—the hand where the thread lives. Thane's eyes travel from the tips of my fingers to the center of my palm where blood-filled crescents accompany scars of the same shape.

"Maybe you need to work on your anger," he says.

Thane's grip feels like steel biting my skin, and I curl my fingers into my aching palm, desperate to hide.

"Let. Go. Of. Me."

He smiles and then asks, "Or what?"

"Do not test me. You have no idea what I can do."

He lets go, and I pull away roughly, rubbing my wrist free of his touch.

"I'm counting on that." He takes a step back just as the bell rings. "Better get to class. Haven't you heard? Mr. Val is a prick."

I glare at him before turning slowly and heading to class. At first, I move away from him at a fast walk, but by the time I make it through Mr. Val's door, I'm running. I come to a stop, slightly out of breath, and realize Mr. Val has been waiting for me. I glance at the students on my right and find they're staring at me too. Natalie appears overzealous that I've been caught breaking another rule.

"Miss Silby," Mr. Val says, his tone patronizing. "So good of you to join us. You're late."

I look behind me. I'm not sure what I expect to find there—maybe my excuse? I open my mouth to defend myself. "I was—"

"Running," Mr. Val finishes, raising a brow. I feel like we're facing each other in a duel, and I know I'm going to lose. As Mr. Val moves to pick up a stack of papers on his desk, he says, "Two days of detention."

"What?"

His eyes cut back to me. "Do you want a third?" Snickers escape from somewhere in the room, and Mr. Val turns his terrible gaze on the class. "Would anyone like to join Miss Silby?"

The class is silent.

"Take your seat."

I keep my eyes on the floor as I find my desk and

slide low in my seat, shoulders weighed down with humiliation.

This day can't get any worse.

Mr. Val begins the lesson. His voice grates like the chalk squeaking against the blackboard as he writes. With each shrill stroke—the sharp turn of a seven, the swift cross of an X—Thane's words run through my head. *What happened to Vera?*

Vera.

The dead girl has a name.

She is well-known at this school where apparently I'm not the only one who can see the dead. *She is missed.*

I wanted to find the coin before, but now I'm desperate.

Who is Thane? Who are these "people" hunting me? Was he telling the truth, or is he one of them?

I should have been more careful, shouldn't have let my fear get in the way of my rules. I used to think if I could get rid of the thread, I could be normal. I tried pulling it out once. There'd been too much blood. Too much pain. Mom found me. I lied and said I cut my hand. The thread is part of me as much as my blood and my veins, and it responds to my fear and my anger…as if it's attached to my heart.

And that makes me afraid. Because I'm tempted to lose control, open my palm, and let the thread sprout like a flower and dance, twist, twirl, thread through Mr. Val's back, twine around his soul, and he'd fall to the floor, dead.

He'd be gone—that mundane suit, the wrinkles on the bottom of his jacket, that thick mustache. *Gone. And I wouldn't just be taking his soul. I'd be killing him.*

And there would be Thane with his coal-black eyes and ever-present smirk, asking me, "What happened to Mr. Val?"

"Miss Silby." Mr. Val's voice cuts through the air. I jump in my seat and meet his stare. "What is the value of y?"

My brain scrambles, and my tongue feels thick and swollen in my mouth. My gaze slides to the problem on the blackboard. It looks like a foreign language. Worse, Mr. Val's black eyes don't move from mine as he waits for an answer.

I think through what I'd been doing before I was called on.

Oh. The thread.

A thing just as alien as the problem on the board.

Mr. Val's eyes remain on me, even when he calls on someone else. "Miss Rivera."

"One," Natalie answers smugly.

"Correct."

At least Mr. Val doesn't seem impressed.

I take copious notes after that, but it isn't until the bell rings that I realize I've been clenching my fist so hard, my hand is shaking. I concentrate on uncurling my fingers one at a time until the pencil falls against the desk and rolls into my lap.

Mr. Val clears his throat, and I look up to find the class empty. He stands behind his desk, staring at me.

"As much as I think more practice would benefit you, Miss Silby, I'm sure you don't want to be late for your next class."

I scramble to my feet, shove my books into my bag, and hit my hip on one of the desks as I go to leave. Just as

I reach the door, Mr. Val calls me back. "Miss Silby." He hands me a slip of paper but does not look at me as he speaks. "Whatever you did before you came here is irrelevant, but you cannot start anew if you do not change the behavior that got you here in the first place." I open my mouth to speak, but I'm cut off. "You're excused."

I swallow hard and turn, leaving the room.

Once I'm outside, the wind runs long, slender fingers through my hair, cooling the back of my neck where sweat has gathered at the base of my scalp. The sun streams into my eyes and they sting. I blink rapidly.

Maybe Thane is right.

Maybe I'm not cut out for this.

But if not this, what?

How is it that my body parts are stitched together with tendon and muscle and ligament and thread? No amount of history or mythology has given me an inkling of hope that there are others like me, who can collect souls with a thread from their palm. Mom isn't like me. This isn't DNA. This is something else—something *other* and unknown.

*I don't know what I am.*

My fists tighten again—not to suppress the rebellious thread but to quash the thoughts running through my head. This isn't about the thread. This isn't about being alone. This is about survival. I have to survive. Mom has to survive, I remind myself. She won't make it without me. That means playing the game—fitting into the mold, bending, twisting, breaking—until nothing's left of the old Anora, the one I was supposed to leave behind before coming here.

I turn on my heels and march toward Hollingsworth, eyes focused on the trees where I'd confronted Vera yesterday. I'll find that damned coin, lock it up tight, and never, ever turn another soul again.

If there's no trail to follow, they can't find me, right?

"Anora!"

I keep walking.

"Anora!" Lennon runs up beside me. Her long, blond hair is pulled into a high ponytail and still manages to spill over her shoulders. "Where are you going? Biology is the other direction."

I halt and stare at her. Sometimes I feel like two completely different people. One Anora wants to admit to a mistake I know I didn't make. Laugh a little and say, "Oh, right," as I turn with Lennon and head to biology. The other Anora wants to remain expressionless. Offer a monotone "I know" and continue on my way. The first means appeasing my mother; the second means doing what I need to.

But I'm kidding myself if I don't admit that I want Lennon to like me. To think I'm normal.

So I smile.

"Oh, right… I guess I forgot my schedule for a moment."

Lennon smiles, but there's a brief sharpness to her eyes—like a lightning strike against a lavender sky—that tells me she doesn't really believe me.

I turn with her and head toward Kline. We walk for a few moments in silence. The air between us feels strained. Maybe it's because I have words at the back of my throat, eager to come out, eager to explain my behavior.

But then Lennon speaks, and I realize it's because she's been holding back.

"You'll never believe what's on Roundtable today."

83

I swallow the words once and for all. They slither down my throat, sour and sharp. I'd almost forgotten about Roundtable.

"What?"

"Nothing about you," she assures me.

Just then, a girl walks toward us along the buckled sidewalk. Her head is down, her blond hair curtains her face, and her books are pressed against her chest, fingers as white as snow. Students move out of her way but turn to stare as she passes—Lennon and I included. I hear whispers all around—*whore* and *slut*, words I hate.

"What's happening?" Because it looks an awful lot like public shaming.

"Remember when I told you something way bigger would overshadow your weirdness in art?"

"Yeah."

"Well, Lily Martin left her phone in English yesterday. Someone read her texts and discovered she's been sexting a guy from Rayon High School. It's all over Roundtable, with *pictures*."

"So?"

"So?" Lennon looks at me, astonished. "She was sexting someone from Rayon High School!"

"Don't you think seventy-five percent of the student body has sexted? Just because Lily got caught doesn't mean she should be ridiculed."

"Oh, you have it all wrong," Lennon explains. "It's not that she was sexting, it's *who*."

"You mean to say it is a crime that she looked outside Nacoma Knight Academy for a love interest?"

Lennon shrugs. "Something like that."

I hate this place already. It's only a matter of time

before Roundtable gets their hands on me beyond just being the new girl…and, well, I haven't decided what exactly I'll do when that happens.

Lily heads toward Walcourt, but my attention is diverted to a figure standing with his hands in his pockets, head inclined, watching Lily. It's Thane, and he's the only one who doesn't move aside as if she's the plague. As she nears him, she glances up momentarily. I can't see her face, but there's hesitation in her step. It's the way Thane looks at her—with soft features and eyes, as if to say *it's okay, I'm here*, and yet Lily doesn't move to him. She continues past him, brushing his shoulder, disappearing into Walcourt.

I look away and start walking. Lennon follows beside me.

"Does Lily have enemies here?" I ask.

Lennon shrugs a lithe shoulder. "It's not about having enemies. Anyone can end up on Roundtable, even the most popular. It's like standing trial and your peers are the jury. Depending on what they read, you'll either retain your rank or fall from grace."

"That's absurd. They need to figure out how to get rid of that app. Who do you think posted the texts?" I ask, glancing at Lennon.

"Who knows. The site is anonymous… That's why Roundtable is so powerful."

I want to laugh at the seriousness of Lennon's words, but I know she's not joking.

"Has anyone ever posted about you?"

Lennon's smile cuts across her face wickedly, and I get the sense someone would rue the day they tried to expose Lennon Ryder.

"Never."

# CHAPTER EIGHT
## Shy and Roundtable

*I'd left home early so I could get to school and search for* Vera, but I haven't exited my Jeep before Natalie shoves her phone in my face. She stands there, glaring at me while I read through a stream of intimate messages between one of my best friends and a human boy from our rival school. I press my lips together, jaw locking tight. A headache's forming at my temple, fueled by the pain pulsing up my arm from the hellhound bite I received last night outside Anora's house. I used a small amount of Mom's medic supplies to doctor my arm, but apparently not enough.

I'm not going to have a good day.

I don't need to ask where Natalie got the screen-shots, I know well enough—Roundtable.

"Has—?"

"Jacobi crashed the site," Natalie says, guessing my thoughts. "It's back up, of course, minus the conversation, but the damage has been done."

Not surprising. I'm sure there are a number of students who saved the images just as Natalie had done. And even though Jacobi can work magic, I've long suspected part of the reason Roundtable isn't taken down for good is someone in the Order finds it beneficial for "gathering information."

"Where is Lily?"

"Bathroom in the library. She won't talk to me."

I sigh, rubbing my temple where the pain has gone from a dull ache to a sharp pain. I get out of the Jeep and reach for my bag.

"Did you know?" Natalie's question takes me by surprise, and I turn to face her.

"What?"

"Did you know she was seeing a human?"

I shoulder my backpack and walk past Natalie toward Covington, where the library is located.

"Why do you think Lily would share that information with me?"

"She shares everything with you." Her voice is tinged with jealousy.

"Not that." Lily and I have a don't-ask-don't-tell policy. It's a safety measure for situations just like this.

Lily was one of Natalie's closest friends, but they'd become distant over the summer. If I had to guess, I'd say that's when her relationship with the human began. Lily probably didn't want to face Natalie's judgment.

"It isn't like I could have kept her from seeing him anyway."

"She should have known better."

"And you wonder why Lily won't talk to you? The righteous prophet."

"Don't be an asshole, Shy. You know the rules just as well as me. This is serious."

I know it's serious, but you can't tell me Lily's the first Valryn to mess around with a human. She just got caught. Now she'll have to face the elites and her father, who is a commander like mine. She will be questioned about the relationship and forced to give details that will only add to her shame. The "severity" of her "disobedience" will determine her punishment, which will range anywhere from probation to exile.

The embarrassment of having her relationship advertised on Roundtable is all extra.

The details of Lily's relationship aren't for me to speculate, and I'm not going to be the one to ask Lily how far things went. She is going to get enough of that just as soon as the Order becomes aware of her... *transgressions.*

Just using that word feels like a betrayal in itself.

Entering Covington is like stepping back in time. The walls alternate between dark wood panels and white stucco. The ceilings are arched, exposing decorative woodwork. As I top the stairs leading to the first floor, I turn to the right and head downstairs. The girl's restroom is directly to the left of the stairwell. I knock on the door and call, "Lily! It's Shy. Open up!"

I pause for a moment, giving her a chance to answer. Just as I start to knock again, the door opens, and Lily appears. Her eyes are watery and swollen. Her usually clear skin is red and patchy, and she holds a shaky hand over her mouth and nose.

Seeing her like this makes everything in my chest hurt.

"Shy—" Her voice breaks, and I pull her to me, turning so her back is to Natalie, who stands aside, hugging herself, looking very much alone.

"It's going to be okay."

Lily buries her head in my chest, and my shirt soaks through with tears and snot and saliva. We stand like this for a long while, and when Lily finally pulls away, Natalie has left, either because I accomplished something she couldn't or because she doesn't want to be late for class.

"I should go," Lily says quietly, not meeting my gaze as she wipes her swollen face with the backs of her hands. She takes a deep breath that trembles as she exhales and then says, "I didn't sleep with him."

"I wouldn't care if you did."

She smiles, but it doesn't touch her eyes. "Sometimes I don't want to be what we are."

I nod. "I know."

There are definitely days when I hate what I am. Yesterday was one of them.

Lily takes a deep breath and retrieves her bag.

I offer to walk her to class, but she insists on going alone. As I approach Emerson, Vera's empty noose remains overhead, and I'm reminded of my agenda for today: Vera is not present over the doors of the building. Her rounds are like clockwork—she hangs until ten and then wanders until school ends at three. I turn and move toward the woods nearest Emerson, sliding my backpack off my shoulder. I shift into my raven form, flying the path Vera takes through the woods, straying from time to time to check thicker brush, but do not find her.

Not that I expected to—I've mostly been hoping. A missing soul isn't good, but there are a number of reasons she might be gone. It is no secret Vera is an old spirit, and her energy attracts all sorts of creatures. What if she summoned a darkling beyond the power of our barrier? Or a death-speaker decided to harness her energy for some dark purpose of their own? There is a third possibility, but with Roth so close to becoming luminary, I don't want to consider it. Not yet.

I'm not looking forward to my next move. I'm going to have to ask Natalie if she reported Vera's absence to the Order, something that is going to open the floor for interrogation. At the very least, she's going to want to know where I was last night. For now, I've got to get to class and at least pretend I'm a normal high school student who cares about being here.

After my last class of the morning, instead of finding Natalie or doing what the Order would expect of me, I go in search of Anora. The tug in my chest is a reminder that she's here, and the need to see her is a clawing, almost desperate thing. There are too many questions spinning through my head, and Anora seems to be at the heart of all of them.

# CHAPTER NINE
# Anora and Detention

*Lunch begins differently today—no Lennon or horde of* zombie students. Instead, I stop by my locker to exchange books and head for detention.

"Hey." Shy's voice startles me, and I drop my books. I attempt to avoid eye contact as I kneel to get them and shove them in my bag, but Shy stoops to my level and helps. I glance at him and find he's watching me. "Sorry to scare you."

"You didn't scare me."

*Lie.* He scares me, but not for the reason he thinks.

As I stand, I hit my head on my locker door. The pain is jarring and brings tears to my eyes.

"Are you okay?" Shy moves toward me but falls back, as if unsure what he meant to do. *I'm* unsure of what he meant to do too.

"Fine," I say between my teeth and slam my locker door shut.

"Do you need me to get an ice pack?"

"I said I'm fine," I say with a little more force than I intend, but Shy doesn't push. I press shaky fingers to the sensitive spot on my head—they come away clean, no blood. Shy still stands in my peripheral, hands in his pockets, staring.

"So…do you want to have lunch today? I thought maybe we could sneak off campus or something."

I gape at him, surprised by his suggestion. It's the first time I've really looked at him head-on since he approached, and it's a mistake. When my eyes meet his, I can't stop my brain from short-circuiting. This boy is teenage heartthrob handsome. His hair is messier today, like maybe he ran out of time getting ready this morning, except instead of looking like a complete slob, he somehow looks…sexier.

God, I hate this reaction to him. This has never happened to me before.

"Are you asking the right person?"

That makes him chuckle, but the humor doesn't touch his eyes. "You are Anora Silby, right? No one walked in and stole your soul?"

Those words make me shiver.

"I can't. I have detention." Then, because I feel like I need to offer an explanation, I say, "I was late to trig."

Shy frowns. "Didn't I warn you? Mr. Val…?"

"Is a prick? You did." So did Thane. Seems everyone is in agreement.

He smiles again, almost sadly, disappointment evident in those eyes, as vivid as morning light breaking through a dark horizon. "Maybe tomorrow, then?"

I don't have the heart to tell him I've been given two days of this purgatory.

I start to leave when he stops me. "Oh, hey. I learned something interesting about you yesterday."

*Oh no.*

"You did?"

"Your mom works for mine," he says.

"Really?"

"Yeah… I thought you said your mom moved here for a job."

"It fell through."

I'm proud of that lie. It's smooth; not a flicker of the uncertainty I feel on the inside manages to make its way free, and yet as Shy watches me, I start to waver in my confidence.

It is just my luck Mom would end up working for one of my classmates' parents. Also my luck that he would be a boy who listens to what I'm saying. I wonder if Shy intended to catch me in a lie.

"Maybe that was for the best. Mom's happy to have her."

I smile. "I'll let her know."

"See you around." The smile he gives me as he steps back pulls at my heart, and as he walks away, it unravels at my feet, like it too is made of thread.

I walk into the detention room and Coach David is there, eating a sandwich and scrolling through his phone with his earbuds in. He barely glances up as he takes a giant bite and tips his head toward the desks in the classroom. You'd think an alternative school would have a fair number of students in detention, but I'm the only one here.

I move toward the back of the room and slip into a seat, riffling through my backpack for a notebook to sketch in. I start to draw a map of campus as Coach

David chews loudly, occasionally laughing at something on his phone.

As I recall the places I walked on my first day, I mark the possible locations my coin could be on the map. The thing is, I'm not really sure what could even happen if someone did find the coin. I've been collecting them, but I don't know what I'm supposed to be doing with them, beyond a feeling deep in my stomach that they shouldn't just be in a box under my bed, that no one should have access to them. The thread and the coins have been given to me for a reason. If only I knew what it was and how it's tied to everything that's been happening over the past few months.

Before I captured her soul, Vera said *they* would come for me. The feeling of being hunted has been with me ever since I made that first coin. Only here, at Nacoma Knight, it's so much worse.

I look down at my map and realize I've doodled ravens all over it. They look like the ones on my coins.

Coach David stands and pulls out his earbuds. "You okay on your own, Silby? I gotta hit the head."

*Gross.* "Yeah. I'm fine."

After he leaves, I stare at the map, my eyes growing heavy as I trace the pattern of ravens. *The lines blur, and then I feel someone touching my hair. I turn quickly to find that I'm no longer in detention but in the wood, my eyes level with a chest covered in black armor, threaded through with gold. My gaze shifts upward, and I meet a pair of dark eyes—Shy, I think, though this isn't him. It's someone slightly older, different, but he feels so much like Shy that my heart squeezes with recognition. I know this man.*

*One of his arms tightens around my waist while the fingers of his other hand skim over my cheek, then he leans forward to kiss me. The press of his mouth to mine ignites a liquid fire in the bottom of my stomach. It fills my veins like my blood and burns hotter as his tongue slips inside my mouth. It's then I realize that I'm holding onto him too, and my fingers tighten against his armor, which is not metal at all but strange and flexible. I pull him closer, our bodies aligning in a familiar way, and I want to lose myself in him, but he breaks it off too soon.*

*He stares down at me, and we hold on to each other.*

*"Come," he says, touching my cheek once more before stepping away. "Charon waits."*

*I hold out my hand to take his offered one, and for a moment, I think I see a thread form between them, gold and silver spooling from our palms.*

"Silby," Coach David says, jarring me awake. "Pack your stuff up. Detention's over."

I sit for a moment, dazed by the dream.

Every touch and every emotion was so real—I could still feel them—each soft caress and press of his lips and the acute desire that had not ceased even now that I was awake, all inspired by the hands of the man who felt like Shy but wasn't.

With a few minutes to spare before art, I deposit my books at my locker and start across campus, hoping for the third time today to retrace my steps and investigate the places I marked on my map. On the way, I try to shake the strange dream from detention, but it swirls around me like a thick cloud, only confusing me more.

As I move slowly past buildings, I watch my feet, searching for a gold gleam in the tangled grass. I'm not even close to Hollingsworth when I hear my name—or at least half of it.

"Miss Silby!"

Is there a rule against using first names here?

I look up to find Mr. Seth strolling toward me; a leather satchel hangs on his shoulder. Without the classroom setting, his juvenile features scream at me—oversize glasses, patchy stubble covering a round chin, and acne splattered across an oily forehead. His presence brings a wave of shame, and all the anxiety of yesterday washes over me. Even the smells are back—the metallic tang of blood, the rancid odor of vomit, the unclean scent of musk.

"Looking for something?" he asks.

"Oh…no." I shake my head.

"I hope you feel better today."

"Uh, yeah. H-how did you know I wasn't feeling well yesterday?"

Thankfully Mr. Seth takes my confusion for surprise. "Mr. Savior suggested you were probably ill from lunch."

*Shy.* Just hearing his name reminds me of that kiss in my dream and makes me feel exposed and embarrassed. I look down. How will I face him now?

Mr. Seth continues, "I'd like to make a request that next time you feel unwell, you excuse yourself and go to the nurse's office."

I nod. "Of course."

Mr. Seth smiles. "Heading to class?"

"Yeah." My voice is small, breathless—full of disappointment, missing another chance to search for the coin. The wind pulls at my skin and my hair as if to drag me away, toward my purpose, but I resist and follow Mr. Seth to Hollingsworth.

# CHAPTER TEN
## Shy and the Web

*Instead of lunch with Anora, Natalie and I are called to* the Compound. There are a plethora of reasons we might be summoned—all things that happened in the time span of the last twenty-four hours. All things the Order would only know about because Natalie reported them. Or maybe they're calling us in because of something to do with Roth. It's hard to predict. I drive with the windows rolled down because the air in the cabin of my Jeep is stretched and suffocating. Plus, the wind keeps conversation at bay for as long as possible, until Natalie takes the liberty of rolling the windows up.

She inhales a few times, the beginning of a sentence poised on the tip of her tongue. She's working up courage. When the words finally come out, they rasp, as if lodged at the back of her throat.

"Where were you last night?" Natalie asks.

I should probably ease my grip on the steering wheel

because my arm is throbbing, but Natalie's question sets me on edge.

When I don't answer, she says, "I didn't tell Elite Cain." As if that'll entice me to spill my guts.

It doesn't.

But I am surprised.

"You used to talk to me."

I glance at her. "And you know why I stopped." *Why we all stopped*, I want to add, but I also don't want to be that much of a jerk. Truth is, Natalie is judgy and way too beholden to the Order. It's why she didn't know about Lily's boyfriend. It's why we all worry she'll run and tell Elite Cain when we aren't following rules. Her determination to become a commander overrides her wish to have friends.

"I said I was sorry," she mutters.

"Doesn't work if you don't mean it."

Her frustration is palpable, twisting in the air toward me like a darkling.

"Blake forgave me," she says through her teeth.

"Because she was about to be sent into exile."

"Because she knew I didn't want to turn her in," Natalie argues. "She was involved with the occult, Shy!"

It was a scandal when it was discovered. Blake was a year older than us and had just entered college when she got tangled up with death-speakers who joined the occult, which is the kind of stuff that happens in New York, not in our close-knit town. She started practicing—small stuff at first, but it quickly got out of control. One night, she came knocking on my door, one of her death-speaker friends dying in her arms. Some spell gone wrong. She asked Mom to help him, and she saved the kid's life, but she was still suspended because "Valryn are not permitted to administer medical attention to humans." The only reason Mom wasn't exiled is because she was technically doing half her job—saving a human soul.

Mom doesn't blame Natalie for what happened. She says the Order would have found out anyway, and she's probably right. And maybe I'm not as mad at Natalie as I am at the Order for turning their back on Blake—someone who needed family and friendship more than the cold shoulder.

"I guess I just never thought Blake was capable of deceit," Natalie says.

Her attitude sets me off.

"There. Right there." My voice stings the air between us. "That's where you're wrong. It's not that she was capable of deceit. She was helping a friend."

"The Order doesn't see it that way, Shy, and whether you like it or not, we're sworn to uphold their laws. Blake knew that."

"You keep telling yourself that."

I turn down a makeshift dirt road and park in a clearing—my usual spot. Natalie and I shift and fly to the Compound. We make our way down white marble halls veined with black toward Elite Cain's office, our feet thudding against the cold stone like a drumbeat ticking off the minutes until our deaths.

Cain's office is cold and hard. The floors are black marble, and where the walls aren't slatelike in color, they are covered in heavy, black drapes. A glossy black desk sits just before a single, exposed window so crowded with trees, no light seeps through, and there Elite Cain stands, one hand behind his back, the other resting lightly on his desk. My father stands to the side.

Natalie and I come to a stop a few feet before them and salute, though Elite Cane doesn't lift his eyes to us.

"It appears I've caught you two in a web." Those words make my heart fall right into my stomach. "Knight-in-Training Rivera, you failed to inform us that Knight-in-Training Savior did not report for patrol last night."

Natalie blanches. Well, at least she wasn't lying when she said she didn't report my absence.

"Where were you?" my father asks.

Simple question with a not-so-simple answer. I can either admit I was checking up on Anora, something that doesn't look good, especially following Lily's transgressions, death-speaker or not, or admit I was attacked by hellhounds and seek medical attention. How much more can I get tangled?

"I was attacked by a hellhound," I say. For effect—and as evidence—I pull up the sleeve of my suit to show off my wounds.

Silence follows my admission, and I feel like I'm standing at the center of a frozen pond, the ice buckling beneath my feet.

"And you didn't think it was important to report the attack? Or seek medical attention?"

That question doesn't really require an answer, so I report what I discovered while fighting the hounds.

"The hellhounds didn't react as they do in simulation," I say.

"Hounds? There was more than one?" Another

100

fact that contradicts my training—we'd been taught hellhounds don't travel in packs.

"One attacked and I skewered its head. When it fell dead, I thought my job was done, but it multiplied, and then, no matter how many times I took a knife to their brains, they did not die."

"And where did they go?"

"They disappeared." Those words are thick on my tongue, like oil, black and sticky. My father and Cain exchange a look, and I wonder what they're thinking.

Cain clears his throat. "In your absence, Knight-in-Training Rivera reported the soul of Vera Bennet missing. Were you aware?"

I'd say yes, but I'm already in deep. "Only this morning when she wasn't in her place over Emerson."

"And neither of you have any idea where she might have gone?"

Just when I am about to say no, Natalie opens her mouth.

"I have suspicions, Elite Cain."

He raises his brows—most likely because of the use of *suspicions* and not *evidence*. The Order is a stickler for evidence before action is taken. "Go on."

"There is a new girl at school. She's supposedly from Chicago, but her last school has no record of her attendance."

"You said she was kicked out of her last school," I argue, recalling the accusation she'd made at lunch in front of all those students.

"Because that's what her record says, but she apparently never even started. And before you suggest it, my father called." Somehow, those words seem even more final by the set of her arms, crossed, one over the other.

"You think this girl has something to do with Vera's disappearance?"

"Within her first day at Nacoma, a soul goes missing. That cannot be coincidence."

"Perhaps not coincidence, but you have no evidence," I remind her—also knowing Elite Cain will agree. "If your father thought this was an issue, he would've said something to the Order. But he doesn't have evidence either."

"I'd have to observe her longer than two days to be sure, but I think I can find the evidence," Natalie says, not taking her eyes off Elite Cain. I know what's she's doing—asking for permission.

"See that you do," Elite Cain says. "Why don't you both work on this assignment together? I'll count it as part of your training."

I'm sort of relieved. If Elite Cain thought Anora might be an issue, he'd send his commanders to deal with her. Still, I'd prefer not having Natalie by my side while I watch her.

"With respect, Elite Cain, I work better alone," I say.

"With respect, Knight-in-Training, you're lucky I'm not putting you on probation for your actions."

A part of me wonders if my dad had something to do with that, but I can't believe he'd go to bat for me with Cain. The Order always comes first.

Elite Cain turns his disfavor to Natalie. "You might think it noble to protect a friend, but you are a shadow knight-in-training first and foremost. You are obligated to report misbehavior."

"Yes, Elite Cain," we say in unison.

"Now that we are understood, were either of you aware of Lily Martin's relationship?"

It's the question I've been waiting for, and it makes my stomach turn, but this is why Lily and I have our rule: We can't get in trouble for what we don't know.

"No, Elite Cain," we say.

He watches us intently, like he thinks we might crack under pressure. After what seems like an eternity, he says, "You are both dismissed."

We salute and turn to leave the room when Elite Cain calls out to me.

"Knight-in-Training Savior, report to the infirmary."

I nod and leave, not waiting for Natalie as I stride down the obsidian halls.

"Shy!" Natalie's feet slap against the marble floor as she hurries after me.

"Why did you put her in the path of the Order without evidence?" I demand, turning to face her.

"Because there's something off about her."

"Something *off*?" I ask, incredulous. "Could it be that you don't like when anyone encroaches on our friend group? Thane bailed on us, Natalie. And Lily's going to be on lockdown with the Order. We have a few vacancies at the moment, so why not Anora?"

"Just because you can't look past a pretty face doesn't mean she's not hiding something, Shy. Besides, you're just mad because you're not the only one keeping tabs on her. Yeah, I know where you were last night—watching *her*."

"You followed me?" I expect a lot of things from Natalie: disdain, disappointment, judgment, but not this. I grit my teeth together and narrow my eyes. "So why not tell Elite Cain I didn't make it to patrol? Why not jump in while I was being attacked by hellhounds?"

"Because I don't want you on probation like Jacobi. And you know how to handle yourself in a fight better than anyone. Besides, you aren't my target. Anora is."

"Anora doesn't have to have a reason to be your target, Nat, and until she starts causing trouble, she isn't your concern."

"Not according to Elite Cain's orders."

"Why do you have to be so damned self-righteous?" I leave her alone in the hallway.

In the infirmary, I sit on a metal table while a medic uses a solution in a clear bottle to clean my wounds, applies a smelly claylike substance to each mark, and then bandages my arm. I'm not there long when my father strides through the curtains. I glance at him and then focus intently on my arm.

"I thought those curtains were there for privacy."

"Do you know the danger in what you're doing?" he asks.

"Infection?"

My father maintains his cold, emotionless façade. "Does your mother know you didn't go on patrol?"

"I wasn't where I was supposed to be last night," I correct. "That doesn't mean I wasn't doing my job."

"Part of doing your job is obeying orders."

"Even when I disagree with them?" I'm aware this conversation has become something very different than I intend.

"You are a knight-in-training. You don't get to have an opinion."

"You sure? Because I actually have a lot of them."

My father takes a step closer and leans in, inches from my face. I want to move away, but I also know it's important to hold my ground, especially since what I've been saying sounds like treason.

"You might think you're standing up for something grand, but when you do it wrong, it's not you who will suffer for your actions, it's the people you love. Do you understand?"

"Are you threatening Mom?" My voice breaks as I speak.

My father straightens as if I slapped him. It's the only indication I have that he's startled by my suggestion, because his features—even his eyes, so like mine—haven't changed.

"That is a display of your ignorance," he says.

"False." I push myself off the metal table and stand. "You're hurting her already, but you wouldn't know that because you're never home."

I honestly don't know what's gotten into me. I've been the good soldier in my father's shadow for so long, but it's like the last few days have flipped a switch inside me.

I await his reprimand, my punishment for defying him, but my father only stares at me, saying nothing, so I start to move past him.

"Shy," he says, and there's something in his voice that makes me turn back. For a second, his expression looks full of regret, but then it's like a gate drops and his cool manner returns.

I shake my head, and then, because this may be the only time I can get away with this, I add, "And you know what? I'll always be here to save Mom, because she's been there to save me. But you—who will be there

105

for you? Elite Cain?" I pause to scoff. "You're just a commander, remember?"

My father's shoulders go rigid, but I don't wait for anything—for words or his scorn. I leave. I promised Mom I'd be home for dinner anyway.

# CHAPTER ELEVEN
## Anora and a New Friend

*I don't get the chance to tell Shy thank you for covering* for me with Mr. Seth because he isn't in class all afternoon, something that bothers me more than it should. I wonder if he found someone else to go to lunch with— maybe another girl, the one who hugged him around his waist yesterday. Maybe they'd lost track of time or ditched to go back to his house.

*Stop!* I order myself.

I can't let a few instances of kindness blind me from things that truly bother me—like Shy's watchful gaze and his perceptive questions. It might seem wrong to be suspicious of him, but some of the greatest threats never set off warning bells.

In contrast, Thane is a walking siren—everything about him screams run the other direction, and what he already knows about me makes him dangerous. I haven't decided what I'll do about him yet, but the only option

I've come up with is fleeing town. I doubt Mom will go for that.

For now, I'm stuck.

Lennon and I make it to the field on time for PE, so we don't have to run extra laps. We start off at a jog. I hope the strain on my lungs will distract me from searching for Shy on the practice field.

It doesn't.

"Looking for Shy?" Lennon asks.

Maybe I should be a little more concerned about how much she's keeping an eye on me.

"He asked me to lunch," I explain. "But he wasn't in class after."

"He left with Natalie," she says.

So I'd been right to think he might have left with another girl—I'd just thought of the wrong one. I don't want to think about what it means that they haven't returned, so I turn my thoughts toward a theory I'd been contemplating since this morning.

"Do you think Natalie had anything to do with posting Lily's texts on Roundtable?"

Lennon laughs, but it sounds a little strangled, as if she choked on the spit in her throat. "No."

"Why not?" I'm a little offended by how quickly she shoots my suggestion down.

"Because Natalie and Lily are friends."

"*Really*?"

"There's a group of them. They grew up together— Shy, Lily, Natalie, Jacobi, Thane."

Thane?

"Shy and Thane don't seem like very good friends."

"They aren't—or at least, not anymore."

"What happened?"

"No one knows. One day, they came to school and they just weren't friends anymore. Didn't hang out at lunch, didn't talk in the hallway, didn't acknowledge their history together."

I can't imagine Shy and Thane ever being very good friends, but now I'm curious—what changed? If I have to guess, it has something to do with the grief Thane carries. Death always inspires change—good or bad.

Lennon and I slow to a walk.

"You're coming to the game Friday, right?" Lennon moves on to another subject, obviously not as interested in Shy and Thane's relationship as I am. "We could get ready together. It'll be fun! Besides, you'll get to see Shy play, and trust me, you don't want to miss that."

I smile because of how normal she sounds—how innocent. She isn't plagued by the dead, by threads or golden coins. I wish I knew what it was like to move through the world as she does. I had once—before things got complicated. I had dreams of attending Princeton or Harvard. I had already started reading about women in space—Sally Ride, Valentina Tereshkova, and Geraldyn Cobb—and studying cosmology, relativity, and gravity. Those dreams were brittle, though, the glass thin, and everything shattered.

Now my plans revolve around hiding. Even now, knowing another mistake means a mental hospital, I have an escape plan.

"Anora?"

My gaze snaps to Lennon. "I'll ask my mom."

Her smile widens, and we continue our laps around the field.

After PE, Lennon and I part ways at Emerson. I pull my phone from my locker and find I have a message from Mom.

Running late. Be there soon.

Maybe someone is looking out for me after all. I shove my books in my backpack and head toward the front office. Mom's delay might not give me time to cross campus again, but I can check lost and found.

When I reach the office, the three ladies from yesterday are still behind the glass. They stand away from the desk so that their whole bodies are visible. Mrs. Cole spots me first and offers a smile, though I still think it's forced.

"Miss Silby, what can we do for you?"

"I wondered if you have a lost and found?"

She maintains that smile. "What did you lose?"

My answer is poised on my tongue. I'd known all along I'd have to say it—a gold coin with the image of a raven—but my whole head pricks, as if my hair wants to free itself from my scalp. The sensation drips down my back, and my gaze slips past Mrs. Cole and her fake smile to the darker presence behind her.

Thane.

He stands in the shadow of the office, watching me curiously, and my whole body feels frozen. I can't seem to clear the words from my throat, especially after the encounter I had with him this morning. He already believes I had something to do with Vera's disappearance, and the fact that he's absolutely right means I can't trust him.

"Miss Silby?" Mrs. Cole asks again, and I offer a smile, though it feels wobbly and just as forced as hers. To make it worse, a breathy laugh escapes from between my lips.

"You know what." I reach into the mesh pocket of my backpack, my fingers closing around my phone. "I'm such an idiot. I found what I thought I lost." I lift the phone, and Mrs. Cole's brows draw together. Clearly, she doesn't believe me, but I take a step away from the counter. As I turn, Mrs. Cole's voice strains through the mechanical filter.

"Take care, Miss Silby."

I don't respond. My feet carry me forward, around the corner, and through the first door on my right—the women's restroom. I take a moment to breathe, releasing the tension knotting my chest before approaching the sink. My reflection looks harsh—pale face, black hair, lips the color of a bitten cherry, chapped. I'm not used to this version of me. I turn on the faucet and splash water on my face, cooling my pink cheeks, when I hear a soft sniffle. I pause and look up but see no one behind me in the mirror.

"Lily?" I venture a guess. I pat my face dry and then bend to see a pair of feet under one of the stall doors. "Are you okay?"

"Leave me alone!" Her voice is thick with mucus, and she clears her throat in the silence.

"I'm not here to laugh at you or judge you," I explain. "I'm Anora Silby, the new girl. I…just want to make sure you're okay."

There is a pause, and I hear the door unlatch. Lily comes out of the stall. Her eyes are rimmed with red and

111

puffy, but she's pulled her hair away from her face, so I have a clear view of her features. She's pretty—blond hair, brown eyes, heart-shaped face.

"This place sucks, you know that?"

I nod. "I'm sorry people were mean to you. You know they've all done worse."

"Yeah, they have. But it doesn't matter. I'm the one everyone is talking about."

I shake my head. "That's ridiculous. It's such a double standard. If you were a guy, no one would care. Or they'd be high-fiving you."

She smiles at me. "You're nice, but you should know they'll eat you alive."

"Thanks for the warning, but I can take care of myself."

"Yeah, I thought that too," she says. Walking to the sink, she turns on the faucet and splashes her face with water. I watch her in the mirror.

"Hey, in a few weeks, no one will remember this, and if not, in the end, this is only high school."

She smiles, but it's sad, and she looks away from me. "I wish that were true." We stand for a moment in awkward silence, and then Lily speaks. "Is it true, what Natalie said? That you got kicked out of your old school?"

"Yeah." The truth is far harder to explain.

Lily tilts her head to the side. "Funny, you don't seem like a troublemaker."

I offer a small laugh. "Yeah, that's what I thought too." There is a pause as I study her, eyes downcast. "Hey…you should come to the game with Lennon and me Friday. It'll be fun."

The ending is tacked on—Lennon's words, not mine.

"Are you sure?" She watches me. Her eyes search my face like she thinks I'll crack under pressure and admit I don't want to be associated with her.

"Why wouldn't I be?"

"Well, you're the new girl. Aren't you worried about your reputation?"

A laugh tears from my throat, and I choke on it. "No. I'd like to be your friend more."

Lily's lips twitch, and I get the sense it's been a long time since she's smiled.

"I'd like that too," Lily replies.

# CHAPTER TWELVE
## Anora and the Telescope

***The next few days are a strange mixture of boring high*** school stuff, ridiculous Roundtable rumors that I completely ignore, and a heightened sense of anticipation that something is wrong. I can't find my coin in spite of combing through most of the campus, even places I didn't visit the first day. But searching for it isn't easy considering the number of people who seem to be keeping an eye on me.

At first, I thought it was "new girl" interest, but it's more than that. Thane seems to show up whenever I'm looking for the coin, but he doesn't approach. I catch him staring in class and at lunch, and he's been outside Emerson Hall every day after school while I wait for Mom to pick me up. Natalie keeps watching me in trig as if she's ready to report any perceived infraction to her father. And Shy is everywhere. Even as I'm trying to actively avoid him. The worst part? He's friendly. As if he doesn't feel the weird tension between us. Which maybe he doesn't. Maybe he hasn't dreamed about me. But I've dreamed about him.

The one I had in detention was almost tame in comparison to last night's. Shy, or rather the man who *feels* like Shy, stood at the center of a lake with me, our bodies bared to the night and skin-to-skin as he kissed me, connected with me, and as our palms touched, a silver and gold thread twined together, wrapping around us, warm and electric, driving the desire between us. When I woke, the dream clung to me as if I had been singed by its hold.

Now, it's past midnight and I'm too afraid to sleep, my body wired. So I'm looking at stars through my telescope and remembering when Poppa and I used to do this together.

It's slightly cloudy tonight, so I decide to take my telescope outside to see if the view is any better. I'm hoping the fresh air might help keep me awake for a little while longer so that when I finally do sleep, I'll be too tired to dream.

But the minute I step outside, I feel someone watching me. I search the trees and see nothing but the ever-present ravens, and while they make me uneasy, it's nothing compared to how I feel about the dogs snoring near my back porch right now. They'd showed up outside our house a few days ago. I thought that maybe they lingered because this had been their home before we arrived. Mom wasn't enthused about their presence and accused me of feeding them. She tried calling the animal shelter to come collect them, but when they showed up, the dogs were nowhere to be found.

They're back now, and while I try to ignore them,

they creep me out like everything else in this town and just make the sense that something is wrong even more pronounced. On the plus side, they're friendly, and if something is hunting me, I'm betting they'd bark their heads off.

Moving to the front lawn to avoid waking them, I set up my telescope, but the view of the stars isn't much better out here. I touch the coin on my neck and whisper to my poppa that I miss him every day. It's like a wound that won't heal.

"You know there's a curfew, right?" a low voice whispers, and I squeak and spin around to find Shy leaning against a tree.

"What are you doing here?" I ask.

Shy grins and I feel it down to my toes. "Breaking curfew."

A raven caws from above and then there's a rustle of wings as it takes off. Shy watches it for a moment, then turns back to me. "How come you're up so late?"

I'm grateful it's dark so he doesn't see my skin flush. "Couldn't sleep," I mumble.

He looks at me speculatively for a second, then rubs his chest. "No, that's not it."

My hackles go up. "Why are you asking *me* questions when you're the one at my house after midnight? What are *you* doing here?"

He scrubs a hand through his hair, the color almost silver in the dark. "Honestly, I don't really know. I just… wanted to see you. I thought maybe…I don't know. I wanted to see you."

His admission stuns me for a moment, and as I stare, I'm once again wrapped in the heat of my dreams. I'm not sure what to say but I still open my mouth to speak when a growl erupts from behind me.

The dogs.

I turn toward the sound, and the whole pack has come around the side of the house, snarling. At first, I think they are targeting me, but then they bolt past toward Shy. I pivot to warn him, but he's nowhere to be found. I scan my surroundings, but he's literally disappeared. Though the dogs bark at the base of the tree he had been standing beneath.

"Knock it off," I hiss at them, and they whine but finally quiet down.

I glance through the trees one more time, feeling even more uneasy than before. There is no way Shy could have escaped that quickly, right?

At least, I hope.

Shaking my head, I pack up my telescope and head back inside, the dogs trotting behind me as if I'm going to invite them in. I can't decide if I'm pissed off or grateful they interrupted my conversation with Shy. All I know is that Shy showing up here, past curfew, and disappearing just as quickly leaves me with more questions than ever.

# CHAPTER THIRTEEN
## Shy and the Council

*Natalie and I spend the next few days searching for Vera* and staking out Anora's house, only to find it more boring than patrolling Nacoma Knight. Natalie was beyond pissed that I risked discovery by changing to my human form while Anora was stargazing. But the strange connection between us compelled me to talk to her in the same way that it draws me to her whenever we're at school. I should be worried about what it means and be more mistrustful of her, but I'm not. Natalie thinks I'm a fool and Anora is putting on a show.

"She doesn't want to draw attention to herself," Natalie argues.

"You're grasping at straws."

"I know she's not who she says she is."

"You can't keep saying that without substantial evidence."

And we have none. The hellhounds have camped

outside her house, but they don't do anything but sleep—something I make sure to include in my reports to Elite Cain at the end of every patrol. Whatever they're doing with Anora, she doesn't seem to be actively causing it.

"I have evidence." Natalie tries to repress a smile, and I hate that she has something to be smug about. "Your *girlfriend's* going by her middle name. According to her forwarded mail, her first name is Lyra."

I should have known Natalie would take the liberty of investigating Anora on her own. She's hoping to prove me wrong and beat me to uncovering some earth-shattering truth about the new girl.

"First, she's not my girlfriend. Second, you went through her mail? Isn't that a federal offense?"

Natalie shrugs. "Only if you open it."

"A lot of people go by their middle name, Nat. It doesn't mean anything." Her eyes narrow. "Besides, you're supposed to be looking for evidence she's practicing the occult."

"It's not just her name, Shy. The school she claims to come from has no record of her enrollment. You don't find that strange?"

Sure, I find it strange, and I'm curious as hell about the truth, and while lying about where you're from is weird, it doesn't actually break *our* laws.

"No matter what reason Anora has for being here, it's not our concern unless she starts practicing the occult."

Whatever she is, she's human and has lived a human life. She could be running from other problems. I haven't seen a man at her house throughout our week of surveillance, which tells me her dad probably isn't in the

119

picture, and if she and her mother are running from him, I doubt she wants him to find her easily.

———

Back at school, I have every intention of keeping my distance from Anora for the week, especially since Natalie has become increasingly clingy. I can't turn a corner without her appearing out of thin air. I don't expect to think about or regret my decision, and yet I discover the longer I go without talking to Anora, the more pressure builds, like someone's stacking stones on my chest. At first, a glance or a smile relieves the tension over my heart, and sitting next to her in class keeps it at bay until patrol, but after one day of avoidance, I'm ready to worship the ground she walks on if it'll make this feeling go away.

So I find reasons to talk to her. I ask her for notes from the day I missed art and arrange to meet her in the library to pick them up. When I find her, she's sitting in one of the large bay windows in Covington. She has a book in her hands, but she's not reading it. She's looking out the window. I stare at her like a creep, but I can't help it. I feel like I've been here before, admiring her from a distance. I like the way her long hair spills down her back, the way her graceful fingers curl around the edges of her book. I wonder how soft her hands are, how it would feel to hold them—to have them on me.

I shake those thoughts from my head, and I approach.

"Hey," I say.

She looks up at me and smiles, offering a breathless, "Hey."

It makes my chest feel lighter, and I think I could spend my whole life making her smile.

"What are you reading?" I ask, nodding to the book in her hands.

"Oh, nothing," she says, closing it and moving her hands over the title.

I reach for the book anyway, brushing my fingers over her skin. She is soft, and a surge of electricity sparks between us. She draws her hands away. I try not to let that disappoint me and instead focus on the book.

I hold it up, reading the title aloud. "*A Simple Guide to Astrophysics*?" The last word comes out as a question because I'm surprised. I look at Anora, then at the book, then at the pile by her feet. They are all books about space. "First the telescope, and now this. Are you into space?"

She blushes. "Yeah, actually. I want to be an astronomer."

"That's so cool."

She laughs and smiles again. "Thanks."

Yeah, I think I'll do just about anything for her smile. We stare at each other for a moment, and then she clears her throat. "Um, you wanted notes, right?"

"Yeah."

She stands and starts gathering her books.

"Are you checking all these out?" I ask.

She surveys the pile. "Maybe just two. We have a lot of English homework this week."

I smirk and walk with her to the copier.

"So back in Chicago...did you have a boyfriend?" After I ask the question, I feel the change in the air between us, and it's not good. This isn't the subject to bring up.

"I did," she says, not looking at me. Making copies just became super interesting. "We're not together anymore."

"Oh," I say, feeling really freaking awkward now. "I'm sorry."

"Don't be."

Once the copies are made, she holds them out to me, and I try to apologize, but before I can get the words out, she says, "I'll see you."

"See you," I say, but I don't think she hears me.

Throughout the rest of the week, I continue to find reasons to talk to her. Stupid reasons. I ask her for pencils or paper or how far she's gotten on *A Simple Guide to Astrophysics*—that question gets a smile. Each interaction eases the tension in my chest. The release is intoxicating.

On Friday, I jog up to her during practice just to ask if she's coming to the game. When she says yes, I smile bigger than I mean to. It's probably the best thing that will come out of today, since I'm not really looking forward to picking Roth up at four, but I'll do it to sit in on Council, even if it means missing half the game.

As I turn to head back to the field, I find Natalie glaring at me.

"Look alive, Savior!"

Unlike Anora on her first day, I'm not fast enough to stop the ball from hitting me square in the face. Blood gushes from my nose.

"That's what you get for daydreaming. Off the field!" Coach Roberts orders.

I don't argue. I need an excuse to leave practice early anyway, though I'd have preferred something less bloody and painful.

*I'm going to be in so much trouble with Coach.*

I go to the bathroom and turn on the faucet, watching blood swirl down the sink as I clean my face and try to stop my nose from bleeding before changing and heading to my Jeep. I hope to slip away unnoticed, but Jacobi calls out.

"Shy!"

I keep walking, pretending I don't hear him, but after a few minutes, Jacobi jogs up beside me.

"Where are you going, man?"

"I've gotta pick up a lockbox for Mom before the game. I promised."

"You know Coach is looking for you?"

"Yeah, not surprising."

I'm not sticking around to get yelled at right now. When Jacobi realizes I'm not turning around, he says, "Need some company?"

"Might be best if you stay behind, explain my absence."

"And let Coach blame me for not keeping you in the locker room? I'll pass."

He continues to walk with me, and I hate that I'm going to have to find a way to ditch my best friend.

"Look, Jacobi." I stop and turn toward him, cutting off his path. "You're second-string quarterback. One of us has to be here."

His smile falters a little. "Sounds like whatever you're leaving for is more than just a lockbox pickup."

"I'll be back. I just might need you to start for me."

"Shy." Jacobi hesitates. "I can't—"

"Jacobi." I clasp his shoulder. "You're good enough to be quarterback…"

"I'm your *backup*, Shy. I'm nowhere near as good as you. I know it, you know it, *they* know it."

Jacobi's confidence in his skills is just one reason I've

kept my appointment as Roth's glorified gofer a secret from my friends. They'd see it as an honor. I've made the mistake of telling them about assignments and scores before. I used to think complaining about them was a way of showing them I'm not as high on the pedestal as they think, but I was wrong. The assignment as Roth's guard—even though it's a hoax—will be seen as just another example of favoritism and my complaints about why I don't want to do it, arrogant.

"Look, don't psych yourself out. I might be back in time. This is all precautionary. Just in case I get held up."

"Getting that lockbox, you mean?" Jacobi asks with a raised brow.

I smile. Jacobi knows I'm lying. He takes a step back but grins, shoving his hands in his pockets.

"All right, but if Coach gives me hell, you're doing my math homework for a week."

I'll do his math homework for a whole month to work off the guilt I feel. Jacobi turns on his heels and heads back to the locker room.

It takes about twenty minutes to get to the airport from Nacoma Knight Academy. I roll up in the passenger pickup lane and park, reaching for my phone. Several messages populate my screen, all from Natalie.

Are you still at the field house?
Where are you?
Hello?

I can tell when she's talked to Jacobi because I get Why didn't you tell me you were running an errand for your mom? As if I have to answer to her for every move.

My phone buzzes in my hand, and another message pops up in the queue: Are you ignoring me?

I debate whether I should answer, but she'll just see that as an invitation to talk, and I don't really want to be bothered right now, so I close out the messages and start a new one for Roth.

Here. Door 3.

I hit Send and wait.

And wait.

Swarms of people come and go with no sign of Roth.

Finally, I start another text. I said I was here.

Just as I hit Send, there's a tap on my window. I look up to find Roth standing outside my passenger door, a coffee in hand.

Somehow, knowing what kept him in the airport just makes me hate him more.

He hasn't changed much, except for a new haircut—short on the sides and long on top. Otherwise, he still resembles the same cheating douchebag I met a few years ago. He's tall and muscular. He takes pride in his physique. I wish I could say it is all for show, but it's not—Roth is a warrior, far more of a soldier than his father ever was. That's about all I respect him for, but he's somehow managed to weasel his way into the hearts of most elites and every female shadow knight. He lays charm on thick—it's his gift.

"Well, if it isn't Shy *the* Savior." He holds up his coffee. "Hope you don't mind—I didn't think you'd want anything."

I start my Jeep and put the car into gear, biting back a comment about his selfishness. "We're going to be late."

It doesn't matter if it's Roth's fault; I'm the one who will get in trouble.

Before he shuts the door, I start moving, a tiny act of defiance. I'm hoping to shorten the drive to town as much as possible. I glance at Roth from the corner of my eye and find him staring down at his phone, a smile cracking across his face.

"You have a girlfriend yet, Savior?" he asks and takes a sip of coffee.

I clench my jaw, trying not to think about Anora, and don't respond.

"I take that as a no."

"Didn't realize you were so interested in my love life."

"I just think you might be a little nicer if you had one."

"So you don't have a girlfriend either?"

"Commitment isn't my thing."

"It's unfortunate you were born Valryn, then."

Roth laughs. "That's the cleverest thing you've ever said, Savior."

"If you're going to be luminary, shouldn't you be loyal to the Order?"

"Not if they're not loyal to me."

I stare at him, not sure what to make of his statement, but I have questions—what exactly is his idea of loyalty?

"If you stare at me any longer, I'll have to assume you've fallen in love, Savior."

I focus on the road again. Silence ensues, and for a

while, all I hear is Roth sipping coffee. It makes me want to punch him in the face. I flex my fingers around my steering wheel.

"You know, as much as I like watching you work, I don't need a bodyguard."

*My thoughts exactly.*

"I'm more than happy to pass off this assignment."

"Except that would ruin any chance you might have at ranking as a shadow knight."

I roll my eyes.

"Has it occurred to you to question why you were chosen to guard me? A knight-in-training?"

"If you think I'm underqualified, you should have said something instead of wasting my time."

He scoffs. "Like you have anything else to do."

"Yeah, actually. I have a life outside the Compound."

"Oh really? Tell me how that's working for you."

He knows perfectly well how it is working for me. I decide it's best if I don't respond.

Council isn't held at the Compound. It's held at a creepy-ass mansion that sits on a hill at the end of Frontage Street. We call it Temple. It was once the home of a wealthy Valryn named Nacoma Knight, our school's namesake. A lot of people in town aren't too fond of the place, say they feel they're being watched...and, well, they are. The mansion's a little more inconspicuous than an obsidian tower. It's used to house members of the Order from all over the world, sort of like a hotel.

On Council, clusters of ravens swarm overhead like storm clouds. People claim it's a sign of bad luck. When I was younger, we used to dare human kids to jump the fence and touch the door. They were almost always escorted off the property by men-in-black types, and we were almost always ratted out and made to dust the library, but it was worth it to see the looks on their faces.

I stop at the gate, enter a four-digit code, and pull around to the back, parking alongside a row of sleek, black SUVs—Roth and I aren't the only Valryn who prefer wheels over wings.

We exit the Jeep and shift. From this point on, I have to remember my etiquette training—keep one step behind your superior at all times…unless there's a door to open.

Freaking annoying.

Inside, Roth and I are escorted upstairs, where a set of double doors open into a room with several elites crowded around an oblong table. Behind them is a wall of windows that overlook a lake at the back of the mansion. I recognize most of them—including my math teacher, Mr. Val—and several of the shadow knights who circle the table. Their wings are exposed, weapons gleaming. I'm the only knight-in-training. Everyone else has been ranked, given a specialty—techs, medics, weapons, tracking, commands. I can tell because of the colors of their threads and how they decorate their uniforms.

As we enter, everyone in the room stands and salutes. That's when I realize Roth and I are the last to arrive. I follow everyone's example, though it causes me physical pain, and salute Roth, falling into rank on the opposite side of the room next to my father. And although he tries to catch my gaze, I avoid it.

"Successor Roth," Elite Cain says. "We are so sorry to hear of your father's ailing health."

Roth offers a curt nod, and his jaw tightens. It's the

first time I've seen Roth react to his father's decline, and I get the sense this might be harder on him than I thought.

Roth moves to the middle of the table but does not sit.

"Shall we begin?" he asks, scanning the room, and I recognize his training kicking into gear. He's assessing, deciding who's a threat and who's not. That move sets me on edge. "I've called this meeting to discuss the Order's efforts to locate the Eurydice."

# CHAPTER FOURTEEN
# Anora and the Game

*On Friday, there's an electricity in the air, spreading* excitement like a current. Even I find it contagious— and I'm only going to the game to give myself an excuse to look for my coin. The halls are decorated with blue and white streamers, and large butcher paper signs read like declarations of battle. It's also, apparently, the only day we don't have to wear our uniforms—a memo I missed. As I walk the hall, black knee-high tights cover-ing my legs, people stare. Two girls continue past me, then turn to whisper to one another.

Did I miss something on Roundtable?

Or is this the result of my friendship with Lily?

Maybe both.

"Hey!" I twist to face Lennon, who is dressed in a blue-and-silver Nacoma Knight shirt, a black skirt, and another oversized cardigan that hangs to her knees. A large blue bow sits atop her ponytail at an angle.

"Do I have something on my face?" I ask.

She studies me for a moment. "No. Why?"

"Because I feel like everyone's staring at me."

"Oh," she says. "You're probably not imagining that."

Lennon doesn't offer an explanation. Instead, she holds up a handful of ribbons—blue, white, silver—and offers to add them to my hair. I let her, since all I did this morning was throw my hair into a ball on top of my head.

"Did someone say something about me on Roundtable?" I ask as she works on my hair, gritting my teeth when she pulls too hard.

"Not that I saw this morning."

I can't tell if Lennon is being intentionally vague or if she's oblivious to how uncomfortable this is, because she's never been the source of whispering before.

"How long does this usually last?"

"What?"

"This," I say, waving my hand. "People talking about you?"

"Oh, well…in your case, it'll probably last until Shy stops paying attention to you."

"What are you talking about?"

Lennon stops fussing with the ribbons and tilts her face to see me. "Anora. Come on."

I blush. *My body is a traitor.* Truth be told, I don't want Shy to stop paying attention to me. I like him, and I like the attention. And I can't help but wonder what he might have said if those dumb dogs hadn't scared him off the other night.

*But I just won't act on anything.*

That way, I can't make the same mistakes I made in New York.

"Has Shy…ever shown interest in anyone?"

"If you mean has he ever dated anyone, there have only been rumors."

"About him and Natalie?"

"And Lily Martin and Leah Thompson and Regan Carmichael…"

"You can stop any time."

"Sorry."

Lennon finally finishes tying ribbons in my hair, and I turn to face her.

"Speaking of Lily…I invited her to hang out with us after school."

"Oh." Lennon sounds surprised, suddenly occupied by her fingernails. "And she said yes?"

"Yeah. Is that a problem?"

"Lily and I don't really get along," she admits.

"Why?"

She contemplates her answer before meeting my gaze. "You could say…we're on different sides."

"What does that mean?"

"I don't think you'd understand."

I admire her for her honesty and cringe at what she says next.

"Just like you don't think I'd understand whatever is going on with you."

I manage a shaky laugh, and it's my turn to look away. "There's not much to understand." But when I look at Lennon again, something makes me think she can see right through me. I decide to change the subject. "I can meet you at the field tonight if you think that'll make things less awkward."

"No, bring Lily! It'll be fun, even if she's not my biggest fan."

"That makes it sound like she's the one with the problem."

Lennon shrugs. "It's not her fault, really. It's ingrained in her. It's ingrained in all of them."

"All of *them*?"

The bell rings, interrupting us. "Better get to class!"

Lennon bounds down the hallway. I've never seen her so excited for school.

The day progresses, and I get the impression no one actually wants to work on Fridays, with the exception of Mr. Val. Students languidly move through lessons, and even Coach David is distracted during PE—not that our class is ever his first priority.

After seventh hour, I walk with Lennon toward the dorms. As we near the front of Emerson, Lennon sticks out her hand to stop me. When I go to open my mouth, she puts her finger to her lips and peers around the side of the building. I follow her example and see Lily and Natalie standing together on the sidewalk.

"Really, Lils, you haven't damaged your reputation that much. You don't need to hang out with those death-speakers."

Based on the fact that Lily is supposed to hang out with me and Lennon tonight, I have to guess Natalie's referring to us when she says "death-speaker."

I lean to whisper to Lennon. "What's a death-speaker?"

She meets my gaze. "It's…a nickname."

What kind of nickname is death-speaker? Not only does it sound archaic, it's very specific. Chills run down my spine, and I have to wonder if Natalie knows more about me than I realize.

Lily continues. "Those *death-speakers* actually asked me if I was okay. That's more than I can say for you."

I can't see Natalie's face, but I can tell by the change in her voice that what Lily said upset her.

"Lily...I..."

"I know what you think," Lily says, and her voice is a whisper, tinged with pain like frost cracking across glass. The silence that follows grows colder too.

I step out from our hiding place and round the corner. Natalie spares me a single, angry glance and leaves. Lily smiles, almost relieved, and I have this feeling she thought I wouldn't come.

"Hey!" I say, smiling. "Sorry we're a little late. Coach David made us run extra laps."

Lily smiles too. "He can be a jerk sometimes." Her gaze slips hesitantly from me to Lennon, who fills the space beside me.

"Tell me about it," Lennon says, rolling her eyes. "I think he has it out for us."

I step forward, looping my arm through Lily's— much like Lennon does with me—and set off toward Emerson.

"Let's get ready for the game."

We make it to Lennon's dorm and meet her roommate, a short, blond girl named Sara who's working on smearing black on her cheeks with a kohl pencil. When she looks at us, her eyelids sparkle with blue glitter. She's also wearing a jersey with the number seven on the front and back.

"Who's seven?" I ask after introductions are made, curious.

"Jacobi Quinn," Lily answers.

"Oh…is he your boyfriend?" I ask Sara.

"I wish," she says with a sigh. "Jacobi's never had a girlfriend…that we know of."

Lily averts her gaze from Sara and surveys the room. The walls are off-white. There's a single rectangular window obscured with a white blind, and the only color in the room comes from the beds, covered in bright blankets and pillows.

"Are you going to the game like that?" Lennon asks me.

I look down at myself—tights, Nacoma Knight uniform, balled-up hair with ribbons… "Yeah."

Everyone in the room is quiet. I don't really need to dress up. I hope to sneak off and find my coin. Its absence has been itching at my skin more every day, coating me with a strange guilt I don't understand but feel to my core.

The girls continue to stare until finally I say, "What?"

"At least let me do your hair a little better. We could curl it and then put the ribbons back in."

I laugh. "You don't have enough time."

"At least change," Sara suggests with a smile. "No one wants to wear a uniform to the game. I have a shirt you can wear." She goes to her drawer and pulls out a jersey with Shy's number on it.

"No," I say quicker than I intend. "I mean…that's okay. I'll just wear my uniform."

Sara's eyes widen. "Why don't you want to wear it?"

"Because…" I'm having a hard enough time blending in with the crowd, and wearing Shy's jersey will just keep those whispers circulating.

It's Lily who speaks up. "I'm sure you won't be the only one wearing the jersey. They're from state last year."

135

"Yeah, we all have one," Sara says.

Encouraged, I take the jersey from Sara and a skirt from Lennon. Sara also convinces me that wearing glitter and smudging a couple of lines on my cheeks isn't such a bad idea. By the time we head to the field, I blend in pretty well with the girls.

Lennon takes me by my hand and pulls me onto the field where a group of students, cheerleaders, and the band have gathered in front of a large, inflatable blue tunnel. A flap over the front is sealed and has the school's initials, NKA, across a shield with a rose on the front. We aren't there long when the drumline starts to play and the cheerleaders chant. Our team runs onto the field from the locker room, disappearing into the tunnel. I stand on the tips of my toes, looking for Shy. When I can't find his number, I think I might have missed him. I turn to Lennon, who matches my stance, straining her long neck. "Did you see Shy?"

"No." She frowns, shaking her head.

# CHAPTER FIFTEEN
# Shy and the Order

*I should have known Roth wants the Eurydice.*

I do my best to control my reaction, but inside, my heart races like it wants to escape the cage of my ribs. The air in the room feels heavy, like someone's sucked all the oxygen out of it.

The Eurydice inspires war like religion because the Valryn are usually split on how to handle her powers. Sure, it's our job to train and support her, but does that mean we let her loose in the world, or do we keep her on a tight leash?

"Efforts, Successor?" Elite Abrams asks. Abrams is tall and lithe and has long black hair. His voice is as imposing as his figure. "Have we confirmed her incarnation?"

Instead of answering, Roth explains, "We believe Shadow Knight-in-Training Lockwood was tracking the Eurydice before his death."

Lockwood? The knight who died in New York a couple months back?

"On what grounds?" Elite Val asks. Valryn around the room exchange looks.

"A journal was discovered among Lockwood's things after he passed. It included information on a girl who captured souls with a thread that he suspected was the Eurydice."

Well, that is pretty incriminating. The Eurydice is the only being who controls the Thread of Fate. She uses it to make resurrection coins. They are her way of ensuring souls pass safely through the Adamantine Gates. Still, there's something in the way Roth keeps glancing to the side that makes me think he's not telling the whole truth.

"Why are we just now hearing about this?" Elite Abrams looks around the room, as if someone other than Roth DuPont can tell him. The Order has never really respected Roth, even if he is the future luminary. They mostly just placate him like a spoiled child. "Shadow Knight-in-Training Lockwood died two months ago."

"The case was being investigated, Elite Abrams," Roth says. "It appears Shadow Knight-in-Training Lockwood went rogue. He was still training, after all." Roth's eyes slither to me. I clench my hands behind my back. "He must have realized he was on the trail of the Eurydice and thought he could bring her in all by himself."

Something about that doesn't sit well with me and not just because Roth looks at me as he speaks.

"Are you suggesting the Eurydice had something to do with Lockwood's death?" Elite Abrams asks.

"Chase Lockwood, a healthy, teenage Valryn, dropped dead out of nowhere, and while the police ruled his death natural causes, the evidence suggests otherwise. Lockwood's soul was stolen."

There's a heavy silence.

"If this is the case, what of the Eurydice? Have we been able to track her movements?" Elite Gwen asks. Her pale hair stands out like a white flame amid the black-clad members.

"We're working on identifying the girl Chase mentioned in his journal, but we believe she'll make her way to one of the other three Compounds in the United States, since the Adamantine Gates once stood at each location before they were destroyed."

It's a good guess. The gates were melted, leaving behind a black lake that gives off high levels of energy, attracting all kinds of things—death-speakers and the dead. Unfortunately, it also attracts Influence.

"And you would like the Order's approval to search for her?" Abrams asks.

"It is our job to locate the Eurydice. We should be searching for her. Clearly, she has demonstrated she's dangerous. She took Lockwood's life."

Oh, hell. I see where this is going now, and it's not good.

"If what you say is true, then the Eurydice should face consequences for misusing her power."

"She is hardly trained," Elite Val argues. "Indeed, as much as you remember it is our job to locate her, you forget it is also our job to train her."

"We can't do that if we do not find her first," Roth argues.

"There is no doubt we need her," Elite Gwen adds. "Without the souls passing into Spirit, Influence is becoming stronger. Just this week, a plane went down in Switzerland. One hundred and fifty people killed."

"I thought Charon opens the gates for mass death," says Ezekiel.

"One hundred and fifty must not have been enough," another adds.

There is a strange, tense silence after that comment. I can practically hear Roth tallying his supporters.

Charon has never been hands-on. He doesn't see us as his children or anything like that. We were created for a simple purpose—to protect human souls, enforce the rule of the Order over death-speakers, and protect the Eurydice. When we fail him, we are punished. Many believe that's what the last seventy years have been, a punishment for our failure to protect the Eurydice in her last life when she was murdered. It was after her death that the Adamantine Gates were dissolved, effectively cutting us off from Spirit.

"I'm assuming this is why you've assembled an army of shadow knights." Elite Abrams's eyes cut to us, lingering longer on me than anyone else. I have a feeling it's from the lack of threading on my uniform.

"I would hardly call them an army," Roth argues.

"Really? Then what do you call several trained soldiers? Sending armed Valryn after the Eurydice will only frighten her away from us. She may not even know what she is—"

"Then what do you expect us to do? Reason with her?" Roth makes the suggestion in jest, even laughing, but Elite Abrams isn't joking.

"That's precisely what I expect. The Eurydice has not incarnated in seventy years due to her murder in her last life. If she is hurt again in this incarnation, we might never get her back."

140

If she's back now, we're lucky. It was Charon who saved her soul in her last life—he opened his own portal into the land of the living. Sometimes I think she might have come back sooner had the Order found her murderer.

"So the Order approves of the search then?" In that moment, Roth reminds me of the child the Order thinks him to be, asking to drive his father's car—not the soon-to-be luminary. It makes me chuckle, and I have to shut my mouth quick after glares from Abrams and my father.

"Not with your army," Abrams says and stands. "Assemble a team—a few knights, that's it. Choose wisely. We'll alert knights at the other Compounds to search for her as well."

Elite Abrams leaves and is followed by several Valryn. Some linger—including Ezekiel—and I know it's because they support Roth's aggressive search for the Eurydice and her prosecution for Chase's death. Roth's dark gaze shifts to the knights around the room. He calls out a few names—Pia, Naava, Idris—all trackers. Emerald thread embroiders the fronts of their uniforms and circles the lengths of their arms. They step forward and salute, accepting their task.

Finally, my father's voice rings out. "Shadow knights, you are dismissed."

I start to leave.

"Shadow Knight-in-Training Savior," Roth says. "Stay."

My first thought is that Roth needs me to drive him to the closest ice cream shop, but a look at my father makes me think otherwise. My heart pounds—surely Roth isn't appointing me to search for the Eurydice too? Hadn't he insulted my training status on the way here?

"Elite Cain tells me you have aspirations of becoming a commander."

This is not new information to Roth. It's one reason he gives me such a hard time.

"I would see the appointment as an honor, Successor," I say, working hard to control my voice and move my jaw. Roth has that stupid glimmer in his eyes that tells me he knows I'm struggling and he's amused.

"Then find the Eurydice for me."

"Excuse me, Successor, but...I don't want to be granted a title without having earned it."

"If you find the Eurydice, then you have earned it, Tracker." Roth turns to Elite Cain. "See that Shadow Knight Savior receives his new uniform promptly...and ensure my team has all the tools required to find the Eurydice. Soon."

And just like that, I'm ranked as a shadow knight. So why don't I feel better? I always imagined this moment would feel better. It would feel...earned. Leave it to Roth to rob me of an experience. Why does he want the Eurydice anyway? He's not the kind to concern himself with Influence's hold over the world unless it affects him. He can't suddenly care about humans now that he's becoming luminary.

No, there has to be another reason.

Those unanswered questions gather in my chest like clouds on the horizon.

A storm is brewing.

A battle.

The worst part? I'm not sure whose side I'm on.

# CHAPTER SIXTEEN
# Anora and Influence

*The fight song begins, and players burst through the banner.* I search for Shy but don't see him. I'm not the only one: several players and coaches turn to look behind them, as if hoping he will appear at any moment. Even Lily seems concerned, brows knitted together in a tight line.

My excitement quickly turns to unease—a feeling that spreads to the crowd as their volume dies down.

We leave the field and take spots in the stands, front and center, where the cheerleaders are positioned on the track. I don't miss the way Natalie glares, both at me and Lily, who doesn't seem fazed by the attention.

Five of our players make their way to the center of the field. Sara leans over. "Looks like Jacobi's our quarterback tonight!"

"Yeah, but…where is Shy?" Lennon asks, looking at Lily expectantly, but all she does is shrug, frowning.

The knot in my stomach tightens.

"Good evening, Knights!" An announcer comes over the intercom. He has one of those made-for-radio voices, and everything he says is drawn out and punctuated with enthusiasm. "Tonight we have a special guest joining us at the center of the field for the coin toss. Please welcome the one and only, Mr. Malachi Black!"

Lennon elbows me. "That's Thane's uncle!"

Malachi strolls onto the turf, smiling and waving at the crowd. He wears a gray business suit, and his long hair is bound at the nape of his neck. The coin toss reminds me of two things—my own coin I've lost and Thane's persistent attention. Self-conscious, I crane my neck, looking for any sign of him.

"Anora?" I turn to find Lily watching me. "Are you looking for someone?"

"No." I smile and shake my head, eyes settling on the field again. "What's the coin toss for?"

"It determines who will be on offense or defense first," Lennon says, leaning toward me.

Once the toss is made, the game begins and spirals out of control within the first fifteen minutes. Jacobi throws two interceptions and fumbles the ball.

"This wouldn't happen if Savior were here. Where's that boy?" a gruff voice says from behind me. I don't turn to look. I feel sorry for Jacobi. I know everyone's thinking the same thing. The excitement I had about being at the game soon wears off, and anxiety gathers in my chest—how am I going to sneak away from my friends?

Behind me, the man mouthing off about Jacobi stands suddenly, yelling about another fumble, and knocks over his drink. The liquid spreads, soaking my shirt. Guess I should be careful what I wish for.

I stand quickly, wringing out my shirt. The loud man hasn't even realized he's made a mess.

"Great!"

"Oh no," I hear Lily say.

"We can go back to the dorm, get you a new shirt," Sara says.

"No, no. It's fine," I say. "I'll just go stand over the hand dryer for a little bit."

"Want me to come with you?" Lennon asks.

"No, that's okay. I won't be long."

I smile at them and hurry away.

The bright lights burn my back as I wander away from the football field. Ahead, the night is illuminated by a few electric lampposts sprinkled across campus. I don't mind the night—I prefer it. When we lived in the city, I used to wish there were fewer lights.

I follow the sidewalk as it weaves across campus, making my way to the trees where I captured Vera's soul. I use my phone as a flashlight, shining it as I step, looking for any sign of the coin. As I get deeper into the woods, farther than I've gone before, I start to feel like my energy is being drained. When I look up, I don't see any dead, but something that strong can't be good.

I resist the urge to investigate, clutching my fist tight, fighting the thread burrowing out of my palm. I came to find the coin, not the dead. I search the ground at my feet but only find dead leaves, twigs, and acorns. No coin.

That's when I encounter the first dead guy. He's standing still, eyes far off and glazed, blood dripping from his nose and drool from his mouth. I step around him, heart racing, only to find another a few feet away. This one has burns covering most of his body. From the corner of my eye, I see another figure and another. They're all around me.

I'm standing on a mass grave, I realize with horror.

The majority of these dead were killed in a fire. Their skin looks like it was attacked by a cheese grater: vibrant red scars, shiny with fresh blood and plasma. There are others with wounds to their heads and wrists, some with rope burns around their necks and tongues that loll out of their mouths.

I hold my breath and navigate around them, wishing myself invisible, hoping none of them are like Vera and follow me, when something grabs my wrist. A scream rises in my throat, and a hand clamps down over my mouth. I bite into the flesh.

"Fuck!" the voice roars, and I twist to find Thane behind me. "You bit me!"

"You snuck up on me! What did you expect?"

"Obviously not your teeth in my skin."

"Oh, it's not that bad. You're lucky. The last guy who snuck up on me got kneed in the crotch."

A ghost of a smile graces Thane's lips. "Too bad. He would have probably preferred your teeth."

"Shut up. What are you doing out here anyway?"

"Following you," he says, taking a quick look around. "I figured you'd need help."

"I'm pretty good at playing dodge the dead, thank you very much," I say.

We stare at each other for a long moment. I know he didn't follow me to help; he followed to spy.

Then we hear the voices.

"Sean, stop!" The voice belongs to a girl. "It's not what it looks like!"

In my experience, it's often what it looks like.

"I can't believe you, man!"

146

Thane surprises me by taking the lead, wandering even deeper into the woods. I follow, led by the voices and that horrible, energetic pull. It makes my insides shake.

"Put that down, Sean!" The other voice is male and alarmed.

*Uh-oh.*

I try to move faster but drag my feet. Maybe I'll scare off whoever's fighting in the woods.

We find them in a clearing—two boys and one girl. The one called Sean is holding a large branch like a baseball bat, and I'm fairly certain he's about to use it like one. His skin glistens with sweat, and he is breathing hard. His eyes move from the boy to the girl and then go dim, like he's not actually present in his body. I've seen the look before—in people who are dying or grieving.

"Sean! No!" the girl screams.

Sean lifts the branch and swings, hitting the other boy square in the face. He falls like a rock. I burst through the trees.

"Stop!"

Sean's back goes ramrod straight, his head snaps back, and a plume of gray erupts from his mouth and gathers in a cloud above his head. I freeze. I've seen this thing before, tangled with my poppa's soul after his death. The *thing* hisses at me and then ripples through the air like the aftershock of an earthquake. Its energy is dark and disturbing. It cuts through the trees, making their branches shake. I run after it, dodging limbs and dead things, but it is dark, and my clothes snag on branches and thorns, and I trip over rocks and raised earth, finally stumbling right through a dead guy.

And it's like I've landed in an inferno—flames

147

scalding, wilting my skin like a flower in winter. I wail, writhing on the ground. My fingers curl into the dirt, and bile rises in the back of my steaming throat.

When the worst of it's over, pain still vibrates through my body. I lie, gasping for breath, unable to move.

Then something lands beside me, and I roll over to find a creature. It's nothing like the thing of shadow that burst from Sean. This has the body of a human and large wings. I roll away, moving onto my hands and knees, blinking rapidly, my head swimming...and find that the person in front of me is just a boy, and the halo of wings I imagined, trees.

"Shy?"

"Are you okay? I thought I heard screaming."

"Y-yeah. I'm fine." I take Shy's hand, head spinning as he helps me to my feet. We're inches apart, and he still has a hold of my fingers.

"How did you..." I start, but I can't think clearly when I'm touching him. I withdraw my hand. I had clearly heard the thump of feet landing beside me, not footfalls. "W-what are you doing out here? You're supposed to be at the game."

"I was just arriving when I heard screams." He's staring down at me, studying me. I feel like he can see the last ten minutes of my life written on my face. "Sean ran out of here like he'd seen a ghost."

*Ha, he doesn't even know he's being funny.*

"Yeah, well, Sean beat that other kid's face in, so he's running from his crime."

Shy frowns. "That doesn't sound like Sean."

"Well, I guess you get jealous when your friend is caught with your girlfriend."

148

"Sean and Ally are brother and sister."

"Well, he didn't like his friend messing around with his sister, then."

A line appears between Shy's brows, still unhappy with my version of things. I can't tell him what I actually saw: something near invisible spewing from Sean's body like an alien. I shiver. I never thought I'd see anything like that again. What was it doing in Sean's body? What had it been doing in my poppa's body?

"What are you doing out here?" Shy asks. His eyes fall to my jersey, and I cross my arms over my chest, feeling self-conscious.

"The same reason you're here. I heard Ally scream."

"All the way from the stadium?" he asks, brow raised.

"Well, no."

"She was looking for me." Thane joins us in the clearing, and the air thickens, suffocating me as I'm caught between the two. I look toward Shy in time to see him clamp his mouth shut. He steps away, putting distance between us, and passes a hand through his hair, pushing it out of his eyes. That's when I see it—the blade sheathed at his side. Mostly hidden under his jacket, it gleams eerily. It's curved like a scythe, but shorter.

I've seen a blade like that before.

Someone tried to kill me with it.

Shy drops his hand and pulls his jacket together.

"The police are on the way," Shy says, not taking his eyes off me. "They'll want a statement from you."

As he leaves, I watch him traverse around the dead—a skilled captain navigating rough seas.

He can see them too.

# CHAPTER SEVENTEEN
# Anora and Thane Treadway

*The game is delayed with the arrival of the police and* ambulance. Sean is put in the back of the squad car while the other kid—whose name is Gage—is loaded up on a stretcher, unconscious. Ally's wrapped in a blanket. During the interrogations, I catch most of the story. The three had gone into the woods to smoke weed when Sean started acting weird—pacing and muttering to himself. I know where this is going before it's over. The police will say the drugs sparked Sean's behavior, and maybe that was a part of it...but that *creature* fueled it.

When we're allowed to leave, Thane walks me back toward the stadium. Unbelievably, the game is still going to continue. Apparently Nacoma Knight is serious about homecoming.

"Eat this," he says, handing me the bread from a hot dog he purchased while I was being questioned.

"I'm good, thanks."

"You have another hour here, and you're about to run low on adrenaline, so I suggest you eat something."

I take the bread. "Fine."

Thane is right about running low on energy. I was keyed up while talking to the police, but as soon as it was over, I felt exhausted. We stop behind the bleachers while I finish eating the bread. I chew slowly, mostly because my stomach feels like it's boiling acid.

Thane steps away from me and lights a cigarette, blasting smoke from his nose and mouth.

"You know your uncle is here?"

"Yep."

"And he lets you do that?"

"As long as I don't smoke near his money, he doesn't care what I do."

*Well, that's sad.*

"Tell me what you saw," he says, leaning against one of the brick columns. It's the first time I've had the chance to really look at him all evening. He seems smaller somehow, in dark jeans and a red flannel shirt.

"A kid trying to beat up his friend."

"What else?"

I watch him a moment, considering my next words, and then say, "I don't think the kid knew what he was doing. This…*thing*…this *creature* erupted out of him and fled. I tried to follow it, but…"

"It's energy. You can't follow energy." He pauses a moment and looks away. "It thrives here with all the dead in the woods."

So the dead fuel the monster. *That's* unsettling.

"You shouldn't try to chase it. It could have gotten you—crawled inside you and possessed you."

"Which is what it was doing to Sean?"

"More or less," Thane says, bringing the cigarette to his lips again. He takes a drag, letting the smoke escape his mouth as he talks. "They have a name for that particular kind of energy—the kind born of the dead." There he goes again, using *they*. They as in the people—or not people at all—who are tracking Vera, the ones who will trace her disappearance back to me. He continues, "It's called Influence. It latches on to insecurities and aggression, feeds them, and then bad things happen."

Like Sean bashing his friend's face in. Like my poppa's suicide.

"But that's not what it's going to look like," I say. "The police are already saying drugs spurred his actions."

"The police aren't death-speakers. They can't see what we see."

I look up. "What did you say?"

Thane blinks and doesn't move to speak.

"Did you just call me a death-speaker?" I ask.

"Yeah. That's what you are, in case you didn't know. Same as me. A human who can see and speak to the dead."

So Natalie's description of me wasn't just a random nickname. She *knows* I can see the dead. Which means Lily does too.

"Is everyone at this school a death-speaker?"

"No, though I can't always spot them as easily as I spotted you, but that's your fault. You act like you just got the sight."

I glare at him.

"Wait," he says, as if just now realizing that might actually be true. "You didn't just start seeing the dead, right?"

"No. It's been a few months now."

Thane stares at me for a long moment. "Who died?"

"What?"

"If you aren't born seeing the dead, usually the death of someone close to you activates the sight. So who died?"

I touch the chain of my necklace but don't pull out Poppa's coin, conscious Thane is watching me. "My poppa," I say. "What about you?"

Thane takes another drag from his cigarette. It's smaller now, and he holds it between his thumb and forefinger. "I was born seeing the dead—shadows, mostly, from the corner of my eye. Then, when my mother died, everything came into focus—in living fucking color."

"I'm sorry."

"Everyone is."

"What about your dad?"

"He might as well be dead too."

I pause a moment and then say, "Mine too."

Thane puts his cigarette out against the brick. "Aren't you going to ask me how she died?"

"Excuse me?"

"I'm assuming you want to know how she died," he says. "Everyone does. Keeps them from googling it later."

I stare at him. I hadn't considered doing any research on Thane in my spare time.

"It was a car wreck," he says. "The driver who hit her was drunk and speeding. He had a really good lawyer and never served time for her murder."

"That's horrible."

"Tell me about it," he says, pulling out another

cigarette. The cherry brightens with his inhale, and as he flicks the ashes away, he says, "Smoking is a bad habit. It smells and will probably give me cancer. But it could be worse. My uncle should be glad I'm not using his money for cocaine."

"Drugs won't help you feel any better."

He smiles, his eyes narrow, amused. "Shows how much you know."

An awkward silence spreads between us. I think about asking Thane about Shy—why aren't they friends anymore? Does it have anything to do with the fact that he's a death-speaker or the blade Shy carries at his side? Is Shy a death-speaker too? Before I can ask, I hear my name.

"Anora."

I twist to find Lennon standing a few feet away.

"What are you doing?" she asks.

"Uh." I look back at Thane. "Just talking."

"Are you okay? You just sort of ran away."

"Yeah. Yeah...I'm fine."

"You better run along," Thane says. "You don't want people to talk."

His eyes don't move from Lennon as he speaks. The tension between them reminds me of the tension between her and Shy, and I have to wonder why everyone's suspicious of Lennon Ryder.

"I'll see you around," I say.

At that, Thane smirks. "I hope that's a promise," he says, and it's clear he likes the idea of becoming friends. I don't know how I feel about it.

I follow Lennon back to the stands. As we go, she explains what I already know—that the game was delayed because of a fight. The police and ambulance were called. I do my part and act both surprised and shocked. I ask all the right questions: Who was involved? Why were they fighting? Is everyone okay?

By the time we make it to our seats, the crowd erupts in applause. Shy jogs onto the field, helmet in one hand, the other raised, waving to the crowd. He runs to the coach, whose exaggerated arms and yelling can't mask his relief. After a few orders, Shy and Jacobi trade places on the field. Shy pumps his arms in the air, urging the crowd to their feet, and like any disciples, they follow his will, chant his name, sing his praise. Everyone but me, who can't quite shake that this kid, this all-American quarterback, carries a scythe, the same weapon used by the boy who tried to kill me before.

As Shy and his now-unified team pull us out of defeat, my gaze settles on Jacobi, who sits alone on a bench near the sidelines, helmet off, hair wet with sweat, evidence of his hard work, all ignored because it didn't mean victory. Despite feeling sorry for him, I still wonder if he carries a scythe too.

"He'll be okay," Lily says. I meet her gaze. "Jacobi's used to this."

"Used to it?"

"We're all used to it," she amends. "Shy's…gifted. He's a seventeen-year-old imbued with the soul of someone much older and practiced."

*Someone older.* My stomach clenches.

"No one's that perfect," I try to joke.

She smiles. "I didn't say he was perfect."

And yet in all his imperfection, Shy leads Nacoma Knight to victory. Teammates fly across the field to lift him on their shoulders, and he takes it all in like a God receiving prayer. Who is Shy Savior? Student, quarterback…assassin?

When his feet touch the ground again, he's crowded by coaches and cheerleaders. Natalie pushes her way forward and throws her arms around his neck. I expect Shy to push her away, but instead he gathers her close, lifting her off the ground in a hug.

A shock of jealousy runs through me, winding tight around my heart. How can I feel jealous of someone I don't completely trust? Someone who carries a scythe? As if Shy senses what's happening inside me, his eyes find mine. There's tension in the look we exchange, the result of our encounter in the woods. He disentangles himself from Natalie, who seems to notice he's distracted and turns my way.

That's when I look away.

"You okay?" Lily asks.

"Yeah," I breathe, feeling the weight of this evening on my shoulders. "I'm just tired."

Lily maintains a soft smile, like she understands everything and everyone.

"We can go."

I don't hesitate to take her up on her offer, and we leave the stadium. As we retreat from the stands, Lennon comes up behind me, looping her arm through mine. She slows down so that Sara and Lily wander ahead of us.

I recognize this behavior. She wants to talk, and out of earshot of our friends. This makes me anxious.

"What's up?" I prompt, trying to sound nonchalant.

"Oh, nothing," she says, pausing. "I was just… curious. Did you…leave to meet up with Thane earlier?"

"What? No. Definitely not."

I should have expected that question.

"Good," she says, sounding relieved.

"What?"

"I mean not good...just..." She sighs, and a smile pulls at my lips.

"Lennon, do you have a crush?" I nudge her a little, but she's quick to respond, and not with embarrassment or disgust—just truth.

"No. I just don't trust Thane."

For some reason, her words arrest me. I stop walking, and so does she.

"Why?"

She takes a deep breath. "Thane's soul is...fractured. After his mother died, he gave up on everyone he loved. Anyone who can do that...can't truly feel for anyone."

A strangled laugh escapes from my mouth. I do my best to swallow it before I hurt Lennon's feelings.

"Look, Lennon. You don't have to worry. I'm not looking for a relationship."

"Thane isn't either. He's looking for a way to bring his mother back from the dead."

# CHAPTER EIGHTEEN
## Shy and the Salt Line

*I wake up with a headache, and my tongue feels swollen.* I roll over in bed and guzzle water before collapsing onto my back again. I patrolled after the game. It was necessary after Influence's attack on Sean and Gage. On the heels of Council, the incident feels like a punch in the gut—as if I need another reminder of Influence's growing power or more pressure to locate the Eurydice.

My eyes are still heavy, and I'd rather go back to sleep, but I have things to do today, so I get up and hop in the shower, turning the water on real hot. It pours over my body, easing my sore muscles. The only thing it doesn't heal is the strange tension knotting up my chest. That's from Anora.

I couldn't admit to her that I'd found her in the woods yesterday because of the weird feeling in my chest. It's like a freaky alarm system, except I still haven't exactly figured out what it means. The only correlation

I've made is that the longer I'm away from her, the worst the feeling gets.

I hate it.

Maybe hate is too strong a word. I like seeing Anora. I like talking to her, but I don't like *needing* her. That's a weakness, and weaknesses are to be conquered.

Maybe what I hate more is Thane showing up to let me know Anora was looking for him. Why are they hanging out together anyway? When did that start? I don't like it.

He's a death-speaker who knows about us and is involved in the Underworld and practices the occult. After his mom died, he became obsessed with learning about reincarnation, which is something I am not willing to support.

I guess I should have expected it. There was no way Thane and I could have remained friends with his interest in the dark practices. At some point, he was bound to do something I disagreed with, and staying friends with him would have gotten me in trouble with the Order.

No one talks about how crappy it is to lose a best friend, but it really freaking sucks.

And part of me wishes I could trust him with Anora.

But I can't.

After my shower, I head downstairs. Mom's shoveling eggs onto a plate. She turns to me and smiles.

"You're up!" She leans forward to kiss my cheek, handing me the plate of eggs. "I made your favorite."

My "favorite" is chocolate-chip pancakes with whipped cream and syrup. Mom always makes it when we're celebrating something. Usually, every Saturday morning, it's a win for my team. Today it's my win and shadow knight appointment to tracker, except I don't feel like celebrating my jump in rank all that much. I still feel uneasy about it, and I dread when Natalie finds out.

Mom and I sit down to eat; Dad's seat remains unsurprisingly empty.

"I heard what happened at the game," Mom says. "Is Gage okay?"

"I think he has a broken nose, but otherwise, he'll be fine."

Mom frowns. "And what about Sean?"

That is a harder question. There is no telling how long Influence had its hold on Sean or what sort of deep-rooted feelings manifested his actions last night. I'd heard all things that are common when dealing with Influence—*he was such a cool guy, he was so funny, I can't believe it*. That's how it works—it's always the people you don't expect doing things you don't expect.

"I don't know."

Mom doesn't say anything, and when I look up, I find her staring at me. "Have any plans today?"

I scrub my hand through my hair. "I…uh…I thought I might go see Anora."

I'd been thinking about approaching her house again since the night with the telescope but hadn't worked up the courage. After last night, today seemed just as good a day as any. The best way to catch someone unaware is to sneak up on them.

It's also a good way to get chased by a hellhound. Thank Charon, they only come out at night. There's also a chance she won't talk to me after last night, but I'm hoping to be invited inside her house. Then I'll have a chance to look for evidence to support—or

160

disprove—Natalie's claim that Anora's responsible for Vera's disappearance.

"Oh." Mom tries to hide her surprise, but she's unsuccessful. At least she didn't spit out her food. "And do what exactly?"

*Make out*, I think sarcastically. Though it's not all that sarcastic. If the opportunity presents itself, I'll kiss Anora. I've wanted to since this feeling in my chest began, just to see if it would ease.

Instead, I shrug. I never like talking about girls with my mom when they're Valryn. I definitely don't like talking about them when they're human. "I don't know. Just…hang out."

"Is your father aware?"

I clamp my teeth together before saying, "He was there when Elite Cain appointed me and Nat to the case."

Elite Cain never specified how Natalie and I should go about observing Anora. And I haven't gotten in trouble yet. So long as I can continue to prove my actions are to benefit the Order, I'm safe. But I know Mom's concerns. The fiasco with Lily is still fresh in everyone's mind.

"I like Jayne well enough, and I'm sure Anora is just as charming." Mom stands and starts clearing away the dishes, so I do the same. As she passes, she stops and looks up at me. "Just…be careful, Shy."

I lean forward and kiss her cheek. "I'm always careful."

———

As I approach Anora's house, I find her outside, crouched low on the ground beneath one of the windows. I come to a stop in the driveway, and she straightens, twisting, hiding something behind her back.

"Shy." Her voice is full of surprise. I'm sure I'm the last person she expected to see in her driveway on a Saturday morning. She's wearing jeans, a gray shirt, and a black jacket. Her hair falls in a thick mass over her shoulder. "What are you doing here?"

"I thought I'd stop by, see if you were doing anything today," I say as I approach her, hands in the pockets of my jacket. I grin at her, hoping she'll smile back. I don't like the disappointment I feel when she doesn't.

"I'm kind of busy," she says, and I glance behind her where a white substance covers the ground. My eyes narrow, but before I can ask, Anora's name is called from inside the house. She goes rigid, and the static in my chest pops. The front door swings open, and the person I assume to be Anora's mom stands there. She has dark, round eyes, and her cheekbones and chin are sharp as knives. She hesitates when she sees me.

"Hi," her mom says, but it sounds more like a question.

"Mom, this is Shy," Anora says quickly, indicating to me with her left hand. The right is still behind her back.

I wave at her and smile. "It's nice to meet you, Ms. Silby."

"Mom, you work for Shy's mother at O'Connor Realty," Anora says, and I can tell by the breathlessness in her voice—and the pinch at my chest—that this is making her anxious.

Ms. Silby smiles and moves closer to us on the porch.

"Oh! You're Guiliana's son? I've heard so much about you."

I sort of laugh—I can just imagine how Mom brags. I've heard her before. "I hope she doesn't talk about me too much."

"She's very proud of you," Ms. Silby says. "But she's not the only one who talks about you. Anora says you're a great football player, practically won last night's game single-handedly."

I look at Anora, whose face has turned an enticing shade of pink. She looks at the ground, kicking at gravel with her foot. It's a small consolation considering she won't smile for me today.

"That's too much credit, Ms. Silby. I'm nothing without my team."

Ms. Silby smiles. It's Anora's smile, but there's something less sincere about it. "Have you had lunch, Shy?"

"No, Ms. Silby."

"Call me Jayne. And you should join us for lunch."

"I'd love to."

When Jayne goes back inside, Anora turns to glare at me.

"Why do you have salt behind your back?" I ask. I'm trying to be playful, but she's not having it.

"To keep the dead away from my house," she says.

It's a challenge to keep a straight face. I'm surprised she's being so direct.

I grin. "Salt's not going to keep anything out... except maybe snails."

"If you have any advice, I'd love to hear it."

I pull my hand from my pocket where I've been rolling a stone between my fingers for the last several minutes and hold it out to her.

"What's that?"

163

"Obsidian. It'll keep evil at a distance for a lot longer than salt."

She tightens her fingers around the rock and says, "Hmm. Must not work. You're still here."

I put my hand to my heart. "You wound me." She glares and I frown. How have I become a bad guy overnight?

I shove my hands in my pockets again, feeling really freaking awkward. "You gonna show me around?"

Anora glances toward her house. "This is my house," she says. "You saw it the other night when you creepily found it on your own."

Yeah. Not scoring any points here. Things have definitely changed after last night.

At least I have a good excuse. "Hey, small town, remember? Everyone at school knows where you live."

"Yeah, but they don't drop by uninvited."

She didn't seem to mind the first time. I almost challenge her, but I'm not sure I want to hear her response.

She sighs. "Fine. Come on."

I follow Anora inside. She leaves me in the entry- way while she returns the salt to the kitchen. When she comes back, we stand facing each other.

"This is the living room." She spreads out her arms and then lets them fall, slapping against her sides.

I raise my brows and maintain a smile. "Nice view."

She turns, heading toward the stairs. They creak as we rise, and her mom calls from somewhere in the house, "Door open!"

Anora cringes, and I'm not sure it's from embarrass- ment or the thought of kissing me. I'm really hoping it's the former.

I follow Anora down the hallway. She turns and walks through a door on the right.

"This is my room," she says.

I brush past her, the scent of roses and rosemary surrounding me as I observe her space. She has a twin bed with a purple comforter, and a four-drawer dresser sits opposite that. There are a couple of boxes in the middle of the floor she hasn't unpacked yet, and the black telescope from the other night sits on a tripod near her window.

"Do you stargaze often?" I ask, already knowing the answer but noting several star posters pinned around her room.

"Sometimes. Mostly, it's too bright."

"How did you get started?"

She hesitates and then admits in a small voice. "My poppa. He bought me that telescope." Her voice catches on the words, like she's not used to saying them in past tense, and something far worse and bottomless opens up in my chest.

I frown. "I'm sorry," I say and decide it's best if I change the subject. I nod to the bookshelves on either side of her window. I knew she read a lot, just by the surveillance we'd conducted. "You have a lot of books."

"It's my goal to have the library in *Beauty and the Beast* one day."

That makes me laugh. "If you could only take one of these with you to a desert island, which one would you bring?"

"That's easy," she says, and I feel her approach—my awareness of her pricks along my skin. "My special edition *Lord of the Rings*."

When I look at her, she's standing just a few steps away.

"What's wrong?" I finally ask, frustrated by how distant she feels. She wasn't like this prior to last night, but now she's looking at me like I'm the enemy, and I don't like it. "You're…different."

"I haven't changed at all," she says.

I twist toward her, closing the distance, but she backs away.

"Are you afraid of me?"

Instead of answering, she says, "Is everyone in this town a death-speaker?"

"I'm not a death-speaker."

"If you aren't a death-speaker, then what are you?"

This conversation is not going the direction I need it to.

"Where'd you learn about death-speakers?" I ask instead, but as soon as that question's out of my mouth, I have an answer for it. "Thane." Her eyes darken at my disdain. "So he's why I'm suddenly a bad guy?"

"Actually, I learned about death-speakers from Natalie," she says. "Thane just clarified, and you're a bad guy because you had a scythe under your jacket last night."

My gut tightens. "Are you absolutely certain you know what you saw?"

"Don't patronize me. Everyone knows what a scythe is. Question is, are you just a weirdo who likes to carry a weapon, or are you—"

Her voice falters, eyes burning, but she's given me what I need.

"Or am I what, Anora?"

Her chest rises and falls quickly, and it's hard not to be aware of her when she's this close. I should step away, leave, but this proximity untangles my chest.

"You've seen the blade before."

And I'm betting the carrier was named Chase Lockwood. And if she knows Chase, then that means...

Before we can continue our conversation, Anora's mom clears her throat. I step away, and we turn to face Jayne in the doorway.

"Lunch is ready."

Jayne waits at the door until Anora and I leave the room in front of her.

Lunch is awkward. I'm not sure if it's because Jayne thinks Anora and I were making out or because Anora avoids my eyes from across the table as she eats. I decide not to let her keep me from enjoying free food.

"This meal is delicious, Ms. Silby."

She smiles, the crow's-feet on either side of her eyes deepening. "Thank you, Shy. Cooking is a bit of a passion of mine."

"My mom loves cooking too," I say. "Nothing frozen ever comes into our house."

"We'll have to have your mother and father over for dinner sometime."

I can't imagine my father sitting down to dinner with me, much less arriving at Anora's to drink wine and chat with Jayne. Still I say, "They would love that." I look at Anora. "Do you cook?"

She seems surprised by my question. "With Mom," she says.

"Anora's being modest. She's a great cook but an even better baker."

"You've been holding out on me," I accuse playfully. "I demand cookies!"

"Mom's exaggerating. I'm not that great."

"I am not!" Jayne laughs. "She likes to bake at night. In New York, she had the whole house smelling like cake at midnight."

Anora goes rigid in her seat at the mention of New York, but Jayne doesn't seem to realize her error. I catch it, hold it tight, and pin Anora with a pointed stare. Was that why Natalie couldn't find Anora's school record in Chicago? Because they were actually from New York? The same state where Chase Lockwood died?

Jayne continues, laughing. "Did I mention she likes to dance too?"

"Dance?" I lift my brow, quirk my lips, watching her. What I'm really asking is: *New York?*

"Mom's...misremembering," she says tightly.

"Nonsense, Anora." Jayne looks at me. "She dances and sings when she bakes. I used to creep into the living room and listen to her. She has the prettiest voice."

Anora seems surprised. Her eyes widen just before they fall to her food, her face flushed. There is silence for a moment, and the lull allows a strange, suffocating tension to settle. I take a deep breath, inhaling the thick air.

"Well, you both surpass me. I can't even cook an egg."

Jayne laughs while I feel Anora's anxiety rise like a tide, swelling. For the remainder of lunch, she's disengaged from conversation and doesn't touch her food, preferring to keep one hand on a gold chain at her neck while she chews her lip. I wonder what is on the end of that necklace.

"It was great having you over, Shy. I'll talk to Guiliana about dinner sometime," Jayne says as we walk to the door.

"I look forward to it, Ms. Silby."

Anora walks me to my car. She's quiet, and I can tell by the look on her face she's still trying to figure me out. She's smart. All that small talk might have convinced another human I wasn't after anything, but Anora has seen things. Experienced things. She knows my tactics.

Because someone's used them before.

"New York?" I finally ask.

"Mom misspoke."

I raise a brow but don't press, because I'm worried if I do, she'll ask me more about the scythe.

"Does your mom know you can see the dead?" I ask.

She sort of laughs, like that's a ludicrous idea. "No. She just thinks I'm a crazy kid."

I nod. All their awkward pauses and tension make sense now.

"I don't know what happened before you got here, but I'm not going to hurt you."

Then she says something that disarms me. "He said that too."

"Chase Lockwood?" I ask.

I'm impressed by her reaction—absolutely nothing. Her jaw doesn't tighten, and her eyes don't narrow.

"Anora," Jayne calls from the front door. "Please come in and do these dishes."

Anora looks relieved at the interruption.

And now I'm even more curious about what happened between her and Chase. I pull the keys to my Jeep out and say, "Put the obsidian in your windowsill."

Then I climb into my Jeep. As I leave, I glance in my rearview mirror. Anora's still standing on the sidewalk outside her house, watching me go. I wrap my fingers around the steering wheel tight, fighting the urge to turn around and stay with her until she trusts me, even as I wonder if I'll ever be able to trust her.

Instead, I put my foot to the gas and speed away.

When I get home, Lily is waiting for me. She sits on the steps, elbows resting on her knees. She's dressed in jeans and a dark-blue sweatshirt. The hood is pulled up, covering her head.

"Hey," I say as I get out of my Jeep. "You know Mom's inside."

"I didn't want to bother her," Lily says, and I know it's because she's embarrassed.

I take a seat beside her. "How long have you been waiting?"

"Not long. Where were you?"

I pause before answering—something I probably shouldn't do, because it implies guilt. "With Anora."

Lily looks confused. "I know we promised each other we wouldn't ask, but I have to, Shy. What are you doing with her?"

"Nothing, Lils. Seriously. I'm just...we're just friends." It is hard to use that word after the interaction I've just had with her, but what am I supposed to say? I feel better when I'm around her, I'm pretty sure she doesn't trust me as far as she can throw me, and I'm also sure she killed Chase Lockwood...which, according to what I learned at Council, would make her the Eurydice and add a whole new layer of complication and mistrust.

"I've never seen you act like this with a human girl.

You're going out of your way to see her—to look at her. Don't think I haven't noticed."

Yeah, because my chest feels like it will implode if I don't.

"Please don't lecture me about this, Lils. I get enough from Nat."

"I'm not going to tell you the same stuff Natalie will tell you, but whatever you're doing better be genuine."

"What do you mean 'genuine'?"

"I know you and Natalie have been ordered to watch her, so whatever you're doing should be because you actually like her and not because Elite Cain told you to do it."

"Lily—"

"It's not right, Shy," she says, her voice rising. She pauses, frustrated. "I'm tired of the control the Order has over our lives. Sometimes…I wonder if Thane was right."

"That's dangerous thinking, Lils."

"Is it?"

"We can't bring people back to life," I say evenly.

"Do we know that for certain? Or do we believe that because the Order told us?"

She's being ridiculous. We know that because we've seen it. Souls that are resurrected are torn from Spirit and forced into a body that fractures the soul. That fracture always manifests itself in the form of anger and beastly behaviors.

"Thane's mother was beyond our reach, Lily. Even if we were to retrieve her soul, it would have been up to her body to heal. She was too damaged."

"But people are resurrected all the time."

171

"And they're not the same. You know this. Why question it?" I narrow my eyes. "You're talking to him, aren't you?"

"Just because you aren't friends with Thane anymore doesn't mean I can't be."

Thane is one of the few death-speakers who actually know about the Valryn. Growing up in the same town with him, it was probably inevitable that he'd learn about us eventually, but he caught Lily in her hybrid form, and after swearing him to secrecy, we told him about us and the Order. Of course, that was before his mom died, before he asked us to help bring her back.

"I've never told you not to be his friend, but you shouldn't encourage his thinking. Don't give him hope where there is none."

"You're one to talk."

"What do you mean?"

"Anora."

"That's not the same thing."

"You keep giving her attention, and she's going to fall for you hard, and what kind of person are you going to be? The shadow knight who breaks her heart or the one that breaks the rules?"

With that, she shifts and flies away, a splash of black against a graying sky.

# CHAPTER NINETEEN
## Shy and the Offer

*The day starts off wrong.*

I wake to my phone going off like a tornado siren sounding in the dead of night, tearing me from sleep. I sit up straight in bed, heart racing, and check my phone: Pick me up at Temple, 5, it says.

Roth.

There are no other details—a why or where we're going.

I glance at the clock at the top of my screen—4:00 a.m.—and scrub my face with the palm of my hand, unable to discern if the feeling in my stomach is alarm from being woken so suddenly or dread.

I don't want to be alone with Roth. He'll want an update on the Eurydice, and I don't have much I want to offer. In the time since Council, Anora has become my prime suspect. I'm positive she lied about being from Chicago, thanks to her mom's slip at lunch, and she recognized my scythe, which means she's seen it before, and at the mention of Chase Lockwood, she stayed silent—I would have been more convinced she didn't know him if she'd said so. I might not completely trust her, but I'm willing to listen to her side.

I've been told to hand everything on the Eurydice over to Elite Cain, but I can't bring myself to do it. It could be because it's Anora and the thought of telling anyone about her feels like betrayal. Or it could just be that I don't like Roth and I think he wants the Eurydice for his own purposes, but I'm just not sure what those purposes are.

One thing is certain—Anora doesn't like or trust what she thinks I am, which means if I were to hand her over to the Order, she won't trust them either, and if she's going to rid the world of Influence's hold, we need her on our side. We need her to believe we really will protect her.

Charon knows *I* have to—there's no telling what sort of damage her distress will do to my body. Her anxiety already has my chest in knots. More unanswered questions: Why do I have a connection to this human? Is it one-sided? I've seen little evidence that she feels the same. Things would probably be a little easier if she did. I wonder if I should ask Jacobi to look into the Eurydice's history, but that might open up more questions I'm not ready to face. It seems that for now, I'll just have to suffer on my own.

When I arrive to pick Roth up, he's standing outside Temple. He throws his bag into the back of my Jeep and says, "Airport."

"You're leaving?" I try not to imbue my voice with too much excitement.

"Dad's taken a turn." He delivers the news colorlessly—as if he were reporting the weather.

My heart pounds, like it's asking to exit my body. I don't have anything to say. I already thought through all the repercussions of Maximus's death. I glance at Roth. His jaw is set, and he stares straight ahead. I manage a whispered "I'm sorry."

And I am—for all of us.

"How long will you be gone?" I ask.

"Depends on when he dies," he says. I flinch, and he continues, "While I'm away, I expect updates on your progress finding the Eurydice. I know Elite Cain told you to report to him, but I'm telling you different."

"I can't ignore Elite Cain's orders."

Roth laughs mockingly. "Even if he plans on stripping you of your title the moment I'm gone?"

"What?"

"Elite Cain and your father don't like that I've appointed you to search for the Eurydice. And they don't respect me as successor. The moment they have cause, you'll be a knight-in-training again, your threads ripped free."

I don't doubt that. I suspected as much when the only orders I was given were to report to Elite Cain. I hadn't been given access to the archive for files on the Eurydice or the Chase Lockwood investigation. I am, essentially, at a disadvantage compared to the other knights appointed to do the same job.

"Why did you choose me?" I ask. "To search for the Eurydice?"

"Because you have something to prove," he says. "Look, Savior, I know your aspirations. You do this for me and I'll give you everything. That position as commander? Yours, tomorrow if you like."

"You just said Elite Cain and my father would strip me of the title you gave me."

"Tomorrow, my father might be dead, and I'll be the new luminary," he says.

I shake my head. "I don't want to owe you anything."

"Oh, come on, Shy. You'll be like your father. Better even. The luminary's guard."

Roth knows me better than I care to admit.

"Did you offer Chase Lockwood the same thing?" I ask, coming to a stop in the passenger drop-off lane at the airport.

"Excuse me?"

"Chase Lockwood—you offered him the same thing, didn't you? In exchange, he was to report only to you about the Eurydice."

"Oh, Savior," he says, offering a humorless chuckle. "You want me to be the bad guy, don't you?"

"If the shoe fits, Roth."

He laughs again, opening his door and grabbing his bag. "You're smart, Savior. But if you're as brilliant as the elites claim, you'll consider my offer and change your attitude to your future luminary. I don't expect an answer now, but I won't ask again." As he retreats, he calls back, "Reports, Savior. You don't want to be on my bad side."

I don't exactly want to be on his good side either.

# CHAPTER TWENTY
# Anora and Lily Martin

*I know something's off when I walk into Mr. Val's class* and notice Natalie, Jasmine, and Michelle glaring at me. I choose to smile at them and slide into my seat. Their gazes burn my back the whole hour. At the end of class, I hope to escape first, but Natalie and her friends have other ideas. They barrel past me, knocking me into my desk. If Mr. Val notices, he doesn't say anything.

Lennon meets me outside Walcourt, bursting with excitement.

"You won!" she cries, her hair dancing as she jumps up and down.

"Won?"

"You're our princess for queen's ransom! It was announced this morning."

*Oh no. I told Shy I didn't want that.*

"Is there a way to…I don't know…relinquish the title?"

Lennon frowns. "Why would you want to? You beat Natalie Rivera! Did you see the look on her face?"

I can't really pinpoint why, but Lennon's excitement at my having beat Natalie seems a little off—almost vengeful.

"I'm not interested."

Lennon blinks at me like she can't comprehend the words that just came out of my mouth. Finally, she shrugs. "Talk to Shy."

*I don't want to talk to Shy.*

He knows things about me. When he looks at me, I see him stitching it together in his head—*sees the dead, knows my weapons, lies.*

After he left on Saturday, I spent the rest of the weekend warding my house against the dead when Mom wasn't holed up in her room. Sprinkling a mix of crushed garlic and cloves under the windows outside and at the front and back doors. I also burned sage in my room. Mom wouldn't let me do it throughout the house. She hates the smell, and I could tell from how little I saw of her that she was having an episode that I didn't want to exacerbate.

I placed Shy's obsidian in my window, because despite the fact that it won't keep people like him away, I believe he knows what he's talking about when it comes to the dead. And if the ones from the mass grave are looking for me, I want to do everything I can to keep them away. After seeing the scythe sheathed at Shy's side, I know he's one of them: the people who hunted me after Chase died.

If ever there is a sign I need to move forward carefully, this is it. I'd already made too many mistakes, but I think I can right this ship so long as I find my coin.

Being named princess for queen's ransom is doing

the exact opposite of what I want, and I'm furious at Shy for ignoring my request. The whole thing is bringing me out of the dark, shoving me under the spotlight where people can see and talk to me. People yell "hey, princess" as I walk from class to class. Some give me high fives, and others invade my space to give hugs.

The first time it happens, I bristle so hard, the thread threatens to explode from my hand. The second time, I consider tossing the guy over my shoulder but refrain.

"I thought you had to be invited to touch royalty," I grumble, rubbing my arms from the last too-tight bear hug.

Lennon laughs. "I see you have no problems embracing the title."

At lunch, I head to the administration office and work up the courage to ask Mrs. Cole if a coin has been turned into lost and found. Today, she's wearing a bright yellow cardigan that reflects off her face.

"It's a piece of my grandfather's collection," I lie. "I lost it my first week here."

"Let me see," she says and dutifully bends to pull a box from under her desk. I hear her rummaging around through the intercom. After a moment, she looks up. "I'm sorry, Miss Silby, but I don't see a coin." I must seem miserable, because Mrs. Cole looks sympathetic and says, "Let me take your information. I'll let you know if anyone turns it in."

I offer her a smile. "Thanks, Mrs. Cole."

Once I give her my phone number, I head outside. I'm not feeling hungry, and I'm not in the mood to hang out in the crowded cafeteria even if I do want to find Shy and lay into him for making me the princess.

The weather is nice today, and there's hardly any wind—an anomaly, I'm told, in Oklahoma. The sun reflects off the white sidewalk, making my eyes water. I keep my head down until I round the corner of Emerson and am in the shadow of the school, but I halt when I find Lily standing a few feet in front of me, staring up at the fire escape ladder on the side of the building.

I hesitate, torn between wanting to talk to her and retreating. I have to be cautious in my friendships, and Lily seems to be linked to everyone who's ever shown interest in me—good and bad. Just as I start to turn away, her head snaps in my direction, and I'm welded to the spot.

Lily looks like she's spent a week buried under brush. Her uniform is dirty and tattered, her blond hair is matted together in clumps, and the skin under her eyes is reddish purple. It's the blood that draws my attention, though—a crimson stain has pooled near her feet. Where is it coming from?

"Lily…what happened?"

I start to move toward her, but something holds me back. Her stare is different—a look I've only seen in the dead. Or maybe it's the thread, sparking to life within my palm: a siren telling me this is wrong. Get rid of it.

I wobble on my feet and take a step back instead.

Lily looks at the blood on the ground and then returns her gaze to the fire escape ladder.

"I'm not supposed to be here," she says. Her voice is gravelly, reminding me of static on an old radio.

"Lily…"

"My name's not Lily!" she seethes, and when she

looks at me, her eyes are finally alight. It's the only thing about her that actually looks alive. "You're just like the rest of them!"

"I'm sorry," I say quickly, holding up my hands as if that will ward her off, but I don't understand. The person I'm staring at is Lily—a battered and beaten Lily. Maybe she fell and has amnesia. I try asking her what happened again.

She doesn't look at me, but her brows knit together. "I don't know. One moment, I was free, and the next, I was trapped."

"Did someone kidnap you?" I ask, trying to understand, but she shakes her head.

"No. A thread trapped me."

My stomach sinks. "A...thread?"

My thread?

"Vera?" Her name comes out as a whisper, but Lily— or the person I thought was Lily—hears it, latches on to it, and exhales, as if I've awakened her.

When she opens her eyes again, she says, "I'm supposed to be up there. They have to see me, to understand what they did to me."

That's why she's staring up at the fire escape. She's trying to figure out how to climb to the roof and hang herself again. She doesn't want to be alive.

I've seen a lot of terrifying things: souls who experienced horrific endings at the end of a knife or a gun. I've seen victims of car wrecks wandering about searching for their head or an arm or leg.

I've never seen a soul inhabit a body where it doesn't belong.

So many questions run through my head: If Vera's

soul is in Lily's body, where is Lily's soul? Is it trapped in my coin? Who could do that? And why Lily?

Vera starts toward the fire escape ladder.

"Vera, no!"

She halts, becoming even more agitated. "They have to see me!" she yells.

"Who?"

"Everyone!" she cries. "They forgot me! But they won't forget me again. I'll hang here forever, a nightmare burned into their memories. I'll haunt them all!"

The words are like chains, binding her to earth in death.

My fingers ache from clenching them so hard. I could capture Vera's soul again, but then what? I'd have a lifeless body on my hands—Lily's lifeless body with a missing soul—and I can't let Vera go through with her plan either.

I need help.

Suddenly, I'm torn between two evils—Thane or Shy. Thane already assumes I had something to do with Vera's disappearance. Will he think I did this to Lily? Will he even know how to help? But Shy carries a scythe, and the last time I saw one of those, the blade was pressed to my neck, and everything I ever loved was threatened.

I'll take the lesser of two evils—Thane.

I start to move, hoping to slip away and find him, when Lily looks at me again. This time, recognition blossoms on her face.

"You!" She jabs a finger in my direction. "You did this to me! Send me back!" she demands and lunges.

I try to dodge but lose my footing on the edge of the

sidewalk, collapsing to the ground, only to feel a sharp pain as Lily grabs a handful of my hair and pulls.

"Send me back!" she shrieks.

I reach for her arm with both hands and yank, sending her over my head and onto her back in the middle of the rose garden. I twist, attempting to scramble to my feet. I have to get out of here before I make another mistake, but Lily grips my ankle, and I fall hard to my knees, scraping my hands against the cement. I kick at her, hitting her square in the face, and she lets me go.

I run.

Thane. I have to find Thane.

It's still lunch, and the past few days, he's been hanging out in the cafeteria. What are the chances he's there today?

I head inside Emerson in search of him, but the bell rings, and the hall fills with students. It's hard to move in the crowd, and the skin on my hands and knees stings as I'm jostled about like a ship on a stormy sea.

Someone grabs my arm and pulls me. I'm about to rip myself free when I realize it's Shy. He looks down at my shirt. It's then I realize I've been holding my bloodied hands to my white top. I meet his gaze. His jaw is set tight.

"What happened?" he demands.

"Please." I try to pull away, but he moves his arms to either side of my shoulders.

"Anora, who did this to you?"

"No one!"

He frowns and releases me. "We both know that's not true."

His eyes drop again, roving, reading my injuries as if they were a map.

183

That's when the chorus begins—a haunting refrain of shrieks and screams.

Oh no. I'm too late.

Shy hurries past me and pushes through the crowd gathering at the entrance of Emerson. I follow after him. I want to reach for him and keep him inside, prevent him from seeing what's happened.

Shy steps outside and twists. His whole body goes rigid, and his eyes widen but in a hard way, like ice. His jaw and throat work as if he's swallowing a scream. I'm not sure how long he stands there, but the sound of a camera snapping draws his attention. I've never seen someone move so fast—he snatches the phone from a student nearby and slams it into the concrete.

"What the hell, man?" the kid demands.

Shy's response is to lift his fist.

"Shy, no!"

I reach for his hand, and he stops but doesn't relax, and his piercing eyes survey the crowd. He says, "This doesn't belong on your fucking phones. It doesn't belong on fucking Roundtable."

His voice sounds different, stripped. When he looks at me, it's at my hand wrapped around his arm. I release him and step away, hyperaware that behind me is a gruesome scene. The knowledge is solid, like a wall closing in. I'm losing my ability to breathe. My chest feels tight. I have to look. I can't go back inside without seeing her.

Shy convinces me to turn—not with anything he says but with the look he gives. It's the look of someone whose heart has broken.

But if he has to face this, I do too.

I start to turn, but he reaches for me and pulls me to him, holding my head against his chest. His lips move toward my ear, and he whispers, "Please, Anora. Don't look."

Guilt slams through me, piercing every part of me—head and heart and stomach and feet. I'm tethered by it, held to the earth by its weight.

This can't be happening.

As I stand there in Shy's arms, my body grows cold and numb. This is my fault. My coin. Whatever happened to it caused this. Lily died because of me.

Within minutes, the crowd is made to disperse, and everyone's directed into the auditorium and offered counseling until their parents can pick them up. I'm called to the administration office and made to wait until my mom shows up. When she arrives, she sits beside me in the hard, wooden chairs.

"Anora, honey, are you okay?" she asks, gripping my hands in hers. She's desperate and slightly manic, but then, so am I. My palms sting, scored from the cement. It's a reminder of the interaction I had with Lily before I ran away, before she somehow got onto the roof of Emerson Hall and jumped. I should have stayed. Even fighting her, I could have ensured she remained alive.

Now she's dead.

Mom looks down at our clasped hands and notices the scrapes. "Honey, what happened?"

She reaches into her purse and withdraws a wad of crumpled tissues just as we're called into Mr. Rivera's office.

This is the first time I've been in the headmaster's office. It's exactly what I pictured: an ornate, cherrywood desk sits in front of a set of bookshelves full of leather-bound volumes. The only decorations on the walls are three framed diplomas. A window overlooks the front of campus. An officer stands slightly behind Mr. Rivera's desk as he takes a seat.

"Please, sit." Mr. Rivera indicates to two chairs in front of his desk, and we do. "Miss Silby, we were notified you were recently in an altercation with Miss Martin."

Those words sound strange, though they are true. Mom stiffens beside me. I glimpse a flash of betrayal in her eyes before it melts into disbelief. As if the officer catches it too, he says, "We have video footage."

"She attacked me," I say in defense, mostly for Mom's sake. She's starting to fidget and tear the tissues. I need her to understand I haven't been walking around here picking fights with people. That I'm not a problem kid.

"Did you have any previous encounters with Lily?"

"No." I shake my head. "We were starting to be friends."

The policeman and Mr. Rivera exchange a glance. "So her behavior toward you was...out of character?"

"Yes."

There is silence, and then Mr. Rivera says, "But you do have a history of breaking rules, Miss Silby."

"Was that supposed to be a question?" Mom interjects. She's frustrated and agitated, and I'm not sure if it's at me or them.

Lennon said Natalie would destroy me with her connections. Is this the beginning? Did she report to her father that she thinks I'm a troublemaker?

Mr. Rivera and the policeman seem to reconsider

where they are taking this conversation. "What happened when you found Miss Martin?"

I shake my head a little. "I ran into her outside at lunch. She...was staring up at the roof, saying she needed to be seen."

The words sound bizarre. I can't tell by anyone's expression whether they believe me.

"What else?" the officer prods.

I don't respond immediately. I'm trying to keep the tears burning my eyes from spilling down my face. I take a shaky breath and say, "She just seemed to think she wasn't supposed to be here."

"Thank you, Miss Silby," Mr. Rivera says. "If we have any more questions, we'll be in touch. If you would like to speak to a counselor, they are available to you. In the meantime, all homecoming events are cancelled. Classes will resume Friday."

Once we're outside Mr. Rivera's office, I glance at Mom, whose face is unreadable.

"I don't want you to think I can't do this," I say. "Please don't send me away."

Her face falters at that. "Oh, honey," she says, wrapping her arm around me. "None of this is your fault."

She has no idea.

From this moment on, I'm not looking for a coin but for the person who took it and put Vera's soul into Lily's body. I'm looking for Lily's murderer.

# CHAPTER TWENTY-ONE
## Shy and the Life That Goes On

*It takes the police too long to get Lily's body down. I* consider doing it myself—just shifting in front of all these people, cradling her against my chest, and cutting her down with my scythe. Jacobi knows what I'm thinking, because he puts his hand on my shoulder. It's his way of anchoring me, yet I feel anything but grounded as I stare up at Lily, lifeless, tethered to the end of that rope, her soul missing. Something is very wrong.

Jacobi and I leave Lily when we're forced inside the school by officers and medics. She hasn't been dead fifteen minutes, and I've already been summoned to the Compound. At some point, I'll have to answer the summons, but right now, I really just want my mom. As I climb into my Jeep to leave, Natalie calls my name, running toward me. I tense, and it makes me realize that anytime I hear her voice, I expect a fight. My stomach clenches.

Damn, that sucks.

"Hey." Her voice is softer than usual, clouded with a throat full of tears. She pauses a moment, studying me with red-rimmed, watery eyes. She doesn't ask if I'm okay, thank Charon. I know it's because she feels like I feel—disoriented, numb, shocked. I hate that it's the only thing we've been able to agree on for the last four months.

"Come over this evening. We can sit outside by the fire at my house. We don't have to talk, but I...want us all together tonight."

We used to go to Natalie's all the time, hang out by the fire, make s'mores, joke about shadow knights who took their jobs too seriously. That was before Natalie became one of them. Still, there's a tribe mentality among Valryn: when something happens to one of us, it happens to all. I don't think any of us are convinced Lily hung herself, and the unknown is already eating at the backs of our minds like a parasite.

I start my car, and Natalie takes a step back. "Yeah," I say at last. "I'll be there."

Her smile is genuine but sad, and it hits me square in the chest. I peel out of the parking lot and race home. After I arrive, it occurs to me that I don't remember how I got here.

My head swims with images of Lily in life and death: Lily laughing loud, turning heads, her joy contagious. Lily hanging over Emerson Hall, head nearly severed, resting on her shoulder. Lily standing up in the passenger side of my Jeep as we roll down the road, singing at the top of her lungs in an off-key rendition of whatever's on the radio. Lily's body twirling to the left and right, like the rope is unwinding. Lily haloed by wings as she fights

189

me in training, the dance she does when she lands a hit. Lily lifeless, arms resting at her sides, palms slightly open, scratched like Anora's were scratched. Lily sitting beside me in my room, playing video games, her laugh echoing through me as she wins. I can't even be mad at her—not with that smile. Lily's blood dripping off her fingertips, staining the concrete at my feet.

My stomach reacts violently, twisting and turning until acid climbs up the back of my throat, and I stumble out of my Jeep to vomit on the gravel. I rest there a moment, hands on my knees, eyes burning. I push the gravel around with my feet to hide the evidence, but the smell is rancid and teases my stomach again. I wipe my mouth with my sleeve and push my hair out of my eyes before heading inside, surprised Mom hasn't noticed my arrival.

Pausing inside the door, I understand why—she's on the phone, and her voice is raised.

"He just lost his best friend—"

She pauses and takes a deep, shaky breath.

"I don't care what Cain wants. He's *my* son!"

She's talking to Dad. I've never heard her raise her voice like this, and I'm both surprised and impressed. Of course, he's only calling because I haven't arrived at the Compound yet. I wonder absently if he started the conversation asking how I was.

Probably not, judging by how angry Mom sounds.

"You know, Bastian, I don't think that really means anything to him anymore."

She's silent after that and inhales. I decide it's time to make my entrance. Normally I'd call out to her at the doorway, to let her know I'm home, but I don't feel like speaking or even attempting to make my mouth work. If I do, I'll probably become a puddle of mush, and I can't afford that right now, because as much as I'd like to tell my father off, I want to go to the Compound because I need to know what they think happened to Lily.

Mom meets me halfway and hugs me tight. I take a deep, quavering breath. She smells like lavender and wildflowers. It's uniquely Mom. Something I can count on for comfort.

I pull away when I'm afraid I won't be able to keep the burn in my eyes from producing real tears.

I clear my throat. "I gotta go to the Compound."

She nods, and I know she's holding back. She doesn't know I overheard the way she spoke to Dad. Now I wonder if this is what's been going on behind my back— if she's been as vocal about his absence as I've become, if she thinks she's just protecting me by pretending it isn't happening.

I used to think nothing was above the Order, but if it came down to them or my mom, I'd choose her, over and over again, even if it means death.

I press a kiss to her cheek, reassurance that I'll be okay, and leave. I transition to my raven form and fly as quickly as I can to the Compound, so no one remarks on my delay. On the way, I think about Lily's body hanging outside exactly as Vera's used to and the implication of that.

When I arrive, I'm directed to the Council chamber. This isn't normally where I would meet Cain or my father, and when I enter, I understand why they're here. There are several holograms crowding the table, members of the Order who couldn't get to Rayon in the few hours after Lily's death. Mixed with these ghostly images are flesh-and-blood Valryn: Elite Val, Elite Abrams, Elite Ezekiel, and Elite Cain.

My father looms behind Cain, eyes ice-blue, cold and critical. I'll credit the added severity of his gaze to the conversation he had with Mom before I left.

"Shadow Knight Savior," Elite Cain says. "It is good you decided to join us. We were just discussing the death of Knight-in-Training Lily Martin."

My insides revolt immediately. I'm not ready for this, I realize. Swallowing the sour taste in my mouth, I manage, "How can I be of service?"

The question makes my palms sweat, and I draw my hands behind my back to wipe them on my sleeves. Elite Cain offers that barely there smirk—his sign of approval. Today it makes me want to scratch out my own eyes.

"I have been informed you were witness to the scene?"

My breath catches. The sound is audible. I hurry to speak. "Yes, after the…incident," I clarify. I have an overwhelming urge to call it murder.

"And what are your observations?"

I shift my footing, unsure of what Elite Cain is asking but also aware that sweat has started to bead on my forehead. They won't miss it.

"I don't know what you mean, Elite."

"Did it appear Knight-in-Training Martin's suicide was assisted?" he asks without pause.

Assisted? Is he asking if I believe someone pushed her?

"I couldn't say," I answer, because I can't. I have no idea, no evidence.

There is silence.

Then Elite Val asks, "Shadow Knight Savior, do you have a theory as to what happened to Miss Martin?"

I meet his gaze, and his dark eyes seem to soften.

"I do."

"Would you share it?" He poses the question as a request, though I know I don't have the option to refuse.

"Lily died in the same manner as Vera Bennet, a resident soul who wandered Nacoma Knight until a week ago when she disappeared."

"Are you suggesting souls were *exchanged* here, Shadow Knight?" Elite Ezekiel asks.

Exchanges are exactly what they sound like—a person's original soul is exchanged for another. They are also illegal and just as bad as resurrections. Both can cause fractures in the soul, which result in unpredictable behavior in the human experiencing the exchange.

They can also only be performed using resurrection coins—coins only the Eurydice can make.

I continue, "There are several consistencies in the manner of death, from the location to the…injuries."

I wince, thinking about the tear at Lily's throat, the blood that dripped to the concrete below her feet.

"These injuries you name as evidence are more than likely consistent with the manner of death," Elite Abrams argues. "It's hardly evidence souls were exchanged."

"Isn't it possible Miss Martin saw the opportunity to end her shame? Was she not recently placed on probation for inappropriate relations with a human boy?" Elite Ezekiel asks.

Man, I really don't like him.

"Lily would never kill herself, and as for the injuries sustained—"

"Shadow Knight Savior." It's my father who interrupts me. I meet his gaze, where quiet anger simmers. "You do not have to continue to describe your friend's death."

"Commander Savior, were you invited to speak?" Elite Cain asks.

"With all due respect, Elite, I do not have to be invited to speak with my son."

A cold tension settles upon the room, making bumps rise on my skin and the sweat on my face dry. Dad's trying to take up for me, and if Lily's death wasn't in danger of being labeled a true suicide, I might take his out, but I can't let anyone think what happened here is because she was ashamed.

"I'm very familiar with the Vera Bennet case," I try again. "The injuries sustained are the same. An exchange isn't far-fetched, given that we believe the Eurydice has incarnated. It should be our first theory."

There is silence, and then Elite Cain speaks.

"Thank you, Shadow Knight," he says. "Until further notice, you are excused from patrol at Nacoma Knight Academy and all other duties as assigned."

"What?" They're benching me from duty? Anger rises from the pit of my stomach. Roth warned me this would happen.

"This is not punishment, Shadow Knight. Think of it as a courtesy, generously granted by your superiors. It will give you time to grieve."

"I don't need time to grieve," I argue. I don't buy their *this isn't punishment* excuse. "I need time to figure out who did this to Lily."

"You forget yourself, Shadow Knight. You are only

provisionally a tracker. Despite what Successor Roth may think, you are not ready for ranks."

*That's* a blow I didn't see coming.

"Does Successor Roth know you are revoking my rank?"

"Successor Roth has no jurisdiction here until he becomes luminary, Shadow Knight. Besides, what progress have you made in locating the Eurydice? Perhaps if you had been more prepared when offered your rank, Lily Martin might not be dead."

The accusation tears through my chest like a scythe—if I'd found the Eurydice sooner, Lily would still be alive.

Problem is, I'm not so sure they're wrong.

I never considered Roth's attention might damn me after graduation, but the fact that I'm only nine months away from placement and I've failed so publicly at this means my goal of becoming a commander is dead.

I place my fist to my chest and bow my head.

"I accept time to grieve. Thank you, Elite Cain."

Those are the hardest words I've ever spoken. I turn and leave.

# CHAPTER TWENTY-TWO
# Anora and the Funeral

*Two days after Lily's death, a memorial is held at Nacoma* Knight Academy. A bruised sky emits a constant film of rain. I walk beneath it, uncovered, heels sinking into the earth.

I didn't go to Chase's funeral, a fact that wasn't received well by anyone at my old school. I succeeded only in appearing insensitive. And it fueled the rumors that I had something to do with his death, since I was the last one to see him. Though they found no evidence, the speculation of my involvement circled me, and my mom, like a swarm of bees. I knew my absence from his service would only add to the talk, but I couldn't bring myself to mourn for the boy who had tried to kill me.

But I mourn for Lily. For the friendship we could have had, for the role I played in her death, though I still don't understand how it happened. I mourn for her friends, who gather here today, red-eyed and pale.

When I reach the auditorium, my clothes feel like they're glued to my skin. Though the hall is filled with people, it's oddly quiet, and the air smells like must, made stronger by wet feet dampening the carpet. Large bouquets of flowers are positioned at each of the auditorium's two entrances, along with an easel holding a large picture of Lily. I stare at her for a long time, attempting to reconcile the Lily who attacked me two days ago with the one in the picture, but I know they're not the same.

The one who attacked me was Vera.

I shiver, wondering if something like this can happen again. My coin is still missing, and I don't know what's happened to Lily's soul.

"Hey." Lennon comes up beside me. Her sudden appearance sets me on edge, but I manage to keep a lock on my instinctual reaction to defend myself. That means keeping the thread at bay.

"Hey," I say.

"This sucks," Lennon says. "We were just getting to know her."

"Yeah."

We're quiet for a moment. I glance at Lennon and find she's searching the crowd of mourners too. After a few moments, she elbows me to get my attention. I'm going to have to talk to her about that habit—it's getting on my nerves.

"I think that's the boy Lily was talking to," she says, nodding to a guy with two long, black braids. He has high cheekbones and bronzed skin. His full lips are set in a tight line. He keeps his body pressed against the wall, hands folded in front of him. He doesn't look up from the floor. He must feel so out of place among so many people he doesn't know and a school that shamed his girlfriend for their relationship.

"His name is Jake Harjo," Lennon says.

I glance at her. "How do you know?"

"There was more information about him on Roundtable this morning."

On the day of Lily's memorial? "That's horrible," I say.

"I warned you."

Why is Lennon even checking the app still?

My gaze shifts back to Jake. He hasn't moved an inch. I want to approach him so he's not alone, but what will I say? I never spoke to Lily about him and what he meant to her. Plus, the coin I created had something to do with Lily's death. I would probably just make him more uncomfortable than he already is.

"There's Shy's parents," Lennon says, redirecting my attention toward a redheaded woman and a tall man with blond hair and black-framed glasses. They are a gorgeous pair, and it's obvious Shy takes after his dad. Speaking of Shy—where is he?

"Maybe he's not here yet," Lennon suggests, reading my mind.

I watch Shy's mom and dad longer than necessary. They interact with several adults, shaking hands, giving hugs, offering and accepting condolences. It makes me feel like an imposter. What *am* I doing here?

I don't belong.

At that moment, Mr. Savior's eyes cut to me, and my breath freezes in my throat. His gaze is unsettling in a way I can't describe, except to say I think he knows exactly what I'm thinking, and he agrees.

I twist toward Lennon. "I'll be back."

I don't give her a chance to ask where I'm going before heading down the hall, unable to shake the weight of Mr. Savior's stare. I don't actually know where I'm going, but when I see a bathroom up ahead, I make a beeline for it.

That is until Thane Treadway comes down the opposite end of the corridor.

I halt, torn between retreating into the bathroom and turning around to find Lennon again.

"I didn't think you would be here," Thane says before I can make a decision to move.

*Dammit.*

"Why wouldn't I come? Lily and I—" I don't finish that sentence. What can I say? Lily and I were friends? But I might've inadvertently killed her?

Thane takes a few deliberate steps toward me.

"She's dead because of you," Thane says harshly. "So don't say you're here for her. You're here because you feel guilty."

I flinch, because maybe he's right. Maybe I don't know the difference between mourning and guilt.

"I didn't kill her!" I hiss.

"You might not have pulled the trigger, but you gave someone the gun. Isn't that how you did it? You trapped Vera's spirit in the coin and then lost it."

How does Thane know this? When I don't answer, he laughs under his breath.

"You have no idea how this all works, do you? This will keep happening, you should know. It can be a never-ending cycle. Is that what you want? More funerals to attend?"

I glare at him, nails digging into the skin of my

199

palms. Thane's eyes fall to my hands, and I jump when he reaches for my arm. "Stop." His touch is like a shock to my joints, forcing my bones to straighten and relax. It takes me a moment, but I finally ask, "How do you know about the coin?"

"Lily told me some things. And then I did my own research," he says, and his smile is like blood smeared across his face. "It's not the first time someone's gotten ahold of resurrection coins. Why do you think we have curfew?"

We stare at one another, and I feel as I did before in Thane's presence—trapped. I don't like being vulnerable.

Still, he's had suspicions about me for over a week and hasn't told anyone. What is his deal?

"What else do you know? And what do you want from me?"

He maintains that smudge of a smile.

"Meet me at June's Café for coffee at three."

"You can't tell me now?"

He shakes his head. "It's best not to talk here, and if you must know, I don't mind getting under Savior's skin."

It's then I notice he's not even looking at me. His gaze has traveled over my head. I twist and find Shy standing in the crowd, frozen in place. He's pale, and his eyes look like glittering diamonds. I'm not sure if they glisten from unshed tears or anger.

I turn back to Thane.

"Getting under his skin?"

"Yeah, I'm guessing he doesn't want you to be friends with me."

"Why would he care?" I shoot back.

"Oh, he cares. Maybe not about you in particular, but he cares about what you are."

Those words hit me hard, like Thane jabbed me in the side with an icepick.

He looks down at me again before pushing past me. "See you at three."

When I turn back toward Shy, he's moved away. I shuffle back into the auditorium and sit in the back with Lennon during Lily's memorial, not wanting to take seats from people who actually knew her well. The memorial consists of a slideshow of pictures, featuring familiar faces—Shy, Natalie, Jacobi, even Thane. There are others too, people I've seen in the hallway between classes or at Shy's lunch table.

Pop music filters through the sound system, setting a surprisingly upbeat tone. I guess it was Lily's favorite band. It conflicts horribly with the symphony of sniffles and sobs present during decrescendo or transitions between songs.

The last half of the memorial, people stand up and share stories about Lily. Jacobi goes first, then Natalie, and then Shy.

He stands under the spotlight, and it washes the color from his face, leaving behind just his bright blue eyes.

He clears his throat before stepping up to the microphone. "This is the hardest thing I've ever done." Shy pauses and swallows. He keeps his hands in the pockets of his slacks and looks down at his feet. When he lifts his gaze again, he searches the crowd. I get the feeling he's looking for me. "Lily believed everyone was worth her time. I don't think she understood how much it meant to people. Maybe that's my fault. I never told her. I guess hindsight is twenty-twenty. I'll spend the rest of my life remembering how lucky I was to have had so much of her time—that she chose to share her smile, her laugh, her love, with us. When you leave here today, consider what you will miss most in the people you love—memorize it—and remember how lucky you are to love and to be loved."

His challenge is morbid, but I understand. I press my hand against my chest where my poppa's coin rests. Feeling the familiar pressure is comforting. I close my eyes and inhale, imagining I smell him—mint from the cream he rubbed on his hands, tobacco from the pouch he kept in his pocket for his pipe. I loved him so much, but it hadn't been enough to keep him here.

My eyes water, and when I open them, Shy's moving off the stage. He pauses to hug Lily's father and then sits.

There's a final prayer given by the headmaster—a strange one that doesn't mention God or heaven—and then it's over and everyone files out of the auditorium. I'm hoping to make a quick exit when Lennon stops me.

"Hey, since all the homecoming events are cancelled and everything sucks right now, would you want to hang out sometime this week? We could eat a bunch of ice cream and veg out or whatever? Maybe tomorrow?"

"Uh, sure," I say. "I'll ask Mom."

Lennon smiles. "I'll text you."

I slip out of the auditorium and cross campus, heading to wait at Emerson Hall for Mom. I also want to check out the scene where Lily attacked me. A part of me hopes I might find my coin there, which is ridiculous, but I still have to look. Thane's words echo in my head: *This will keep happening...*

202

That's the last thing I want, so I have to do everything in my power to get my coin back and find the person who did this to Lily.

As I come around the side of Emerson, I stop, finding someone already there.

*Shy.*

He stands, staring up at the place over the doors where Lily hanged herself and where Vera had hung before that. Now there is nothing—not even the phantom noose. His hands are in his pockets, and while he appears casual, I sense his aggression.

I start to back up, hoping he hasn't seen me, when I hear my name. I hesitate, too late to pretend I didn't hear him. I have to get better at this, but it is the way he says my name: breathlessly.

"What are you doing here?"

I pause and turn, explaining, "I'm waiting for my mom."

"Then why were you leaving?"

"I thought you might want to be alone," I say.

He shakes his head. "That's the opposite of what I want."

"Then why come out here? Don't you know all those people back at the auditorium?"

"I don't necessarily want to hear how sorry everyone is," he says. "Apologies don't bring people back to life." He looks back up at the building. "I thought I might find something here. Anything."

"Any luck?" I ask.

"No."

I don't believe him. That's the difference between him and Thane. Thane tells me everything he's thinking,

203

even if it hurts me. Shy keeps his cards close to his heart. I can't decide which I prefer.

Shy stares at me for a long moment. His gaze isn't searching, just piercing.

"Where did you learn to defend yourself?" he asks, and it's clear he's figured out I had an altercation with Lily.

"I didn't."

That is the truth. I hadn't learned how to defend myself. I hadn't taken any classes.

"You just naturally know how to kick ass?" he asks, quirking one eyebrow.

I hate denying I know how to kick ass, but this girl—the new and improved Anora—isn't supposed to have those skills, much less *need* them.

It's my turn to ask questions. "Where did you learn to defend yourself?"

"I've been training since I was twelve," he says, and I'm surprised by his honesty.

"That seems a little extreme, don't you think? We're not going into battle."

"*You* might not be."

Those words make me shiver. I narrow my eyes and look him up and down. "Are you wearing a scythe?"

He smiles. "I'm always wearing a scythe."

"I can't imagine where you keep it."

He lifts his head a little, and his eyes flame. "I'd let you search me, but I don't want to be on the receiving end of my own blade."

Just like that, it's harder to breathe. I'm glad for the weather. The mist lands on my face, cooling my heated skin.

"You weren't this eager to admit anything when you came to my house," I point out.

"That was before my best friend died."

Shy reaches into his pocket, and I go rigid, but he pulls out his cell phone and looks at the screen before pocketing it.

"I have to go."

He starts past me, but at the last minute, I feel him turn so he faces my back. I know this move: he'll snake his arm around my neck, pull me to him, and press something sharp into my skin—probably that scythe. Before he can get his arm hooked around me, I grab it and twist to face him, gripping his wrist. Shy smiles— I've done exactly what he wanted.

"If you want me to believe you aren't trained, you're going to have to stop doing that."

I let him go with a little push, but he doesn't budge.

"If you don't want your nose broken, you're going to have to stop doing that."

Shy laughs. How can I find his smile so endearing when there's so much mistrust between us?

"I'd rather our fights not end in pain." He takes a step away. "Bye, Lyra."

The use of my first name steals my breath. He's done some digging on me. I watch him retreat until I can no longer see him, swallowed by a thick crowd spilling out of the auditorium. The more distance he puts between us, the colder I get. I end up huddled under the awning near the doors of Emerson Hall, shivering, scanning the ground on the off chance I'll spy my lost coin.

Shy gave me a little of himself, but it didn't come without a price. I feel as if I'm in a race. First one to discover the other's secret wins a prize—preferably a normal life and absolutely no involvement in whatever battle Shy hinted at.

———

Mom takes me home, and she's unusually quiet on the drive home. At three, I take off on foot to Main Street, not even bothering to tell Mom I'm leaving since she's holed up in her room again. I wonder what Shy's mom will think of her new employee if she has another full-blown episode and can't get out of bed for a week.

June's Café is not far from my house—just a walk down the broken sidewalk in my neighborhood and a right turn. The ground beneath my feet is slick with rain, and a light mist coats everything in a haze. Several cars are parked at an angle before old, brick shop fronts. Despite the weather, clusters of people stand outside, including Thane, who leans against the building, one foot drawn up to steady himself. His phone is in one hand, and he is distracted by it; a cigarette is in the other. He hasn't noticed me yet, and I watch as he brings the cancer stick to his mouth.

"That's going to kill you."

Thane looks up at me and flashes a smile. It's probably the sincerest one he's ever given me, and it makes his face look warm and friendly, until he blasts smoke out of his nose and mouth.

"I have other vices that'll kill me first." He leans away from the wall, putting his phone in his pocket. Taking one last drag from the cigarette, he puts it out against the bricks and flicks it away into the street. Then he opens the door. "After you."

Given the conversation we had earlier and the reason I'm here, I don't take his chivalry too seriously. I enter ahead of him and find several teenagers in the shop. Some are doing homework; others attempt to flirt and show off. None of them look familiar.

"Kids from Rayon High School," Thane explains. "Most of them hate us, think we're snotty rich kids."

"Aren't you?"

He raises a brow. "Are you?"

*Fair point.*

Thane directs me to the counter. "Order."

I ask for tea, hoping it will calm my roiling stomach. Thane orders coffee after me and pays. When our drinks are ready, he grabs a handful of sugar packets and cream and carries the cups to a booth near the window. A table of kids from Rayon High stop talking as we pass, and I'm well-enough acquainted with that behavior to guess they're talking about us.

As Thane sits, he pushes the cup of hot tea toward me. He's like a viper rising to strike, and his eyes flicker like smothered flames in the night. I don't reach for the drink; instead, I bring my knees up, hiding my hands in the hollow between my chest and legs.

"For each of my questions you answer, I'll answer one of yours," he says, tearing open the first packet of sugar and emptying it into his drink.

"What if I don't want to answer?"

"You fucked up." He takes a sip of his coffee, testing, then adds more sugar. "You don't have a choice."

"I always have a choice."

"Right. Except you're clearly involved in something you don't understand."

"How can you be sure I don't understand?"

He sits forward, stirring his coffee, but at my question, he pauses and looks at me, brows raised. "So you're saying what happened to Lily was intentional on your part?"

I set my teeth.

Thane sips his coffee, testing, then continues to pour packet after packet of sugar in.

"Didn't think so."

I have to remember this can be just as beneficial to me as it is to Thane. Whether or not he has an agenda of his own, at least he's not lying about why he's giving me the time of day.

"Fine. What do you want to know?"

His smile curls, triumphant. He sits back in his seat, as if preparing to watch a movie unfold on screen. I'm just glad he's stopped emptying sugar into his coffee.

"Why did you leave Chicago?"

*Easy.* "You can only be different for so long before someone notices."

His eyes darken. He doesn't like my answer.

"How did you know about the coin?" I ask, and he smirks, shrugging a shoulder.

"It's not the first time it's happened."

"You said that earlier."

"What's the matter? You don't like vague answers?"

"If that's your next question, then no, I don't. If this has happened before, then explain."

He leans forward, elbows on the table. "In the twenties, people started turning up dead unexpectedly, like Lily. Anyone who knew Lily knows she wouldn't have killed herself. Back then, there were eight cases in total, mostly undetermined deaths, but there were suicides too. The police started to enforce curfew. Turns out a few resurrection coins made it into the wrong hands."

Who else can make coins? Does this mean I'm not the only one?

He sits back. "Where did you get a resurrection coin?"

"I don't even know what that is," I say, though clearly he means the coins I make with my thread.

Thane studies me for a moment. He doesn't blink. I wonder if he knows how uncomfortable his eyes make me, if he knows the paleness of his skin makes his lips look freshly bitten.

"Resurrection coins give a person the ability to resurrect or exchange a person's soul. Souls trapped inside can be brought back or swapped out for another soul. The coins are distinct, having an image of a raven on one side and nothing on the back. Symbolism, I think—but the idea is that it's also a one-way ticket into Spirit. You know, the afterlife? It's illegal to be in possession of one unless you're the Eurydice, but one will pop up now and again from out of nowhere and causes havoc for the Order. Case in point," he says and indicates to me.

*The Order.*

So my hunters have a name.

He continues, "They'll want to know where you got the coin too, and how Vera got inside."

Well. I definitely can't say I have a whole box full under my bed.

Thane leans over the table again. "You want to know what I think?" he asks.

"No."

"I think you make them."

I scoff. "You think I make resurrection coins?"

He nods. "And if I'm right, you had better be prepared, because the Order's after you, *Eurydice*."

I shiver involuntarily. It's the words he uses—*after you*, not *looking for you*. It's exactly how I've felt the last few months, *hunted*.

"That's the second time you've said that. What's the Eurydice?" I ask.

"It's your title," he says. "The name of the one who can turn souls into coins and offer them safe passage into Spirit."

"It's not my title. I'm not the Eurydice," I counter.

He shrugs. "You say tomato, I say to-mah-to. A resurrection coin means two things: you either got it from the black market, or you created it. So far, you have demonstrated virtually no knowledge of the death-speaker world, so forgive me for coming to the alternate conclusion that you are the Eurydice."

I uncurl myself from my position in the booth and lean forward, wiping sweaty palms on my jeans. I need to know more about the Eurydice without giving myself away. "You said the Eurydice can turn souls into coins, that she's supposed to offer safe passage into Spirit. How?"

"She summons the Adamantine Gates and offers the coin to Charon, the gatekeeper."

"Whoa, whoa, whoa, wait," I say, holding up my hands. This is too much. "Charon? The ferryman from Greek myth?"

"The very one. Except he's not a ferryman. He's a gatekeeper. Always has been, always will be."

A flash from my dream flickers in the back of my mind. A gate. No. It's not possible. I stare at Thane for what seems like an eternity, waiting for him to say this is all a joke.

"I can't really blame them for looking for you," Thane says. "You've been gone so long...you're practically responsible for creating Influence."

*Influence.* That was what he called the thing that possessed Sean. Is it also what corrupted my poppa? I can't be responsible for that.

"I can't believe I'm the first one to discover the Eurydice," Thane says, almost to himself.

"What?" I realize Thane's already made his mind up that I'm the Eurydice. For now, I'm going to let it go in favor of learning more. "How am I responsible for that?"

"You didn't incarnate for seventy years. Lost souls can't move into Spirit, so they just stay. You know what their energy is like. It does crazy things to people, and it feeds darklings—monsters—and death-speaker magic. It also spawns new darklings, and all those darklings create Influence."

"Why didn't the Eurydice incarnate?"

"Remember how curfew began? With all those murders? Well, it started with the Eurydice's murder. They say, as punishment, Charon dissolved the gates and prevented the Eurydice from incarnating."

"But...why would he choose to let her incarnate now?"

Thane shrugs. "Things are pretty bad, Anora. Just turn on the news—plane crashes and riots and natural disasters. It's all Influence. The more chaos, the more doubt, the stronger Influence gets."

It feels like Thane just placed the weight of the world on my shoulders. Being responsible for Lily's death is hard enough, but suddenly I'm also responsible for every bad thing happening in the world?

"Even if you aren't the Eurydice, you won't escape the Order. They keep tabs on those who can see and speak to the dead. We fall under their rule, and trust me, they think death-speakers are the scum of the earth. Though, they really only worry about the ones who practice death magic, the occult."

"But I don't practice death magic."

"Soul exchanges are death magic, Anora. Vera's soul is gone for good now."

"I didn't...*exchange*...anyone's soul. I lost the coin."

"So you were in possession of a resurrection coin and lost it. Still illegal. Worse, reckless!"

He's right.

"What are you? Their bounty hunter?"

Thane laughs. "Trust me, I'm as far from the Order as you can get. I didn't even know they existed until Lily risked getting into a whole lot of trouble by telling me."

"Why did she tell you?"

"Because we were friends."

He watches me for a moment. I note the way he sits, poised on the edge of his seat, hands resting by his legs, rigid. He thinks I'm going to bolt. I wonder what he would do if I went for it in front of all these people? He couldn't exactly restrain me without drawing a crowd.

"Look, I don't care if you're the Eurydice, but you had something to do with Lily's death, and I want to get to the bottom of it. I can help you," he says, taking his rigid arms and resting them on the table. He leans so far over, he's practically lying on the table. He explains, "I can get you an appointment with someone. She might be able to trace Lily's soul, which means we can find your coin."

My heart rises into my throat. All I've wanted is to find this coin, but I'm immediately suspicious of Thane.

"Why would you help me?"

"You want your coin, and I want to find out who did this to Lily. We need each other to do that. If we can track that coin, we both have what we want."

"How do I know you won't turn me over to the Order?"

I don't know anything about Thane; he could be pulling one over on me.

"Do you want the appointment or not?"

"Who is this person you want me to meet?"

"All you need to know is that she might be able to help. It's either this or soul exchanges keep happening and more people die, Anora—your call."

I don't like the way he says my name, but the mention of more people dying makes my chest hurt. If any more guilt lands on my shoulders, I'll be crippled.

I might not trust Thane, but he is the only one who's given me real answers, and it's likely the more I'm around him, the more I'll learn about myself, my powers, and Influence.

"Fine. Make the appointment."

The corners of his mouth turn up. "I'll be in contact."

He stands, and I follow.

"Do you have a ride home?"

"I'll walk."

"In the rain?"

"Y–yes," I say as I look toward the window and notice it's pouring.

Keys jingle in Thane's hand. "I'll take you home."

We leave the coffeehouse, and Thane holds the door open for me.

"Hold up," he instructs once we are outside under the awning. He moves to take off his jacket for me. "Use it as an umbrella."

The drive to my house is short, especially since I tell Thane not to drop me off directly in front.

"But it's still pouring," he says.

"That's okay. I like the rain." He doesn't look convinced but doesn't argue. I add, "Thanks for the ride."

"Anytime, especially if it's raining."

I start to get out and leave his jacket behind.

"Take it." He holds it to me. "You can give it to me at school on Friday."

"I'll be fine."

"Just do it. I'm already wet. It won't help me."

I take the jacket and put it over my head as I get out of the car. "See you Friday."

I close the door and walk the rest of the way to my house in the pouring rain with Thane's jacket covering my head, smelling of cigarettes.

# CHAPTER TWENTY-THREE
## Anora and the Witch

**When Thane said we would be in contact, I thought that** meant I wouldn't hear from him for a couple days. Instead, I get a text near midnight. The buzz of my phone startles me, and I sit, staring at the message. It's simple. I'm here. I contemplate whether I should meet him, claim I was asleep come Friday, though if he's parked close to my house, chances are he can see the light on in my room and me in the window.

I spent the evening googling a combination of words I'd learned today: *Eurydice, the Order, death-speaker*. I came up with nothing useful. Seems like these people do a good job of keeping their world a secret. When that produced no answers, I started a list of reasons why I'm not the Eurydice and a list of reasons I could be the Eurydice. So far, the list of reasons I could be the Eurydice outnumber the other six to one—one being a measly *it's just impossible*.

The other list includes the thread, turning souls into

coins, seeing the dead, unexplained ass-kicking abilities, weird scythe-wielding boys stalking me...

I imagine the list will get longer too. I feel an odd mix of relief and fear, knowing what I am has a name, that others know it, that they want me. I tell myself I should be freaking out more. I should have spent the evening packing all my things, enacting my escape plan, with the weight of the Eurydice, the Order, and Influence driving me.

And then I think of the priorities. I can't leave until I know who killed Lily, until my coin is in my possession once again. I can't let this happen to anyone else. Plus, Mom is still locked in her room, and there's no way I could leave without her. Our relationship is complicated, and sometimes it seems like I'm more the parent than she is, but we've always had each other.

My phone dings again, reminding me I have a message I've ignored. I shrug into my jacket before climbing out my bedroom window and wriggling down the trellis. The thread pricks my palm, poised and ready for what comes out with the dark. The streetlights flicker, and the wind picks up. It's like a scene from a horror movie, foreshadowing the appearance of the killer.

I walk a little way down the street to where Thane's black Charger waits, headlights off, and slip into the passenger seat.

"What took you so long?" he asks.

"I was making a decision."

"To trust me?"

"I don't trust you, but you've given me answers. This might give me more."

"I bet you trust Savior." The words, strung together

as they are, should sound jealous, but Thane doesn't say them with venom. His tone is almost passive, like he intended to keep the comment inside his head. "It's how he looks. All bright-eyed and cheerful. People trust him."

"Actually, I trust him less than I trust you."

"You're only saying that because you're mad at him."

"I'm pretty sure I know when I don't trust someone."

"Well, at least that's one thing you've gotten right." Thane observes me for a moment and then starts his car. He waits until we are turned around to switch on the lights.

"Where are we going?"

"Not far."

I'm not a fan of Thane's indirect answers, but I'm also not interested in talking any more for fear of being questioned, so I sit quietly, unable to relax in the slick leather seat. The only sound in the cab is from air blowing through the vents. It hits me in one continuous stream, freezing patches of skin. Any other time, I might reach up to close the vent or turn it away from me, but the chill blast gives me something to train my thoughts on rather than the scenario that might play out if we fail to find Lily's soul before it's exchanged with someone else's.

Thane isn't lying when he says we aren't going far. He pulls left onto Main and drives about half a mile out of town before turning down a slim, makeshift road crowded with trees and brush. I'm not prepared for the fact that it leads to a cemetery. My body's already reacting to the energy suck straight ahead. It's like my soul wants to come out of my body, and my heart throbs sickly in my chest. I hate cemeteries.

"What are we doing here?"

"We have an appointment."

"In the cemetery?" My voice sounds shrill in my ears.

Thane gets out of the car, and I scramble after him. If there's one thing I hate more than graveyards, it's being alone in them.

I hurry to catch up with him. "You never said *who* we were meeting here!"

"We're meeting a witch," he says.

"A *witch*?" I try not to let my voice rise, but I'm not successful. Thane looks amused. "Why didn't you tell me?"

"Obviously because of the way you *just* reacted."

"How is a witch supposed to help us find Lily?"

"They are just as connected with the dead as you are and even more capable of finding a soul. Besides, she's the only witch I trust, so we're going to use her."

"What's this witch's name?"

"A name won't help your prejudices," he says.

"I'm not...prejudiced!"

Thane gives me the side-eye.

"Okay, I guess I am a little prejudiced, but you can't blame me. The only witches I've ever seen are in movies."

A small smile graces his lips. "Trust me, this witch wouldn't waste time with threats and flying monkeys. She would have poisoned you within seconds of seeing you."

"That's not magic. That's murder."

"Who said there is a difference?"

"If you're trying to make me feel better, you're doing a miserable job."

"We've established that I'm not the warm and fuzzy type. If you want this sugarcoated, you'll have to talk to Shy."

"I think we already established that I don't trust Shy."

218

Another ghost of a smile. It touches parts of his face I've never noticed before: smile lines under his eyes, a dimple on his right cheek—a phantom of who Thane used to be. I want to approach that subject, ask him how things changed once his mom was gone, ask him if he's helping me because he's hoping to bring her back, but my gaze has slipped from him to the graveyard.

For someone who can see the dead, graveyards are like walking through a creepy wax museum. Bodies freckle the landscape, frozen in states of death and time, and they're all lost—suicides and the murdered, those who faced death suddenly or unexpectedly. They come in all forms: men and women, the old and the young, but the thing I can never quite come to terms with are the children—little girls with braided hair and white dresses, boys with smooth hair and small suits. It makes the push and pull of the energy they stir harder to bear.

Thane must notice because he grabs my arm, pulling me toward him.

"You okay?"

"Yeah," I breathe.

He slides his hand down my arm, wrapping his fingers around mine, and leads me through the graves.

At the back of the cemetery near the tree line sits a mausoleum. The marble structure resembles a house with a tall, steepled roof, and two windows flank a door with an image of a cross entangled in iron vines.

Thane approaches the mausoleum, digs his phone out of his pocket, and shines the light on the door. After studying the lock, he withdraws a thin silver spike from the pocket of his jacket and jams it into the keyhole.

*Pretty sure this counts as desecration.*

"What are you doing?"

"Picking a lock."

"Is this something you do on a regular basis?"

"Not a regular basis," he says none too confidently as the lock clicks. After pocketing his phone and the piece of silver, he pulls the door open, and we enter the mausoleum.

I expect a room of statues and crypts. Instead, the inside looks like a hotel lobby. There is a red rug that runs the length of the hall and two couches at the center, flanked by a set of side tables with wrought-iron lamps. At the very end, rising like a headstone, is a stained-glass window. Moonlight streams through, casting a kaleidoscope of colors over marble walls, highlighting the names of the dead.

"I thought this was a mausoleum." My voice sounds ragged in the quiet of the hall.

"It is."

"Why does it look so...relaxing?"

Thane gives me a look I can't quite place until he speaks—it's understanding, born from experience.

"It's hard to let go. Having a place to come and visit makes things...easier over time."

Thane isn't looking at me as he speaks. He's staring at the walls of names, but I'm reminded his coldness was built from grief.

"Come on."

We continue through the mausoleum, passing several more private corridors. The sense of loss here weighs on my shoulders, made heavier by the light, which only seems to illuminate us from the waist down. I find myself clutching Poppa's coin through my shirt.

Finally, we come to the back of the mausoleum where the hall splits into a T, and both sides plunge into darkness. Thane takes a turn to the right, but I pause, falling back as the air from the void caresses my skin. Thane must sense my hesitation, because he turns, reaching out to clasp my hand. His fingers are just as cold as the air. He says nothing as he digs his phone out again, using the light to descend.

The steps spiral, and the walls around us narrow, as if they're closing in, making my chest feel tight and my breath shallow. Thankfully, the descent to even ground is quick, but the darkness continues, thick and heavy, pressing against my eyes. Thane pulls me forward without pause. Now and then, the light from his phone illuminates smooth concrete walls.

"Are we...underground?" I ask.

"Yes. This is a tunnel—one of many. There is a network of them under Rayon."

I pause a moment and then ask, "How do you know about them?"

"Like everyone else... I inherited the information."

"Well, where did they come from? What are they for?"

"I guess they were built when the town was built," he says. "There are a lot of theories. The most popular is that they were used as a way for important men to sneak back and forth between the local bar and brothel, but more than likely, they were used to smuggle alcohol during Prohibition."

We continue on. At first, I can tell when the tunnel curves and when we change direction, but over time, in the silence and the darkness, I lose my way. Relief washes over me when I finally spot a light at the end of tunnel—literally. It provides no illumination and is more like a beacon, signaling refuge in a storm.

As we near the light, I realize it's an elevator. Thane clicks the button, and the doors open with a ding. Inside there are a few options for floors, ranging from a negative one to five. Thane chooses negative one as our destination.

"What's on the other floors?"

"People you'd never want to meet."

When the doors open, we're at the end of a long hall. The walls are white, stained and scuffed. The air smells sterile, like a hospital, but with a tinge of blood lingering. It puts me on edge and makes me feel tainted. I glance at Thane, who doesn't seem to notice, because his eyes are on the figure of a man with dark, stringy hair and a messy, curling beard. His shirt is tinged yellow, like he'd shut himself in a room of cigarette smoke for months.

*Gross.*

"We're here to see Samael," Thane says.

The man looks us up and down. There's something strange about his eyes—there is no gleam or glassiness. For a moment, I don't think he's going to let us pass, but then he says, "She has a client. You'll have to wait."

"We'll wait."

The man inclines his head and turns. We follow.

We are led to a set of chairs at the end of the hallway.

"Coffee's around the corner," he says, pointing with his thumb, then whirls around, making his way back down the hallway. It isn't until he's out of sight that Thane lets go of my hand and takes a seat. It was nice

222

having him to hold on to, like a strange truce between us, one borne out of grief and solace.

"What's up with that guy?" I ask, signaling down the hall.

"He practices death magic," Thane says. "Consequence of using? It takes from you—your mind, your health, your youth. Whatever it wants."

I swallow a thickness building in my throat and then sit down. There's a small table beside me covered in magazines: *Witches & Pagans*, *Spirituality & Health*, and *Psychology Today*.

"Well, this is weird."

"It's a business," Thane says. "We're here on business. What did you expect?"

I shrug. "I don't know. Maybe a yellow brick road and an emerald castle. You think Samael melts in the rain?"

"I'd advise you to test that theory if I didn't think she'd also curse your ass."

The door beside Thane opens, and a man stumbles out as if he's been pushed. He's balding and wears a gray windbreaker. He stands for a moment, blinking, before a woman follows him out.

"Sa'id!" Her voice is sharp—a command.

The man who let us in comes out of his room.

"Show the man out."

"Wait! H-how do I know it will work?" The man spins on her.

The woman narrows her eyes, and then the man's phone rings. "That call is very important," she advises. "You had better answer it."

Sa'id has the man by his arm. As they turn, he answers his phone and begins to sob. What did he ask of Samael?

The woman turns to us, eyes rimmed in kohl. She has long, black hair and wears a layered skirt and a loose-fitting shirt. Bangles on her wrists clash together as she moves, and several gold rings sparkle on fingers firmly planted on her hips.

"What happened to him?" I ask.

If she thinks it's inappropriate, she doesn't say anything. She doesn't even blink.

"He asked for revenge on his cheating wife," Samael explains. Then she twists and enters the room.

Thane and I exchange a look before rising to our feet and following. Behind us, the man lets out a guttural sob. "This isn't what I meant!"

Samael closes the door behind us, muffling his cries.

She walks around us and takes a moment to light incense. The smell makes my head spin, a mix of sage and jasmine. After, she positions herself on a bed of pillows in the corner of the room.

"Sit." Samael directs us to pillows on the floor, and I do as she instructs. "You will not sit?" she asks Thane.

"I prefer to stand."

She shrugs, dragging her eyes back to me. Her berry lips pull back into a smile, and yet there's something cold about her. Maybe it's her heavily lined eyes, studying me like a difficult spell.

"What can I do for you?"

I open my mouth to answer, but Thane takes the lead. "We're looking for a soul."

Samael's lips part, and she nods once in understanding. She holds out her hand, and Thane drops money into it before I can register what she's asking for. She reaches for a glass bowl and pours various substances inside—powders and liquids. I wonder how often people come to her for this sort of thing.

"Do you have an item of theirs? Something they wore, perhaps?"

Thane steps forward. "It's not something she wore… but it was a gift from her."

He drops a necklace into Samael's palm, and a heavy weight settles in my chest. I wonder when Lily had given it to him—was it before or after the falling-out with Shy?

Thane doesn't look at me as he returns to his spot behind me. Samael drops the necklace into the mixture and lights the contents on fire.

I gasp as dark red flames erupt from the bowl. "What are you doing?"

"She gave a part of herself to the boy when she gave him the necklace. If I can resurrect that part of her, perhaps she will tell us where she is."

"But…I thought resurrection was illegal."

Samael looks at me, part in challenge, part in annoyance, and answers, "It is."

I sit in silence, sorry I interrupted her, and watch the flames. A single form rises from the fire—beautiful, like a doll with long limbs and graceful steps.

"She felt safe when she died," Samael says at last. "Relieved."

"Relief?" Thane echoes her.

"Yes. She felt like something had been made right."

A second image materializes. This form is outlined in bright orange, but the middle is darker. The two flames embrace, twining together in a crackle of spark and smoke, and when they part, the bright, doll-like

225

flame has waned so thin, it flickers until it is nothing more than a thin rivulet of vapor.

"The last thing she felt was shock."

The other flame remains, and a high-pitched whistle fills the air. Samael retrieves a pitcher of water, dousing the fire, filling the air with the smell of sulfur. I cover my nose with the sleeve of my jacket.

The witch reaches into the sludge, retrieving Thane's necklace, and drops it into the center of a cloth. As she starts to massage away the evidence of her spell, she speaks.

"The girl you seek is at the train yard."

Thane and I exchange a look. I'm not familiar enough with Rayon to know where the train yard is located, and now I'm curious. Why would Lily go there?

"Are you aware of your responsibility once you do find her?" Samael asks.

"Very much," Thane says evenly, almost angrily, but I still don't understand. What's his responsibility?

Samael doesn't look convinced and says, "She must be returned to Spirit."

"I said I understood," Thane snaps.

But Samael isn't looking at him. She's looking at me.

"How does she return to Spirit?" I ask.

"You must summon the Adamantine Gates. That is the only way lost souls can find their way home."

A hand presses against my shoulder, and I jump, looking up at Thane.

"Let's go," he says.

He helps me to my feet, and I sway, dizzy and unstable. Thane steadies me, but before we leave the office, Samael says, "They always come back wrong, Thane. Always."

We leave the witch's office.

Once we're in the elevator, I take deep breaths in an attempt to clear my swimming head. I slide to the floor, and Thane crouches before me.

"You all right?"

"I think so."

"Just keep taking deep breaths."

"What did she do?"

"It's the incense. She uses it to confuse you in hopes you'll give away something she wants."

I glare at him. "You didn't stop her?"

"Have you ever tried to tell a witch not to do something in her own shop?"

My stomach sours. Sometimes I wish Thane would sugarcoat things. After a few more breaths, the smell of sage and jasmine is replaced by Thane's musk and stale water.

"Thane," I say after a long pause. "I don't know how to open the gates."

Admitting that feels like admitting to Thane that I am the Eurydice, even though he already knows.

"I know."

"Then what do we do when we find my coin?"

At first, I don't think he'll respond, but after a moment, he says matter-of-factly, "You learn."

# CHAPTER TWENTY-FOUR
## Anora and the Train Yard

*Once we're back in Thane's car, he twists toward me in* his seat.

"Samael said Lily is at the train yard. Are you up for investigating?"

"T-tonight?"

"Do you really think we have the luxury of time, Anora? Who's to say Lily's murderer won't exchange another soul?"

Yeah, like his or mine.

I hesitate. If Mom discovers I snuck out, I'll be grounded forever, but that's far better than another murder. Also, there's a better than good chance that Mom will be in her room for another few days.

"I'll go."

On the way to the train yard, I think about what Thane said—I need to learn to open the gates, to save souls, to rid the world of Influence. For such a heavy burden, I wonder why I was so alone in the discovery of my power. It had been just after I found Poppa dead and witnessed a plume of black explode from his body. Influence, I now know, but then, I'd been so afraid. So fearful. The thread had burst from me then and every time after that, responding to those same emotions. This can't be how it's meant to be, summoning the thread when I feel the most distress.

I know I need to learn to control it, and it would be best if I could summon the gates. Having a box of coins lying around is dangerous. Look at the chaos losing one caused. But how am I supposed to learn? How am I supposed to stay under the radar practicing?

The headlights of Thane's Charger only provide a few feet of visibility against the night as we approach the train yard, protected by a locked gate and a tall fence. Thane stops, exits the car, and unlocks the padlock.

"What?" he asks when he returns to the driver's seat.

"Where did you get that key?"

"My uncle owns this property," he says, as if that explains everything.

I look at him suspiciously. "That's…convenient."

"Don't overthink this, Anora. My uncle owns half the town."

"So you stole his keys?"

"I *borrowed* them," he corrects. "Don't make everything I do sound like a crime."

He inches the car forward until it's inside the gate and then shuts the engine off. I follow him as he exits the car; the wind roars around me, picking my hair up, tangling it around my neck. It also carries the distinct smell of rot. It's faint, still some distance away, but chills spider down my arms and back, making my skin feel like canvas stretched too tight. Thane doesn't seem to notice as he walks, the crunch of loose gravel grating under his feet.

We make our way to the thick of the yard, moving over the outlines of tracks, overgrown with patches of grass. Streetlights spill blue-tinted light over parts of the property. Worn and broken locomotives sit abandoned to our left, and I swear the way the light hits them, they have faces, angry and disfigured. Metal silos and warehouses rise like guards, obscuring anything beyond the yard. It's clear by the size of this place that it used to be the hub of town, now just a phantom, and Rayon has grown around it.

I pause, standing at the center of a set of tracks. Behind me, a train with an ugly face stares back at me, while the rails at my feet create a path straight to a grid of warehouses with vacant, black windows.

"Why would Lily come here?" I ask.

Thane doesn't answer immediately. He stands ahead of me, staring into the dark, shoulders rigid, like he's had wire shoved up his back and arms.

"We came here before…" He pauses, and I can finish that sentence: before his mother died, before he severed his relationship with everyone he knew. "It was just a place to escape."

Thane starts off toward the locomotives, and at first, I want to follow, but the wind picks up, blowing my hair in my face again, and as I turn toward it, a light flickers in the distance. The only reason it draws my attention is because it's coming from inside one of the warehouses. Has it been on since we got here? An uneasy feeling crawls up my back, like claws tiptoeing along my skin. Maybe Lily's last moments were spent inside that

230

building, but if that's the case, what sort of clues remain? Among them, the killer?

Worse is the feeling that I need to move forward. Like I'm being reeled in—a creature at sea, caught on a line. I twist to look for Thane and tell him where I'm going, but he's already disappeared behind the train cars. I take the bait, more curious than anything, and start toward the building. Each step makes my heart beat harder in my chest. A sheen of perspiration bubbles on my forehead, and I squeeze my fingers into a tight fist. I've gone into a lot of fights knowing I'm not defenseless, and yet that only makes me more afraid.

I stop before one of the warehouse buildings. Lights flicker from within, illuminating the dusty windows. Why would anyone need light in an abandoned building? Unless they were doing something illegal? Like selling drugs or…resurrecting people from the dead.

I wander to the side of the building and find a window I can easily climb through. I know I should find Thane and tell him to come with me, but the compulsion forward is too great. At first, I think the window's open, but glass crunches beneath my feet, and I realize it's been knocked out of the frame. This is beyond stupid and I know I shouldn't venture in alone, but if there's evidence inside that might tell me what happened to Lily, I want to find it, so I climb through, slicing my palm.

"Jesus!"

The word slips out, a harsh curse in this dark atmosphere. When I inhale, it's sawdust I taste on my tongue. I close my fingers around the cut, feeling sticky blood pool in the crevices of my palm.

I stand for a moment to get my bearings as the lights

flicker and fade. The warehouse is nothing spectacular, just a concrete floor scattered with broken pieces of wood and metal. Overhead, heavy beams create a pattern that holds up the metal roof, and windows are set high up to allow in as much light as possible during the day. Still, there's something about this place that's familiar. I can't place it, but I feel it, like energy vibrating around me, raising the hair on my arms, pricking along my neck.

I pull my phone out to text Thane to meet me here, but before I can, the lights go out, and something crashes to the ground, startling me. I whirl, facing the sound just as the lights come back on, and find a large black bird flying toward me. I lift my hands to cover my face, but at the last minute, it turns upward and flies toward the rafters. It tilts its head, watching me. I can't say whether it's the same one I saw at Nacoma Knight my first day or one of the ones in the trees outside my house, but it's definitely a raven.

The bird's beady black eyes glint in the dark, and an involuntary shiver runs down my spine.

"Stupid bird," I mumble under my breath before continuing to explore the warehouse under the watchful gaze of my unwanted companion. I text Thane, but it churns and ultimately bounces back as undeliverable. No bars inside this building. For now, I'm on my own.

I've inspected most of the warehouse when I hear it—movement from somewhere distant. There's a door in the corner of the room. As I step toward it, a harsh caw erupts from the darkness, and that stupid bird swoops down in front of me. Startled, I drop my phone. I can't shake the feeling that this thing wants to peck my eyes out. Instead, it perches on the windowsill closest to me.

As I bend to pick up my phone, I grab a piece of scrap wood to throw at the creature.

"Go away!"

The bird dodges and screams back at me, rising toward the rafters.

When I look at my phone, the screen is broken.

*Great.* Just something else for Mom to get upset about.

After the commotion, I wait in the silence at the door, thinking that whatever's in the basement might move again, but I hear nothing.

*If it's another bird, I swear I'll hit it with a board.*

Gingerly, I turn the knob. It's cold and gritty, and when I open the door, the air around me changes—thickens—and it's tinged with the faintest chemical smell. I stand at the edge of the darkness, using my phone flashlight. For a long moment, I can't move. I guess I'm waiting for something to creep out of the shadows.

But nothing happens.

And yet I get the sense that something's happened here. Something dark. It sticks to my skin like dust, seeps into my pores, spreading unease. I should turn around and leave this place, but I can't help thinking that this feeling is guiding me to my coin.

I take a deep breath and step into the dark, shutting the door behind me so that damned raven can't follow.

As I come to the end of the steps, I find a light switch on the wall beside me. The buzz of electricity sounds overhead, but the lights don't come on. Instead, I rely on the pocket of light my phone creates as I move forward. Columns run along each side of the room. Between each column are metal shelves and a collection of glass jars. It isn't until I move closer that I see something inside them. Brushing a thick layer of dirt from the glass, a dead crow stares back at me. My breath catches in my throat, and I jump away from the shelves. Shining my light from this distance, I can tell the other jars are full of dead things too.

And then I hear a familiar laugh.

It rushes into my ears like water and suffocates my lungs.

I twist toward the sound—that glorious baritone—and *smell* him.

Pipe tobacco.

Life Savers.

*Poppa.*

And when I turn, he's standing there at the center of this horrible basement amid all the dead things in his flannel shirt and high-waisted pants. He smiles at me, and his skin, thin like paper, crinkles.

This can't be real. I close my eyes and open them. He's still there.

"Poppa?"

He laughs again, then mimics taking off an invisible hat and bows before shuffling his feet along in an odd dance he used to do to cheer me up. He would reach for my hands, hold them lightly in his own, and then we'd take a turn around the room while he hummed a tune. The nearer he comes, the more details I notice: the bottom pearl snap of his shirt is undone, like always. The faded tattoo of an anchor on his inner arm, overgrown with wild hair. The patch of fuzz on his chin he never seems to scrape with his razor. He reaches for me but doesn't grab me. He waits for me to take his hands.

My heart races, and my throat feels tight, and there's pressure in my eyes that might make me go blind.

I want him to be real.

I reach for him, and when his hands clasp mine, they're warm and the skin is rough.

"Poppa," I say again, my voice a half whisper.

This time, Poppa smiles, but his lips pull back, revealing a set of jagged, sharp teeth.

# CHAPTER TWENTY-FIVE
## Shy and the Tracker

*I can't sleep. Every time I close my eyes, I see Lily's dead* body hanging behind my eyelids. I can't stop thinking about how similar her death was to Vera's, how there's a strong possibility Lily's soul was exchanged with Vera's. And right now, I'm pretty freaking sure Anora is the Eurydice.

But is she capable of killing Lily?

A better question: Is Anora in control of her power enough to execute something like an exchange?

It's a question only she can answer. And since I'm still on leave from my knight-in-training duty, I'll have to wait to talk to her until school.

I grab my phone and find myself scrolling through photos from digital albums my mom created. I'm realizing now I'm lucky Mom liked to take so many pictures of me and my friends growing up. I have a timeline of my friendship with Lily, Jacobi, Natalie…even Thane. There are photos of all five of us outside Rayon Elementary.

My eyes linger longest on Lily, who is smiling so big, her eyes are closed. When we entered our freshman year, we all transferred to Nacoma Knight Academy for training. And of course, Thane followed us. Mom made us take the same photo but outside Emerson Hall. Lily has the same smile.

I have photos from birthday parties, dances, and school. I finally choose a photo of me and Lily to set as the background image on my phone. It was taken the night I got my Jeep. Once Dad gave me the keys, I drove to Lily's to show her. She hopped in the passenger seat, leaned over the console, and snapped this photo before we went backroading.

She never judged me for wanting to do more and more "human" things.

"Hey." I look up to find Mom standing in the doorway. "What are you smiling at?"

I turn the phone around so she can see. She smiles too, but it's sad. Mom's mourned Lily's death just as much as me. She's used to my friends coming over unannounced, hanging out for hours at a time. They're just as much her kids as I am.

I clear my throat, mostly to make sure when I speak, my voice is clear.

"What's up?"

"I came when I saw your light on to see what you were up to," she says. "And to say I'm heading to the Compound for a few hours."

"Are you being reinstated?"

She looks uncertain. "I'm meeting with Elite Cain to discuss reinstatement."

"Oh." I don't know much about the process of being

237

reinstated once a shadow knight is placed on probation. I imagine it has to do with how severe the offense is.

She crosses my room and kisses the top of my head before heading out.

I set my phone aside, stand, and shift into my raven form. At first, I think I'll take a break, fly to the lake, and sit a while, but I find myself en route to Anora's.

*Questions only Anora can answer.*

I'm ready for answers.

If I have to show up in her bedroom in my hybrid form just to get them, I will.

As I near her house, I know something's off, because the usually snoozing hellhounds are sniffing the ground as if they're trying to catch a scent. I fly in circles over their heads. The hounds look up at me, glowing red eyes like lasers, and gnash their teeth. One of the hounds lets out an ear-splitting howl, and at first, I think it's reacting to me, but it darts down the road into the darkness. The other two follow. Something's not right here.

My hand goes to my blade as my feet touch the ground. I take a step toward the house, but the air around me changes, and I twist to find Natalie shifting into her Valryn form.

"She's not home."

"How long have you been here?"

"Only a few minutes more than you. Seems we both had the same idea."

*I sincerely doubt that.*

"And what idea is that?"

"To find evidence Anora's exchanging souls."

I glance at the house. "And how did you plan on finding evidence?"

Natalie shrugs. "We're not bound by human law."

"You can't just break into her house, Natalie."

"I'm a little beyond the point of respecting boundaries, Shy. Lily's dead, and Anora was the last person to see her alive. We both know Lily didn't kill herself. What else has to happen before you accept Anora's responsible?"

I'm not sure, but I know something has to change… and maybe that's Anora's anonymity, even if I don't trust what Roth's planning for the Eurydice. At least the Order has the final say and might be able to help her.

"Shouldn't you be a little more discerning now that you're a *tracker*?" Natalie glares at the green threads on my suit. "Why?"

"What do you mean 'why'?"

"No one gets promoted before training, Shy. Not even you. I'd think real hard about why Roth wants you as a tracker. Real. Hard."

The thing is, I have been thinking real hard about it, and it bothers me just as much as Anora's absence. A shrill cry sends my heart beating in my chest, until I realize it's my phone.

Good thing I'm not hunting darklings tonight.

Fumbling, I pull it out of my pocket and answer.

"Yes?" My voice sounds more like a hiss than anything else.

"Shy, where are you?" I can hear the tap, tap, tap of Jacobi's fingers against the keyboard. It sounds like heavy rain on the window.

"Home." I would tell him the truth, but Jacobi's on probation, and he would want to join us.

"Liar. You're outside, 222 Foley… Isn't that the new girl's house?"

I pause a moment. "How did you know?"

"I traced your phone." His voice is tinged with humor. Of course. Ever the tech, ever the hacker. The tempo of his fingers continues at a steady pace. "Just in case you were wondering, hanging out outside a girl's house is no way to make her like you."

"Uh, first, Nat's here with me, and second, we were appointed—"

"To stalk her. I know," he says.

"What do you want, Jacobi?" I ask quickly, in no mood for his commentary.

"I thought you'd want to know, I pinged Lily's cell phone."

My chest feels like it's collapsed. I hadn't even thought about Lily's phone. I assumed it was with her body.

"And?"

"It hasn't been used since Sunday," he says. That was the day before she died. "And she was all over the place that day. School, the lake, June's…"

"You said you tracked it, which I assume means it's not at her house," I say, growing impatient. "So where is it *now*?"

"The train yard."

"What was she doing there?"

Jacobi's still typing. "I mean, we used to hang out there when we were still friends with—"

"Thane." Thane's uncle, Malachi Black, owns the property, but being abandoned, it became a popular hangout for death-speakers looking to perform the occult. Thane and I had actually been there one night when we happened upon a séance, which aren't always bad…except when we were caught, the kids chased us.

One caught me and punched me so hard in the face, I blacked out for a moment. When I came to, a patrolling shadow knight had arrived and shut everything down, and I wasn't allowed to go back to the yard.

Lily admitted she'd been hanging out with Thane again, so the fact that her phone is at the train yard could be coincidence. I'm not so sure she wanted it in her possession when her father or the other elites questioned her about her relationship with the human. Maybe she left it there on purpose until after she faced the Order. Still, it is worth investigating.

Jacobi continues, "I don't know the exact location of the phone, but we can call it once we get there."

"We? Jacobi, you're on probation."

"Exactly," he says. "This isn't patrol, so I can't get in trouble."

"Jacobi—" I start.

"I'll be there in five," he says, interrupting me, and before he hangs up the phone, I'm in the air. Natalie follows close behind.

The train yard sits against a curtain of dense wood, and a stagnant reservoir makes the place smell like rotten eggs. It is connected to a network of brick and metal warehouse buildings that once housed factories. Railroad tracks twine through the property, unused. I land atop one of several skeletal locomotives. The wind rustles the grass and the trees, carrying the scent of death: distinct, raw, and strong. I turn, staring off toward the warehouse. Two streetlights pour yellow light on the ground, and one warehouse window is lit. It's that light—ugly, orange, and bright—that makes me feel uneasy.

Something's wrong—I can sense it in the air. A strong current of energy is here, which means there are either a lot of souls or a few darklings about.

"You feel that?" I ask Natalie.

"Yeah." She looks around.

"Stay alert."

Jacobi lands beside us atop the locomotive. As he shifts, he pulls out his phone, staring down at a map where a glowing red dot pulses on the screen.

"I think it's in the woods," he says, and I follow his gaze to the tree line, a wall of solid black.

"Can you call it?" I ask.

Jacobi nods, and soon a low ringtone sounds from somewhere ahead of us. We jump from the roof of the train, swallowed by the overgrowth. I draw my scythe, hating the way the ground moves beneath my feet. It's wet and marsh-like, making it difficult to move forward. It will also make fighting anyone out here harder and more dangerous.

"Do you smell that?" Jacobi asks.

Natalie coughs. "It's awful."

The smell of decay gets stronger as we move forward, invading my nostrils and spilling down my throat. Ahead I notice a disturbance in the grass—tall tendrils lying flat, forced down with weight. The ringtone goes silent just as I break through the wall of blades to find a pile of animal corpses in various states of decay.

"What the…" Bile rises in the back of my throat, and I swallow it down.

Jacobi kneels close to the corpses, examining them. There are a variety of species: squirrels and birds, cats and dogs, raccoons and opossums, basically any unlucky

242

creatures that might live in the woods beyond or wandered onto the property. "No wounds," he says.

There are too many corpses to assume these animals died naturally. No, their souls had been stolen.

"You think this is practice?" Natalie asks.

"I don't know, but that seems like the only logical explanation," I say.

"I don't understand. If this is the work of a death-speaker, why would they leave the corpses out in the open? Why not bury their evidence?" Jacobi says.

"No one said we were dealing with a death-speaker." I feel guilty for even thinking it, but I have to. What if this is the work of the Eurydice? Is this how she is gaining control of her powers? Practice?

"We should report this," Natalie says at last.

"Uh, in case you forgot, me and Jacobi are not supposed to be here," I say.

"If you want me to take the fall for it, I will," Jacobi says, and in return, Natalie and I glare at him.

"Don't be a martyr, Jacobi," I say evenly. "I'll report it. We can't risk more time added to your probation."

"It's not so bad, Shy," Jacobi says with a small smile. "Besides, it's a waste if you get sidelined for even longer."

"It's just as much a waste to lose your talents," I argue.

"Flattery will get you nowhere," he says. "Besides, you don't have to lie. I've seen my file."

I stop myself from asking how, realizing he's hacked the archive. I have no idea what his file says, but I can guess that his prospects for ranking as a shadow knight aren't great. "Jacobi. You shouldn't have done that."

He shrugs. "At least I know their plans. It's easier to make my own now."

243

"Jacobi—" Natalie starts.

Just then, a light ignites in the darkness beyond the trees, small, faint. Jacobi steps toward it when a scream breaks the night—high, shrill, full of fear. My heart feels like it's going to tear from my chest. Anora. The scream is coming from one of the warehouses a distance away.

Jacobi, Natalie, and I exchange a look.

"Go!" I command.

We race for the warehouse, and I try not to think about what will happen if we're too late. We won't have the killer at all, just another victim. One I don't think I can live without.

# CHAPTER TWENTY-SIX
# Anora and the Cercatore

*Another scream tears from my throat, and I try to pull* away, but the creature has my hands held tight in its own, and it's pulling me closer. It turns its head upward toward the ceiling in an unnatural way, unhinging its jaw so its mouth opens wide. It no longer resembles my grandpa. It's a tall creature made of darkness, with long limbs as pointed as its teeth.

Glass breaks somewhere in the distance, and something heavy knocks into me. I hit the ground hard, landing on my back with Natalie over me, hands holding down my arms, her legs clamped tight against mine. I recognize this control. She's trying to incapacitate me.

"Get off me or I swear—"

"What? You'll kill me too?"

For a moment, I go completely still and glare at her, then I realize something's off about her appearance— most notably, the large black wings sprouting from her back. That's when I lose it.

"Get off of me! Get away from me!" I thrash, trying to loosen her hold. The thread ignites between us, and Natalie springs away. I scramble to my feet and get a good look at her. She's Natalie all right, but different. She's leaner, but maybe I never noticed before because she doesn't wear skin-tight black suits to school. Her hair is slick and straight, falling over her shoulders in a sheet. Then there are the wings—huge sweeping black-metallic things that surround her like a halo.

"Get her out of here!"

I freeze—I'd know that voice anywhere.

*Shy.*

I twist to find him, but he doesn't look like the Shy I know—his blond hair is silver and falls to his shoulders, and black wings sprout from his back. He takes my place in front of the thing that looked like my poppa moments earlier, two long blades clasped in his hands.

What is going on?

"Go!" Natalie pushes me forward, and someone grabs my wrist. I try to pull away but recognize the voice.

"It's me," Thane says. "Do what they say!"

*What the actual hell?* Did he just tell me to do what they say? Shouldn't he be helping me fight them?

Thane drags me toward the door, but the creature of shadow screams, and tentacles explode from it, stretching out and knocking us to the ground. Something flies past me—another one of the bird creatures. I scramble to my feet and find the three poised before the creature, blades exposed in the pale light filtering through the thin windows above.

They cut and stab at the creature, but their blades only make it angry, and the angrier it gets, the more damage it does, knocking into shelves and the concrete columns. Jars crash to the ground, choking the air with formaldehyde and dust.

"This isn't working, Shy!" Natalie says, and my stomach knots painfully, but I don't have time to comprehend what's happening here, because the creature's tentacles flail, and I have to duck to keep from being flung across the room. Thane's in front of me again, pulling my arm.

"We have to get out of here!"

"Look out!" I push him forward and fall with him, landing as one of the creature's tentacles rushes over us and crashes into a column. There's a cracking sound as it comes loose from its place and falls toward us. Thane and I scramble to our feet and away, finding ourselves closer to the fight than we wanted to be.

"Jacobi!" Shy's voice is harsh as Jacobi propels from his position on the floor. Scythe in hand, he cuts a blow across the creature's tooth-filled face. Its scream grows louder, and one of its tentacles lifts, smacking into Jacobi and sending him flying against the wall. Shy twists, searching, until his eyes meet mine.

And something in my chest pulls so tight, I lose my ability to breathe.

*I know him.*

And not in the way I've gotten to know him the last week. This is different, deeper. It goes beyond his skin and blood and bones. It's like my dreams.

*I know his soul.*

The knowledge shivers through me, and my mind strains to place him. I chase tendrils of memories, but they slip from my grasp, teasing, playful, brutal—and they smell like smoke and jasmine.

*What did that witch do to me?*

Shy's harsh voice brings me back to the present. "Get her out of here! She's making it stronger!"

"Shy!" Natalie warns, but it's too late. He goes flying, his body flipping unnaturally as he lands in a pile of his own feathers. I don't go to him, and I don't run away. I stand, rooted to the spot. Anger, white and hot, washes over me, burning my eyes and skin. I want to smash this thing to pieces for giving me hope, for lifting me from darkness just to crush me.

*I want to kill it.*

And the thread responds, rising to fit my palm like the hilt of a blade. I don't know what it does to creatures like this, but I unleash it anyway. It twirls through the air, lancing the creature, looping throughout its limbs. It writhes, jerking and hissing, its body splitting so that light pours through cracks in its shadow skin.

I see it all in slow motion: how the thread twists and tightens, moving methodically through each arm and then diving down into a mouth of teeth, only to burst from its stomach, spewing black oil, but it happens in an instant. The creature groans and falls into a puddle, and my thread reels back in, coating my hand in sticky black tar.

As I stand there, catching my breath, the anger melts, replaced with something far more urgent.

*Oh God.* What have I done?

I turn to find everyone staring at me—Shy, Natalie, Jacobi, all still in those strange, tight suits, feather wings sprouting on either side of their heads. Even Thane hasn't managed to close his mouth.

Then the building groans, and pieces of the ceiling come loose.

"Go!" Another quick command from Shy's lips.

There's no hesitation this time. We spill outside into the streetlight, and for a moment, the only sound is our harsh breath. Then, Natalie's voice.

"Shy…"

Growls sound from around us, and when I look up, we are surrounded by five large hounds.

"Oh, come on!" I hear Jacobi say.

While he and Natalie prepare to fight, Shy moves so the hounds have a clear path to me and says, "She's not hurt. We're not going to hurt her."

He seems to think these things are protecting me.

They stay poised for attack, bent low, their jowls pulled away from sharp teeth. Shy cocks his head toward me but keeps his eyes on the hounds.

"*Tell them*," he orders me.

These people are crazy.

But my heart is racing, my hand sticky with black blood from a creature that looked like my grandfather come back to life, and I'm surrounded by creatures with wings.

*So what the hell.*

"I…I'm not hurt. They won't hurt me." I repeat what he says.

"You could sound a little more convincing," Natalie says sharply.

She's probably right. Problem is, I don't believe what I'm saying.

I move forward slowly, coming to stand beside Shy, and try again. "I'm not hurt. They helped me… Please… you can go."

There's a change in the rumble of their growl, and

finally they go quiet and ease up. The five exchange looks and then meld with the shadows.

*Well, that was weird.*

"They're not gone," Jacobi says.

"Of course not." Natalie's glaring at me. "Haven't you figured it out? They're here for *her*."

"Oh my God," I say. My hands go to my head, and I stare at the four of them, Thane included, because he completes the arc in front of me, an extension of them, hands crossed over his chest, unaffected by their appearance.

"Uh-oh. Quick, shift before she explodes," Thane says.

I glare at him.

"Can we just talk about the fact that you aren't freaking out right now?" I ask.

"Oh, for Charon's sake!" Natalie curses. "He already knows what we are!"

Of course. Lily must have told him this part too. Thane's arms tighten across his chest. I guess that shouldn't be surprising—they're all former friends, right?

"So...did you have a falling-out before or after you discovered all your friends were crows?"

"I resent that," Jacobi says. "We're ravens. A little more graceful, definitely bigger."

"Whatever. The fact is you have wings."

"We need to get out of here," Shy says, ignoring me. "The Order will send knights in. That creature consumed a lot of energy. It had to show up on their radar."

"That's perfect," Natalie says. "We can turn her over when they get here."

"What?" I instantly feel the thread rise to the surface of my palm.

"No," Shy says.

250

Natalie gets that look about her. The one where I imagine she's envisioning tearing someone apart limb by limb.

"Shy, *she's* the Eurydice! The Order's been looking for *her*!"

"So is Roth, and I don't trust him." He turns to me. "I want to hear your story first. Why you're here. What happened in New York."

I swallow hard. "New York?"

"We know you're not from Chicago," Natalie says. "Figured that out pretty fast."

My fingers tighten into fists.

Thane looks at me. "I'm not a fan of any of them, but it's not such a bad thing to have them on your side, especially as the Eurydice."

It takes effort, but I'm able to uncurl my fists. I take a deep breath. "Fine. Where are we going?"

When I look at Shy, his face seems so severe, I flinch.

"My house." He turns, spreading his large wings and taking flight. The sight is oddly beautiful. Natalie and Jacobi follow.

I'm left standing with Thane.

"That's why you know their rules so well," I say, sounding a little accusatory. "You never mentioned that they were frickin' birds!"

He shrugs. "You didn't need to know so long as they didn't know you were the Eurydice." He pauses, letting that sink in, and then says, "Let's go. I hate to admit it, but Shy's right. This place will be swarming with knights soon."

*Swarming.*

Suddenly, all I can think is that I made a huge mistake coming here.

251

# CHAPTER TWENTY-SEVEN
## Anora and the Valryn

**Before we leave, Thane pulls a water bottle from his car** and a stack of napkins from his glove compartment. He helps me clean the black blood from my hands, and I remember the cut I had gotten when I climbed through the window. It stings, and I hope I'm not in danger of contracting any weird diseases. If so, Thane doesn't choose this moment to start naming them off.

As he pours water over my hands, I notice several scratches on his wrist where his shirt sleeve has lifted.

"What's on your wrist?" I ask.

"What?" Thane asks.

"Your wrist. It looks like you scratched yourself." I say scratched, but what I mean is cut. It looks like he cut himself. The line is too precise. I reach for his hand and pull it toward me, twisting his palm upright and pushing back his sleeve. There, on his pale skin, are a series of angry, red marks. Some of them are scabbed over; others are fresh.

"Thane," I breathe, and when I meet his gaze, he yanks his hand away.

"Mind your own fucking business, Anora," he snaps and climbs into his black Charger. I scramble into the passenger side before he speeds off, heading for Shy's.

Thane's knuckles are white as he grips the steering wheel, his eyes focused on the dark road ahead. I can almost taste the air around him—shadowed and sad, tortured and adrift. I think he's been drowning so long, he doesn't want the comfort of solid ground beneath his feet.

When he finally speaks, his voice shakes, his hatred barely restrained.

"I was with Shy the night I found out my mom was in the accident. His mom called him, and he gave me the news. I demanded he take me to her, and when he refused, I ran there." I must look shocked, because Thane adds, "It wasn't far. This town isn't very big, remember? I broke through the police barriers, calling her name, before I saw her lying motionless on the ground. She was surrounded by paramedics trying to revive her, but she was already dead. I knew because her soul stood a few steps away from me."

He pauses a moment, and his next words are pained but thoughtful. "You know they usually wear their deaths, but she...she looked perfect." He clears his throat, and I shiver, swallowing hard. "Later, I found out it was because her insides had exploded."

"I'm sorry."

"Everyone is," he says. "But no one's sorry enough to do anything about it."

"What do you mean?"

"In those few moments after her death, with that perfect body, her soul could have been returned, and no one would have known the better of it. She might have been called a miracle. But no one—not Shy or Natalie or Jacobi—would help me."

I remember what Lennon said about Thane—he wants his mother brought back to life. I shiver at the thought. *Buffy the Vampire Slayer* taught me resurrection is a bad idea. People always come back wrong.

"But…resurrection is illegal."

Thane looks at me. "Keeping you from the Order is illegal too, and they don't see that as a problem."

"Would they even have known how to resurrect her?" I ask softly.

He turns to me, and the look on his face is hard. "Certainly someone seems to know, don't they, Anora?"

I decide not to say anything else, but I wonder why he's still here, offering to take me to Shy's, if all this reminds him of the day his mother died.

Shy's house is a charming two-story cottage. I try imagining Shy and the others fitting their massive wings through the doorway of such a normal-looking structure, but I can't. Even with everything I am and everything I saw tonight, I find it hard to accept shape-shifters. Maybe it's because I can make sense of everything else. Souls are lost, and their energy creates creatures like the one I saw tonight, but whatever Shy, Natalie, and Jacobi are, well…that has no explanation.

We exit the car and approach the house. The windows are open, and I can hear Natalie's raised voice.

"What are you thinking? Not turning her over to the Order?"

"I told you. I want to hear her story," Shy responds.

"As if that changes anything! She's still the Eurydice. She's still the Order's responsibility."

"We're part of the Order, and we're being responsible."

Thane slams the door closed behind me, announcing our presence, and all goes quiet. After a moment, Shy appears in the entryway. I meet his gaze, finding it angrier than I anticipated. That earlier feeling of recognition is back, knotting up my chest. Why does his disapproval hurt? His eyes slide behind me to Thane, who's standing so close, I can feel the brush of his body against mine. His gaze falls to our feet.

"Shoes off."

He turns and goes into the living room. I glance at Thane, who has already stooped to unlace his boots. I follow his example, shucking off my shoes beside the others piled close to the door. I guess everyone but me is used to this when visiting Shy's house.

We meet the others in the living room. Jacobi's sitting on the couch, bent over a laptop. Natalie's beside him, and Shy's in the armchair across from me. We stare at each other, not even trying to hide it. I don't know his excuse, but I'm trying to figure out why I suddenly feel like I'm having déjà vu.

Thane clears his throat. "Get your interrogation over, Savior," he says.

"First, I want to know what that thing was and why it looked like my poppa," I say.

Shy's eyes seem to soften at the use of my endearment.

"The creature is called a cercatore," he responds. "It morphs into what you want most, to set a trap and drain your blood."

The statement makes me feel angry and violated. Not only had that creature somehow reached into me and pulled out my greatest wish, but I'd also given a

255

piece of myself to everyone in this room without ever intending to.

"Of course, it wouldn't have been a problem if you had obeyed curfew," Natalie cuts in. "You should know better, Thane."

"Fuck off, Natalie. We were investigating."

Shy glares at Thane and then at me. "Investigating what?"

"Lily's killer is out there, and none of you have done anything to find him," says Thane.

"Or her," Natalie corrects. "How do you know she isn't sitting in this room right now?"

I straighten. "Excuse me?"

"She wouldn't be your first victim, would she?"

"Natalie," Shy warns.

"I didn't kill Lily."

"What about Chase Lockwood?"

This is what Shy meant when he said he wanted to hear my story. Moisture burns my eyes, blurring my vision, and I swallow.

"I killed him."

I let those words hang in the air, creating a barrier between me and everyone else in the room. I expect them to look horrified, to jump to their feet and draw those sickening, curved blades, threaten me like Chase did, but none of them move.

"How?" Natalie asks.

"With the thread," I say, though it's obvious. It's the only weapon I own.

"The correct question is why?" Shy says crossly.

Why?

"Because he tried to kidnap me."

256

# CHAPTER TWENTY-EIGHT
# Anora and Chase Lockwood

*Four months ago*

**"Mom, I see dead people."**

I shake my head. No, she'll just think I'm quoting *The Sixth Sense.*

*"Mom…I see ghosts."*

"I still sound crazy," I mutter under my breath. Okay, how about, *"Mom, I see souls."*

This is going to be a disaster.

I look at my report card. The D beside chemistry looks like the mark of Satan. How am I supposed to show this to Mom? I've never gotten a D. I think about the last few months and what's led to my failing grades. Chemistry isn't the only class that's taken a hit. Trigonometry's a low B, and history's a C. This is the worst report card I've ever received.

And I know why.

I reach for the chain around my neck and clutch

my poppa's coin. It's only been two months since he died. Two months since I witnessed his soul leave his body, tangled with some black substance that I can only describe as wrong. It has been two months since a gold thread erupted from my palm and consumed my poppa's soul, turning it into a coin.

After the incident, everything just got worse. The dead are literally everywhere, and sometimes they look like real, living people. Sometimes my route home looks like a scene from *The Walking Dead*.

So yeah, school's been rough.

I haven't told anyone about my experiences because, let's face it, no one's going to believe me.

But I really, really want someone to understand.

"Earth to Lyra." Emma waves her hand in front of my face.

"Huh?" I blink at her and fold my report card quickly, feeling embarrassed by the letters written on the page.

"Did you hear anything I said?"

I bite my lip and offer a sheepish, "No."

She frowns, those big blue eyes studying me. "You sure you're all right? You've seemed…more stressed than usual."

"Yeah, I'm fine." I don't look at her as I respond, focusing instead on choosing the right notebook and textbook from my locker. When I face her again, she doesn't look convinced.

"What?"

"You're lying," she accuses as we start walking to class.

"Look, I'm just not sleeping very well, that's all."

It's the truth. Since Poppa died and I can see the

dead, I've discovered I can hear them too. Apparently, someone who liked to sing at the top of their lungs died in my apartment complex at some point.

Sometimes the dead suck.

"What were you saying?" I ask Emma, because I don't want to talk about myself anymore, and I'm genuinely curious about what she was saying before I zoned out looking at my report card.

The worry instantly evaporates from her face, and she smiles, showing her dimples. I love Emma's smile. So do most of the boys in our school.

"We have a new student, and Olivia says he's gorgeous!"

"Olivia thinks every new guy is gorgeous," I complain.

"Lyra, you don't understand. I saw this one!"

"Close up?"

"Well, no," she admits. "But I don't need to see him close up to know that bone structure is only for gods."

I roll my eyes. "If he looks like a god, he's probably a jerk too, and I'm not interested—"

I slam into a body and drop my books. The person I ran into turns around, and suddenly I'm face-to-face with a literal god. I mean, he's too beautiful to walk the halls of Mount St. Mary for the Gifted. He's so tall, I have to crane my neck to get a good look at his strong jaw, chiseled cheekbones, and full lips. When I meet his eyes, I can't look away. I've never seen anyone with those eyes. They're light green and rimmed with black.

"Hi," I manage to squeak.

He smiles, and oh god, my heart races in my chest. "Hi."

Then he bends to scoop up my books, and as he rises, I swear he inches closer. I can't breathe.

I'm not sure how long I stare at him before he clears his throat. "Are you...heading to class?"

"Yeah." Then I realize he's still holding my books. I go to reach for them. "You probably don't want to keep holding those."

But he moves them out of my reach, clutching them tighter to his chest—his well-defined, muscly chest.

What kind of workouts is he doing outside school, and how long has it taken him to get that body?

"Why don't I walk you to class?"

I just nod. Beside me, Emma giggles, and suddenly I remember I'm not alone. And from the way she's looking at me, I'm apparently acting like a starry-eyed schoolgirl from a Disney show.

The god and I look at her. She smiles, all cute with her dimples and blond curls. She holds out her hand. "I'm Emma."

How is she coherent in front of this guy?

He smiles and takes her hand. "Chase. Chase Lockwood."

He looks at me. By the time I understand he's waiting for me to say my name, Emma beats me to it.

"This is Lyra. Lyra Silby."

Chase's smile widens, and he walks Emma and I to our class. On the way, Emma asks him questions—*Where are you from? Upstate New York. What school did you transfer from? Midwood. Are you a senior? Yes. Do you play sports? Lacrosse. Do you have a girlfriend?* Chase glances at me and answers, "No."

I don't think I've blushed so much in my life, and as I

walk between Chase and Emma, I realize this is the longest I've gone without thinking about Poppa being gone.

When we make it to our room, Chase hands me my books.

"It was nice meeting you!" Emma says and disappears into class, leaving Chase and I alone. He's studying me with those strange eyes, and it makes my chest feel all fluttery.

"It was nice meeting you, Lyra," he says. "I'll see you around."

I watch him leave, all swagger and confidence as if he's been at this school for years. For once, Olivia was right about the god on campus.

I barely register walking into class and finding my seat. I feel like I'm floating, and every time I think about how Chase looked at me, I blush.

Then Mr. Ray returns my chemistry test from Friday.

F.

I'm screwed.

———

It's almost a month later when Chase discovers my ability to see the dead. A man with a lacerated face has wandered on campus. It's lunchtime. I'm sitting on the top of a picnic table. Chase sits on the bench, facing me. He keeps trying to tell me how lacrosse works, but I can't help watching the dead man. His eyes have been on me the entire time, and he continues to stumble toward us. I'm trying to think of excuses to leave before he gets too close. Sometimes I swear they want something from me.

Bathroom. The bathroom is always the best excuse. I can feel his energy pulling at my skin, stealing my breath, and I play with the evil eye on my backpack.

After a moment, Chase pauses, looks over his shoulder, and then takes my hand.

"Hey." His voice is quiet. "Are you okay?"

"Yeah," I manage, but the word escapes my lips breathlessly, so I smile.

"You know they can't hurt you."

My smiles fades fast. "What?"

"The dead. They can't hurt you."

There is silence between us for a long moment and then, "You can see them too?"

He smiles that warm smile I've become so familiar with over the last few weeks. It makes my chest feel like it's on fire.

"Yeah."

Until this moment, I've never met anyone who can see the dead. I burst into tears. Chase's brows knit together, and his hands cup either side of my face.

"Hey, hey, hey." His voice is gentle as he brushes my tears away. "It's okay."

"I know," I say, sobbing. "It's just…I've felt crazy, you know?"

He sits beside me on the table and pulls me to him. "You're not crazy."

Later that night, I sit at the kitchen table with my chemistry book and notes spread out before me. I have two more exams before the end of the school year, and I need to ace both of them to bring up my failing grade. I've managed to avoid the topic of my report card because Mom's been too busy with work to realize it's midsemester. I'm hoping I can make it to the end of the year before she even thinks about grades.

My phone vibrates on the table. Before I look at the screen, my heart starts to race in my chest.

Chase.

I smile as I pick up the phone.

What are you up to? he asks.

Studying.
Want a break?
I just started.
Did you eat first?

I laugh. No, why?

You'll need fuel to keep you going. Come eat with me.

I'm about to reply I can't, Mom's cooking dinner when she enters the kitchen.

"Lyra, what's this?"

Mom holds a piece of crumpled paper. It's my report card. My smile evaporates, and I feel the color drain from my face. I put my phone down and meet her gaze, even though I want to run far, far away. Why didn't I take Chase up on his offer? I could have been out the door moments before she walked in.

"It's my report card."

"And why was it in your trash can?"

"Why were you going through my trash?"

"Lyra," she warns.

"You know the answer, Mom!" She can read. Why does she have to rub it in?

"I want you to tell me."

Why are parents the worst?

"Because I got a D, okay?" I can still save my grade. That's why I'm sitting here with my chem book and my notes.

But things have been so hard.

"Why didn't you tell me?" Mom asks, sitting down at the table.

"Because I knew you would be mad."

"Honey, I know things have been hard for you."

"You have no idea."

Mom flinches, and she sets her jaw. "I think I have some idea. You lost Poppa, and I lost my father, Lyra."

"It's not just that! There are other things, Mom. You've been in your own world too. You wouldn't understand."

I push away from the table. I don't even know where I'm going, but I don't want to be here anymore.

"Lyra, don't walk away. Please. I want to help."

I pause at the door, hands fisted.

"Please give me a chance," Mom pleads. It makes my heart feel like it's being ripped into tiny pieces. In this moment, I can see how tired she is, how this is beyond a depressive episode and is true grief. We've both just been going through the motions to get by.

"You won't believe me," I whisper.

"Honey, of course I'll believe you."

And when I turn to look at her, I know she will. I know it deep in my heart, and I'll have someone to share this burden with. So I sit down at the table again, and she takes my hands in hers. They are as cold as a corpse.

"Promise you'll believe me?"

"Yes." She nods, and her voice shakes a little.

"Mom." I start to cry. I can't even say it for a long moment; all I can do is choke on my sobs. "I can see the dead. I saw Poppa!"

She lets go of my hands, and her chair scrapes against the floor as she stands. "Lyra Anora Silby, that is enough."

"You said you'd believe me!"

"Not when you are spouting nonsense! Not when you're throwing my father's death in my face."

"It isn't nonsense! I see spirits, Mom! As real as I see you. You have to believe me!"

"I will believe no such thing!" Her voice is shrill. "Are you telling me this is why you got a D?"

"I swear, I found Poppa!" I scream. "I saw his soul come out of his body. I saw something black and horrible fighting—"

"Enough!" She matches my tone. "Don't speak another word or I'll have you hospitalized, Lyra."

Neither of us speak after her threat, and just as much as I believed a moment ago that I could tell her the truth, I now believe she's completely capable of committing me to a mental institution. My mom can turn on a dime, just like that.

I should have known things would end this way.

"You know what? Fine," I say, grabbing my phone. I leave the kitchen and head for the door.

"Where are you going?" Mom demands.

I don't answer.

"Lyra, don't you dare leave this apartment."

I'm out the door.

"Lyra!"

I slam the door in her face.

Once outside, I send Chase a text, asking him to

265

meet me at the park. As I walk, my eyes blur with tears. It was too good to be true to think I could trust Mom with the truth. Chase had warned me. He'd said that she would never believe me. That no one would. He had been right.

What am I supposed to do now? When I go home, will Mom have already looked up therapists or psychiatric hospitals? I don't want to be put on medication.

As I approach the park, Chase is leaning against his car, parked near a streetlamp. The light pours over his body. He looks harsh under it, but I run to him anyway. He wraps his arms around me, and I cry into his chest. He doesn't say anything. He waits for me, and when I'm ready, I tell him everything—about my fight with Mom and her threat to commit me. I tell him things I've never told him before, about the coins and how I make them with a thread that comes out of my palm.

He wipes my tears away. "I told you she'll never understand. She can't. She doesn't see what you see."

"I know."

"But I understand. I see what you see."

"What am I going to do?" I ask, not expecting him to answer, but he does.

"Leave with me," he says.

"What?" I pull away and meet his gaze.

"Leave with me," he says again, and his arms tighten around me.

"I...I can't."

I might be mad at Mom and scared that she will stay true to her threat, but I can't leave her. Poppa just died. She would be all alone, and besides, as much as running away would make me feel better right now, in the long run, I'd only feel guilty. I need Mom just as much as she needs me.

"Lyra," Chase says, taking my hands. "Your mom will never understand you. She'll never believe you."

I tear away from him. He's no longer helping me feel better. He's just making me mad.

"Shut up!"

He moves toward me. "I'm not trying to hurt you. I'm only using your words, Lyra."

I feel like he's slapped me, and I flinch.

"You know what? Never mind."

I start to turn, but he grabs my arm. His fingers dig into my skin. He's never touched me this way, and it has warning bells going off in my head. "Where are you going?" he demands.

"Home!" I try to pull away, but he won't let go.

"Why would you go home? You just ran away."

"Because I should have never come here." I jerk away again, and once I'm free, I start to run.

"Lyra!" Chase calls. Then closer, "Lyra!"

That's when he grabs me and something sharp digs into my neck.

His breath, hot against my ear, threatens, "I can't let you leave. We've been waiting for you for too long."

My heart races in my chest, and adrenaline rushes through me as he starts to drag me back to his car. I can feel the thread rising to the surface of my palm. It's not painful, but the feeling is distinct, like holding a sharp rock tight in my palm.

"Stop!" I scream at both Chase and the thread, but it's too late. The blade loosens around my neck, and his weight eases off me as he falls to his knees. I twist to find my thread skewering his eyes, erupting through his nose, and entering his mouth. It continues to lance his body until he's consumed in golden light, and when it fades, a glittering gold coin lies a few feet from the body.

Chase Lockwood is dead.

# CHAPTER TWENTY-NINE
## Shy and the Lake

*My chest aches.*

But this is unlike the feeling that connects me to Anora. This is something angry and primal and raw. Halfway through her story, I can't sit still anymore. When I get to my feet, Anora's eyes meet mine, her gaze like an arrow through my heart. Her eyes are haunted, her face pale.

Even Natalie is affected by Anora's story, leaning forward in her chair with her fingers pressed to her lips. Jacobi's set aside his computer and can't even look at her. None of us expected this. It's a betrayal of our oath as shadow knights. We're supposed to protect humans; we're supposed to protect the Eurydice. The only explanation is not only had Chase gone rogue, but he was connected with the occult.

I've never wanted to comfort someone so much in all my life, and yet I'm sure that's the last thing she wants—comfort from a Valryn, comfort from me. There's an ugly feeling associated with that thought as I observe Thane standing behind Anora like some dark guardian, and I stuff it down quick. I'm no better than Chase if I act on this…connection I have with Anora.

I pace, hating Chase with every word she speaks.

"After Chase died, it felt like eyes were always on me. Like I was being hunted. Maybe I was. I stayed at Mount St. Mary's for one more month before Mom got a brochure about Nacoma Knight Academy. She thought I could start over in a place where people wouldn't recognize me, wouldn't be suspicious of me."

"So when you got here and encountered Vera…" Natalie starts. Her words aren't vicious anymore but full of understanding.

"She followed me. She said *they* would find me. I thought she meant people like Chase. It scared me, and the thread reacted." Anora pauses. "I didn't mean to… I didn't want—"

"We know," I say as gently as I can. She meets my gaze. "It was the day you ran out of art?"

She nods. I found her near the tree line. She looked hysterical, but I assumed she was just suffering from the effects of walking through Vera's soul. Even now, I shudder at what that must have felt like.

"But how did Vera's soul end up in Lily's body?" Natalie asks.

"I lost the coin," Anora admits, looking at her feet.

"Are you sure it was lost?" Thane asks. "Isn't it possible someone stole it?"

"Either way, whoever has it knows how to use it, and they practiced," Jacobi says.

"Practiced?" Anora asks.

"We found several dead animals at the train yard," Natalie says.

Anora looks paler than before. Her lips stand out, red like a rose.

"The coin was at the train yard tonight," Thane says. "That's why Anora and I were there."

I grind my teeth together so hard, I think my molars will crack. Every time Thane opens his mouth about what happened tonight, I want to throttle him even more. "You mean when you let her wander off alone?"

"I can take care of myself," Anora argues.

"Oh yeah? With what? The thread?" Natalie snaps.

"Do you need a reminder of my skills?" Anora asks, her eyes alight with fire.

"How did you know the coin was at the train yard?" Jacobi asks quickly, easing the tension rising in the room.

Thane and Anora exchange a look, and I sort of hate that they have secrets.

"A witch told us."

I glare at Thane, and he glares right back. I know him well enough that I can practically hear his thoughts. *What? She wanted answers, so I took her with me. It's more than you'd do for her.* And he's right. I'd never introduce the death-speaker world to the Eurydice. There are too many people in the Underworld who want her powers and know ways to get them.

"What about you? What's your excuse?" Thane asks.

"I tracked Lily's phone there," Jacobi says. "But after our encounter with the cercatore, I lost the trace. It must have died."

We're all quiet, realizing we've hit a dead end—all of us except Anora. "Well...can't we just go back to the witch?"

"No," we say in unison, with the exception of Thane, who I'm sure would be glad to lead her back to the Underworld.

That firelight returns to her eyes. "But she told us exactly where the coin was!"

"And look how that turned out," Natalie snaps. "You were attacked by a cercatore and have nothing to show for it. How do you even know she was telling the truth? This whole thing sounds like a setup, and she's a death-speaker practicing death magic."

"*I'm* a death-speaker," Anora argues.

"You're the Eurydice. There's a difference."

Anora doesn't reply, but I can tell there's a response bubbling under the surface.

"What Nat is trying to say"—I glance at her—"is we'll help you find the coin. We don't know why the killer chose Lily, and we don't know who they'll target next."

She doesn't argue, so we make a plan for tomorrow that includes a list of places Jacobi was able to track Lily's phone to the day she died: the school, her home, June's, a beach near the lake, and the train yard.

"We'll split up. Look for clues and interview as many people as possible about Lily's behaviors. Anora's with me," I say. Thane's dark eyes meet mine. "She's the Eurydice. She's to have a shadow knight with her at all times."

I expect an argument, but Thane says, "Whatever. I can't help tomorrow anyway. Uncle Malachi wants me in the city. He wants to show off at...some gala."

Once we have our assignments, Thane and Anora get up to leave. As she follows Thane to the door, I call her name. She turns and looks at me. My heart beats hard in my chest.

"I'm sorry for what Chase did."

"Don't apologize for him," she says, almost frustrated, then pauses and clears her throat. When she speaks again, her voice is soft. "Thank you. For letting me tell my story."

"You're welcome."

We stare at each other for a moment before she turns, gets in Thane's car, and leaves.

———

After Natalie, Jacobi, Anora, and Thane leave, I lie awake, staring at the ceiling.

*Anora and Thane.*

I don't even like saying their names in succession. They left my house together. I wanted to follow, to make sure she made it home safe. I mean, Thane *led* her into the Underworld and into the hands of a cercatore. Can I really trust him with the Eurydice? I try to tell myself it's because she's the Eurydice that I care so much—she's like a gold mine, far too valuable to lose—but in reality, I know if anything happens to her, I will never be the same again.

And it makes me feel crazy. It makes me feel like this thread connecting us is wound tight around my heart. I need to tell Jacobi about it so he can research it in the archive. I've kept it from him for too long.

I get up, climb out of my window, and shift, flying into the night. The air is cool, the sky is clear, and a full moon lights up the night. It's only a few hours until dawn. At first, I think I'll take a quick flight around the lake to clear my head, but then I find myself heading in the direction of Anora's house. Just as I consider turning around, I spot her sitting on the roof, knees drawn to her chest.

*Screw it. Might as well see what she's up to.*

273

I shift and land beside her. She jumps.

"Jesus Christ! You scared me!" she hisses, and I can't help grinning.

"Sorry," I offer, but I'm more amused than anything else.

She's quiet for a moment, probably trying to calm down after I frightened her, and then she asks, "You're not checking up on me, are you?"

I raise a brow. "That makes me think you're thinking about doing something you're not supposed to."

She smiles just a little and turns her head away. "That night when you came here before because you wanted to…" She waves a hand vaguely. "Whatever you wanted to do. Were you one of the ravens in my tree?"

"Yeah. We were ordered to watch over you. Shadow knights protect the Eurydice. But we didn't know…" I take a seat beside her. My legs dangle off the edge of the roof, which elicits a growl from one of her hounds. It's clear they've made it their job to protect her. I wonder if they've always done that, but I assume the Order would have known if they did. Perhaps there's something about her being close to the site of the gates that has brought them out.

"And now? Why are you here now?" she asks.

"Truth is, I couldn't sleep," I admit.

I feel her eyes on me. "Me either."

Another moment of silence and then I ask, "How are you holding up?"

"I should be asking you that question." She peeks at me through her lashes.

"I have never really had to deal with death," I admit. "My grandparents all died either before I was born or

274

shortly after. Lily is the first person I've lost. I think I thought it would never happen to me. Stupid, I know."

"It's not stupid," she whispers.

When I look at her, her eyes have softened. It makes me feel like I can share my deepest secrets with her.

"It's weird, you know? Because the things that make me think of her are so unpredictable."

I opened the wound wide today by looking through pictures. Now every memory I ever shared with Lily is fresh in my mind—my thirteenth birthday party when she shoved cake in my face and pushed me in the pool. That time we went to the eighth grade dance together because we were best friends and we could. The day we stood side by side as we took our oaths as shadow knights-in-training and proceeded to duel each other. The dance she did when she won (I let her).

"I understand," she says, and for a moment, I think she might share something about how she experiences grief, but she's quiet.

Before, I'd only glimpsed her sorrow. Tonight, it tore free, and yet she remained upright, and I wonder when I'll be able to handle the weight. When will Lily's loss not feel like a stab to the gut?

After a moment, I get to my feet. "Can I show you something?" She looks wary, so I add, "It's not far. Promise."

She regards me for a moment. Her ever-changing eyes study me in a way that makes me feel like she's trying to figure out every word I never said. Then she slips her fingers into mine, and I shift into my Valryn form. Her eyes widen slightly as she watches me transform.

"I don't know if I'll ever get used to that."

I smile like an idiot, reading too much into her statement, but it suggests that she plans to stick around, and that makes my chest feel lighter. I scoop her up and take off. Her hounds scramble after us, baying their way through the streets, but soon we're flying over woods, their branches thick with leaves.

Anora's arms tighten around my neck, her cheek brushing my own. "You could have warned me!" she cries against my ear.

"There's no fun in that."

I keep my promise, and just as quickly as we take flight, we land. I set Anora on her feet in a grove of willow trees.

"Call off your hounds," I say.

"Why do you keep calling them mine?" she asks.

"Because they are clearly yours. They seem to want to protect you, just as the Valryn are here to support and train you."

The hounds bound out of the darkness, slipping through the trees like ghosts themselves. I only wish they moved like ghosts. They could wake the dead with all the noise they make. Good thing normal humans can't hear them.

I stay a few feet away from Anora when she turns to face them.

"I'm fine," she says, easily this time, no hesitancy in her voice.

They halt and sit, a low chorus of growls rumbling in disapproval.

"They don't seem to trust you," Anora says, tilting her head as she studies them.

"I think they know I don't like them," I say, preferring not to admit that I'm a little afraid of them.

"Why don't you like them?"

"Other than the fact that they smell like a pit of dead bodies, I was attacked by a dog when I was five." I press my finger to my lips where a faint scar remains from the attack. "I don't even really like to be around the nice ones."

She looks at my lips a lot longer than I expect, and I want to lean in and kiss her, but one of her hounds barks, making us jump.

"Go!" Anora commands, pointing to the woods. The hounds' growls turn into whimpers, and they sulk away, melding with the dark.

"Come on." I grab her hand. This is the most I have touched her since I met her, and I'm soaking up every bit of it—the feel of her fingers laced with mine, the heat of her skin, the faint blush that colors her cheeks almost every time she looks at me.

"What did you want to show me?" she asks as we step through a curtain of willow branches. "*Oh.*"

We're at the lake, far away from light and anything that might pollute the natural beauty of the landscape. The water is so calm and so dark, it mirrors the star-clustered sky. There's a faint breeze picking up the smell of roses. It envelops me and makes me shiver.

"It's beautiful here," she whispers.

*She's* beautiful.

The moonlight spills over her delicate nose and full lips. Her fingers are still twined with mine. It's strange, standing next to this girl who had, just hours earlier, wielded the Thread of Fate as her weapon.

"The lake is one of my favorite places. Being near the water, it helps me think."

"Do you come here often?"

"Yeah, mostly after patrol."

"How often do you patrol?"

"Most nights," I say with a sigh. "Well, except recently. I've been…excused."

She doesn't ask why. We are quiet for a moment, and then she says, "At Lily's memorial, you said you'd been training since you were twelve. Training to do what, exactly?"

"To fight and defend," I say. "Being anything other than a shadow knight really isn't an option when you're Valryn. It's just what you do. We take the oath at twelve, then we begin training. We learn our history and then our enemies. We learn to fight, and we learn weaponry. Our last year, we are given a patrol and tested. This is my last year. If the elites think I'm ready, I'll be ranked and given an assignment as a full-fledged shadow knight."

"I want to learn to control the thread," she says.

"We can teach you."

My fingers tighten around hers, but she lets go, and I feel the loss of her immediately.

"That would mean telling the Order I exist."

"Well, yeah…that's inevitable. You've seen Influence's work. You're the only one who can stop it."

She takes a breath.

"Anora." I whisper her name, coaxing her to look at me. "I'm not going to let anything happen to you."

She looks frustrated and fierce. I want to kiss her so badly. "I don't want to trust you."

"I know," I say, stepping closer. She doesn't move away. Instead, her head tilts back as she holds my gaze before her eyes fall to my lips, and I don't think as I press my mouth to hers. I'm not sure what I expected, but it isn't what this becomes—something heated and frantic. My hands settle on her hips, and I pull her to me as I kiss her before guiding her back until she rests against the trunk of the willow tree. Her hands press to my chest and then twine into my hair, and when I lean into her, she gasps. My tongue clashes with hers, and she is sweet and new and familiar. She fuels the heat in the bottom of my stomach.

I could drown in her and die happy.

I hitch her leg over my hip, wishing to be closer, and then images flash through my mind: heated kisses and bodies coming together, desperate to feel, and suddenly we're not close enough. I'm not kissing her enough, and there are too many layers between us.

And for some reason, Chase is in the back of my head. I think about how he gained her trust and broke her heart. How often he embraced her and kissed her. How many lies he told her.

And how am I different?

I'm not.

Because at the end of the day, she is human, and I am Valryn, and we can never be together.

I pull away from her, studying her beautiful face, wanting to memorize every part of her.

"Why are you looking at me like that?"

I blink, unsure of what she means. "Like what?"

"You look so intense," she says and touches my cheek. My eyes fall to her kiss-bruised lips.

"I don't mean to," I say, but the truth is, I'm struck by this feeling that she's the embodiment of my heart, and she's walking around outside my chest, and I'd do anything to protect her, no matter the cost.

Even if I can't be with her.

# CHAPTER THIRTY
## Shy and the Past Life

*By morning, I haven't slept a wink.*

I stayed out with Anora another hour until the sun peeked over the edge of the horizon. Then I returned her home with the promise that I'd see her in a few hours so we could retrace Lily's steps, but I'm already eager to be near her again.

We sat by the lake and talked about everything. She told me about what it was like living in New York with her poppa and the times he'd take her into the country to watch the stars.

"What about your dad?" I asked, because in all honesty, I was curious.

"He left when I was two," she says. "Mom says he was on drugs. It's probably good he didn't stick around. After, we moved in with Poppa."

I told her about what it was like growing up in this small town.

"My dad knows everyone," I said.

"He can't know everyone."

"You wanna bet? I can't do anything without it getting back to him. Right after I got my Jeep, Jacobi and I skipped school to go backroading. Dad found out, and I got grounded."

Sitting there beneath the willow trees, I never felt so…normal, and it was intoxicating.

As I come downstairs for breakfast, the television blares, interrupting my thoughts. It puts me on edge. This isn't like Mom. She despises technology, especially around mealtimes.

"Mom!" I call, reaching for the remote, about to turn the TV off, when I see what's being reported: the deaths of at least seventy-four people in a London apartment block set ablaze in the early hours of the morning. An anchor describes the horrific scene as trapped residents screamed from inside the building while the fire raged. The number of fatalities cannot be confirmed due to the scale of the building, but the death toll is expected to be high. There is no word on what caused the fire, but foul play isn't being ruled out.

"It's getting worse," Mom says from behind me. The segment on the fire feeds into a report on the unusual number of earthquakes we've experienced in the last year and an update on the mental health of the pilot who took down the plane in Switzerland.

*Influence, again.*

"It's getting stronger," I say.

And nothing—no one—is off-limits, as evidenced by the range of conflict it controls: Gage and Sean, the weather, the fire, the plane crash, and that's just the beginning. Influence knows no boundaries. It will stop at nothing to ensure complete chaos, utter darkness, a world where it consumes, feeding off the dead. Last night, I finally discovered our only hope for destroying it—the Eurydice.

*Anora Silby.*

She is flesh and blood and human and something *other*.

She used the Thread of Fate like it was an extension of her emotions, lashing out at the cercatore in anger, taking revenge. She was beautiful and strong, and I find I feel just as terrified as I do hopeful.

What if she *doesn't* choose our side?

What if she gives in to grief and, subsequently, Influence?

I push that thought away, but another, equally depressing thought replaces it—I have to tell the Order about Anora soon. Which means all the fantasies I had about spending every night after patrol talking to her by the lake are just that.

I turn the television off.

"Shy." Mom's voice is low. "Where were you?"

"What do you mean?"

She levels her gaze with mine. "When I came home last night, you weren't in your room. You weren't in this house."

"I was with Natalie and Jacobi," I say. It mostly isn't a lie.

She watches me for a long moment, long enough that I know I'm not fooling her.

"Elite Cain excused you from patrol, Shy," she says. I'm just relieved she assumes I was on patrol. "Have you stopped to consider he might have a very good reason?"

They certainly feel they have a good reason. "They never thought I was ready to be a tracker."

"Or maybe they're worried about your well-being, like I am."

I don't mean to laugh, but I can't help it, and Mom pales. "I really doubt that, Mom. The only thing Elite Cain or Dad will manage to say if I'm killed on patrol is that I should have trained harder."

"That is ridiculous, Shy." Her voice shakes, and I realize I shouldn't talk about my death in front of her. One of our own just died. This is as real for her as it is for me. "This is hard enough!"

"Don't you think I know that?" I snap. Mom flinches, and then her eyes harden. My only motivation for getting out of bed each day is finding Lily's killer and now Anora's coin, and it pisses me off to think the Order would imply she might have been suicidal. It pisses me off that half the school thinks it, that they will always communicate it that way—*Remember that girl? The one who killed herself on campus? It was because of Roundtable.*

Fuck Roundtable and fuck the Order.

I stare at my mom. Fighting her will do no good, and after a moment, I hang my head in my hands and scrub my face.

"I'm sorry."

She exhales and wraps her arms around me. I don't hug her back. When she pulls away, my phone vibrates in my pocket. I pull it out and find two messages:

The first one was just sent: I'm coming back. Meet me at June's tonight.

It's Roth.

I should text back, notifying him of Elite Cain's

decision to excuse me from my duties. I assume that also includes my obligation as Roth's errand boy.

I haven't had time to decide how I'm going to approach the subject of the Eurydice with him. There's no way to avoid it, since that's the only reason Roth's keeping me around. Still, I'd like to have the advantage walking into this and figure out why Roth wants Anora, because I'm still certain it isn't for the same reason the Order does.

The second message is from Jacobi and was sent around four in the morning when I was with Anora. All it says is When you wake up, come over. I found something.

Those words settle in my stomach like a stone.

"What's wrong, Shy?" Mom asks.

I shove my phone in my pocket and clear my throat. Suddenly, I have a headache. "Nothing. I'm…uh…just going to head to Jacobi's."

Mom studies me a moment. I bite back the instinct to ask when she decided she didn't trust what I say.

"Be safe," she says as I make my way to the door.

I head to Jacobi's and send a quick text when I'm in his driveway.

"Shy!"

I look up to see Jacobi's little sister, Lydia, run from the house.

"Hey, little one!" I climb out of my Jeep and capture her in a hug, spinning her around. She giggles, and I place her on her feet. She grabs onto my shirt and pulls.

"Come play with me!"

Jacobi saves me from disappointing my number one fan.

"He's not here to play, Lydia." Jacobi emerges from

284

the house, dressed in a pair of jeans and a school hoodie. "Mom says come inside."

"But—" she tries to argue.

"Not now, Lydia." Jacobi's annoyed, and Lydia turns her gaze to me.

"I'll come back soon," I assure her.

She narrows her eyes and puts her tiny hands on her hips. "Pinkie promise?"

I smile and hold out my pinkie. "Pinkie promise."

She accepts and bounces off toward the house, sticking her tongue out at Jacobi as she goes. He tries not to laugh as he climbs into the passenger side of my Jeep.

"She's smitten with you."

"She's five. She loves anyone who will play with her."

"I don't know, man. You have a gift."

I drive aimlessly, and for a while, neither one of us talk. I think we both miss this—the ease of a ride down country roads—but this sense of freedom doesn't last long, and soon the realities of the last few days creep back in. I need to tell him about my strange connection with Anora, but I'm not sure how to start.

"Roth's coming back," I say instead.

"What are you going to tell him?"

"I don't know. Some version of the truth. He won't believe me if I say I haven't found anything at all."

Jacobi moves uncomfortably in his seat.

"What?"

"Look, man," he says. "Just...be careful with this. Roth might be playing you."

He sounds like Natalie. After I was promoted to tracker, she'd told me to consider why Roth had asked me. The promotion couldn't be based on talent.

I scoff to myself. Even I don't believe that.

"Have you been talking to Natalie?" I ask.

"No…no…just…what if Roth already knows who the Eurydice is?"

I want to shoot this down, claim there is no way Roth's observant enough to guess. And the Order wouldn't likely be reporting on what's been happening here over the past few days. They try to keep Roth out of things as much as possible. But he may know something anyway. Why else would he have me searching for her? There's something in Jacobi's face that's telling me he knows more than he's letting on.

"What did you find?" I ask tightly, my impatience growing.

He looks away, opening and closing his mouth.

"Jacobi…"

"I did some research on the Eurydice…on her past lives. In the process, I discovered she's always incarnated with another person. A protector…a lover."

This is new information. I know a lot about the Eurydice's past lives, mostly how she was killed, which is super depressing.

I wait. He waits. My heart beats so hard in my chest, it hurts.

"I hacked the records." The records are a restricted part of the archive that track reincarnations from the beginning of time. There are a few missing pieces, strands Valryn have missed, but for the most part, they're comprehensive. And they're only accessible by the records keeper, a designated shadow knight who apparently has the ability to see and read the threads of Valryn past lives.

He continues. "I followed the threads."

I know what he's going to say before he continues, know it like I know the feel of my blades in my hands, but it still somehow manages to cut right through me.

"It's you."

He says it like he's delivering a death sentence, and from what we know about the Eurydice, I guess he sort of is.

"In your last incarnation, you were captured and murdered. Whoever did it sent the Eurydice clues to your whereabouts, and once she got there, they attacked her too."

So I'd been the trap that ended her life—and that would prevent her from incarnating for seventy years. All those annoying questions from Roth about whether I have a girlfriend make sense now. He's guessing I'll be attracted to the Eurydice. Problem is, he is right.

"The other lifetimes aren't any better," Jacobi says, his voice gritty and unfamiliar. Whatever he'd read must have been horrible. "I got suspicious when Roth appointed you as tracker. I mean...you're talented but..."

"No one gets promoted before training," I finish. "Roth knows."

We're silent for a long moment. Then Jacobi says, "At least you know why you like her so much now. You can just...stop."

"What?"

"Come on, Shy. She's still human. You can't have a relationship with her anyway."

I haven't been able to sort out my feelings for Anora, between the incessant pull and all the drama surrounding her, but being told I can't like her—*being told I can just stop*—infuriates me.

"I don't need a reminder from you, Jacobi. Natalie does that enough."

He looks a little pale. "All I'm saying is it's bad for both of you!"

I'm quiet for a moment. "Don't tell anyone what you found, Jacobi. Do you understand? The fewer people who know, the better."

He nods. "Okay, fair enough, but what are you going to do?"

"I don't know," I admit. "Keep it to myself. The longer Roth goes without realizing we've caught on to him, the better chance we have of figuring out what he really wants with the Eurydice."

I take a deep breath, mostly to ensure the next thing out of my mouth doesn't sound bitter. Maybe this is why I didn't want to tell Jacobi about the pull between me and Anora in the first place.

"Thanks, Jacobi."

# CHAPTER THIRTY-ONE
# Anora and the Queen's Ransom

**Shy picks me up at one that afternoon. When I shut the** door of his Jeep, he offers an easy smile, and yet I feel his tension. It corners me, stealing my breath, and I can't help asking, "Are you okay?"

He seems surprised by that question. "Yeah. Why?"

I shake my head, trying to form words. "I just thought I'd ask. You know, after last night."

His smile broadens, and it reaches deep into my heart. "I'm more than okay after last night."

I blush and look away, though I know he's not being completely honest. I can feel that he is troubled. Like tendrils of smoke, it surrounds me, caressing my skin. It makes me want to touch him, to feel his energy deep in my bones, because somehow, I know it will comfort us both.

The thought keeps slicing through me, sharp and startling. Something changed between us last night, and it didn't even start with the kiss. My dreams suddenly make more sense.

*I know his soul.*

He was my calm in all the chaos.

It was the last thing I wanted to feel for a shadow knight, especially after Chase.

Why do I feel this way now? Was it Samael's incense or seeing Shy in his Valryn form that created this connection? Both make me uneasy.

"What about you?" he asks.

"Huh?"

"What about you?" he says again. "Are you okay?"

"Yeah," I breathe. "Sleepy."

He smiles. "Me too."

He puts his Jeep in gear, and we start retracing Lily's steps. While Shy drives to our first location—a beach called Peter's Point—he explains Jacobi's plans to gain access to the security office to review footage from the day before Lily died.

"By gain access—"

"I mean he'll probably hack the server."

I shake my head. "How in the world did he learn how to do that?"

"You can find anything on the internet."

I still don't understand why we can't just go back to Samael and ask her to trace Lily's soul again. It seems like the fastest way to get what we need, and without wasting more precious time. Plus, I could ask Samael if she did anything to my brain last night when she lit that incense.

Peter's Point is uneventful. It's a small peninsula with several parking spaces for vehicles and boat trailers. A road curves around, offering access to various camping, fishing, and swimming areas.

Shy and I get out and walk. It's hard not to reach

for him. My body feels magnetized, and every time I bump him, an electric current shudders through me. Our fingers brush, but he never slips his hand into mine. I try to ignore the way it makes me feel—like this is all temporary, like it's an act.

Is it an act?

Did I fall for the same trap Chase set?

I shake my head. *A kiss doesn't mean you're together*, I remind myself.

"Did Lily like the lake too?" I ask.

"Not really. She hates—hated"—the correction makes my chest ache—"not being able to see her feet when she swam."

"Why do you think she was here?"

He's quiet a moment and then looks around, squinting against the bright sky.

"I think she was probably meeting her boyfriend here."

I can't help thinking about last night.

"You mean she was meeting him in secret?"

Shy doesn't say anything.

"Was there something wrong? Was she not allowed to date?"

"Something like that."

I know he's not telling me everything, and it's just another reminder of why I need to keep my wits about me when I'm around Shy. I slip my hand in the pocket of my jacket. Thane gave me the necklace Lily had given him. *You know, just in case you don't find anything tomorrow*, he'd said last night before dropping me off at my house.

And it's looking like we aren't.

Shy and I walk the loop around the lake and then get

back in the Jeep. After, we head to June's, and when Shy parks, I feel a resurgence of his anxiety.

"What's wrong?"

He looks at me quizzically, as if he can't figure out why I asked.

"Nothing." He pauses, rubbing his hands on his thighs. "I can go in alone if you don't wanna come in."

What is he hiding?

"No, I want to come in. I could use some coffee." I feel like the walking dead.

He nods once, and we head inside.

I'm familiar enough with June's now to expect several kids from Rayon High to be here, but I don't expect them to look up all at once when we enter. I don't like it, and I have a feeling it is because the star of the Nacoma Knight football team has arrived.

Shy places his hand on the small of my back, sending shivers up my spine, and guides me to the counter. We order two coffees, and after the transaction, Shy asks the barista, "Hey, man, did you happen to see Lily in here about a week ago?"

I assume Shy knows the barista. He's a short, round kid with glasses. His name tag says Jorden. "Maybe? She came in here a lot. It's hard to say."

"Was she talking to anyone you didn't recognize?"

"No, not really. Just the same people."

I watch Shy's face, and he raises a brow. "Like?"

"You know, Thane Treadway and her boyfriend, Jake."

"Thanks, man. Tell your dad I said hi."

"Sure."

Shy retrieves our coffees, but just as he turns around,

two muscly boys approach. One has locs that come to his shoulders, and one is trying to grow a mustache, but it just looks like he missed spots shaving.

"Savior," says the one with locs.

"Jeremy."

The kid's eyes slide to me, and he smiles, nodding. "This your girlfriend?"

"We're actually pretty busy at the moment, Jeremy," Shy says, handing me a coffee. He places his hand on the small of my back again and starts to guide me to the door.

"Sure, sure," Jeremy says and then, "Heard you were backing out of the queen's ransom."

"We're not backing out. It was cancelled," I snap, frustrated that this kid would bring up something so superficial in the face of Shy's loss.

The kid's smile widens. "Who said it was cancelled, princess?"

Shy pulls me closer and directs me toward the door. Outside, he walks me to the passenger side of the Jeep. He's never done this before. I want to tell him not to worry, I won't disappear getting into his car, but I watch his face as he closes the door, and I know what Jeremy said has made him mad.

"You okay?" I ask as he starts his Jeep.

"Yeah," he says. "Let's get you home. I bet you want a nap."

It's something I feel he should say with a smile, but he doesn't even look at me. He just backs out and heads to my house. Before I get out, he stops me.

"Anora," he says. "I don't trust Jeremy. Don't go outside tonight."

I start to laugh, but there's something in the way he's looking at me and the way he feels that makes me nod.

"Okay."

Shy reaches across the console, laces his fingers through my hair, and kisses me. Everything about it feels perfect and familiar, and I wish I could stay like this forever. That it could just be me and Shy and none of the other things that seem to be conspiring against us. He pulls away and looks at me as if I'm everything he ever wanted, but then his expression goes cold and he offers me a tight "Be careful."

———

It's dark when I decide to leave for the graveyard.

I clutch Thane's necklace in my palm, studying the pendant. It's a flat circle with the letters L and T carved into the silver. It must be some sort of friendship necklace. It feels wrong to have it in my possession—just as personal as my poppa's coin. I should have refused to take it, but I know why Thane gave it to me. Finding out what happened to Lily and her soul is more important. Besides, I'm partly responsible for this. I have to fix it if I can.

I take a deep breath, shove the necklace in my pocket, and climb out of my bedroom window. When my feet hit the ground, I come face-to-face with the hellhounds. They sit in a V, and I know they're prepared to follow me, but if I'm going to keep any Valryn from realizing I'm gone, they're going to have to stay put.

"Stay," I say.

They whimper in unison, which makes me feel strangely guilty, but they lie down, resting their heads on their paws.

After a moment, I extend my hand, and the one closest to me inches forward until his wet nose touches my fingers. I scratch his muzzle and whisper, "I'll be back. I promise."

I grab my bike and walk it to the road. I cast one last glance over my shoulder. The hounds watch me, but they haven't moved from their spots.

I head toward the graveyard. I can tell when I'm close because I can feel the energy of the dead growing stronger. I navigate the souls faster this time and approach the mausoleum. The door is still ajar, the lock broken from Thane's handiwork. I start up the stairs when someone grabs me from behind.

I react, slamming my head into their face. Whoever has a hold of me lets go.

"Fuck! I think she broke my nose."

I spin and run. The thread is trying to burrow out of my palm, reacting to my fear. *No*, I think. *You've caused so much trouble already.*

"Get her!" another voice calls.

Someone knocks into me, and I fall—straight through a dead person. Whatever they died from causes my head to spin, and as everything goes dark, I hear a third, familiar voice in the mix.

"Shit. Is she okay?"

*Jeremy.*

Then, nothing.

# CHAPTER THIRTY-TWO
# Shy and Roth's Return

*After I drop Anora off, I head home to sleep a little before* meeting Roth. The streetlights glare through my windshield as I drive to June's. As much as I'd have liked to disregard Roth's message, it doesn't do me any good. I'm already in deep with the Order. Ignoring the soon-to-be luminary will just get me in more trouble.

Luckily when I return, Jeremy is gone. I really don't like him, and not just because he's my rival. The kid's been trouble in the past. He was caught on security cameras spray-painting our gym. His anger has led to several penalties and suspensions for unsportsmanlike conduct and targeting. Most of all, I don't like that he knows Anora was selected as the princess for queen's ransom. It makes me think he's plotting something. I hope Anora listens to me about tonight.

I find Roth at a small, round table in the corner, bent over a latte with a foam art cat on the surface.

"I didn't know you were a cat person," I say.

Roth looks at me and smiles. "There're a lot of things you don't know about me, Savior."

"What do you want, Roth?"

He nods to the chair in front of him. "Sit down."

Begrudgingly, I take a seat.

"What's new?"

"What's new?" I echo his question. He poses it like we're friends.

"Yeah," he says, shrugging and then leaning forward. "You have a girlfriend yet?"

Instinctually, I want to flinch, because now I know why he asks—because it is inevitable that I'll attract the Eurydice. And I'm pretty sure it's inevitable that I will love her.

"Why are you so worried about my relationship status? You interested?"

He grins. "Now you're learning, Savior."

Roth focuses on his coffee for a moment. The foam barely resembles a cat anymore.

"My father died."

My whole body feels shaky at his news, and my stomach coils. Death usually inspires sympathy, but I feel fear. Before, Roth's commands could be blocked by the Order. Now as luminary, there is little he can't influence.

"When?"

"This morning."

"Does anyone know?"

"You," Roth says, still looking at his coffee.

"And…?"

"Just you."

"Why?" I don't understand. How am I the first to

know of Maximus's death? Why is Roth choosing to share this information with me?

"Everyone else will find out soon enough. Besides"—he shrugs—"we're friends, right?"

"We're not friends." He stares at me, his eyes darkening, and the most frustrating part is I can't tell if he's joking or under the delusion we're actually buddies. My skin starts to feel like it's made of wool, hot and itchy.

"We shouldn't suffer grief," he says, then slams his hand on the table. I tense, wondering if this will turn into a fight. "It should be our power to summon Charon, walk into Spirit, and take everyone back we've lost."

"It's not that simple, Roth. Even the Eurydice has limits."

"You don't think she would bring someone back to life if she could?" he asks.

I know she would. The real question is, does Roth?

"Is that why you want the Eurydice? To bring your father back?"

"My father?" He scoffs like that's the most ludicrous idea in the world. "No. Never him. I'd have no power then. I barely have any now."

There's too much wrong with that statement.

"Being luminary isn't powerful enough for you?"

"What is the luminary but a lawmaker? There's untapped potential among the Valryn. We could rule the passage to Spirit, offer life and death, all with the Eurydice's help."

And just like that, I understand why he wants her, and it makes me sick. He wants her as a power play to control who lives and dies. To force people to bargain with him, sacrifice for him. He wants to play god.

"The Order won't support that."

Roth chuckles. "Look, Savior, I'm not here to ask your opinion. I'm here to see if you've considered my offer."

The offer of commander—my dream.

I thought so often of what it would be like as commander. To stand beside my father, my arms banded with red thread, marking me as someone who's earned the title.

And there is the problem. I didn't earn anything.

"I thought you didn't ask twice," I say.

Roth's smile is barely there. He stands, takes a final drink from his mug, and says, "I hate to see wasted potential." Then he walks out the door with all the swagger of a man intent on ruling the world.

I sit in June's for a long time after Roth leaves, thinking about what he shared. Who exactly did he want to bring back from Spirit if not his father? Roth had hinted at his weakness tonight, and I want to learn more about it before he discovers mine.

As I stand to leave, Jacobi enters June's, and I know something's wrong.

"Shy, you're going to want to see this." Jacobi shoves his phone in my face. The Roundtable app is open. Anora's staring back at me. She's furious, her jaw set in a tight line. There's a caption at the bottom of the photos that reads: Queen's ransom is on. Come and get your princess, Nacoma Knight.

"No."

So many thoughts pass through my head at once. At

the forefront—can Anora contain her anger and keep the thread in check?

"Can you track her phone?"

"Already on it." He takes his phone back, and his fingers fly over the small keyboard. "It's at the cemetery."

"Call Nat. We're going to need help."

# CHAPTER THIRTY-THREE
## Anora and the Beginning of the End

*I recovered from the fall through the dead person pretty* quick but not fast enough, because when I come to, I'm in the back seat of a stranger's car. There are two boys in the front seat and one sitting beside me. He holds a bloodied, balled-up shirt to his nose. When he sees I'm awake, he scoots away, leaning against the door. I reach into my pocket for my phone so I can call someone—the police, Shy, my mom—but it's not there.

"Where's my phone?" I ask curtly.

"Glad you're awake, princess." The boy in the driver's seat, who I recognize as Jeremy, looks at me through his rearview mirror.

"I asked you a question."

"We left it behind in the cemetery. Don't worry. We have a picture of the gravestone where you can find it after this is over."

"Where am I?"

"Well, we can't exactly answer you. That would take all the fun out of it."

"You think this is fun?" I spit the words like venom.

"Well, yeah. Nacoma Knight might have cancelled queen's ransom, but as far as we're concerned, it's still on."

"I'm not a willing participant in your pissing contest, which means you've kidnapped me."

The boy in the passenger seat looks at Jeremy, and I can tell he's worried. "Man, I don't want to go to jail."

"No one's going to jail!" Jeremy says and then glares at me in the mirror. "Don't be fucking dramatic. Savior will be along to rescue you soon, and it'll all be over."

Jeremy takes a sharp turn onto a gravel road, driving like he's trying to lose someone. After a couple of miles, he turns off the dirt road and cuts through a space in the trees, coming to a hard stop. He exits the car, leaving the engine running, and walks around the front. As he does, the boy sitting beside me and the one sitting in the passenger seat turn and look at me.

The door opens, and Jeremy offers a mock bow. "We've arrived, princess."

I really, really want to send my thread right though his eye, but I keep my fist clenched and exit the car cautiously. There's another truck in the clearing. A boy stands in the headlights. He has black hair past his shoulders and skin like tanned leather. He's pretty and statuesque. I recognize him from the memorial: Jake Harjo.

He's staring at me like he recognizes me too. I wonder if he was paying more attention at the memorial than I thought.

"Jake," Jeremy says as he approaches. The two exchange a bro shake. "This is Anora. You gotta watch her. She's already broken Devon's nose. He wants to go home."

"Then we have something in common," I say curtly.

Jeremy and Jake both look at me, and Jeremy says, "You can go home. As soon as your boyfriend finds you."

Jeremy and the others drive away, and I'm left with Jake.

"I'm sorry about him," Jake says, and I jump. I didn't expect him to speak to me. His voice is pleasant, deep. "He's pretty terrible."

"Why did you agree to this if you think he's terrible?"

Jake kicks the ground. "If I didn't agree, he'd have someone else here waiting with you, and I...didn't want that."

"But...you don't know me."

"But I know you're important to Shy, and Shy was important to Lily." He takes a seat on his tailgate. "Sorry."

I don't say anything. I pace, hoping Shy shows up soon. It's getting colder.

Something rattles behind me, and I turn to see Jake reaching into a cooler.

"Capri Sun?" he asks, holding a pouch.

I look at him, wary, but accept the drink. I'm thirsty.

Jake reaches behind him again and produces a blanket. "Here. I can tell you're cold."

"You've done this before, haven't you?"

"Never this way," he says. "It's always been official. But yes."

I put the Capri Sun down and wrap the blanket around me, taking a seat beside him on the tailgate. It creaks with my weight. We're quiet for several moments when I say, "I saw you at Lily's memorial."

He nods.

"How long were you together?"

"Through the summer," he says. "She wasn't allowed to have a boyfriend. I was a secret, so we got creative with our hiding spots. It was exciting at first, and then one day, it wasn't. I didn't want to be a secret anymore. She…ended it before she…" He doesn't finish his sentence, but I know what he was going to say—before she killed herself. So he believes that. "I didn't know she was struggling."

She wasn't.

My heart aches for him, for his belief in her unhappiness and suicide, for his wish to be visible beside her. I wonder if he cares now, if he'd be her secret if it meant she were alive again. I wonder if I could do it—be someone's secret. Isn't that what I am now? In a different way?

"I think she was seeing someone else," he says at last.

"What?"

"I saw her with this kid from your school," he says. "He didn't look so nice. Kind of severe, and he smoked."

*Thane.*

"Were you following her?"

"No, they were out," he says. "*He* wasn't a secret. I know this sounds bad but…I can't help thinking he convinced her to…to…you know, kill herself."

I hold back the protest climbing up my throat.

"Why do you think that?"

"Because of the way he looked at her when she wasn't looking at him. Or I guess that he never looked at her at all. He was always glancing at his phone like it was more interesting than the girl beside him." He pauses a moment. "You know I found her at June's the day before she died?

She was sitting in the corner booth, crying her eyes out. I tried to talk to her, but she wouldn't say a word, wouldn't look at me. Finally, that kid—her new boyfriend or whatever—came along and told me he'd take it from here."

Thane never mentioned being with Lily the day before she died.

"What time were you there?" I ask.

Jake looks confused for a moment. "I don't know... late. Toward closing time."

The Capri Sun sours on my tongue.

I can't imagine Thane taking me to Samael, helping me search the train yard for clues, or spending time with the Valryn if he were involved in Lily's death. After all, it makes sense he would be with her. They were best friends. Still, was he the last person to see Lily as Lily?

We are silent for a few moments, and then I say, "His name is Thane. She wasn't dating him."

And when we're quiet again, I notice the world has gone quiet too. The hair on the back of my neck and arms stands up. Then there's a rustle in the trees beyond.

"It's probably your rescue party," he says and reaches for his flashlight. "All right, you found her."

But when he shines the light into the trees, it isn't the face of a student staring back. It's not even the face of a living person.

It's a dead person.

It's Lily.

"Oh no."

"What the hell..." Jake can see her. He pushes off the tailgate, starting forward, but I grab his arm, and he stops. Lily hasn't moved from the tree line. She stands as if she might implode, like a doll held up with string.

Her shoulders fall forward into her chest, and her knees buckle. She peers at us through a curtain of stringy hair, face streaked with dirt and bloody tears.

And the smell—decay and something chemical that burns my nose.

Souls don't smell.

"Is this some sort of sick joke?" Jake asks.

"Jake, get in your truck," I say.

But he's not listening, and he doesn't understand what he's looking at either.

"You aren't funny, Jeremy! Come out of there!"

Lily moans, lifts her head, and it lolls to the side. "Jake?" she whispers. Blood spills from her mouth. "Anora? What are you doing here? Together?"

I squeeze Jake's arm, hoping it's enough of a signal to keep him quiet.

"It's queen's ransom," I say, trying to swallow down my shock and think on my feet. "You found us."

She doesn't blink, and after a moment, her broken head falls forward, and she makes a gurgling sound.

"What…happened…to…me?"

I push Jake back and whisper, "Get in the truck, Jake."

Lily looks up. The yellow light from the flashlight casts shadows on her cheeks, making her features look sharp and demon-like.

"You."

"Lily." I spread my feet apart, the presence of the thread at the surface of my palm.

"*You!*"

The wind picks up, carrying her odor, moving the grass, so I don't notice the insects until they're climbing on my shoes and up my jeans. I yelp and brush them off.

"What the fuck!" Jake cries and starts an odd dance, hopping onto the bed of his pickup, but the insects reach him there too. Jake picks up a shovel and starts squishing them, which only enrages Lily.

The bugs take my focus away from the thread, and Lily catapults forward like a beast, knocking me to the ground. She holds me down, and her hands shove my palms into the earth, keeping the thread smothered, like she knows what I am.

Her fingernails dig into my arms, and at the breaking of my skin, the bugs ascend, mouths attaching to my body with a jab. My screams join Lily's shrieking.

And then Jake is over us, the shovel in hand.

"Jake! No!"

But it's too late. The shovel makes a loud thud as it comes into contact with Lily's head. Bones crunch, and she twists, vaulting toward Jake. He uses the shovel like a baseball bat and hits her again midflight. She goes down, but on bent legs, springing toward him again.

I scramble to my feet and brush the latched bugs off me in a fury, my body stinging. Lily launches at Jake, navigating the swing of his shovel. As soon as he hits the ground, his screams fill the air, then he is silent.

I reach for the flashlight in the grass and hold it up. Lily twists on Jake's chest, blood and bits of skin hanging from her mouth.

She's ready to come after me again when something lands in front of me. Crouching low, it rises, wings stretching. The moon illuminates a silver halo of hair.

*Shy.*

He draws both blades from the sheathes on his back.

"Lily," he says.

307

Another Valryn lands behind her—Jacobi. Lily, still crouching on Jake's chest, acts like an animal, caged. Her head bobs back and forth between the two Valryn, and her mouth pulls back into a fierce growl.

*They always come back wrong.*

Something grabs me from behind, and I scream, twisting to find Natalie.

"Come on!" she commands.

We rush to help Jake, but it's pointless. Lily tore his throat out.

I turn from him, vomiting in the grass, and when there's nothing else in my stomach, I dry heave.

"Get in the truck, Anora!" Natalie commands as she laces her arms under Jake's and drags him toward the pickup. I take several deep breaths before I join her, helping her settle Jake in the bed of the pickup.

"Get in the truck!" Her voice is raw, thick with fear.

I scramble into the passenger side, and Natalie slides into the driver's seat, starting the engine. The headlights flood the field, and she floors it. I fumble for my seat belt as we bounce over the pasture. Natalie makes a sharp turn, and the engine revs. She's moving faster, on a path straight for Shy, Jacobi, and Lily, locked in battle.

"What are you doing?" I scream.

At the last minute, Shy and Jacobi zoom into the air, and there's a bang as we hit Lily head-on.

Natalie brakes, throwing me painfully against the seat belt. She backs up, and the truck jolts as we roll over Lily's body again. Then we sit. The only sound is our breathing. I can't take my eyes off Lily's motionless body, heaped in the headlights of Jake's truck.

And then my passenger side door opens, and I scream.

"Shh!" Shy says, grabbing my wrists and holding them to his chest. I throw my arms around his neck, and he holds me close. He's sweaty and breathing hard, but his nearness comforts me. How did all this happen? How did we get here? Minutes ago, Jake was sitting beside me on the bed of his pickup, sharing his blanket and Capri Sun. Now he is dead in the back of his own pickup, and Lily lies on the ground in front of it.

I'm close to breaking. My chest shudders with unshed tears, and the only thing holding me together is Shy's embrace.

"Shy," Natalie says. "We have a problem."

We look up to find six pairs of eyes in the darkness, followed by a chorus of howls.

My hellhounds have found me.

Then Lily's corpse twitches.

"Dammit." Shy looks at me. "Stay."

When he shuts the door, Lily is on her feet again, and the hounds have come into the ring of light.

"W-why won't she die?"

"Because she's already dead," Natalie says. "Her soul's just been resurrected, which gives her the ability to fight but none of her humanity."

*Lily's murderer has struck again.*

"Why does he keep fighting her? If he can't kill her?"

"Because all we can do is subdue her until the Order arrives."

"But—" As much as I want this to end, I can't be here when the Order arrives.

"Stay," Natalie says and gets out of the cab. She joins Shy and Jacobi, creating a triangle around Lily.

All that talk about why resurrection is illegal makes

sense to me now. Surely Thane wouldn't want his mother back like this? This isn't even a shell of what Lily used to be. This is something different, a monster, more animalistic than my hellhounds.

Lily bares her teeth and lashes out. All three Valryn jump back and rise off the ground, their wings spread wide. That's when my hounds descend upon Lily. The sounds filling the air are horrific—a mix of growls and howls and whining. Their teeth clash and snap, biting down on Lily's limbs, tearing into her dead flesh, and yet she gives as much as she takes, clawing at my hounds and biting into their flesh.

Then Lily jumps, moving above the hounds' heads. She grabs onto one of Jacobi's wings and jerks him to the ground. He lands headfirst and is still. I'm out of the car in an instant, running toward Jacobi. He can't end up like Jake. I won't let that happen. I have to end this.

"Jacobi!"

I grab the shovel, discarded in the grass, and run for them. Lily twists toward me, and I hit her with the shovel. She doesn't budge but prepares to leap at me, so I call the only defense I have—the thread.

Shy calls after me. "Anora! No!"

The thread cuts through the air toward Lily. She dodges it, and I reel it back in as she charges for me. Her weight knocks the breath out of me, but my palm faces her chest as we go down, and the thread breaks through her back. As it consumes, I expect her soul to transform into a coin and land on my chest.

But something different happens as I capture this soul. As the thread wraps in and out of her body, it begins to break apart, and gold flecks fall into my eyes, mouth, and hair. It's pieces of the coin that are supposed to contain her soul.

When it's over, Lily lies on top of me, dead weight and decay. I scream, pushing against her until I free myself of her bulk and scramble away. Then I sit, shaking, staring at her corpse. What have I done to her soul? Why did the thread refuse to create a coin? What does that mean for Lily?

My skin crawls, covered in bug bites and bits of coin dust. I brush at myself frantically, wanting to remove all traces of this night.

"If you don't want the Order to find her, you had better get her out of here," Natalie says. Shy hesitates, going for Jacobi, but Natalie shoos him away. "Don't worry. I'll check on Jacobi."

"Come on," Shy says, gathering me into his arms and launching into the air.

I can't breathe right, and I keep shivering and passing my hands over my face and arms, like I walked through a spiderweb and can still feel the phantom of their silk on my skin.

"Stop moving," Shy warns, and I freeze, mostly at the tone of his voice. There's an edge to it. Part of it inspired by this night, part of it directed at me. Then he adds softly, "I don't want to drop you."

He doesn't look at me as he speaks, and the only thing I see from this angle is his jaw and sharp cheekbones.

"I'm sorry I didn't find you in time," he says and then looks over his shoulder.

He descends, landing in another field, setting me on my feet. What did he see that made him stop? I start to turn my head to the sky, but he prevents me, placing his hands on either side of my face.

"Anora, this is important. You are going to be taken by the Order. I am sorry I can't keep you from them, but I won't be far away."

He leans forward and kisses my forehead. The move is intimate and steals my breath.

Then he's torn from me, pulled away by a very tall and very angry shadow knight who looks just like him—his father.

"No!" Shy struggles but is held back by the larger version of himself, and there's a prick in my neck and a gush of liquid that feels like fire rushing into my veins. I sway and am caught, held in the arms of an angel haloed in black wings.

# CHAPTER THIRTY-FOUR
## Shy and the Aftermath

*I've seen the inside of Elite Cain's office more times in the* last month than I have since I took my oath to become a shadow knight-in-training at twelve. The marble from the wall presses into my skin, and my arms sting where Lily's nails pierced it.

I am in so much trouble.

We all are—me, Natalie, Jacobi, and he's not even conscious.

An innocent kid died tonight, and Lily's corpse was reanimated with her soul—a soul that was subsequently shattered. Anora was trying to help, but her ignorance about her powers means Lily is tethered to this world in *pieces*, pieces that can never be reclaimed. Someone's going to have to tell Lily's father. How many people in the world have to experience the death of their daughter twice? My chest hurts.

I sag against the cold marble. It's an awkward angle, but I don't care, because it's the only thing I feel at the moment, and it's the only thing grounding me to this spot.

Beside me, Natalie leans forward, elbows on her knees. Her eyes glisten. I haven't seen her cry often, but tonight did us all in. There are things we've seen on our patrols—monsters and soul stealing and dead bodies—but never the horror of this night, and we weren't trained enough to handle any of it. We fumbled about like idiots trying to take down a resurrected Valryn. Lily had the memory of her training from her time as a knight-in-training but she had none of the humanity.

Jacobi was taken to the infirmary barely breathing. He looked dead.

*Please, Charon, don't take another one of my friends.*

Elite Cain bangs into his office, throwing open the doors. Natalie and I get to our feet and salute.

"Probation!" he yells. "All of you, including the unconscious one! Probation until I say otherwise, and I'll tell you it isn't looking like you'll get off in the next year."

I try not to flinch. I've never seen Elite Cain angry.

"What the hell were you all thinking? As soon as you saw the situation, you should have alerted your superiors. None of you were equipped to handle this. Now we have a dead kid, and I have to tell Commander Martin his daughter will never know Spirit. Careless!"

We keep our heads bowed, feeling lower than low. Worse, we both know he's right.

God, my chest *hurts*. It's like it's split in two—one side pounds with anxiety, the other with fear.

"Who wants to tell me what happened first?" Cain asks, but it's not a question; it's a demand.

It's not often I'm unable to speak, but I'm ashamed and afraid. I keep my jaw pressed tight so my chin doesn't tremble.

"We learned Anora Silby was kidnapped. When we finally found her, she was fighting a resurrected Lily," Natalie says. "The boy—Jake—was already dead. We just wanted to get Anora out of there."

"Was that before or after you learned she was the Eurydice?"

Neither of us speak. As far as Elite Cain is concerned, we all learned Anora was the Eurydice tonight. If he finds out it happened any other way, probation could turn into suspension, and I don't think Anora's safe among the Order with Roth as luminary.

"Before tonight, I'd have said you were both the best of your class. Now, I realize my mistake. You have so much to learn. I'm releasing you to your parents. Go."

Our gazes shift toward the door where both of our fathers stand still and at attention. Natalie moves first; her dad gestures to have her exit in front of him. Then I'm left under my father's cold gaze.

"Infirmary," he says.

The medic cleans and bandages the scratches on my arm and a set on my face I didn't notice until she starts spraying my cheek with sanitizer. Dad has stepped out to make a phone call. I can hear the timbre of his voice through the curtain. He's talking to Mom, describing the scene—one human dead, Jacobi injured and unconscious, Natalie and I bruised up but okay, and Anora. He doesn't mention our punishments, just says we're all okay. While he doesn't indicate when he'll be home, he does say in the sincerest voice that he loves her.

315

As the call ends, the medic finishes up and switches places with my father. His presence fills the small, curtained compartment to bursting.

Before, I always thought my father never gave me the benefit of the doubt, but now I feel like maybe he's been right all along. Maybe I am just an idiot.

"How long have you known Anora Silby was the Eurydice?" he asks.

I look at my wrist, pretending to read the time, and say, "Three hours."

"Don't you dare lie to me," he says, and the threat in his voice makes me cold.

I grind my teeth together so hard, my jaw hurts. "For certain? A day."

"How long have you had suspicions?"

"Since Vera disappeared. I just…I don't trust Roth."

"Trusting Roth has nothing to do with your job. Your orders are orders, and you obey them, even if you disagree." He's given me this lecture before. I hated it then, and as if sensing my protest, he closes the distance between us, hissing, "This is important, Shy. Do you remember what I told you?"

*You might think you're standing up for something grand, but when you do it wrong, it's not you who will suffer for your actions; it's the people you love.*

I remember.

And he is right. I lost Lily, and she suffered, again and again. Lily is dead in a way that means she is never, ever coming back—not through reincarnation even. It feels like someone's smashing my chest with a sledgehammer. Shame and embarrassment are there too, undercurrents heating my skin.

"Think for a moment what we could have helped prevent if only you'd have told us about Anora."

*Nothing!* I want to scream at him. You could have prevented *nothing* because Anora's not the one who killed Lily, and she's not the one who resurrected her. But I don't want to get into that with him. Not with Roth having his own agenda. If he can't control Anora, he may try to find someone else to bring back the dead.

"What could you have prevented?" I ask bitterly, pushing myself off the gurney. "What could you have done better?"

For a moment, I hate him, and I want to make him feel it.

"I'm never good enough for you. I'm not good enough for anyone. The only reason Roth chose to promote me to tracker is because of Anora. I know you didn't think I was ready. Well, guess what, you were right. I screwed up."

"You're wrong," my dad says. His voice settles on me like snow, making me shiver.

"Who are you to tell me I'm wrong? What have you done to prove me otherwise? Have you been home the last two months? When was the last time you sat down to dinner with me and Mom? You don't know? I do—it was August!"

"I don't know where all this sudden defiance is coming from. There are things I have to do here, Shy. Things you don't understand right now—"

"Try me, Dad!" I yell and then beg, "Trust me."

But he doesn't. He doesn't say a word. Just looks at me with those eyes—*my eyes*. I hate it.

"Forget this."

317

As I go to leave, he says, "I do trust you, and I believed you were ready long before you were promoted, but don't think for a second I didn't know what Roth was doing when he chose you to track the Eurydice."

I stop and face him.

"What are you saying?"

Dad stares for a moment, as if trying to communicate wordlessly. Funny, I know what he's saying: *You know exactly what I'm talking about.* "We know Jacobi hacks the archive, Shy. We know he entered the records. I'm assuming he told you what he found."

He's talking about my and Anora's past lives.

"You knew and you didn't tell me?"

My father puts his hands up, as if he's afraid this will send me over the edge, and for a moment, I think it might, but instead, I realize I want someone to know. Someone who isn't Jacobi or Natalie. Someone like my dad. Because, for Charon's sake...I can't do this on my own.

"My sixteen-year-old son's...*lover*...from a past life reincarnated and just so happens to be the Eurydice."

*Never mind. This is the worst. I take it back—I don't want him to know anything.*

"What do you expect from me?" my father continues. "I knew what Roth would do when he found out, and I was right. You think I wanted my spoiled superior to use my son?"

"But...you could have told me!"

Or at least tried to warn me in subtle ways. Instead, all he does is make me feel inferior and keep me from my assignments...

*Oh.*

318

We stare at each other for a long moment. Then he says, "I guess it was too much to hope you'd keep your distance from the Eurydice, given she's a human and you're Valryn."

There it is. I should have expected the blow. I should have been prepared for how bad it hurts, but I'm not.

Dad continues, "I understand why you have the instinct to protect her."

But he doesn't. Not really. Because I don't.

"Forget that this is against the Order. What could you possibly know about someone you met less than two weeks ago?"

It's not like I'm marrying her. I'm *learning* her. I might not know the material things—roses or lilies or no flowers at all, favorite music, movies, or books—but I know she loves the stars and wants to be an astrophysicist, all inspired by the love she has for her poppa. I know she grieves for him deeply, that if she lost anyone else, she would shatter. I want to protect her from that, because Anora might be the Eurydice, but she grew up human and is human, and even Valryn cannot escape pain.

Greater things connect us—horror and struggle and fear and love. I might never learn her in other ways, but I'll know her in the ways that count.

"Dad...I can't have this conversation right now."

He doesn't press, and I'm relieved. I feel like we have a truce, and I don't want it to end so soon, even knowing at some point, he's going to want to have that conversation with me. The one where he tells me I can't see Anora.

Right now, I'm hoping he won't tell me that.

"Where is she?"

"She'll go before the Order soon."

"Dad, she has a life outside this place, outside being the Eurydice. Keeping her here would be kidnapping her—"

Dad reaches out, and I flinch. He hesitates but decides to place his hand on my shoulder anyway.

"Mistrusting one part of the Order doesn't mean you should mistrust all of it."

"Then let the Order prove me wrong."

# CHAPTER THIRTY-FIVE
# Anora and the Order

*I wake up stuffed inside covers. Blankets are tucked under* my shoulders, arms, and legs. The feel of them against my skin is like being restrained. I shove them aside, thrashing to release my limbs. Once I'm free, I lie there breathing hard. My mind picks up where it left off before everything went dark—Lily coming to life and feral, Jake lifeless, looking like something out of a horror movie, Jacobi landing on his head, unmoving, and Shy, Natalie, the hellhounds, all arriving too late.

Because even after they were all assembled, they couldn't kill Lily.

So I did.

But at what price?

Lily's soul shattered.

*That's what happens when you use powers you don't understand.* Thane's words echo in my mind. Why does he have to be right all the time?

I start to clench my fist, but pain prevents me. When

I look at my hand, I find something metal molded around my palm. Prongs dig into the top of my hand, like a diamond set in a mount, except there's nothing pretty about this contraption.

Hysterical, I sit up, trying to pry the thing from my hand, but I only make it worse. The prongs dig into my skin and bleed. A wave of dizziness washes over me, and I stop, focusing instead on my cage.

I can see nothing, save a large glass door that opens into a hallway flooded with sterile light. I start to rise from the bed and go to it when a voice erupts from the darkness.

"Comfortable?"

I spin to face the sound.

"Who the hell are you?" I demand.

A laugh and then lights. Dim, ugly lights that illuminate the cell and a creature—a Valryn with a pretty face, dark eyes, and a devastating, infuriating smile. His body is long and lean, and his muscles are contoured by his skin-tight suit. Weapons are arranged strategically on his body: a knife at his thigh, blades crisscrossed on his back. He's haloed by large, iridescent-black wings.

"Forgive me, Eurydice. I did not introduce myself." He places his hand to his chest. "I am Luminary Roth DuPont, the head of the Order."

I just stare at him. That name means nothing.

"I'm disappointed," he says. "Savior hasn't told you about me?"

"Guess he didn't think you were worth mentioning."

Roth offers a charming smile, and I hate it. "Shy didn't think you were worth mentioning either. But I think you and I understand things of value. Things like this." He holds up my necklace, and I go rigid.

My grandfather's coin spins, glinting under the lights. In this sterile room, it's magic. I reach for it, but Roth pulls back, and the coin thuds against his chest. A surge of anger rushes through me, that he possesses something so important to me. That he would dare hold it that close to *his* heart.

"If truth be told, you have nothing to fear from the Order. They think you should be trained, and I agree. You are more useful once you reach your potential. It is likely you'll leave here tonight having lost nothing of real value—with the exception of this."

I watch my coin, not Roth.

"You can't keep that. I won't let you," I say through gritted teeth.

"You won't let me?" He laughs, raising his brows, and then glances at my hand. "What are you going to do? Steal my soul?"

Instinctively, I curl my fingers into fists, but the metal claw digs into my skin, making me flinch.

"You can hardly blame me, Eurydice. I can't chance you running off again. And while the Order's under the impression they can appoint a shadow knight to patrol, we know you're not above killing one of us."

Roth stands and starts toward the door with my poppa's coin. I want to attack him, and I might have had I not been in Valryn custody. Chances are, assaulting the person in charge won't lead to my freedom, and then I will be stuck here and still not have my coin back.

Roth pauses at the door. "Just remember, Eurydice, the Order may grant you freedom, but you are under my control."

As soon as he's gone, I search my cell for a weapon.

The bed is bolted to the ground and solid metal. There is nothing on the walls, and even the small bathroom is empty. The shower doesn't even have a curtain, and there are no towels. I'm still looking when the door to my cell opens, and a shadow knight steps through.

It's Shy's father.

"My name is Bastian," he says. "I've come to collect you for the Order."

I stiffen.

"I want my mom," I say.

"You will see her soon enough," he replies. "We do not plan to keep you here."

"How can I trust you?"

"You don't have to trust us now," Bastian says. "You can trust us later, when you're home safe."

I know I'm not getting out of here without going before the Order, so I relent and leave with Bastian. He walks a step or two behind me. Now and then, he'll call out an order—left, turn right here, and then stop when we arrive at a stainless-steel elevator. We ride to the fourteenth floor.

"Where am I?"

"You are at the Compound." Bastian doesn't look at me as he speaks. "The fortress of the Valryn."

If I were in another situation, I might laugh at his use of the word *fortress*, but in the last few days, I've discovered nearly everyone I've met is a shape-shifter, the other half are death-speakers, and I'm some sort of modern ferryman. I am in no place to critique vocabulary.

I'm led to a room with a large, oblong table, already crowded with a mix of flesh-and-blood Valryn and holograms. These must be the elites Shy talked about, the leaders of the Valryn. Among them is Roth, who makes eye contact with me; his fingers play with a chain at his neck. My poppa's coin—a reminder of the power he has over me.

Bastian directs me to a seat at the head of the table. My back is to a large, dark window. If that isn't enough to make me uncomfortable, everyone is looking at me, assessing, wondering if I'm capable of the accusations leveled against me. I study them too. Some are surprised and others hostile. No one appears friendly, not even the most familiar face among them. When my eyes land on him, I can't stop myself from blurting, "Mr. Val? *You're* Valryn?"

He is reactionless except for a single raised brow, as if he wants to be amused but his face forgot how.

"Yes, Miss Silby," he says. "I'm equally surprised *you're* the Eurydice."

My face heats, and for some reason, I find myself wanting to prove Mr. Val wrong, but not just him—all these people.

Roth clears his throat and stands.

"You've all been briefed on tonight's events, along with the disappearance of soul Vera Bennet and the deaths of Chase Lockwood and Lily Martin for which the Eurydice is responsible," he says.

I have the urge to protest—just what exactly have they been told? But I bite my tongue—I'll have my chance...I hope.

"It is my opinion that Anora Silby is a danger to herself and others," Roth continues.

I set my teeth so hard, my jaw hurts, and my hands, resting on the arms of the too-large chair, clench, even the one caught in the claw.

"And what evidence have you to present, Luminary?" the elite sitting closest to me asks.

*Yes, what evidence? I want to hear it too.*

"You already know the story, Elite Cain," says another Valryn. "Chase Lockwood's soul was stolen right from his body—we have proof of that. Is that not evidence enough?"

"It is a start, Elite Ezekiel," says Elite Cain. "But overall, it proves nothing."

"Eurydice," says a white-haired woman who introduced herself as Elite Gwen. "Did you know Chase Lockwood?"

"My *name* is Anora."

"Actually, your name is Lyra, isn't it?" Elite Cain asks, pressing something on the screen in front of him. A hologram pops up at the center of the table, projecting from a tiny box. There, a photo from my previous school appears. "You started going by your middle name when you moved here. Is that because you were on the run, Eurydice?"

"I started going by my middle name for anonymity," I say, trying to keep my voice as even as possible. It's hard not to betray how angry I am, how hostile I wish to be, with Roth's gaze searing into me. "There were a lot of rumors I was involved in Chase's death at my school. None could be proven, but people still talk. *Mom* didn't want that to follow me here."

I emphasize Mom. I want these people to know I have someone waiting for me at home.

"Would those rumors happen to have any truth, Eurydice?"

"You tell me what the evidence says."

The elites around the table exchange glances. I can guess a few words they might use to describe me: *know-it-all*, *stubborn*, *entitled*, but I don't care. I wasn't born in their world, I was forced into it, and Chase Lockwood started the whole thing.

"This is what makes her dangerous!" Elite Ezekiel exclaims. "It's possible more have died by her hand and we have no way of knowing! She should be kept under constant supervision, the thread contained!"

My heart seizes. Contained? Do they mean to make me wear this claw forever? They can't!

"At what cost?" another elite says. "Charon has already dissolved the gates. He has hellhounds pacing outside our walls, apparently assigned to protect the Eurydice. His orders are clear: we support the Eurydice, not imprison her."

"Someone has to think about the souls!" Elite Ezekiel argues. "Charon won't summon the gates for one hundred and fifty dead in a plane crash, and this *girl* has taken life!"

"That has yet to be proven," Elite Cain reminds them.

Suddenly, all eyes are on me again.

"Eurydice," Elite Gwen says. "If Lockwood attacked you, we need to hear it."

I recognize this tactic, know she is playing good cop, and yet I cave, swearing to God or Charon or whoever in the hell is responsible for life on earth that I will never tell this story again.

I begin the same way I began when I told Shy and the others, except I use more details. Use the words he used to lead me into his snare—beautiful and toxic and breathtaking. I tell of warm kisses and heated touches that spun me in silk. I tell of the cold press of his blade that drew blood and tarnished his web forever.

"I used the only weapon I had," I say. "The thread."

There is silence for a very long time, and then Elite Cain speaks. "In the matter of Chase Lockwood's death, does the Order find the Eurydice at fault?"

Everyone raises their hands, and my stomach falls straight to my toes.

Elite Cain says, "As far as I'm concerned, the Eurydice killed Chase Lockwood in self-defense. Her actions, while dangerous, were appropriate, and she used the only weapon she had against a nearly fully trained shadow knight. All in agreement of this statement…"

A little over half the Order raises their hands.

"With respect, Elite Cain," says Roth. "Chase Lockwood swore an oath to the shadow knights and had authority to bring her in."

"That would be correct if Chase had notified the Order once he discovered she was the Eurydice. As far as we understand, he was working alone," Elite Cain states.

Roth crosses his arms. "What of Lily Martin, then?"

Hearing Lily's name wasn't easy before. It's harder now.

"Eurydice, if you captured Vera's soul, you were just doing your job," Gwen says.

Her good cop routine will only go so far. There are people here who want me under their thumb, and admitting I got angry and captured Vera's soul in a coin I subsequently lost will only give those in favor of my imprisonment fuel for their argument.

"I wasn't doing my job," I say. "Because I haven't accepted your offer."

Elite Ezekiel laughs. "This isn't an offer of employment, Eurydice. You cannot refuse."

"I am not Valryn. You can't tell me what to do."

"But you see the dead, you speak to them, and by all accounts, controlling the Thread of Fate can be considered death magic. By definition, you are a death-speaker and fall under our jurisdiction."

"So you would treat me like an enemy?"

"Death-speakers are not our enemies, Eurydice, *unless* they are doing something wrong, like stealing souls."

I glare at him. "I didn't steal Lily's soul, and I didn't resurrect her."

"We're fully aware you didn't resurrect her, Eurydice," Elite Cain says.

"You are?" I ask, a little surprised.

"Yes, even you have limits. Giving life, no matter how crude, is not a power you possess. Charon forbids it. Whoever gave Lily's corpse life did so with power from the occult. We believe whoever reanimated Lily was in possession of a resurrection coin you made." He is quiet as he lets the information sink in, and then he asks, "Where are the coins, Eurydice?"

"What?"

"You captured Chase's and Vera's souls. Where are the coins?"

"Why do you want them?" I ask.

He ignores my question. "We know you haven't opened the gates since your incarnation here on earth. Which means the coins are either in your possession or…"

"I lost them," I lie quickly. I can't let them know

329

I still have Chase's coin—or a whole box full at home under my bed. I glance at Roth, who smiles gleefully.

The silence that follows my admission slices through me. What have I done? For some reason, I repeat myself, as if I haven't driven the point home. "I lost them."

"You...*lost* them?"

"Whoever has them...killed and resurrected Lily."

More silence. Elite Cain's gaze is hard as he studies me, and I get the sense he doesn't believe me.

"And you expect this child to navigate her duties alone?" Elite Ezekiel explodes. "Clearly she has demonstrated she cannot be trusted outside the walls of the Compound."

"She will not be alone. Besides, we cannot keep a sixteen-year-old girl hostage, Elite Ezekiel," says Gwen.

I have suddenly become invisible. Part of me wonders if I can sneak away, but as I glance around the table, I find Mr. Val watching me—the only elite paying attention.

"Her lack of responsibility for something so important should be punished," said Elite Ezekiel.

"And yet it is the Order's duty to find, train, and support the Eurydice." Gwen's voice rises above the rest. "We did none of those things. Can she be blamed for decisions made untrained?"

Elite Ezekiel definitely thinks so.

"Eurydice," Elite Cain says in the gentlest voice he can muster. "We are offering you training and protection. We wish to teach you how to use your powers. If you let us, we will be your support."

"Not all of you seem to be in agreement," I say, glaring at Elite Ezekiel.

"We are a democracy, Eurydice. Majority rules," says Elite Gwen.

And as she speaks, more than half the room raises their hand in agreement.

Elite Cain says, "The Order will move forward as planned and train you. In exchange, you will fulfill your duty and lead lost souls into Spirit, so we may offset the power of Influence. Think of it as…redemption for the coins you lost."

*I can't lead anything into Spirit*, I want to say. I don't know how to summon the gates, but I keep my mouth shut just in case they all decide in the next few seconds that setting me free is too risky. Let them think they have me now.

"This Council is dismissed," Elite Cain says. "Commander Savior, please escort the Eurydice to the infirmary."

Shy's father stands in the small room where a medic removes the claw from my hand. I wince as the prongs come free. The medic treats the four punctures and then binds my hand. Bastian is quiet; the only question he directs toward me is about the bites all over my skin. When I tell him Lily was able to summon the bugs, his brows rise in surprise.

I think about how this night started—all I wanted to do was track Lily's soul. Now I'm in the Order's custody. Of all the things that upset me the most, it isn't the interrogation or that I'll now fill the role as Eurydice. It's that Roth has my poppa's coin and thinks to use it as a snare to keep me in Rayon.

I will get my coin back, one way or the other, but first, I have to find my lost coin and Lily's murderer.

Once the medic is through, I follow Bastian out of the infirmary. Before he exits into the waiting room, he pauses at the door.

"Before you leave, your trainer would like to speak with you."

"My trainer?"

Shadow knights don't mess around. The fact that they already have someone assigned to teach me makes me think they decided this a long time ago.

"Shall I introduce you?"

I get the feeling it is one of those rhetorical questions I can't refuse, so I nod.

He pushes through the door and steps out of the way, and I'm face-to-face with Mr. Val.

"Oh no. *You're* my trainer?"

# CHAPTER THIRTY-SIX
## Shy and the Ritual Site

*I take Anora home after the Order is finished questioning* her. Now and then, I catch a glimpse of reddish-brown fur in the tree line. Anora's hellhounds are following. I don't think she notices as she seethes in my passenger seat, sitting as far away from me as possible. In response, I keep one of my hands clutched around the steering wheel of my Jeep and the other pressed against my chest where the thread connects us across lifetimes. It pinches and pulls. The feeling isn't as severe as when she was in trouble, but it's not the normal level of anxiety I'm used to with her. I want to snap at her, tell her to stop—but stop what? Feeling?

I can't blame her for feeling right now—anger, fear, betrayal.

The Order found a way to make the Eurydice compliant. She will pay for her sins by serving them. They'd done exactly what she'd feared from the beginning— taken away her choice.

"Stop doing that!" she snaps at me, finally breaking the silence straining between us.

I jerk. I don't like that she startled me. It means I'm not paying as much attention as I need to be, but how can I help it? I can't shake her discomfort, and the cab of my Jeep is small and compact, thick with all her feelings and her smell. There are a million other things I'd prefer to do in this car rather than fight with her.

"What?"

"You keep rubbing your chest, and it's making a noise, and it's driving me crazy."

I crush my fingers together and drop my hand, leaving it in a fist on my thigh. She watches it for a moment, and I think she might touch me, ease the tension and frustration, but she doesn't.

That only increases my irritation.

"You do that a lot, you know," she says.

"What?"

"Rub your chest."

*Because you're always worried*, I want to snap.

"Do you have a rash?"

"I don't have a rash." At this point, I can't tell if she's joking with me, because everything she says comes out between gritted teeth and sounds hostile.

She doesn't say anything for a long moment.

"What is Mr. Val in your society? Why was he chosen as my trainer?" she asks.

"He chose to train you," I say. "Elites are the best among the Valryn."

"And elites make the rules," she says. It's not a question. "Rules like humans and Valryn can't be together."

"Yes." I pause, and now my insides feel twisted. "Who told you?"

"I guessed," she says. "Jake said he was a secret. Why is that a rule?"

"Because our DNA—what makes you up and what makes me up—doesn't mesh. We make monsters. *Abominations.*"

She shivers, and suddenly I wish I had a better way to explain this, but I don't. I bite down hard on the inside of my cheek, hoping she doesn't ask another question about abominations. This conversation won't do anything to improve her opinion of me—or us.

"What happens to abominations?"

"A number of things," I say, pausing so long, I'm not even sure I'll finish explaining. "Sometimes they are killed. It depends on the severity of their deformity… if they can live with it. Some are placed in servitude for Compounds across the nation."

I'm really just repeating something I've been told.

"Have you ever met an abomination?"

"No."

"So you don't know what one looks like? If they are actually… 'deformed' as you say."

I don't, and I say so.

"So how do you know there's any truth to the claim that human and Valryn DNA doesn't mix?"

I can't answer that either.

"You obey this rule? Without evidence to support its truth?" she asks.

I open my mouth because I want to tell her no, I don't obey that rule, because if she could hear the things

335

I think about her, she'd know I don't really care that she's human, but no words come out.

"Why did you kiss me?" she asks, not looking at me.

I flex my fingers, crushing them into a fist. "Because...I wanted to."

And I don't regret it.

Even as I reiterate, much to my body's complete disagreement, "Nothing good comes from a human and Valryn relationship."

When we arrive at Anora's house, she sits up in her seat. "Oh no."

Her mom is outside on the porch, standing with her arms crossed. Her face is all harsh lines. It's obvious she's angry, and she has plenty of reasons—it's about three in the morning, and Anora's coming home in a boy's Jeep.

"I can stick around. Help you explain where you've been." I come to a stop in her driveway, but she's already on her way out of the passenger seat.

"No, that's okay." She sounds defeated and tired. "See you."

She closes the door and heads toward the porch. I roll down my window.

"Hey, Ms. Silby," I say with a wave.

"Shy," she says with a nod. Her arms tighten across her chest, and I'm pretty sure she doesn't like me as much as she did a week ago.

"Sorry for bringing Anora home late. We fell asleep watching movies."

Anora's mom raises a brow. "I'll be sure to talk to your mother. Good night, Shy."

"Night," I say, rolling up the window. As I leave,

I spot the red-eyed gazes of Anora's hellhounds in the shadows around her house.

I head back to the Compound to see Jacobi. I expect to see Malee, Jacobi's mom, when I enter the infirmary. Instead, Natalie is sitting at his side, holding his hand.

"Where's Malee?" I ask.

"She stepped out for coffee," Natalie says. "I haven't been here long."

I watch their laced hands for a long moment. It reminds me of our childhood pre-training days when Natalie had a crush on Jacobi. It was one of the reasons she followed us around so much. Then I think about how obsessed Jacobi's always been with the newest technology, how he would spend hours telling me about new game enhancements he researched when all I wanted to do was play the damn thing. Standing here in this dark room with beeping machines and a silent Jacobi, I regret being so impatient with him, because just as I can't imagine living a life without Lily's laugh and smile, I can't imagine living without Jacobi's technobabble.

I would miss it.

*Don't you dare die on me.*

"Malee says he woke up briefly. The medics say he has a severe concussion. He will have a long road to recovery."

I don't know what that means. Will Jacobi be different when he wakes fully? How will this affect his tech skills? His fighting skills? His progress toward graduation?

After a long moment, Natalie says what I'm thinking. "What if he doesn't recover?"

Her voice sounds hollow, and the only thing I can think to say is, "He will."

I say it like an oath, a promise that can't be broken.

"There are things I still need to say," she says. "I need to apologize for thinking rules are more important than friends." She inhales sharply, and I come to stand beside her. "I'm sorry for what happened with Blake and your mom. You were right. Blake never did really forgive me. She just said it. I think maybe she hoped she could believe the words one day."

"Blake blamed the Order, not you, Nat," I say quietly.

She shakes her head and then looks up at me. Her eyes are red, and tears slide down her cheeks. I brush them away. I hate seeing her cry. "I lost Lily even before she died... I'll never forgive myself for that," and then she falls into me and sobs.

Sometime later, after Natalie's tears have subsided, we leave. Shifting into our hybrid forms, we land in the clearing where I parked my Jeep after leaving Anora's. I look at Natalie. "I want to go back to where we found Lily. What if she was resurrected nearby?"

Natalie stares at me for a moment and then says, "Are you asking me to come along?"

"If you're up for it," I say.

She smiles. "More than ever."

We shift and take off together. The Rayon High students chose to hide Anora in a pocket of wood near the graveyard. Guess they didn't want to take Anora too far from where they abducted her.

We land in the field. Natalie and I pause a moment, observing our surroundings before we make a plan. Evidence of Lily's animalistic state are everywhere—in the blood pooled on the ground where Jake fell, the earth torn apart by her savage attacks. The Order will brush

Jake's death under the rug, claim it was an animal attack, and only a few of us will ever know what really happened. It's hard to be back here so soon, but necessary. Someone reanimated Lily's corpse, and with the graveyard so close, I'm guessing the ritual was completed nearby. All that energy from lost souls probably fed the spell.

Natalie and I split up. She heads for the graveyard, and I follow a set of hellhound tracks into the woods in the opposite direction. Their prints are deep and fierce, evidence of their desperation to reach Anora. At some point, the tracks diverge—two on the left, two on the right, and one straight ahead. I follow the tracks in front of me, thinking they will probably lead straight to the ritual site. The other sets make me think the hounds got distracted by a scent or a chase. I'll check them later.

It's the smell that gives the ritual location away—a mix of wax and sage and blood. Thin black candles identify the barrier of the spell, a place for the magic to gather over the body. Whoever conducted the spell hadn't had time to remove any of the evidence.

I stand outside the circle, studying the impressions in the ground: where Lily's body lay, where she rose and dragged her feet, awakening from an eternal sleep that should have never been disturbed. Somehow, she managed not to bother the circle of candles. I stoop to study them. They hum with a faint vibration—energy, what humans call magic. I shiver involuntarily.

It's just another reason Anora—the Eurydice—is so important to us. The more dead on earth means more energy—power—for death-speakers in the occult to work with. We have a name for it, *death essence*: the energy of the dead.

As I step into the center of the circle, my whole body shakes, and I feel cold. Something latches on to my arm, and it goes numb. It's a phantom, residue left over from the spell cast hours earlier. It takes a moment, but soon I'm free of its icy grip, though my arm is still numb, and my chest feels like ice. I look up and find a clear view to the starry sky above. There's a full moon tonight, and I'd bet anything it shone right through that opening hours ago.

"It's impossible to tell if Lily's grave was disturbed. It's...fresh." Natalie's voice comes from behind me. I glance at her. She's looking at the ritual site. "I swear to Charon...I hate the feel of the occult." She shivers involuntarily. "It's..."

"Creepy," I provide.

"*Wrong.*"

I nod in agreement. It is wrong—contrary to the rules of life, death, and rebirth.

Natalie's looking around in the trees outside the circle. "What's that?" she asks and shifts, reappearing in front of me with something black.

"Where did you see that?" I ask.

"It was tangled in the branches."

I wonder if our culprit hid in the trees to escape the hellhounds.

"Whoever this belongs to, they're walking around with a pretty bad injury. There's blood all over it. Plus..." She holds up the sweater. There are four gashes across the back where a hound's claws bit into the fabric and the body wearing it.

I inhale sharply. Being bitten by a hellhound is pretty painful, but these gashes? They have to be excruciating.

"At least we have something to connect whoever did this to the scene," I say.

"Yeah, but unless they're shirtless, we won't be able to tell," Natalie says, frowning at the sweater.

"What's wrong?"

She hesitates for a moment. "I just…well, there's one name that comes to mind when I see cardigans, especially this one, because I'm pretty sure I've seen it before…on Lennon Ryder."

# CHAPTER THIRTY-SEVEN
## Anora and Roundtable

**My sleep is restless, plagued with nightmares that feel** more like memories.

*I'm afraid.*

My whole body feels alive, hypersensitive, like a live wire. Everything that should provide a cloak to keep me hidden encroaches like a maze. The wind, the night, the stars, feel like a weight, and I'm moving through it, following a path *they* created.

But I'm not afraid of *them.*

I'm afraid of what they left for me.

A warehouse with an ugly yellow light spilling down the front appears before me. A weapon materializes in my right hand. The feeling is familiar, comforting. The blade is a part of me, like my flesh, blood, and bones, and I think—*If anything has happened to him, I will kill.*

Inside, I find him. A pile of bones and skin and hair crumpled on the floor.

My chest squeezes so tight, I think it might explode. He's dead. His soul has already fled his body.

That happens when a death has been particularly traumatic.

That's the last logical thought I have before I start to hyperventilate and a horrible, searing pain spreads through me. A blade explodes through my front—a curved scythe I recognize. I twist and shove my own blade through my attacker, but even as he falls, another enemy takes his place, cutting me down the front. I fall to my knees when I'm struck on the head.

Struck everywhere.

Over and over again.

Until there's nothing.

———

I wake up with the sound of bones crushing and smelling smoke and jasmine. The taste of tears coats my tongue in a salty sludge. My sheets are tangled around my legs. My clothes cling to my skin, damp with sweat. The aftermath of the nightmare has my stomach churning. Shoving off the sheets, I stumble from bed into the bathroom and vomit. The acid burns the back of my throat and my nose, drawing tears.

"Anora!" Mom calls, and I scramble to my feet, shutting and locking the bathroom door.

"I'm up!" I call.

I should tell her I'm sick and skip school today, but after coming home so late, there's no way she'll let me. Last night, it was clear that whatever had been keeping her in her room was over, and she was in full-on Mom mode. Not only had she already told me that I'd be going to school no matter how little sleep I get, but she also said I'm grounded for a month.

Truth be told, I can't afford to miss school. I have some questions for Thane—like why didn't he tell me he was one of the last people to see Lily alive?

Standing under a scalding stream of water is cleansing, and by the time I'm finished, my skin no longer feels clammy. The bites on my arms from Lily's bugs have faded from a bright red to a dull pink. My hand still aches. When I start to trust the Order, I'll remember the claw and think twice.

I wipe the mirror free of fog. I miss my necklace, miss the weight of its chain around my neck, the press of the coin against my skin. I miss the comfort it brings. Roth took that from me. He touched me—unclasped the chain, let it slide along my collarbone until it was free of me and in his possession.

I squeeze my fist tight. The thread reacts to my anger, pushing at the surface of my palm. I wonder what it means to be the Eurydice with Roth at my back, hanging my poppa's coin over my head. What plan does he have for me? Shivering, I shove that question from my head. For now, I have to focus on finding the coin and Lily's killer.

As a reminder, the television is on when I come downstairs for breakfast, screaming a report on Jake's death. Hearing his name and seeing his pictures on local news make my stomach ache, and I let my cereal turn soggy in the milk. They manage to blame it on a bobcat attack while he was playing a game in the woods. The anchor describes queen's ransom as a decade-long tradition between rivals, Rayon High School and private school Nacoma Knight Academy, an event that was cancelled by school officials after Lily's death. The students who chose to play did so of their own accord. Inexplicably, my name is kept out of it, and I wonder if that's the work of the Order.

The screen cuts to Natalie's father, standing with Emerson Hall in the background. His hair blows like a wispy cloud.

"We are devastated by all this tragedy," he says. "It is a horrible time for all of us."

Then the anchor, "This is not the first death to haunt Headmaster Rivera or the students of Nacoma Knight Academy. Earlier this week, the campus was shut down due to an apparent suicide outside the administration hall."

The segment transitions into international news where anchors summarize the continued investigation into the London block fire and the Switzerland plane crash.

Mom shakes her head, unable to peel her eyes from the screen.

"All those poor people," she says. "It sort of feels like something bad is happening every day, doesn't it?"

Ever since the night Sean attacked Gage, all I see is Influence's hold over the world, and since learning I'm the Eurydice, I have a hard time not blaming myself. At least when I start training with the Valryn, I'll have some control over its strength. I think that's the only part of this job I'll actually like. It means I'm doing something good.

Mom drops me off at school early, and it's the first time I'm able to stroll across campus at a leisurely pace. I notice things I didn't before, like the leaves changing to

345

red and orange and yellow. The wind is crisp and kisses my cheeks. The air smells like decay—the earthy kind, not the dead kind.

I make it all the way to Walcourt when I bump into Mr. Val in the hallway outside his classroom. He has keys in hand and is locking the door to his room.

"Miss Silby." He turns to me. I fight the urge to run away. Yesterday, Mr. Val was my least favorite teacher at Nacoma Knight Academy. Today, he is supposed to train me in all things death.

"Is…something wrong, Mr. Val?"

"There is an assembly this morning. Headmaster Rivera thinks it wise to review rules after the events of the last week. You would know that if you ever arrived to school on time."

"I was on time!" I defend as the first bell rings.

"Let's not argue, Miss Silby. Shall I escort you to the auditorium?"

Uh, no. I'm perfectly capable of making it there on my own.

"I wouldn't want you to go out of your way," I say.

"I'm heading there anyway."

Great.

I set out with the intention of staying one step ahead of Mr. Val the entire time, but he has longer legs and keeps stride. While I prefer not to hear his condescending tone any more today, there's a question burning on the tip of my tongue, and before we reach the auditorium, I ask, "Why agree to train me?"

Mr. Val gives me a hard look, and I think he won't answer, but he says, "I'd hate to lose another student, Miss Silby."

He leaves me at the doors of the auditorium. I stand just inside, watching as students find seats. I have yet to spot anyone I know—not Lennon or Thane, Shy, Natalie or…Jacobi.

Right. Jacobi won't be here. He's still in the infirmary. I'm anxious for an update—had Shy heard anything else last night after he dropped me off? I would text him, but I still don't have a phone since mine was lost at the graveyard.

Someone crashes into my shoulder and I stumble, catching myself on the arm of a chair. Two girls pass and turn to glare at me. *What's your problem?* I want to ask, but someone's calling my name.

"Anora!"

I turn my head to find Thane standing, waving me to him.

As I approach, he says, "Jesus Christ, you're out of it today. I've been calling your name—" He pauses and looks at me—really looks at me. "You look awful."

"Thanks," I say mildly, taking a seat beside him. I know from the quick glance I had in the mirror this morning that I don't look my best: my eyes are sunk in a pool of purple-black. I rub them with the palms of my hands and am surprised when Thane pulls my hand away from my eyes.

"Don't do that."

"I didn't sleep much."

I explain what happened, including my trip to the Compound, the claw, my trial before the Order, and my new training instructor. I leave out that Roth has taken my poppa's coin. It doesn't seem relevant.

Thane frowns and doesn't say anything, so I do.

"Why didn't you tell me you were one of the last people to see Lily alive?"

"It wasn't necessary," he says and then looks at me. "I didn't kill her."

Mr. Rivera takes the stage, microphone screeching as he adjusts his hold, quieting the auditorium.

"As I am sure you all know, we lost one of our own earlier this week." He clears his throat into the microphone. "Lily Martin is no longer with us, and we will be holding a vigil in her honor this evening. Over the next few weeks, you will see an increase in security on campus. Any who wish may have access to crisis counseling. We will take this time to go over safety procedures, rules, and regulations regarding various locations around school..."

As Mr. Rivera drones on, I notice phones illuminating like lighters across the entire auditorium. Students turn their heads to whisper to one another and twist to search the crowd. Something's just been posted to Roundtable. Call me paranoid, but I can't help thinking it has to do with me.

When one person finds me, others do too, and it isn't long before everyone's attention is fixated on me.

What is on that stupid app?

If I had my phone, I would download it just to check. I lean toward Thane.

"Do you have access—?"

Even as I ask, he's opening Roundtable on his phone.

The first headline is: Anora Silby moved to Oklahoma because she killed someone.

A horrible high-pitched sound fills my ears, and my stomach feels sick. Who posted this? There are four people who know my identity. One is sitting beside me, one is in the infirmary, and the other two are Natalie and Shy.

I take slow, even breaths. Thane keeps scrolling.

Her real name is Lyra. There's a link to a news article about Chase's death that uses my name liberally, even has a picture.

Then:

Anora Silby was the last person to see Lily Martin and Jake Harjo alive. It isn't a coincidence. She's a murderer. She is a fake.

The app closes without warning. For a moment, I think someone's managed to take it down, but Thane says, "There are too many people on it right now."

Great.

The whispers continue, and people turn to stare. I feel like I'm in a room with the walls closing in. My chest tightens, and I can't take in air. I want to run, and I think Thane knows it, because he keeps his hand wrapped tight around mine.

Who made these posts? I don't have a very long list of suspects. There are four people who know my background, excluding the Order, and while I won't put something as petty as this past them, I'm assuming adults weren't involved. That leaves Natalie, Jacobi, Thane, and Shy. Jacobi is ruled out for obvious reasons, and Thane was sitting right beside me when the information went live. Shy has done his best to protect me from the Order—or rather, Roth—and he hates Roundtable. Those reasons aren't as strong, but they have more weight than what I have on Natalie, which is nothing.

She hates me.

After the assembly, Mrs. Cole's voice crackles over the intercom: "Anora Silby, come to administration. Anora Silby."

I want to sink lower in my seat, but Thane pulls me up.

"It's going to be okay," he says.

"How do you know?"

"I don't know that, but most of the Order is on your side, right? They'll protect you."

I can't tell if he's being snide or not. Nearly half of the Order would rather see me pay for Chase Lockwood's death. I wonder how many Valryn out there feel the same. On top of that, the student body at Nacoma Knight seems ever eager to believe anything posted on Roundtable.

What had Lennon said about Roundtable? *You'll either retain your rank or fall from grace.*

At least I don't have far to fall.

———

My stomach is queasy as I head to the administration office. Mrs. Cole is in her usual place behind the glass. When I tell her I'm here to see Mr. Rivera, she says he'll be out in a moment.

"Did you find your coin, Miss Silby?" she asks while I wait.

"My coin?" I ask, hysteria rising inside me until I remember I'd asked her to check the lost and found at the beginning of the week. "Oh, my coin." I laugh weakly. "No, not yet."

"I'll keep a lookout," she promises.

"Thanks."

A door opens, and Mr. Rivera appears.

"Miss Silby," he says, stepping aside so I can slip past him into his office. Mr. Val stands there looking out the window.

Mr. Rivera closes the door behind him. "Please, sit."

I glance at Mr. Val as I do, but he acts like I haven't even entered the room. I guess he's here because he decided to take responsibility for me yesterday.

Mr. Rivera takes a seat behind his desk.

"My daughter made me aware of a post on Roundtable that compromises your safety."

I bet she did.

"We have managed to shut the site down and are working on gathering the IP addresses of everyone who's accessed it. Still, until we're sure this leak is under control, you are in danger, Eurydice."

"Roundtable has put a lot of students in danger. The Order could have, and should have, shut it down. Why didn't they?"

I suspect I know the answer to that question—the Order needs Roundtable for intel. They don't want to shut it down. It's only a problem now because it's me. Because my soul somehow makes me more important than anyone else who fell victim to Roundtable.

"We're not discussing other students. We are discussing you," he says. "We have already made arrangements for you to stay at Temple through the weekend. Just as a precaution, until we can neutralize this threat."

I blink. Did he just say what I think he said?

"What's Temple?"

"Temple is home to several Valryn and the temporary home to others. It's far more accommodating than the Compound. Indeed, there are no cells, just bedrooms."

Ironic they think to disguise a prison with comfort. I'm not buying it. Thane warned me about this. Besides, I have more important things to do. I need to find out who posted my life on Roundtable, who reanimated Lily and took my coin, but I know their argument: I'll have plenty of time for that at Temple. Alone. In a room that's not my own.

"What about my mom?"

"We'll post guards at your house."

It doesn't feel right, to be stuffed away in some sort of supernatural sanctuary while my mom is left out in the open.

"Can't I just go home? You'll have guards there anyway."

"We can protect you better at Temple. Rest assured, no harm will come to your mother."

What he's saying doesn't make sense in my head. If that's true, why can't I just stay home? But I get it... It's a way to control me.

"And what happens if you don't contain the threat? Does a few days turn into a week, then a month, then a year?"

"Miss Silby, we do not wish to keep you there any longer than you wish to stay there," Mr. Val says, turning to face me. "But we will do what we must to keep you safe."

"Good luck convincing my mother," I mutter, crossing my arms.

"We have already taken the liberty of contacting her," Mr. Rivera says. "She believes you are attending a student retreat for extra credit."

My heart falls. They cover all their bases. And as mistrusting as my mom is, she's not going to question the headmaster of my school. She needs me to make it work at Nacoma Knight.

"But...what about the vigil?" I ask. I want to go for a lot of reasons, and it also gives me enough time to think of a way out of spending the weekend at Temple.

Mr. Rivera and Mr. Val exchange a look.

"Of course you can attend," Mr. Rivera says. "But with a guard."

"You want me to walk around with a shadow knight?"

"We are ravens, Miss Silby," Mr. Val says. "We'll be watching."

I hate shape-shifters.

―――――

Campus looks like a still from an Alfred Hitchcock film. Ravens hang out in the grass and trees, on electric lines and roofs. They spread their wings as if stretching, like they're stiff from perching. Sometimes they caw together, like one of them told a joke and everyone thinks it's hilarious. They watch me as I go from class to class. They're just as bad as the students, who can't seem to keep their eyes to themselves.

I use class to consider my options for escape. There aren't many. I'm convinced Natalie posted my past on Roundtable, Shy will side with the Order, and I prefer to keep Lennon out of this mess. That leaves Thane.

It's times like this I wish I had a car.

In history, Lennon nudges me with her elbow, her body swallowed by one of her many huge cardigans. "You okay?" It's her way of asking me about Roundtable. I've been waiting, wound tight.

I let out a breath. "Yeah, I guess."

She nods, pursing her lips. She looks pale today, and a sheen of sweat glistens on her forehead. I start to ask her if she's okay when she asks, "So…is it true?"

I don't look at her as I admit, "Parts of it."

She nods and keeps her gaze on the teacher at the front of the room. "I've been following Chase Lockwood's case since it broke national news."

"What?" I exclaim. I can't help it. She's known about Chase this whole time?

Everyone's eyes snap to me, and Mrs. Wilson frowns. "Is everything all right, Miss Silby?"

"Yes. I'm sorry."

She glares at me before returning to her lecture.

Lennon waits a few moments longer to explain. "When a shadow knight dies, it puts everyone on edge, even death-speakers."

Wait. "You're a death-speaker?"

"Technically? No. I didn't inherit my mother's gift of seeing the dead."

I'm still reeling. "Why didn't you tell me before?"

She raises a shoulder. "It didn't seem like you under-stood any of it. I figured you'd talk to me when you were ready and I'd explain then."

Part of me is hurt Lennon knew what I'd been going through and didn't offer to help, but the other part of me understands. She'd tried to reach out. She'd invited me to hang out this week, and I blew it off.

"I'm guessing you're the reason for all the ravens?" she says.

I nod once and give a shortened version of what happened last night during and after the forced queen's ransom and the Order's belief I will be safe at Temple this weekend. I leave out Lily's resurrection and that I'm the Eurydice.

After a moment, Lennon asks, "Do you want to escape?"

Yes...but something keeps me from saying that out loud.

"I can help you," she adds.

"Why? They'll just come after you."

She smiles, but it's a strange smile—challenging, as if she's saying *I'd like to see them try*. I shiver.

"I hate shadow knights," she says at last. The use of the word *hate* surprises me, but then she says, "They killed my mom."

Her words slice through me and settle in my stomach, sharp as knives, and yet my brain can't comprehend. Did she just say a shadow knight killed her mom? Why? When? How long has she lived with this secret? How long has she known she's surrounded by shadow knights?

"Lennon...I..."

"Don't be sorry," she says quickly. "Just don't trust the Order."

# CHAPTER THIRTY-EIGHT

# Shy and the Revelation

*I know something bad has happened when I arrive at* school because Natalie's waiting in the parking lot for me. It reminds me of the day she broke the news that Lily's relationship with a human was posted on Roundtable.

I immediately think of Anora.

Turns out, I'm not far from the mark. She shows me a series of posts about Anora that reveal her real name and link her to the murder of Chase Lockwood. This has negative consequences for Anora on all levels but also puts her in danger from human and Valryn alike—really, anyone who wants revenge for Chase's death. There are Valryn who care very little that she was defending herself when one of their own died, and they think she should be punished.

I meet Natalie's gaze. "Where is she?"

She hesitates. "Don't get mad at me."

My heart beats hard in my chest. *Oh no.* "What did you do?"

"I told Dad about the posts," she admits.

I start to push past her with the intention of heading straight to Headmaster Rivera's office, but Natalie grabs my arm.

"Shy, think about it," she begs. "Jacobi isn't here to take down the site, and Anora's in danger. She's known to the Order now. Who best to protect her? They'll take her to Temple and keep an eye on her."

*I'm supposed to protect her*, I want to argue, but Natalie's right. It will be easier if I don't have to worry about whether Anora's safe. Still, putting her well-being in the hands of someone else feels wrong.

"In the meantime, we can do some research," Natalie says. "Figure out who made those posts, who reanimated Lily's corpse. We have work to do."

I relent. "Right. Okay. I went by Jacobi's house this morning and snagged his laptop."

Well, one of his three laptops.

"I have his phone," Natalie says. When I give her a look, she shrugs. "What? He's got a lot of stuff on here, including that app he used to track Lily's phone. We might need it."

Fair enough.

Natalie and I find a spot in the library to camp out. We're supposed to be in class, and we'll probably get in trouble for skipping, but right now, I couldn't care less.

I pull out Jacobi's laptop, and Natalie and I sit side by side as I open the archive. Jacobi gained commander-level access, probably using his mom's codes. And luckily, the Order hasn't locked him out yet. I understand why Jacobi looked up his own file; it's hard to keep myself from doing the same, especially having access as I do

357

right now. After discovering my father was aware of my connection to Anora, I want to research the records and follow the threads of my past lives—of Anora's past lives…

And I will, but I have priorities, and one of those is figuring out who reanimated Lily's corpse. So I start with the small lead we'd gotten last night in the cardigan Natalie found at the ritual site. We don't have a way to prove it is Lennon's, but at this point, everyone's a suspect, and it's best to start eliminating.

I search Lennon Ryder.

The inquiry gives no results, which isn't surprising considering I don't think Lennon's ever been arrested for practicing the occult.

"What about her mother? Her father?" Natalie presses.

"I don't know their names," I say.

"Jacobi's got access to school records."

I look at her, brow raised. "How do you know?"

"This isn't the first time I've used his computer," she says. She takes it from me and starts clicking around, navigating the interface like she's done this a million times.

"So what? You just…head over to his house and look up whoever you want?"

"No," she says, annoyed. "We've been trying to figure out who's responsible for Roundtable."

I try to imagine them together without me. Funny enough, it's hard to do, but apparently it's been happening. "And that's…*all* you do?"

"Shut up, Shy," Natalie complains, shoving me hard with her shoulder.

I laugh. "Hey, it's a fair question."

She glares at me, but she's blushing, and the corners of her lips are turning up. After a moment, she's in the school's records, pulling up Lennon's name.

"Looks like she lives with her grandmother," Natalie says. "There's a restraining order against her father—Goliath Markov."

My blood runs cold. Natalie must see I'm startled by the name because she asks, "What?"

"I know that name. I've heard my dad mention him," I say and take the computer back. Once I'm in the archive again, I search Goliath's name. He has a profile and not just any profile: Goliath Markov is Valryn. He's also been incarcerated at the Compound for the last seventeen years—the whole of Lennon's life—for several reasons, one of them being impregnating a human woman.

That would make Lennon an abomination.

"How does the Order not know?" Natalie asks beside me as the realization settles upon her. If Goliath was in prison for his relationship with a human, the Order definitely knew about Lennon at one point.

"Maybe they do know about her?" I offer. "Maybe they decided not to do anything about her as long as she stays hidden?" There's nothing about Lennon that screams abomination. She looks like any other human. But if the Order knows about her and are letting her live, why have they been telling us horrible things about abominations for so many years?

Anora's questions flood my mind...

*Have you ever met an abomination?*

*You don't know what they look like?*

*If they are actually...deformed?*

It's Natalie who dares say what I'm thinking out loud. "She has to hate us."

She probably does, and while that doesn't make her a murderer, it does give her motive.

I push the computer aside, standing suddenly.

"Dammit."

"What?" Natalie asks, and I start to pace.

"The day Anora captured Vera's soul, I found her in the woods. As we were leaving, I noticed a raven in the trees. Any other time, I would have followed it because I didn't recognize it. What if it was…"

"Lennon."

# CHAPTER THIRTY-NINE

# Anora and the Standoff

*Lennon convinces me I should eat lunch in the cafeteria.* She says running makes me look guilty and is useless since the Order will find me. Ravens are everywhere on campus at the moment, which I guess is supposed to keep me safe until after the vigil when they take me to Temple.

I can't quite wrap my mind around Lennon's admission and what it means. Before today, she had spoken so highly of Shy. She had included Lily in our circle, gone to her funeral, and mourned that we would never be close friends, and she had known the whole time they were Valryn. Was all of that a ruse? A way of protecting herself?

She's watching the room. My first day, I assumed she was looking for someone, but now I know she's just watching people. She warned me: *Learn their secrets so when they come after you, you're untouchable.*

The words make me shiver, and I want to know:

What does she do with those secrets? How has she made herself untouchable? But I think I know the answer to that—she doesn't share her secrets.

Today is rare.

I wonder how soon before she regrets sharing. Or if there's a reason she finally decided to tell me the truth. The thought makes me shiver.

"What was your mother like?" I ask. It's a question I like to answer about my poppa, but Lennon looks surprised. Like no one has ever asked.

"I don't remember," she admits. "She died shortly after I was born."

That answer makes me hate the Order more. I know they have ridiculous rules and expectations, but taking a mother away from her child? Unforgivable.

We move through the line quickly. With our trays in hand, Lennon and I start looking for a place to sit in the packed cafeteria when I'm hit hard from behind.

"Oops," a girl mocks.

My tray flies from my hands, and I stumble, but before I hit the ground, I'm caught by the waist and pulled against a hard body. When I look up, I'm staring into Shy's bright, angry eyes. My heart moves into my throat.

The whole cafeteria has gone quiet. I twist to look at the person who pushed me when Natalie says, "Don't be a bitch, Jasmine."

Jasmine looks just as shocked as me that her move didn't win praise from Natalie.

Then Lennon says, "Really, Jasmine, you could easily be in Anora's place."

What's that supposed to mean? Does Lennon know something about Jasmine the rest of us don't? Is she threatening to post it on Roundtable? After all the damage she's seen that stupid app do? An uneasy feeling creeps over me.

"You should probably say sorry," Shy says.

"S-sorry," Jasmine manages, her face turning pink. She backs away, fleeing the cafeteria. I can't help feeling bad for her. She hasn't been very nice, but she was just shamed in front of everyone.

Natalie looks around, noticing we have the attention of the whole school. "What are you all staring at?" she barks. "Nothing to see here."

*Is that true?* I wonder. After queen's ransom and Roundtable, this is probably like a reality television show. Anyone within a one-mile radius can feel the tension coming off us. They're probably waiting for a fight to break out.

Speaking of tension, I feel Shy against my back. His arm is wrapped around my waist like the hook of a scythe. There's a brief moment when I want to reach behind me, snake my hand around his neck, and kiss him, but that yearning feels like a distant memory. Reality is, someone posted my past on Roundtable, and these are two of the four people I haven't ruled out. Besides, I'm having a hard time coming to terms with the fact that the Order killed Lennon's mother.

I place my hands on Shy's arm and pry it loose, stepping out of his embrace. When I turn to face him and Natalie, his jaw tightens.

"You didn't have to embarrass her," I say.

"She embarrassed you," Natalie says defensively.

"You'll turn your back on anyone, even your so-called friends," I tell her.

Natalie's brows shoot up, but her surprise at my words doesn't last long before she decides she's angry with me.

"What's that supposed to mean?"

I start to speak, to accuse her of the Roundtable post, but Shy stops me. "We're not here to argue."

"Anora's had a rough day," Lennon says. "She doesn't need this."

"We're not here to talk to Anora." Shy doesn't look at me. He's looking at Lennon. So is Natalie. What's going on here?

"Oh?" Lennon mocks. "And what could you possibly have to say to me?"

"Why don't we step outside," Shy suggests.

For a moment, I don't think Lennon will agree, but she maintains this unsettling smirk as we exit, stepping into the cool, fall air.

"What's this about?" I ask, but Shy and Natalie pretend I'm not there.

"Where were you last night, Lennon?" Natalie asks.

"Why don't you just accuse me of whatever you're going to accuse me of and get it over with?"

"Someone tell me what's going on," I demand, angry I'm being ignored.

Shy's gaze cuts to me. "Lennon stole your coin. You watched Anora capture Vera's soul, didn't you? Swooped in and stole it in raven form. Did you kill Lily too?"

I look from Shy to Lennon. She's emotionless and cold, but I expect that. She was just accused of murder. The problem is, I don't know who to believe, so I ask for the only thing I can, though my voice rasps as I do, as if in protest. "Do you have proof?"

"What?" Shy's question is sharp and surprised; it tangles my chest and makes me feel wrong.

"Proof," I say again. "You've accused her of murder, Shy. You must have proof."

Isn't that what the Order's always asking for? Evidence?

He opens his mouth, but the only thing he manages is, "You don't trust me?"

If my heart were glass, it would shatter. He looks at me with solid frustration, jaw tight, eyes like lamplights... like he can see all my flaws and fears. It hurts my chest.

I manage to scoff, but it takes a lot of energy to stay angry with him. "This isn't about trust. You're targeting Lennon, which is an insult when the Order's responsible for her mother's death."

Lennon's pain and anger are palpable. She lost her mother. How can I not say something to Shy and Natalie about their precious Order?

"We've done nothing but help you and risked everything for it!"

"I'm not arguing about whether you've helped me, but murder is a serious accusation, one you seem to be willing to just throw around whenever you please."

Natalie takes a step forward. "You'd insult the only people who've kept you alive?"

"Arguably," I say, "you've almost gotten me killed."

"You're not dead, and that's more than we can say for Lily."

It's obvious Natalie wants to keep questioning Lennon, but Shy pulls her away. The stark look of betrayal on his face feels like a slice to my heart.

They leave, entering the school again. When I look

up, I see students staring out the windows, watching our exchange.

*Bet this will end up on Roundtable.*

In the aftermath, Lennon says, "She's lucky Lily's the only friend she's lost."

I turn to face Lennon, surprised those horrible words came out of her mouth. "Lily's dead, Lennon. That's not funny."

Lennon shrugs. "I didn't say it to be funny."

It's another threat.

Then it hits me: Lennon predicted the posts that would destroy Lily's reputation. She'd said they would *overshadow my weirdness in art.* Now that I know her better, I'd say she was...excited.

She also hadn't thought it was ridiculous that Lily was being publicly shamed for her relationship with a human. At the time, I didn't think much about her response—

*It's not that she was sexting. It's who...*

"You posted Lily's texts on Roundtable," I say. Lennon doesn't move to deny it, and I feel my heart sink further into my stomach. "Why?"

She shrugs. "I had to show her she couldn't trust the Order, just like I had to show you."

Then she walks away as if she hasn't just upended everything and left me with no one to trust.

# CHAPTER FORTY
# Anora and the Betrayal

**By the last hour of the day, I'm desperate for the comfort of** my room. I want to be close to my poppa's things. I want the weight of his soul around my neck. I think about what he might say if he were here, but I already know: *Admit to your mistake. There's nothing wrong with an apology.*

I should have believed Shy and Natalie when they confronted Lennon. In the moment, I'd been so certain standing up for her was the right thing to do, but I was blind.

She'd been behind the posts. That's why she watched people, learned their secrets. That's why she was untouchable.

But did that also mean she took my coin and killed Lily? I can't say, and that makes me afraid.

Instead of going to PE where I'll have to face her, Shy, and Natalie, I head to the library. If I can't go home, I'll surround myself with one thing that brings me comfort—books.

The library is quiet, and only a few people turn to stare at me. I head into the stacks, searching for a place to hide and read. As I navigate the maze of shelves, I halt, heart jumping into my throat. A man sits, slumped over in the corner, head resting against his chest. He's too pale to be asleep. The lights create a shiny spot at the center of his head where his hair has thinned. His arms lie at his sides, both palms up. He's dressed in a blue checkered shirt and brown pants. He doesn't have any outward injuries, but he's fallen in such a way that it looks like he was pushed.

As I stand here, the spirit disappears and reappears inches from where I stand. Stumbling away, I stifle a scream and watch as he plucks a book from the shelf. He leafs through the pages for a moment before dropping the book, hands going to his chest, which rises and falls quickly. He stumbles back, landing against the wall. His eyes meet mine, round and full of fear. He slides to the floor, breathing fast until his head falls forward on his chest and his arms unfold to rest at his sides.

He's dead.

I twist to flee and run straight into a body. Pushing away, I come face to face with Thane. With my heart still racing, I can't keep from cursing.

"God! Why are you always where I don't want you to be?"

Thane raises a dark brow. "Who pissed in your Cheerios?"

Then he seems to notice the man behind me.

"I see you found Mr. Richardson."

"You know him?"

"He's one of the school ghosts, but most of us forget

about him because he keeps to the library. He died about ten years ago from a heart attack."

I shiver.

"The rumor is he was found by a couple students who came here to have sex. If you ask me, the faculty keeps that one going."

Thane says it in jest, but I feel sad for Mr. Richardson. I twist to see him flicker and fade, reappearing a few steps away. The urge to capture his soul rises inside me, like a flower blooming before the first frost. I know it would be a mistake, since I can't open the gates, but I also know that the faculty and students who have made him into a ghost story keep him here, bound to this one spot, reliving his death over and over again.

I twist, facing Thane again.

"What are you doing here?" I ask.

"I came to find you," he says. "I heard you haven't had a very good day."

"That's an understatement."

He smiles a little. "Maybe I can make it better?"

"Unless you can get me home without an army of shadow knights noticing, you can't."

He shrugs one shoulder. "I can't promise anything. Fucking Valryn are everywhere—in raven form and in human form…but I'm willing to try."

"Really?"

"Don't get your hopes up," he says. "We can't leave now anyway. We'll have to wait until after the vigil starts, when people are a little more distracted."

I can wait if it means getting to go home tonight.

———

I arrive to the vigil with Thane around seven, and as the sun sets, a sea of candlelight erupts in the dark. There are people everywhere, living and dead, on the field, on the track, and in the stands. This vigil goes beyond Nacoma Knight and Lily. It goes to Rayon High and Jake. It extends to the community.

*I did this*, I think as Thane and I find an open spot to stand. *I'm a goddess of chaos.*

Thane nudges me. "I know what you're thinking. Stop."

"You can't know," I say.

"This isn't your fault."

I don't argue with him. No matter what Thane says, I'll always feel responsible.

The sight of black birds flying overhead catches my attention. They land on the light poles and the stadium.

More shadow knights.

"They're here to pay their respects just as much as they're here to watch you," Thane says.

I know that, and their presence has me searching the crowd for Shy. I haven't seen him since lunch. I spot him surrounded by several students. He's dressed in a Nacoma Knight hoodie and jeans. His head is bowed, and his blond hair falls into his eyes. I think about how his features change when he shifts into Valryn form— how his hair turns to silver and makes his eyes look bluer. How fit he looks in that black suit.

He rolls his shoulders and then his neck, and I get the feeling he's trying to shake the feel of me watching him.

Natalie stands nearby, ever in his shadow. When I first met them, I might have assumed it was because she liked him. Now, I know differently. It's Natalie who meets my gaze first—fierce and indignant. She turns her head to Shy and whispers something in his ear. Whatever it is, it makes him look up.

His stare hurts my heart. Even at this distance, I can tell his eyes are red and glistening. The reality is, he's been reliving Lily's death every day since it happened, and it's all because of me. Tonight's just another repackaging.

He has to be sick of me.

I look away and hold my candle to Thane. "I have to go to the bathroom."

He nods, taking the candle. Once I'm off the field and behind the stadium, a hand clamps down on my shoulder. I reach for it and twist, coming face-to-face with a man I've never seen. Judging by the hard set of his jaw, he's a guard.

"I have to go to the bathroom," I say and shove him off. "Are you going to follow me?"

The answer is yes.

Except when I get to the restrooms behind the stadium, there's an out-of-order sign posted on the women's door. I turn to look at the guard, who raises a brow and glances at the men's.

"I'm not going in there," I say and stalk toward Emerson. The knight remains behind me, silent. I don't like having him at my back; something about it feels wrong. Then I see red eyes ignite in the dark—my hellhounds are here, and their low growl causes me to slow. When I turn, the shadow knight attacks, striking me across the face. I stumble, and he draws his scythe just as one of my hounds rushes forward, vaulting over my head.

The knight shoves his scythe into the dog's eye. It yelps, and the sound freezes my blood. I can feel my

371

other four hounds fall into formation behind me. I've come to sense their presence just as I sense Shy's.

"Stop!" I yell as the knight continues to stab my hound until it no longer moves. The knight straightens, breathing hard, and my other hounds let out a chorus of growls, the blood of their brother covering his weapon and hands.

"They told me you were a good fighter, Eurydice. No one said you let your hounds fight for you."

I clench my fist, and his eyes narrow on my hand.

"What are you going to do? Steal my soul and call it self-defense?"

"Stay," I command my hounds, and they whine in protest. I step forward, and the knight smiles, slicing at me with his scythe. I dodge, landing on the ground. As he approaches, I tangle my feet with his, and he trips. I roll out of the way before he can fall on me, and once he's on the ground, I strike, digging my knee into his back and swiping the blade from his hand. I'm on my feet again, armed.

The knight stands, breathing hard. "Bitch!" He charges toward me but stops short when the hound he stabbed pounces. The knight's screams fill the air as his body is mauled. Then someone grabs my hand, and for a moment, I think it's another knight, but when I turn, I come face-to-face with Thane.

"Come on!"

He drags me from the hounds and the body of the knight, toward the parking lot.

He opens the passenger side door and shoves me inside the car. "Tell your hounds to go so they don't draw attention to you. Stay here until I get back!"

Then he disappears. My hounds pace outside the car, prowling, but I do as Thane says and ask them to leave. They obey.

I'm shaking, and the car is stuffy and oddly quiet. The silence presses against my ears like my head's been placed in a vise, then I hear a muffled beep. I look in the console that separates me from the driver's side and then the glove compartment. That's where I find it—Lily's phone. The color and warmth drain from my body. What is it doing in his car?

I fumble with the phone, heart racing as I look through Lily's messages. At the very top—the last person she texted—was Thane.

He said: Come to the train yard.

She responded: Be there soon.

She'd trusted Thane.

And he killed her.

I look up in time to see Thane coming into view.

Damn. And I sent my hounds away.

I shove the glove compartment closed and slip the phone in my pocket, but I can't school my features fast enough to put on a show for Thane, because as soon as he gets into the driver's seat of his car, he asks, "What's wrong?"

"Nothing," I say too fast. "You know, I'm just going to go..."

As my hand lands on the door handle, the locks click into place. I turn to face Thane.

"I'm sorry, Anora," he says, but there's something superficial about his apology and a darkness to his gaze I recognize: Influence. "I can't let you leave."

I don't have a lot of room to fight, and I don't want

to use the thread on Thane. Still, I give it my best and fling my left arm out, toward his face. It's more of a distraction than anything. My right goes for his stomach. The blow lands, and he grunts, but it doesn't keep him from wrapping an arm around my neck and crushing me against him. His hand claps over my mouth and nose, and the only thing I become aware of is the pressure around my neck, the raw pain of having my body starved of oxygen. My vision blurs with hot tears, and saliva seeps into my throat and out of my mouth.

The sensation builds until it feels like his bones are cutting into mine, slicing through the arteries, detaching my head from my body.

And then there's nothing.

# CHAPTER FORTY-ONE
## Shy and the Abomination

*I know the moment Anora steps on the field because the* thread connecting us makes my chest ache. I have to clench my fists just to have something else to focus on. I could solve this easily if I'd just go stand by her, but I'm still angry about earlier—even angrier when I glance in her direction and see she's standing with Thane. Why does she keep hanging out with him? He gave her answers, but I did too, and without putting her in danger.

*She trusts him more than me.*

If Chase were still alive, I might kill him myself for making the Eurydice afraid of the only people who can protect her.

But it's not just Chase. It's Lennon too.

She'd given Anora that story about her mom being killed by the Order. I still can't find any evidence that it's true, though I'm more willing to believe something like that considering Lennon's an abomination and I'm not ignorant. I know the Order does some shady stuff. They're a government.

But Anora blamed *me*.

She called me a murderer.

And after all the ways I've tried to protect her, that sucked. Bad.

*Something's wrong.*

The feeling slices through me, clean and sharp like a new blade. My gaze snaps to the space where Anora stood a few moments ago, but she's not there, and neither is Thane. I start to cut through the crowd looking for her, unable to ignore the urgency of this pull.

"Shy?" Natalie calls, but the longer I go without seeing Anora, the more frantic I become. People step in front of me and attempt to offer their condolences. I interact with the first few, but then there are too many, and I push through them. I'm at the edge of the field when Natalie catches up to me.

"Shy!"

I twist toward her. "Where's Anora?"

Then I notice the set of her jaw, the burn of her eyes.

"I just did a scan. Lily's phone is on," she says.

"For how long?"

"Ten minutes."

I scan the crowd again, but I know in my heart Anora's not here. I turn back to Natalie.

"Will you track it?" I ask.

She seems surprised that I asked. "Don't you—"

"Once you get a trace, notify Elite Cain," I instruct. "Don't go alone, Nat."

"But…where are you going?"

I'm not paying attention to her anymore. I've found

Lennon in the crowd, and she smiles at me. I've always had an aversion to her, but now I understand it—that smile is evil. Whatever she's done—and it has to be bad—she's excited about it.

Then she bolts, and I do too.

"Track that phone, Nat!" I call as I take off, rounding the corner of the stadium to find Lennon. She twists toward me, smiles, then wings sprout from her back, and she jumps, shifting into a raven, and is gone.

I shift and chase after her.

Lennon navigates the night like she's done this for years, and I bet she has, right under the nose of the Order. She twists and turns, dipping below trees and zipping between branches. It's almost like she's toying with me. When she goes down, it's in an alleyway off Main Street. I recognize it because I know there's an entrance to the Underworld used by death-speakers.

I shift and land, but Lennon is nowhere in sight. I draw my blades and start down the alley. There's little light from the streetlamps near the road, but it's enough that I catch shadows squirming on the walls. This place is infested with occulates—they stain the walls with their shadows. I shove my blades into them, and their screams sound around me, their tar-like bodies oozing into pools at my feet. I've never seen so many darklings saturate one area. They've been placed like wards. Occulates not only act as spies but alarm systems, and they are sending signals in every direction that I'm here.

The air changes, and I twist to find Lennon standing behind me.

"Boo," she says and swings a long, jagged blade toward me. I block her attack. The blow is harsh. It makes my arms throb. In that moment, I understand two things about her: she moves to kill, and she is strong.

"Good," she says, critiquing my counterattack, as if she's my instructor and I'm the student. We stare at each other over our blades. Neither of us move to disengage.

"Where'd you get the blade?" I ask.

"A death-speaker made it for me. You like?"

"I didn't know you were so connected to the death-speaker Underworld."

"I have a feeling you don't know much about me."

I have a feeling she's right.

She steps back, disengaging her blade carefully, gingerly, as if it might disintegrate if she moves too fast. It is both a graceful and deceiving move. The jagged parts of that blade can catch on mine at any moment and rip it from my hands.

"How did you find out what I am?" she asks.

"It wasn't that hard," I say. "It's well known why your father is incarcerated at the Compound."

"So you must know the Order is aware of my existence too."

I stumble. I did wonder, but I can't believe my parents wouldn't have told me the truth.

"Interesting. It must be more of a need-to-know thing when it comes to what they tell trainees about abominations." She narrows her eyes a fraction. "I'm surprised you haven't changed your mind about us, given how you feel about Anora."

Sometimes how I feel about Anora doesn't feel like a choice.

"Us?" I ask. It's strange hearing that word describe a group of people I haven't assigned a number to. I've never really thought much about abominations, but clearly that was my first mistake. It is true that after Anora arrived, I've been reminding myself on a daily basis why humans and Valryn can't be together, but all the reasons I come up with for why it is bad disappear when I'm near her.

And Anora is right—I have never been presented with any sort of proof that what the Order refers to as abominations are bad.

Although as Lennon paces around me, her dark blade drawn, I'm beginning to wonder about what they've been hiding and why.

Her laugh escapes like a bark. "What do you think? I'm the only one in existence? The Last Samurai?"

I don't respond, mostly because that's what I had assumed.

"But you've been working alone?"

"Not alone."

"Right. Thane," I say.

That's how she knew about Anora's background. Anora trusted him and he betrayed her.

Lennon laughs again. It's like a chime—pretty, soft. She even throws back her head, and all I can think is that's a good way to get your throat slashed. My hand tightens on my blade.

"He's an easy puppet. So malleable."

"What's your plan?" I ask. "Because you don't have much time to execute it. The Order will be here soon."

"You expect me to believe you've learned there's power in numbers?" she asks. "You work alone; for some reason, you think it's best. It's like you're trying to prove yourself or something."

Those words sting.

She's a little right, of course, but she discounts my friendship with Natalie, and Natalie believes in teams and the power of the Order, and she'll find me.

"So the plan," I say. "What do you want with Anora?"

"She's not really good for anything but her power."

I flinch at the words. How could Anora ever have assumed this person was her friend? But I know the answer...Lennon deceived her, and it makes me angry.

"If I control the Eurydice, I control everything."

How can she possibly think she can control Anora?

She laughs then, her smile wide. "Can you imagine? The Order having to bow to me? An abomination?"

Her bone-like shoulders shake with laughter.

"The Order doesn't bow."

She finally stops circling me and says, "They will. To me."

And then I'm under attack, but not by her—by the occulates that were scurrying across the walls. They circle me like sharks. When they erupt from their shadow forms, they stick to me like tar. They're smart too, because the first thing they cover is the scythe at my thigh—the only blade that has any effect on their bodies.

"Dammit!" I curse.

I can hold them off with my double blades, but there are so many darklings, I won't be able to do it for long. Not to mention the ones on my leg are squeezing tighter and tighter. Soon they'll cut off my circulation. I hack at them as they rise from the floor, conscious that Lennon stands near like a wraith, her skeletal body draped in black, her strange blade at her side. I catch a glimpse of her, eyes narrow and focused. She's controlling the occulates...but how?

I'll figure that out later. Until then, I grip the hilt of my blade like a spear and aim. It lodges right in her shoulder. She's jarred from her concentration, and the occulates release their hold enough for me to withdraw my scythe. They scream as I pierce them, and once I'm free, my wings unfurl, and I rise off the ground.

Lennon removes my blade from her shoulder, and it clatters to the ground. She rises with me.

"Who taught you to fly?" I ask.

We'd been lucky in the Compound. They pushed us off a cliff and said fly. At least we'd landed on something soft at the bottom.

"It took a while," she says with a savage smirk. "But I find I can make my body do just about anything if I'm scared enough."

I admire her. She trained herself under the radar all these years.

She attacks, giving weight to her blow by letting herself drop and pushing off the hard floor. I counter, letting her deliver the blows, letting her think she has the strength and the advantage. She relents and puts distance between us.

"Come on, Savior!" she says. She's out of breath. "I've been waiting for this moment."

"I don't want to fight you."

She laughs, throwing back her head. "Don't give me that bullshit."

"I don't," I say. "I just want Anora."

"Oh, we know already," she says, irritated. "You've wanted her from the moment she stepped into your space. She's all you can think about, all you can *feel*." She lifts her blade. "But what makes you think you can have a happy ending? My father doesn't get to live in a world where he knows his love is alive, and that means you don't get to either!"

She attacks again, and I block. Then her blade latches on to mine, and I'm jerked forward. I swing at her with my scythe, and she jumps back, disengaging our weapons. She tries the same move again, but I'm ready, and as her sword hooks into mine, I twist my blade. Her black knife comes free from her hands and falls to the ground. She's quick to retrieve it. I stay in the air, hovering.

"Where's Anora?"

Her answer is to withdraw a gun. I shift into raven form in an attempt to move faster, but she fires, and the bullet goes straight through my wing, and I am blown backward. I land hard on the ground, shifting into my Valryn form. My wing droops, and blood drips on the floor.

"You've had that the whole time?" I ask, getting to my feet. Blood covers my hand as I try to put pressure on my wound. "Why the hell did you fight me with a blade?"

"I just wanted to spar." She pauses, looking at her weapon. "Guns are so much better."

A pain I've never experienced before hits me square in the chest. It takes the breath out of me and burns at the same time. It's nothing compared to the pain in my wing. I could stand before, but this drives me to my knees. I have no experience resisting it—this is Anora's pain.

"No!" Lennon screams. "No, no, no!" She grabs a fist full of my hair. "What's happening?" she demands. "Tell me what's happening!"

The pain in my chest restricts my words. Lennon lifts her gun to shoot.

But something barrels into her. She pulls the trigger, and as she goes flying, her bullet lands in my shoulder.

*Damn*, this is the worst.

We hit the ground at the same time, groaning, and stare up at Roth DuPont.

"What are you doing here?" I manage between painful breaths.

"I thought it was obvious. Saving your life," he says, reaching down to give me a hand.

"I was fine without you," I say as he drags me to my feet.

"There was a gun to your head, Savior."

"I was handling it," I say, and as we both look in Lennon's direction, she's reclaimed her gun and aims it at us.

"Down!" Roth commands, and we hit the floor as she fires at us and flees. "You were handling it, huh?" Roth asks as we scramble after her.

"Why are you even here?"

It takes him a moment to answer, but when he does, it's enough to make me glad for his help. "I know what it's like to lose something important."

# CHAPTER FORTY-TWO
## Anora and the Eurydice

*When I come to consciousness, someone's tapping my* cheek hard.

"Anora," the voice says.

My throat feels raw, and I'm aware of a band of bruising around my neck, like Thane's arm is still there, cutting into my skin. My hands are bound in front of me, palms pressed tight together. I don't know where I am, but this place feels familiar. The air carries the weight of the dead. It settles over me like some sort of soul sucker, draining my energy. That tells me one thing: I have to be near a lot of dead people.

The tapping continues. "Open those eyes," the voice coaxes.

I do and jerk away from Thane, who's crouched in front of me. I can still feel his cold fingers on my face—the same fingers that crushed my windpipe.

"I wasn't sure you'd wake up," he says and stands, taking a lighter and a pack of cigarettes out of his pocket.

Once one is lit, he says with a smile, "I thought I might have done too good a job."

I hate him.

But I don't.

I can't help thinking this isn't Thane. He doesn't *look* the same. This Thane is angrier, scarier, darker. This Thane is controlled by Influence.

"Thane...please."

"Don't beg, Anora. It doesn't become you," he says, taking a long drag from his cigarette. He acts so casual standing there, as if he hadn't strangled and kidnapped me. It's then I realize he's brought me to the mausoleum—the entrance to Samael's office. I knew it felt familiar. We're in the main room, the one with the large stained-glass window. I'm resting on one of the red couches. The upholstery is soft but dusty and makes my skin crawl.

"Why then?" I demand.

"You're going to help me get my mother back."

"What?"

"I've been honest with you from the beginning about what I want," he says. "When I was sure you were the Eurydice, I knew I had my bargaining chip. Charon will raise the gates for you if you are dying, and I can demand my mother's soul is returned to me."

"You have my coin," I accuse, and he shakes his head.

"Lennon has your coin," he says, and I'm not sure I can feel any worse. Shy was right, which means...

"She killed Lily?" I whisper. "And...you knew?"

Thane shrugs. "I didn't want Lily to die, but she knew too much. Lennon felt she had to get rid of her."

"You work together?"

"I don't know the occult like Lennon does," Thane says. "Once I'm able to open the gates and obtain my mother's soul, she's going to help me resurrect her."

"With what?" I demand. "You don't have a body!"

"There's a whole cemetery full. We've been watching for the newly deceased. Lennon says it's best to have a fresh one."

Things are suddenly falling into place. With the coin, it's possible Lennon can obtain a soul from Spirit. She'd resurrected Lily's soul into her body for practice.

"You can't be serious. Thane, your mom won't come back right."

He sucks in a breath. "I knew you'd say that, but Lennon's been perfecting her spell."

He's delusional.

"I do hate this, Anora. I'd like to think we might have been friends."

I grit my teeth. *We were friends*, I want to say, but I know now that's not true. Instead, I ask, "How long?"

"How long what? How long have I been working with Lennon, or do you want to know when Influence took me?"

It is strange to hear him talk of Influence, as if he's fully aware of the darkling inside him. I stare, waiting. Answers to both questions will suffice.

"Influence took hold the day my mom died," he says. "Lennon approached me shortly after. We are united by our hatred of the Order. I introduced her to the death-speaker Underworld. She has a following there."

A following? I try imagining Lennon rallying the death-speaker troops to defeat the Order. Prior to tonight, I'd have said it wasn't possible, but you never know who or what you're dealing with. The Lennon I witnessed today is completely capable of such a feat.

But it's not even her presence that makes her a threat. It's her story. She lost her mother to the Order. She was rejected by Valryn society, forced to go underground. Yet she's survived.

People rally behind stories, and hers—it is powerful.

"You didn't have to do this. You had friends."

"You never consider that I might like what I've become."

"Do you?" I challenge.

"It wouldn't have worked anyway, Anora. We have two different perspectives on the world. You think it's worth saving. I do not."

I didn't always care. Before coming to Rayon, I wanted to hide, lead a normal life, let the world spiral out of control around me if it meant I could continue going to school.

But I can't live each day turning on the news to another horrific disaster perpetrated by Influence, knowing I can change it.

What kind of person would that make me?

No better than the thing that killed my poppa. No better than Influence.

Thane lingers in my periphery like the dead on the edge of campus. I wait until I catch him on his phone and bolt, charging out the mausoleum door. I slide on the slick cement, wet from dew, and land right in the middle of a dead man standing at the end of the steps. My chest seizes, and I can't breathe. My arm goes numb, and I think for a moment that my heart might explode. I manage to stagger to my feet but don't gain my balance before falling again. This time, I tumble through a dead woman in a long skirt. My stomach turns, and I hit the ground, vomit, and black out.

I wake to Thane lifting me from the ground. I feel like a child, cradled against his chest, my hands bound in front of me.

He returns me to the mausoleum and sets me down on top of a tomb in one of the adjoining rooms. From outside the mausoleum, I hear the howls of my hounds. They've found me. It means two things—the Valryn can find me faster, but Thane's also running out of time.

He leans over me, eyes wandering over my face as if he's trying to memorize me. I wonder if, for a moment, Influence has lessened its hold. Then he says, "I really do care about you, Anora."

For a moment, I spy the other Thane, the one buried deep under Influence's control.

Then he says, "Which is why I'm going to try and do this without killing you."

Then Thane lifts a knife and brings it down into my shoulder.

I scream as the blade pierces my skin and hits the tomb beneath me with a clunk. He draws back and waits, as if expecting something to happen—and suddenly, I understand what he's trying to do...summon Charon with my death.

My face is wet, stained with tears, and hot blood gushes from my wound, soaking my clothes and matting my hair.

I think of stupid things like how much blood I have to lose before it's too much and where major arteries are located. This can't be my end. Where the hell are Shy and Natalie? Mr. Val? The Order?

He draws the blade over his head again, aiming for the other shoulder. When the knife breaks skin, I swear it hits bone, and the impact makes my screams a thousand times louder. My ears ring.

"Stop, please, please, please." My words turn into a whispered, breathless prayer, and Charon doesn't come.

"Fuck!" he says, and his dark eyes contain a frantic fire. He lifts the blade to strike when a blur of black charges into him, knocking him off his feet. The next moment, Natalie is standing over me, reaching for my bound hands with a knife.

"Look out!" I shriek as Thane comes forward, swiping at Natalie with his bloodied blade. She springs away, dodging his blow. With Thane distracted, I roll off the stone slab and land hard on the floor. I try prying my wrists from the restraints, but the tape bunches and pulls painfully against my skin.

Thane and Natalie are locked in a knife fight. While Natalie fights like a dancer, her thrusts graceful and deliberate, Thane is full of rage, slicing and cleaving, backing her into a corner. At the last second, she shifts into her raven form and takes flight overhead, but Thane is quick and grabs her claw, jerking her from the air and slamming her into the wall. She reverts to her hybrid form, a heap of feathers on the floor.

"No!" I scream, and Thane advances on me. I bite at the tape around my wrists to loosen it. He lifts the blade over his head with both hands, and as it comes down, my hands are free and the thread comes to life in my palm. It lances him, piercing his chest. His eyes and mouth go wide as the thread passes through his throat and pops out one eye, then the other.

When he's consumed, Thane's body falls, lifeless, to the floor, and the coin lands on my chest with a thud, but I barely register the feeling, because a dark cloud stands in the place where Thane was. It is powerful and crackles with the energy of the dead. Influence hisses at me, and I swear to Charon it rears back as if to punch me and charges forward. The sensation of it inside me is something I don't quite have words for. It's like the sensation of falling when you're upright and haven't even moved. It's the sensation that someone's in the room with you but you're alone.

It's searching for something to latch on to—a dark seed it can fertilize and grow into something all-consuming and terrible.

It finds what it's looking for in the form of my poppa's death. The day I found him dead after he put a gun to his head and blew his brains out. It's a day I've never forgotten but one I don't bring to the surface often, yet Influence pulls it out of the dark pool of my mind, sets it high upon a pedestal, and tells me to worship it.

I scream.

My brain feels divided in two: one side rational, the other desperate for death. Tears rush down my face, and I feel split into a thousand jagged pieces. I'll never be put back together again. Too much of myself has been lost. With this new sadness comes a power I've never felt, a pump of adrenaline, motivated by a wish to kill myself.

I cannot continue.

I have to end the pain and suffering…

*Now.*

The pain in my shoulders where Thane stabbed me is nothing compared to the way my heart seizes at the memory of Poppa's death.

I push Thane's lifeless body on the floor. He had a knife. *Where is it?*

*There!*

Just a few feet from me. I grab for it, but someone kicks it out of my reach.

"No, no, no!" I howl. Disappointment crashes into me hard. I try following the blade as it slides across the floor, but someone stomps down on my leg, then grabs a handful of hair.

I meet Lennon's icelike eyes. My right hand is free to defend, and I send my sharp nails down her face. Her skin comes loose under my nails, and she screams, casting me aside.

"Bitch!"

Influence continues to invade my body, like thick oil, coating and suffocating all the parts of me that like the light.

"Your soul is mine!" Lennon hisses, reaching for me again. I grab her arms and pull hard. She tumbles over me and onto the ground. The impact jars her hold, and then I'm free. I stumble to my feet. My mind still feels split in two, and I understand that as much as I need to be free of Lennon, I also need to be free of Influence. I call the thread forth, just as shadowlike creatures circle me like sharks smelling blood. When they rise to the surface, it's as thick, tar-like glue. I'm lodged in a puddle of darkling quicksand. I stumble, and my hands are consumed, quashing the thread.

I scream, trying to free myself, when I hear Lennon

laugh. She bends so that her eyes are even with mine. "This is for your own good. Once Influence takes hold, you won't feel so desperate to die. You'll be used to this feeling of hopelessness and easier to control. Just like Thane."

At the mention of Thane, I recall the marks on his wrists. Times when he'd cut himself, probably as a result of Influence taking hold.

Suddenly, it feels like someone's cracking my head open, and I have this renewed determination to win, to defeat Lennon and Influence. I know how Influence corrupts. Grief might be all-consuming, but there are pockets of light, memories that bring a flood of feeling—sadness, yes, but also happiness and love and warmth. Sensations that make the darkness a little more worth it. All I have to do is knock some holes into his darkness.

And so I think about all the nights spent with Poppa on the old quilt Grandma Poppy made, watching the stars. He would spread it out, his crepe-paper hands decorated with brown spots and raised veins.

*"Gotta bring Poppy," he says and winks. "Help me set up the telescope."*

A chasm forms between my mind and Influence. Tendrils of its being reach out, stroking, testing my resolve.

*I prepare the tripod. Poppa assembles the telescope. I sit on the quilt, the dew-stained grass already soaking through the blanket to dampen my clothes.*

*"Tonight I spy with my little eye," Poppa says as he closes one eye to focus on something in the sky. He pauses and turns to look at me. "Well, why don't you tell me."*

The tendrils draw back as if burned. Influences hisses.

*I imitate him, drawing close to the telescope, closing one eye to gaze at what he's located in the sky. I inhale sharply and exclaim, "Mars!"*

*Poppa laughs, his wrinkled face a map of his happiness and sadness.*

*"How right you are, my little astronomer!" He hands me a Twinkie, and I rest my head on his shoulder as I eat.*

My eyes fly open as Influence tears from my mind. Lennon stands in front of me, a gun in her hand. When she realizes what's happening, her eyes go wide, and she lifts her weapon.

"No!"

Influence races for her. The impact causes her to stagger as she absorbs the darkling. Before she can regain her stance, a black shape zooms before my vision. It crashes into Lennon and transforms as they tumble to the ground. The spell's interrupted, and the coin and the gun go flying.

It's Shy! I've never felt such joy. I want to collapse with relief, but another black shape enters the mausoleum and shifts. I'm caught in strong arms and held up.

"Oh no, you don't," a familiar voice says.

"Roth?"

"If you fall, the occulates will consume you," he says. "Stay up."

I obey, shaking as Roth unsheathes his scythe and starts stabbing at the occulate pool at my feet and hands. The creatures hiss and steam, and soon my hand and feet are free.

"Get the coins," I order Roth as I stand.

I call the thread forward and move toward Lennon. She's clawing at Shy, reaching for his hair and ripping feathers from his wings. Then she rears back and hits him hard in the side. He cries out and falls, breathless. Lennon scrambles to her feet and reaches for him, but she freezes when she notices me.

"You wouldn't," she says.

"Anora." My name escapes Shy's lips in a harsh breath, and he shakes his head.

I glance at his hand, and I swear I see a flicker of a silver thread in his palm. I can almost see the connection between us. But then it disappears.

My fist shakes, and as bad as I want to watch her soul being consumed, I know it's not right—the thread has caused enough damage. As my thread reels back into my palm, Lennon reaches for a nearby scythe. A shot rings out, and she falls backward, hitting the ground hard.

I twist to find Roth holding her gun.

"Damn," he says. "We should use these more often."

Then I collapse. My vision blurs, and the last thing I remember is the sight of ravens swarming overhead.

# CHAPTER FORTY-THREE
## Anora and a New Set of Rules

**It's been two days since the mausoleum.**

I pace the room even though my body resists. I'm not fully recovered. I'm sluggish, and most movement causes extreme nausea...or maybe the nausea comes from the anxiety boiling in the pit of my stomach at the thought of facing the Order. Maybe it's the anticipation of returning home to Mom, not knowing how to explain any of this to her and knowing I probably won't ever be able to anyways.

My stomach roils. It's Sunday, which means Mom still thinks I'm at Temple. Thank God for small miracles. Still, I'm desperate to see her, because though Bastian and Mr. Val have assured me she is safe, I won't believe it until I see her with my own eyes.

I turn my thoughts to the present moment and the task at hand. The elite of the Order are assembling in the Council chamber as we speak—every single member, no holograms this time. They're here to interview me, Shy, and Natalie about the events of Friday night.

I'm not sure what more they think to discover through another interrogation. Once I'd woken up late Saturday morning, I'd been questioned by Elite Cain for hours. I have no more answers left in me, nothing more to say. Thane killed the Valryn who attacked me at the vigil and kidnapped me. He was possessed by Influence and tried to kill me, so I killed him. He worked with Lennon, who also tried to kill me and can apparently control occulates. She is half Valryn. She has some crazy powers. I told them, "You better watch your back, because I'm pretty sure there are more like her."

They didn't like that, and they'd demanded more information about what she was capable of.

I smiled and said, "Ask Lennon."

She is still alive, imprisoned like her father.

"You should rest," Shy says. He's sitting on the marble bench a few feet away in his human form, arm in a sling, blond hair a mess. His bright blue eyes practically smolder. He's been staring at me differently since Friday night, like if he doesn't pin me with an incredibly unnerving gaze, I might disappear, and I guess he has a lot of reasons to believe that.

"I'm fine," I snap.

He lifts his head a little, expression unreadable. I don't know what he thinks of me. We haven't talked since Friday when I defended Lennon and said I didn't trust him. Standing in the aftermath of what happened that night, I know I'm wrong, and I owe him and Natalie an apology—so many apologies.

"It's not like the Order's discussing your future this

time," he says. "You can relax a little. They just want to question you about Lennon and Thane."

I'd like to repeat what I said—that I have nothing new to add—but I don't. The Order wants to know how many followers Lennon has in the Underworld, and what exactly is the extent of her powers.

I want to know that too, but for a very different reason.

Now that everyone knows about Lennon being an abomination, will the Order continue to demonize half human, half Valryn? Or do they hope to use the powers Lennon possesses in some way? Was that why they kept her alive all along? To study her?

"What will they do to her?" I ask.

Shy mistakes my question for concern. "Don't think about her. She can't hurt you."

"I'm not saying what Lennon did was right, but… experimentation, torture…those aren't punishments, Shy."

He doesn't respond. Clearly, we think differently. After a moment, he rises to his feet and approaches me. Every bit of me comes alive in his presence, and it's hard to breathe. He reaches for me, places his free hand on my waist, drawing me close so our bodies touch.

I stare at his chest, not wanting to meet his gaze. There are things we haven't discussed, understandings we haven't made, relationships we haven't defined. I feel his fingers under my chin. He tilts my head upward, and then I'm caught in his gaze—a fly in a spider's web.

"Just worry about today," he says.

He removes his fingers from my chin, but I don't look away.

"I'm sorry." My mouth quivers as I speak, and Shy's gaze melts me.

"I know," he says and kisses me. He doesn't pull me any closer or crush me to him, conscious of our wounds, but his lips on mine are warm and solid. Heat rushes through me, and I lean farther into him, rising onto the tips of my toes just to have more, to taste deeper. I sigh into his mouth, and the urge to crush myself to him is overwhelming. Too bad the pain in my shoulder overrides me.

Someone clears their throat, and we break apart to find Bastian in the doorway. He is in his Valryn form. I have only seen Bastian in his human form once—blond and blue-eyed, he looks far more grounded sporting black-framed glasses than he does sporting weapons and long, silver hair.

"It will never be a good idea for you two to stand that close, but it is an especially bad idea here."

It's easy to forget that this Valryn is both knight and parent. Bastian's features are cold. Shy says his father always looks like this, that it doesn't mean he dislikes me. I want to disagree. Part of the reason I don't know where I stand with Shy is the Order and their rules against me—a human—being with him—a Valryn—in any sort of romantic way. Lennon's powers don't exactly instill confidence that they can control abominations. And being the Eurydice or our past connection doesn't seem to matter. Needless to say, Bastian has a reason to dislike me.

"Need I remind you what might have happened—"

"Had someone else found us?" Shy finishes quickly, the implication being no. "They didn't."

Bastian narrows his eyes, promising a conversation later. Just the thought of what it might include embarrasses me.

"The Order is ready for you, Eurydice."

I think about correcting him, requesting that he call me Anora, but I don't want the Order to be informal with me. The goal is respect, and they can start by using my title, and after that, they can start by obeying my rules. I'm done with letting others control my life. The Order needs me if they want to stop Influence, and I am not going to let them forget that.

Anxiety knots my stomach. No one—not Elite Cain, not Bastian, not even Shy—knows what I have planned for the Order. It will throw everyone off balance, and maybe, in the end, they will kneel.

Bastian turns, holding the door open as we pass through. We walk, escorted, down marble halls toward the Council chamber. It looks the same, except the large window is crowded with thick greenery, and all twelve seats in the chamber are full.

I have to say I prefer the elites when they are mostly holograms. Facing people who are whole and solid, people with unfriendly eyes and stone-carved faces, is way more intimidating, and somehow, I feel they're even more disapproving of me. The projection at the middle of the table moving through images of Friday night isn't helping. They include pictures of Thane's lifeless body, two resurrection coins, Lennon's winged body, pools of liquid occulate... It had been one hell of a night, that's for sure.

I take the same seat I had before, at the head of the table.

"Eurydice," Roth purrs when he sees me. "I speak for all of us when I say we are glad to see you recovering."

I want to scoff at his formality, but I manage a civil "Thank you" as I sweep a glance up his frame, wondering where he might be keeping Poppa's coin.

"It is our understanding you owe your life to Luminary Roth," says Elite Ezekiel.

I glance at Roth. I owe my life to Natalie and Shy—and mostly to myself—but clearly a different set of events has been communicated to the Order.

"You must be eternally grateful to him."

"Very," I say tightly.

"Eurydice," says Elite Cain. His eyes remain on the projection at the center of the table a moment longer before someone switches it off. Now there is a clear view across the table. "Why don't you tell us the events of Friday?"

"I have told you everything I know," I say. "I'm not sure what more I can bring to the conversation."

"Just your perspective, Eurydice," Elite Cain says. I have a feeling those words are supposed to be encouraging. They aren't.

I begin with the fight in the cafeteria between me, Shy, and Natalie, realizing Lennon was responsible for revealing Lily's secret and my life on Roundtable, then move on to the vigil when the Valryn guard attacked me. Some looks are exchanged, as if to say *How can you believe this child?* I ignore them and plow through to the part where Thane kidnapped me instead of taking me home to my mother.

Elite Ezekiel interrupts me.

"So you willingly left with him because you did not think we had your best interest in mind?"

"Well, one of your own did attack me twice," I say. "And you wanted to keep me away from my mother, the only person I have left in this world. What if something happened to her?"

"We wouldn't let that happen, Eurydice."

"Well, I don't believe you." I experience a pang in my chest, and I have this gut feeling that my words hurt Shy, but he doesn't understand.

The elites are silent for several moments.

"Please continue, Eurydice," Elite Gwen says.

I do. Explaining where I'd woken up, the conversation I had with Thane, that he was eaten alive by Influence and wanted his mother back. Then we move on to Lennon.

"And you say there were no signs prior to Friday night that Lennon Ryder was an abomination?" Elite Ezekiel asks.

There were signs she disliked the Valryn, but they were subtle, comments she made about Lily and Shy that suggested the two were on different sides.

"No." I'm surprised when Mr. Val answers for me. "Lennon Ryder was one of my students. She showed no obvious signs of being anything other than human."

I nod. "My first impression of her was that she couldn't see the dead. She seemed bored, and I guess, in a way, she was."

And she'd found entertainment with my coin, which translated to devastation for the rest of us.

"Tell us what you saw of her demonstrated powers," Elite Cain prompts.

"She seemed to be able to manipulate the occulates."

"But not Influence?"

"No. I think…it was too strong."

"And you were possessed by Influence briefly?" Elite Ezekiel asks.

"I was."

"How do we know you're not possessed?"

"Because I'm not." It's a weak response, but I'm not

sure how else I'm supposed to convince someone I'm not controlled by Influence.

"How was Influence removed from your mind?"

"I can't…explain it." It was too personal of an experience, and I don't want to give these people any more of myself.

"Eurydice, you realize expelling Influence from a host is a valuable weapon?" Elite Gwen asks. I don't like the way she looks at me, like I'm some marvel—a rare insect to study.

"Yes," I say. "And I can't really tell you how I did it, but I did."

Elite Cain and Mr. Val exchange a look—a wordless conversation that says: *Figure it out*.

"Eurydice, you have told Elite Cain that Lennon has a following," Elite Ezekiel says. "Have you seen it?"

"No."

"And yet you believe this?"

"Lennon is captivating, and she has a story. Anyone jaded by the Order would follow her."

"Including you?"

"What?" First they question whether I'm possessed by Influence, and now I'm being openly accused of treason.

"You make it no secret you despise us."

That is a strong word. "Are you ignoring the part where she tried to kill me? Why would I follow someone who wants me dead?"

"We're just trying to determine where your loyalties lie, Eurydice," says Roth. I glance at him. He's been silent this whole time. I don't like that he's chosen now to speak up, especially since he's sealed my *allegiance* by stealing my poppa's coin.

402

"My loyalty lies with myself," I say.

Everyone is quiet, and my gaze sweeps the faces surrounding me. There is a mix of reactions. Some mistrust me. Others seem smug, almost proud. Some I can't read, including Mr. Val.

"Very well, Eurydice," Elite Cain begins. "You are—"

"Before I'm dismissed, I have requests for the Order." It's time for new rules.

The whole room tenses, even Shy, who I can feel behind me.

"You have *requests*?" Elite Ezekiel asks. "To make of *us*?"

I just stare. I won't repeat myself.

The Valryn laughs. "This is ridiculous. You do not get to make demands of us."

"I don't threaten to abandon you to Influence's power or leave lost souls on earth. I don't even threaten to take your soul," I say. "But you will do me this courtesy because you respect me. Is that understood?"

Another peal of laughter. It's Elite Gwen. When I meet her gaze, her eyes sparkle. She says, "Please, Eurydice, continue."

"First, you will grant me a patrol and access to your records. I can't know what's going on in my town without it. Second, I get to choose my partners. Third…"

"This is insane!" Elite Ezekiel exclaims.

"With all due respect, Elite Zeke, *shut up*," Elite Gwen says.

"Third," I say pointedly, glaring at Elite Ezekiel. "I want to be trained as a shadow knight."

"*That* is absurd! You are not Valryn. We cannot teach you!" he argues.

"Why not? Is there something that prevents me from

using your weapons? Will the hilts burn my hands if I touch them? Will the world come down around us if you spill the secrets of your weapons' mastery?"

*Man, I love mocking the Order.*

"I don't see the problem," Mr. Val says. "I can easily add weapons training to her schedule. She should fight like us, especially if she is to patrol. She will be a liability otherwise, or worse, she'll just keep using the Thread of Fate as a weapon."

I meet his gaze, shocked that he sided with me.

*Thank you, thank you, thank you.*

His eyes say: *Don't thank me yet.*

"We will grant these requests, Eurydice," Elite Cain says. "Are you finished?"

"No," I say, smiling. "I have rules for how you are to use my powers."

No one says a thing, so I continue.

"Resurrection coins *aren't* to be kept by the Order, even for research purposes," I say, looking directly at Roth. "I will *never* be used as an assassin, and I am on the side of good. If I feel you have corrupted your purpose, I will no longer help you. Are we understood?"

No one responds, but I smile anyway and say, "Great. Should I draw up the contract myself?"

"Contract, Eurydice?" Elite Cain doesn't sound surprised, just tired.

"Yes, it will be harder for you to twist any of our agreement if it is in writing, not to mention it's likely you'll remember my requests better in the form of a contract you must sign."

"We will draw up the contract, Eurydice," Roth says. "After all, we have expectations of you as well."

I don't like that, but at least it means they are accepting my terms. "Very well, but I plan to read it thoroughly."

"As you wish. Is that all, Eurydice?" Elite Cain tries again.

"Just one more thing," I say, standing. "I told you I wanted to choose my own knights. I will offer those names now: Jacobi Quinn, Natalie Rivera, and Shy Savior."

"Eurydice, the three knights you chose are in training, not to mention on probation."

I shrug. "We go to school together. They're my friends. They are least likely to cause suspicion. No offense, but one of you hanging out around me is going to look creepy."

Elite Cain pinches the bridge of his nose. I like the idea that I might give him a headache.

"I will discuss it with the commanders," he says.

I want an answer before I leave, but I figure they're running out of patience fast.

"Thank you," I say.

I'm escorted out of the chamber by Bastian. Shy's at my side. We don't speak as we head back to Elite Cain's office. Once the doors are shut, I find father and son staring at me like I've grown two heads and tentacles.

"What?" I ask.

"That was…" Shy begins but doesn't finish.

Bastian shakes his head.

I think that's as close to approval as I'm going to get.

# CHAPTER FORTY-FOUR
## Anora and the Stars

*Mom says I'm still grounded, but she deducts time for* attending the retreat over the weekend. I find I'm not really all that upset. Maybe it's because things at home have been pretty stable since I returned from my horrific weekend. Maybe it's because I prefer the company of books over my cell phone, or that my only friends happen to double as birds and can fly into my room at any point they wish, or that I'm going to be sneaking out my window most nights to patrol Rayon with Jacobi (once he recovers), Natalie, and Shy and to train with Mr. Val.

Granted, if I am ever caught, I'm probably grounded for infinity plus two, but I'll take my chances. I have work to do. I'm going to climb up in this world that lives beneath the living, learn all there is to know about it. I'm going to gain allies and study my enemies. I'm going to learn to open the gates and reclaim my poppa's coin.

By the time I'm through, no one—not Roth or Lennon or Influence—will have power over me.

For now, though, I need to make it through my return to school.

As Mom navigates the curved driveway toward Nacoma Knight, I realize this is it. Not many people get a chance at a fresh start, and this one is mine. If I don't do it right, I'm screwed.

So I swallow my nerves and lean across the middle of the car to kiss Mom on the cheek.

"Thanks for the ride, Mom. I'll see you after school!" I get out of the car and pause before closing the door. "I love you."

Mom smiles. "I love you too."

I head inside Emerson Hall to exchange books at my locker. An ache forms in my chest as I wander down the halls I once shared with Lily, Thane, and Lennon. Two of the three might have ended up as my enemies, but for a time, I thought they were my friends.

The news doesn't report Thane's death but instead calls it a disappearance. I asked Shy why, and he said his uncle wants it that way. The knowledge makes me uncomfortable, like he is expecting him to come back to life. His coin is with the Order in a vault.

There is no word on Lennon, though she's still imprisoned at the Compound. If anyone asks, we're to say she has moved. I'm not sure of the Order's plans for her. Shy assumes they will kill her. I assume they will want to learn everything about her power and her following.

I want to learn the extent of her power too. I want to know how many half human, half Valryn are in existence.

Those are just a few things on my long to-do list, which includes other things like studying for Mr.

Val's tests and preparing for his first lesson in all things Eurydice. He's told me weapons will come with time. I want them now.

Maybe I can convince Shy to train me early.

Just thinking that makes my face flood with heat. I exhale, trying to shake the sudden warmth flushing my skin, but can't manage it before he appears beside me.

"Hey," he says.

"Hey," I breathe.

"What are you doing tonight?"

"That depends—what do you have planned?"

I'm thinking he's going to tell me about a patrol assignment. I haven't officially been assigned anything yet, but instead he says, "I was hoping I could come over...before patrol."

"I'm grounded—forever. Besides, I don't think Mom's forgiven you for bringing me home at three o'clock in the morning."

"I'm sure she doesn't believe we were watching movies," he says. The reality of that night was much, much worse. "But I didn't say she has to know I'm there."

"I can't leave my house," I warn. I am determined to do better moving forward. I came here with a goal to blend in, to live as normal a life as possible. I still want that, even if I am moonlighting as the Eurydice.

"We're not leaving the house...this time," he says, and a thrill rushes through me. The bell rings, and Shy takes a step away, one side of his mouth quirking upward. As he retreats, he takes his warmth with him. If I were brave, I'd reach for him and draw him back to me. "Tonight. Eleven. Leave your window open."

Eleven. That leaves us an hour before he has patrol.

The farther he walks away from me, the more my smile grows.

I run across campus, hoping I can make it to Walcourt before the second bell rings. I blow through the doors and slow to a walk as I stroll into Mr. Val's classroom just as the bell sounds.

"Miss Silby," he says, a pink slip between his fingers. He holds it out to me. "So good of you to join us."

I have yet to take my seat or catch my breath. "I was on time!" I argue.

"Running," he says.

I take it back. I'm not looking forward to training.

———

I'm reading on my bed when Shy arrives at eleven. I'm trying to look chill, but in reality, I've reread the first line of this book fifty times since I picked it up. My heart's been racing since he asked to come over, and my whole body is on fire, like I'm made of starlight.

"Hey," he says, smiling.

"Hey." I smile too.

He's changed into jeans, a white button-up, and a dark jacket. With his arm still in a sling, it's the only kind of shirt he can wear. Freshly showered, he smells like spice, and though he runs his fingers through his hair to keep it in place, pieces come loose, falling around his face in waves. I slide off the bed and move toward him, stopping when we're a breath away from each other. I brush his hair out of his face when he clasps my hand and kisses my palm. The touch sends threads of heat through my bond. He twines his fingers with mine, pulling me flush against him, kissing me. His lips are soft

409

and feverish, and he tastes sweet. The best part is that he's alive, warm and real and solid beneath my hands.

"Ready?" he asks.

"If Mom—"

"Not leaving your house, remember?"

He climbs out the window and starts up to the roof. I'm impressed by his one-handed scaling of the wall. It makes me realize just how much upper body strength he has.

I follow behind him, thrilled, ignoring the red eyes of my hellhounds illuminating in the hedges around my house. Their low growls signal their disapproval, but this night isn't about the Eurydice, the Order, or the differences between me and Shy.

It's about us.

When I reach the roof, I find him standing beside a new telescope.

He clears his throat. "I thought you might like to stargaze."

"Where did you get that?" My voice quivers as I point to the telescope.

He glances at it and rubs the back of his head. "I… uh…bought it. For you."

I take a few deep breaths to keep from crying and move toward the telescope. It's similar to the one my grandfather owned, the one we had to sell when we moved here. I touch it gingerly, afraid it might disintegrate.

"It's…mine?"

He nods, his face like carved marble, and I realize he's not sure what to make of my reaction, so I reach for him, wrapping my arms around his waist tightly.

"Thank you," I whisper against his chest.

His good arm circles me, squeezing tight.

"You're welcome," he murmurs, and I feel his lips brush my hair.

*You are amazing*, I want to say, but the words stick in my throat. He studies me for a long moment and then looks at the telescope.

"So find something," he encourages.

It takes me a moment to locate the Dog Star, the brightest star in the sky. Shy looks through and mutters *wow* under his breath. When he draws away, he meets my gaze and says, "Beautiful."

We share the same space, the same breath, the same warmth.

"If I could give you anything in this life," he says, his voice vibrating, "it would be the happiness you feel when you look at the stars." He leans forward to press his mouth against mine. When he pulls away, his lips touch my ear. "I want to know everything about you."

I melt into him. I want to know everything about him too. How he thinks, feels, and tastes. I start from the beginning. My words flood the air between us far past midnight, when stars come out and monsters come to life.

# About the Author

SCARLETT ST. CLAIR is the bestselling author of the Hades X Persephone Saga, the Hades Saga, *King of Battle and Blood*, and *When Stars Come Out*. She has a master's degree in library science and information studies and a bachelor's in English writing. She is also a proud citizen of the Muscogee Nation. She is obsessed with Greek mythology, murder mysteries, and the afterlife. Scarlett is based in Oklahoma City, Oklahoma. You can find pictures of her adorable dog, Adelaide, on her Instagram at @authorscarlettstclair and updates on her books at scarlettstclair.com.